A MISPLACED HOPE

HEATHER MICHELLE

Books by Heather Michelle

The Misplaced Children Series

A Misplaced Child

A Misplaced Hope (you are here)

A Misplaced Life

Novellas

Forever Misplaced

Unseen Consequences

The Unseen Series

A Girl Unseen (Coming soon)

Late for Dinner Press LLC
P.O. Box 982
Acworth, GA 30101

Edited by Nicole Schuette: www.nicoleschuette.com

Cover Design by Heather Michelle

First Edition: May 2021
ISBN 978-1-952857-08-9

To everyone who's ever felt lost

A MISPLACED HOPE

Book Two in the Misplaced Children Series

HEATHER MICHELLE

Chapter One

ELODIE SAT AT HER DESK, thumb tapping a quick pace against her leg, torn between telling her class the truth or the lie that had become her reality. The assignment required each student to present a personal history to the class, and Mr. Baker left it very open ended. She, like most of her classmates, did research into her family history and wrote a paper based on her family tree, but the boring telling of grandparents and familial anecdotes left her unsatisfied.

It wasn't even her family after all.

Last night as she looked over her finished presentation, that small place of rebellion she'd never been able to extinguish rose, and she wrote an alternative history, a story. Short, sweet, and authentic.

While she waited her turn to stand before the class and give her speech, both versions sat side by side on her desk. Two sheets of paper, both true, but telling vastly different versions of her history.

Her best friend had loved her short story when she'd read it before school, though Vanessa would support Elodie in anything she did. They both acknowledged reading it in class would cause problems, but it had been therapeutic to write.

Elodie was used to the jokes and names by now. They hadn't disappeared when she reached high school. There was no reason to read her creative story when it would only add ammunition to fire back at her later. She would read the boring report instead.

"All right, Elodie. You're up," Mr. Baker called from his seat at the back of the room.

Elodie stood from her desk. Her chest tightened, and she was a little out of breath. She looked down at the different essays one last time. Hands shaking, she picked up her paper and walked to the front of the room. She kept her eyes on the stained, faded carpet and set her paper on the podium in front of the class.

She took a deep breath and let it out, releasing the panic and anxiety with the air.

"Gather in close, and I'll tell you my tale," she started.

No magic wound through the surrounding air, nothing rose with her words to bind her to her listeners, allowing her to share her thoughts and memories.

This was a mistake.

Her stomach turned and the words swam before her eyes. She focused harder on the paper in front of her and forced the words out.

"The day the baby came was as perfect as a storybook. The sun was bright in the blue sky, with big puffy clouds to add a lovely contrast. Birds sang and bees buzzed as the soon to be parents rushed to the car.

"'Hurry, the baby will be ready soon,' Cynthia Harper called to her husband as she slid into the front seat.

"Frank Harper, for all of his cool planning, ran back and forth from the house to the car grabbing inconsequential items. 'I just want everything to be perfect!' he shouted to his wife as he threw the car seat into the back of the safety-rated SUV and slid behind the wheel. After a frantic search for the keys already in the ignition, Frank made sure his wife buckled in before putting the car in drive.

"The couple held hands and gazed lovingly at each other all the way to the adoption agency.

"The Harpers had wanted a baby for years. Cynthia grew up believing deeply in her responsibility to prove herself in both the professional and maternal world, and she already had a successful career as a wedding consultant, a perfect marriage, and an idealistic home. Naturally, a baby was the next achievement she had to conquer. Unfortunately, nature was against her and conception seemed out of her control. That, of course, would not do for her plan and so adoption became her solution.

"Frank Harper just wanted a little princess. His life had gone according to plan thus far. Graduated top ten percent of his class. Check. Working for a large firm in the city. Check. Perfect, beautiful wife running his perfect respectable home. Check. Now all he needed was a perfect princess daughter he could spoil and protect and show off at family work functions without having to do his day-to-day share. He saw a child as the next prize on his mantle, and thanks to his wife's determination, he was now getting it with little work on his part.

"The adoption process had been long and tedious, following the typical path of paperwork, loads of money, home inspections, waiting, more waiting. They then refused a few children for not meeting their race and gender criteria, until finally they were offered the baby girl of their dreams. The baby was young enough not to be too messed up by the birth family, while still being past the intimidating infant age.

"After a few face-to-face visits with the cute, light-haired, blue-eyed baby girl, the Harpers finalized the adoption. It had been an extensive process, and the couple was ready to start their picture-perfect family.

"I was asleep when my parents drove me home that first day. They read all the books, attended all the classes, and felt prepared for anything I could throw at them. I spent the next three days crying more than anything else as my new parents attempted to show me my new room full of toys. While they spent the time feeding me, changing me, rocking me, doing anything to get me to stop crying, they regretted their decision every moment I wasn't peacefully asleep. Eventually I must have grown used to the strange new world. Day by day, those first few months of my old life were encouraged to sink into the back of my memory and be forgotten.

"It was a week after my arrival before Dad, with relief, went back to his world of suits and business meetings and let Mom take full responsibility for their new bundle of joy. It took a month and a half for Mom to break down and hire a nanny. And it was just over a year before I began worrying my mother by acting differently from all my playdate friends: playing with sticks and talking to trees, ignoring dolls and princess movies. I had a pet caterpillar named Alby that I kept in a large jar filled with freshly picked mulberry leaves from the backyard. Behavior perfectly normal for a little kid, but for Cynthia and Frank's image of their little princess, it would not do.

"Over the years there were many moments this little girl worried her mother with her make-believe ideas of trees with feelings and plants who were her friends, but it wasn't until a fortnight before I started kindergarten that I first saw the broken-adopted-kid look in my mom's eyes.

"The day started with the usual call. 'Elodie darling, come inside before you get dirty!' Mom had a way of singing it in a sickly-sweet voice as she shook her head in disappointment watching me play in the trees at the edge of the backyard. She called a second time, a third, and a fourth with a little more bite in each word until the act was dropped, and she called in a voice bordering on disgust. This was the signal my time was up, and I left the fortress of leaves and raced across the yard, brushing off dirt and grass as I went. She inspected me with her nose wrinkled and I could see the disappointment of adopting a broken kid in her eyes. She scolded me for the mess but promised ice cream after errands if I washed up and changed.

"The perfect balance of disappointment and guilt gifts, courtesy of the Harpers.

"That ice cream parlor, after a long day of shopping and fake smiles, was where it happened the first time. I sat in a chair by the window spinning a plastic top from a quarter machine and eating my Gravenstein apple crisp ice cream cone, as my mother stood by the door talking with someone she ran into. I gave the top one good spin, and it fell off and under the table. Slipping out of my chair, I crouched down after it.

"The moment my knees hit the floor, I was struck with the oddest sensation of my life. I ducked under the table carefully so my head didn't bump any of the gum stuck underneath and noticed a shimmer floating just above the floor. It was like the air over the street on a hot day, yet thick and tangible.

"Setting down my ice cream, I reached for the shimmer and was met with a cool breeze. I could smell fresh air and old leaves, quite unexpected in a stuffy shop filled with the scent of waffle cones and old sugar. A moment later, I was pulled to the left as if something had a hold of my bones and tugged. Then I was falling.

"The shimmer surrounded me and gave a tight squeeze before I landed on my back on the soft plant life and dead leaves of a forest floor.

"I can go on and on if you let me, talking about the white trees with bright blue star-shaped leaves filtering the evening sunlight in the most eerie yet magical way, or the bright red bushes with twigs as hard as bits of steel that smelled like peppermint and tore my legs as I wandered through this peculiar wood. But the crucial part was the man that I met there. I knew, at first sight, he must be a brave knight from a storybook. His clothes and the sword glinting under his cloak said so. He was taller than my dad, his hair was thick, black, and streaked with gray at the sides. His eyes were sad with a few tears in the corners, but they were kind and bright blue. He showed me a birthmark on his forearm in the shape of a bird, and I excitedly showed him my own, in the same shape."

Elodie paused her speech and tapped on the mark showing on her collarbone. She didn't look up to see the reactions. She usually wore shirts to cover the mark and tried to stem the rumors that it was a tattoo, but today she had unzipped her hoodie before the presentation. She continued.

"The knight smiled and said I was like him, marked with a future. He told me many things over the hours I spent in that world, the world of Eres, on a continent known as the Twoshy. He told me about spells, prophecies, and traps, many things I wouldn't understand for years, but he impressed upon my small five-year-old mind that this land where I now stood was my home. I, and a few other children, had been stolen and trapped in a magical spell.

5

We'd been misplaced from time but would return to the Twoshy for short trips over the years until one day the spell would be broken.

"The knight told me he would never see me again. He would be gone by the time I returned, but a friend would always be there to watch over me and help me when I arrived.

"He led me to a small clearing on the edge of a cliff overlooking a vast breadth of land. Spectacular hills climbed and fell in an unobstructed way that overwhelmed me. The land stretched for miles, and in the center of it all was an enormous castle rising out of a village. This was my home, he said. Aluna, my kingdom, would wait for me.

"I soon felt a familiar tugging as the shimmer rose. The knight, a complete stranger who now felt closer and more real than anyone I'd ever known, said a rushed goodbye before the shimmer surrounded me, pressing in from all around. It filled every corner of me, my eyes, the feeling of my own skin, the stinging of my scratched legs from the peppermintsteel bush. Every sensation was drowned in the shimmer until quite suddenly I was back under the table, my ice cream turning into a small puddle by my knee.

"It took a few moments of shaking my head, trying to remind myself where I was before my mom saw me on the floor, ice cream staining my dress. She shrieked before remembering she was in public, then attacked me with napkins. She was too angry at my mess and too afraid for the car upholstery to listen to a word of my grand adventure as I rambled on and on.

"I puzzled over my healed legs in the car but found a bit of blue leaf in my braid to corroborate my story. But still, she didn't listen. It wasn't until I was home, trying to tell my dad about the knight I met, that my mom finally told me to stop telling stories and leave my dad to some peace and quiet. I persisted for days and days that it was real until the broken-adopted-kid look came back and stayed in my mom's eyes.

"I traveled to the land of my birth several times after that. I never met the knight again, but an old man with knowledge of magic and things unimaginable would always meet me, guide me, teach me. The great Wizard Gediminas became my mentor, taking me on adventures and teaching me about the world I came from. I would stay for months or a few years at a time in Aluna, never knowing for sure how long I would be there. Whenever I returned, it would be as though no time, or maybe an hour, or a day or two had passed since I'd left. My hair might be longer, or my shoes might be leather boots, but mostly, the shimmer would stick me back in this world as it had found me. I could be gone for two years, but when I returned I would be the same age as when I left, though the experience gained never left me.

"My disappearances and the truth I gave as explanation always got me into trouble. Attention seeking, a cry for help, out of touch with reality, just plain bonkers. This is who I became to my parents, my teachers, and my classmates. So I learned to shut my mouth, and I stopped telling the truth. Until reality became a lie, and this lie became my life. My name is Elodie Harper, and this is my history."

Elodie looked up from her report, the paper creased from her sweaty hands clutching the edges. The room was stuffy as the early summer sun beat down on the closed windows of the classroom. Students, lazy with the boredom that came from peer oral reports, began a delayed smattering of applause, although a few hid smirks and quiet laughter behind their hands. In the back corner of the room, the new kid sat glaring at her with an anger she didn't understand.

Elodie gave a little satirical bow as the teacher stood in the back of the class and came forward. Students hid phones in their laps and sat up to attention as he passed. He too was clapping hesitantly, a disapproving smile on his face.

"All right, thank you, Elodie, for that . . . uh . . . unique report," Mr. Baker said as he gestured to her seat. "Next up is Hanna."

The class clapped louder as Elodie moved to her desk, and a pretty brunette girl in a kimono stood and walked to the front. She took deep calming breaths and whipped her hair to the side as she passed Elodie, smacking her in the face.

Elodie sighed. She took her seat and started doodling on a copy of her report, making the title *Family History* as illegible as possible. Hanna began reciting her report in a bright and peppy voice. "The History of my family dates back to 523 AD in the Ming Dynasty."

The boy in the seat before Elodie leaned back over his chair, bumping into her desk. "Hey, I loved that report, Harpy. Very fact filled and informative." A few other students snickered.

Elodie's stomach fell, but she gave him a winning smile her mother would approve of.

"Thanks, Jackson. I can give you some pointers next time if you'd like. You know, so everyone doesn't fall asleep again."

Jackson glared at her with his sharp blue eyes and turned back to the game lighting up his phone under his desk.

Elodie sighed and returned to her doodling only to be revived by the occasional applause she instinctively joined in on.

She knew telling her short story was a mistake, but she'd still done it. It was a stupid choice, but she wouldn't live in regret.

It had been four years since the last time Elodie had traveled to Aluna, the Twoshy. There was a crazy few months in her life where she'd traveled six times. It was exciting, frustrating, and exhausting and left her with a few lingering nightmares. When she'd returned to this world, Earth, she'd wanted nothing more than to stay, at least for a little while. When she was away in Eres, Earth and her friends and family and life all felt far away and distant like a dream. She'd always believed Earth was an illusion—part of a spell used to trap her—but when she was here it felt so real. It was hard to care about resolutions and decisions she'd made back in Eres.

A part of her missed the Twoshy and wanted to go back, but it was a wistful, sleepy part. The active part of her was comfortable in the normalcy of her life on Earth and was quietly afraid of returning to Aluna and seeing the mess things had become in her absence.

Last night when she'd written the story version of her history, that wistful part of her spirit had taken over, and now she needed to deal with the consequences and prepare for the ridicule that was sure to follow.

It was too much to hope her short story would be taken as ingenious, but with any luck, the repercussions wouldn't be too bad. She thought about sending out a silent prayer to Reza, the god of knowledge, or Cooric, the god of fools, wondering if the gods of the Twoshy could reach her through the illusion, but she stayed silent.

The gods were powerful beings in the Twoshy, and her mentor Wizard Gediminas, Gedas to her, always advised against attracting their attention.

Praying wasn't worth the risk. If her peers thought her crazy, at least the crazy would be on her terms this time.

Chapter Two

BY THE TIME the lunch bell rang, Elodie's spare paper had doodles of star-leafed trees branching up the side margins and thunder clouds filling the header. Elodie shoved the paper into her English binder. She zipped up her backpack and slid it over her shoulder as she stood in one smooth, practiced movement. Joining the stream of bodies making their way out of the classroom, she set a clean copy of her report on the teacher's desk as she exited and entered the river of students in the dense hallway. Students laughed and banged lockers. A few guys in letterman's jackets pushed past, yelling to each other about sports ball, and Elodie headed for the quiet corner by the side door where her locker stood.

The path to her locker opened up like the sea before Moses, and Elodie rushed into the gap before it closed. An elbow collided with her and a backpack swung into her path as it transitioned from floor to shoulder. She dodged and bumped down the hall, with the grace of a half-blind puma, but eventually made it through the horde.

Leaning against her locker was a girl with long black braids tied up in a knot on the crown of her head. From the dark amber glow of her complexion to her long willowy form, she was beautiful. Today she had on bright blue leggings under her black-and-white-striped skirt. She wore a galaxy cat T-shirt with a burnt orange cardigan on top. As Elodie approached, her big brown eyes left the phone in her hands and fell on Elodie.

"Oh my God, did you hear? No, what am I saying, you never talk to anyone other than me. Kevin broke up with Nicky! Apparently, it was epic. He caught her cheating with Mitch over the weekend, and I guess he didn't even say a word, just walked away. Then today during homeroom, she was trying to kiss up to him and tell him how sorry she was. She said it was only once and she would never do it again. Yeah right, I mean come on. Everyone knew she'd been cheating for like a month. But that's another story. While she was apologizing Kevin freaked! Started yelling that they were over, and she should get her dirty, cheating hands away from him. Mr. Kirkland just looked up from the papers he was grading and watched it all unfold. Once Kevin finished yelling and Nicky was crying at her desk, Mr. Kirkland handed Nicky a note for the nurse's office and told the class to get back to their reading." The girl continued her breakdown of the day's events as Elodie listened and spun the combination for her locker.

Vanessa was Elodie's favorite person in any world. The stunning, eccentric girl blended in well with a school where half the kids were trying to be original and unique and the other half passed for trendy, striving their hardest to fit in. Vanessa was part of the unique category with her hair in any style that made her happy, and her bright contrasting colors and patterned clothes that worked in a way most people wouldn't dare try. Everything from the clothes she picked, the jewelry she wore, and the way she did her hair were purposely designed to say *I don't care what you think and I don't care how that makes you feel*. But in the same breath, it had to be stated that Vanessa's favorite hobby was talking about the thoughts, feelings, and actions of everyone around her. She was the perfect example of a high school paradigm.

Elodie on the other hand dressed and acted in whatever way would help her go unnoticed. At least, she usually tried to go unnoticed, temporary insanity during oral reports excluded. Elodie listened and asked clarifying questions about her classmates as she switched out her books and binders for the second half of the day.

She didn't speak to most of her classmates, but thanks to Vanessa, Elodie knew more about them than anyone would guess.

She had just closed the locker, lunch bag in hand, when something Vanessa said raised an alarm. "Wait! Vanessa, go back. What did you just say?"

Vanessa froze midword and closed her mouth, smiling smugly. She leveled a knowing gaze at Elodie. "I said, the word on the street is James Nelson has a crush on someone. He told Monty all about it after playoffs last week. He said it's someone he's liked for a while. He's going to ask her out now that basketball season is over and his parents have lifted his no dating until you're older rule." Vanessa said this with slow deliberate pacing, stretching out each word and pronouncing each syllable with care.

This was how Vanessa worked. She rambled through the news and gossip of the day, spreading all she gleaned, keeping the best bits somewhere in the middle as if to say they didn't matter at all.

But, of course, it mattered. Every girl in school cared about James and his long-awaited dating life. All it took was one look at his light brown hair and big blue eyes and they were lost. Every girl had been swooning in his presence since he'd turned seventeen over the summer, but James had stayed single. It was a mark of his character that he hadn't jumped into a bad relationship the same day his dating hiatus was lifted. Instead, he'd taken his time, using his athletic career as an excuse.

But now, the word was out: he was looking to start dating and the look on Vanessa's face said it all. She had on a silly grin that really made no sense. What were the chances James would have his eye on either of them? But Vanessa could hope. Elodie personally hoped the change in James's dating habits would mean his best friend, Matthew Moreno, would also be on the prowl.

As soon as she thought it, she frowned and ignored the fluttering in her stomach. At worst she was a pariah, at best, she was invisible. Not the kind of girl who would draw a boy's eye. If Matt started dating, he wouldn't be looking toward Elodie. James was top of every sports team, a star of the school, and Matt ran in the same circles. He was a little chubby and a little nerdy, and oh so cute.

He was also hilarious.

And crazy smart.

He always found a way to make those around him smile when they were having a bad day. Elodie had spent a semester last year being lab partners with him in chemistry. Even though he was a year ahead of her, he'd always been cool, making her laugh, talking about TV shows and books Elodie loved, and never treating her as a brainiac underclassman for being in an advanced science class. Besides, it wasn't like Elodie was that brainy, she just really liked chemistry.

It wasn't magic, but it came close.

Something was waving in front of her face, and Elodie's eyes refocused on Vanessa's snapping fingers and glittery blue nail polish inches from her nose.

"Hello? Ground control to Major Elodie? Are you back with me now? Gosh, I thought you'd slipped off to the Twoshy."

Elodie rolled her eyes. Vanessa was the only person Elodie had told about the Twoshy who completely and totally believed her. When they were younger Elodie would always tell Vanessa about her trips and adventures, and it had been the catalyst for their friendship. They were still friends for so many more reasons, but the Twoshy had brought them together in a weird way. When Elodie would return from a trip, she would find Vanessa and tell her all about it.

They hadn't talked about it in a while since Elodie hadn't traveled there in so long, and a part of Elodie wondered if Vanessa still believed her, or if she thought it was all something Elodie made up when they were kids.

In the end, Elodie didn't think she could handle knowing how Vanessa really felt.

"Anyway, my bet is that James is going to ask *me* out," Vanessa said with a sideways grin.

Elodie grinned back. "You two did get pretty close in photography."

"Right?" Vanessa grinned again and shook her head. "But I'm trying not to dwell on it. If he doesn't ask me, I will be totally broken-hearted. Promise to come over to my house this weekend if he asks someone else out?"

"I'll bring the ice cream," Elodie said. "But I doubt it will come to that since you two will totally be a thing by the weekend."

"Do you think so?" Vanessa asked, grabbing Elodie's arm as they dreamed together. "We can totally double date! You and Matt would be so cute together."

Elodie signed. "Now you're getting delusional, Ness."

"You stop! I mean, you two got close in that science class of yours, all of those completely unnecessary study sessions after class and all. No way he would have asked you to give him some chem tips outside of class so often if he wasn't into you."

Vanessa said this in a matter-of-fact way, but Elodie shrugged it off.

"Oh, come on, can't I get a little more excitement than that? I was under the impression you thought he was foxy, but if not, I'll just let him know to move on I guess." Vanessa pulled her backpack over her shoulder as if dismissing the thought.

"I do like him, that's not the point. It's just . . ." Elodie trailed off and they headed down the nearly deserted hallway toward the quad to eat lunch.

"Please don't say complicated. There is nothing complicated about it. He thinks you're hot, the feeling is mutual, go for it, girl!"

"Vanessa, you don't even know he likes me. You're still just speculating, right?" She peered at Vanessa to double-check that her friend didn't know more than she was admitting, but her face was neutral.

"Yeah, but you know I've always been an expert on the human soul. Teenagers are way too predictable. Like, for example, even though you told me you were going to scrap your short story and present the boring report you wrote up instead, I predicted that was a lie and that you would go on ahead and tell your story regardless of the fact everyone will be talking about it by the end of the day."

Elodie grimaced. "How did you find out so fast? I came straight here from class. Did you set up listening spells all over the school or something?"

Vanessa beamed, "You know I'm not one of your mages. Besides, I don't need spells and magic. You, my friend, are way too predictable."

Elodie shook her head and exhaled her frustration as the two of them sat down under the big weeping oak tree in the middle of the open quad to eat their lunch.

The oak was a member of the beech family. Trees were reservoirs of power and strength, but an oak provided stability and peace.

Elodie listed the facts in her mind as she attempted to relax in the shade of the thick branches. The oak bark, prepared as a decoction, could be used to remedy a sore throat, tonsillitis, or digestive issues. As a lotion, it could treat various skin ailments. When influenced by ruakh, the magical force that filled the Twoshy, the properties of an oak magnify extensively. Acorns from a strong oak provide stability and strength to poultices, ointments, potions, and spells, while the leaves that stayed on the tree through a harsh winter season would have advanced healing properties.

While Elodie knew all this was true, there was a part of her that shrank from the knowledge and tried to avoid thoughts of magic. Surviving high school was hard enough without magic clouding her mind. She pushed away the feeling of heat radiating from the tree. Not quite heat, it was more like a sunbeam falling through a window but more familiar and unique, like a close friend standing just behind her.

For her to feel the tree so well, the ruakh must be close, bleeding through the spell into the illusion like it would just before she traveled. Elodie pushed again against the sensation and got out her lunch.

"So how did the report go?" Vanessa asked with a concerned look.

Elodie sighed. "As expected. Everyone laughed. Jackson made a joke. And that new kid, Allen, gave me this super pissy look like my story offended him or something. Have you gotten a read on him yet?"

A deep look came over Vanessa as if she was peering through one of the many file cabinets in her mind. "Taking advanced physics and trig but he talks down to teachers like he knows better than them. He hasn't made any friends either. He's a foster kid, apparently bounces around a ton. His last home kicked him out about three months ago for unknown reasons, and there's a few unverified rumors he bounced in and out of juvie a few times." Vanessa smiled. "That last part is probably not true. He seems like a kid who's way too smart for his own good and wants everyone to know it. I don't know why your report would piss him off. Maybe he wanted to tell a story and seem all existential and you showed him up." Vanessa shrugged and took a bite of a carrot covered in hummus. "I don't know, there aren't enough facts for me to make a realistic guess about him, just rumors and I don't rely on those. He doesn't talk to anyone, and he probably just needs a good friend."

Elodie sighed and drank her orange juice. "I shouldn't have read that paper. It was stupid. I should have stuck with some stupid facts. But last week Mr. Baker pissed me off so bad when he said I don't have a normal family history so I should use this report as an opportunity to express myself and my 'troubled past'. Like he actually expected me to talk all about being adopted in front of the class and bare my emotions or something. He acted like he was full of righteous justice, that this was some grand opportunity for self-actualization."

"But you did talk about being adopted," Vanessa pointed out.

"Yeah, but I did it on my terms. I told him what I really believe, not what everyone else believes."

"Well, I think it was brilliant," Vanessa said. "Whatever the fall-out, we can deal with it, we've dealt with worse. Don't let that asshat get to you."

"Vanessa! Please don't make me give you detention this early in the week," Mrs. Butler, the art teacher, said without breaking her stride as she carried a pile of very heavy canvases toward the art building. Elodie knew the teacher didn't mean the threat of detention, Vanessa was her favorite student.

"Sorry Mrs. Butler," Vanessa called to the teacher's retreating form. Vanessa grimaced at Elodie before continuing. "Anyway, did you hear that last week Mr. Baker told Donald to get his parents to buy him some nice clothes, not something from a thrift store, because physical appearance would be counted in the final grade for the presentation? He even offered to send a note home."

Elodie groaned. "He really is the worst."

"Well, not to change the subject or anything, but what are you going to do when Matt asks you out?"

Elodie didn't respond as her stomach lurched. She took a bite of her roast beef sandwich, chewing as slowly as she could. The food felt dry in her mouth and her hunger disappeared.

Luckily, a swarm of girls looking to spread and glean their wealth of gossip descended upon Vanessa, and Elodie could escape to her thoughts. She liked Matt; she had for a while, but every time she thought about his lightheartedness and warm brown eyes, thoughts of her responsibilities in the Twoshy filled her mind and wiped away any dreams about a funny schoolboy at the top of their class.

If only she really knew he existed. If only she knew without a shadow of a doubt that Matt wasn't just another part of a complex illusion wrapped around a spell to trap her.

Maybe the Twoshy really was all a delusion, and she should let go of it and embrace this world and this boy. Decisions.

Elodie laughed to herself. There was no decision. Matt wasn't going to ask her out, regardless of what Vanessa thought.

Elodie took another bite of her lunch and turned her attention to the chatter of her fellow self-obsessed peers. She spent the rest of lunch talking about shoes and clothes and everything else that was meaningless in the Twoshy, trying her hardest to convince her mind that this was reality, this was the real world. She should go out with Matt, if he asked, and just be normal for once. Forget about prophecies and responsibility and handsome squires with green eyes who Matt could never compare to, and just live for today.

Now if only she could convince her heart to go along.

Chapter Three

AFTER SCHOOL, Elodie walked with Vanessa to the ice cream parlor where Vanessa worked. It was the same shop Elodie first found the ruakh and was pulled into the Twoshy. She picked a table near the counter and set out her homework while Vanessa started her shift.

The parlor was slow on Tuesday afternoons, and Elodie liked to keep Vanessa company while she cleaned counters or scooped the occasional cone.

They had a paper for English due that Friday about a book Vanessa hated and refused to finish, so while she worked Elodie told Vanessa the finer points of the plot and Vanessa jotted down notes in the notebook she had propped behind the cash register. No one cared. The manager working tonight was nineteen and currently on the phone with his girlfriend in the back room, so no one complained if Elodie and Vanessa discussed colorful metaphors of death and sacrifice while Vanessa served ice cream to small children.

Elodie was explaining a rather grim part when the little bell on the front door chimed again.

"Hey!" Vanessa said loudly, cutting Elodie off. "How's it going, guys?"

That was odd. Vanessa usually didn't greet people until they were looking over the flavors. Elodie twisted in her seat just in time to see Matthew Moreno holding the door open for a little boy with big brown eyes and a dazzling grin. He could have been a miniature version of Matt.

Elodie turned back to Vanessa and made pleading eyes at her friend. Vanessa shot her a grin and wiggled her eyebrows.

"What's that about decapitation?" Matt asked, grinning.

"Elodie and I were just arguing about the likelihood of someone being decapitated with a sword," Vanessa explained.

The little boy, maybe four or five, crossed to the row of ice cream coolers in the low refrigerated unit and stuck his face against the glass.

"Mark, don't touch the glass, then my friend here just has to wash it when you leave."

"Sorry!" the boy called as he slid sideways down the row of ice cream, leaving a long smear as he squeaked by.

Matt sighed. "Sorry about him."

"Don't worry about it. My job is literally just cleaning face prints from the glass all day," Vanessa said.

Matt chuckled. "Right, so back to decapitation. It's possible, like with an axe, but with a sword the force required just wouldn't be there."

He crossed to Elodie's table and picked up her English book, flipping through the pages with his slender fingers. His hands were too soft for sword work. It would take ages to build up the proper calluses.

"God, I hated this book," Matt said.

"Same!" Vanessa called before giving a tiny sample spoon heaped with ice cream to Mark.

"So what do you think, Elodie?" Matt asked. Elodie glanced up at him a little unsure where the conversation had gone. "About decapitation," he said. "What's your opinion?"

"Oh, well." She cleared her throat and looked away from his clear brown eyes so she could think properly. "It comes down to weaponry, force, and skill. If the blade was sharp and well cared for, it will always have an easier time. When talking about force you need to think of the strength of the man, the weight of the weapon. And skill. Does he know the proper angles, will he hesitate when he connects or carry through on the movement? A proper knight would have the training and would care for his weapon, making sure it's always sharp. But a trained warrior would also know his own abilities and if he was capable of carrying out the strike before attempting it. Totally possible in a very specific set of circumstances."

Matt grinned at her, and her cheeks got hot. He held the book up by opposite corners and gave it a little spin. "But in this book, he's not a knight."

"Right." Elodie frowned. She'd gotten carried away and her cheeks were on fire. "In the book, he's just some regular dude who grabs a decorative sword off a wall. The likelihood of him actually decapitating someone is super unrealistic."

"What's decapitation?" Mark asked, coming over to Elodie's table, his tongue blue from his ice cream.

"We should go," Matt said, grinning. He set down the book and paid for the ice cream, leaving a big tip for Vanessa. "Will I see you at school tomorrow?" he asked Elodie.

"Every day!" she said.

"Great." Matt smiled and held the door open for his brother.

When the door closed behind them, Elodie unscrewed her smile and dropped her head onto the table. "Every day? What does that even mean? I don't go to school every day," she complained into the table.

"I think that went great," Vanessa said.

Elodie lifted her head and stared at her friend. Vanessa was leaning against the counter, smiling fondly at the closed door.

"Ness, were you even there for the same conversation? I went off on a tangent about knights and their weapon care."

"I bet he thought it was cute. Don't you roll your eyes at me. He totally engaged you in the conversation, and he played with your book. Those are all signs of interest." Vanessa grabbed the glass cleaner and came around the counter, spraying an ample amount of liquid on the glass before wiping it up. The scent of rubbing alcohol and vinegar filled the air, overwhelming the warm sugar smell for just a moment. "If he wasn't into you, he would have just got the ice cream and left."

"Ness, sometimes conversation is just conversation. Reading

into things too much just leads to heartache when nothing comes from it."

"But if you don't hope for something, wishing and dreaming, what's even the point? Life is so boring without a little hope. Even if it does get crushed from time to time."

Elodie sighed and leaned back in her chair. "I've had enough of dreams lately."

Vanessa put away the cleaning supplies and washed her hands. "I thought you took care of your dreams, are they back?"

Elodie grimaced. She'd always been prone to vivid dreams, but they got worse as she got older. When she was twelve, she'd started hanging tarragon behind her headboard, the herb sometimes able to ward off such dreams. She replaced it every few months when she woke up sweating from another dream. Her current batch wasn't old, yet she'd woken every night from bad dreams in the last week.

Vanessa came back around the counter and sat across from her, her expression sympathetic. "That's why you told the short story, isn't it? The dreams made everything fresh and sharp in your head."

Elodie sighed. "Usually, I can forget about the Twoshy. It's not hard to just ignore the thoughts and memories, just like ignoring my thoughts and feelings for"—she gestured toward the closed door. "Things are just so much easier if I put my head down and ignore everything else. And just get through the day."

"Easier maybe, but a lot less fun." Vanessa smiled. "You should try being impulsive for a few days. Just do whatever comes to mind and see where it gets you by the end of the week."

Elodie laughed. "I don't know how that will go over with my mom."

Vanessa shrugged. "If it causes issues, I will help you come up with a reasonable excuse. Come on, it will be fun."

The door chimed again, and Vanessa got up to help the new customers while Elodie thought over the idea.

On her walk home, Elodie stopped by the store to buy a new bundle of tarragon. She could be impulsive without waking up from nightmares.

Chapter Four

IN A SMALL, bare, hardly lit room, a boy sat at a wooden desk pushed up against the wall. A light globe hung just above his head, illuminating scrolls and books on his desk. Hunched over, he scribbled furiously on parchment when the door burst open, and an identical boy walked in.

Sort of.

The new boy looked very similar, but the differences grew more and more apparent by the moment. Both had the same figure, the same dark hair, and gray eyes, but there were differences to the shape of the face, the tilt of the nose, the size of the forehead.

"I've been working on a curse." The new boy, his nose a little pointier than the first, flapped a piece of parchment in the air before jumping back on the bed.

"I don't know why you insist on wasting time on such nonsense when you got a P on your last assignment," the first boy drawled, not looking up from his parchment.

"I got a P because Professor Froggsnar has no imagination. Now, do you want to see?" He waved the parchment again, and his classmate set down his quill with a sigh. Pointy nose grinned and threw the paper. It floated through the air helped along by a small blue spark. The first boy snatched it from the air, rolling his eyes and reading over the marks and symbols on the paper.

He frowned. "Is this a phono cortex built in?"

Pointy nose smiled. "Did you notice the cortex is holding a trap as well? It is a sort of illusion, a little fantasy not of my own creation, that I found reference too in an old script."

The first boy's frown deepened. "Lan, this is dark magic. You could get expelled for something like this."

Lan waved his hand as if the thought were trivial. "But did you look at the focal where I created the vortex?" Lan scooted to the edge of the bed and pointed out shapes and figures, a small grin on his face. "It will close like a trap, imprisoning someone in a fantasy world far out of reach, that was all my ingenuity. I was thinking of trying it out on Professor Froggsnar. I'll show him 'lack of structure and refinement in technique.'"

"Why even work on this if you know it's not the sort of magic you can turn in? Don't you have enough work to do?"

"I have to have something more interesting to break up the monotony. Besides, the teachers only share the boring magic with us. Don't you want to go further?" Lan's face was wistful as he looked down on the paper.

The first boy brought the parchment closer to his nose. "The structural integrity of the transporting vortex doesn't seem very stable to me. It looks like this whole thing will unravel if just the right string is cut. Perhaps if you changed the bonding material to a mineral, say white sapphire, it would give you the added boost to bind them together."

Lan ripped the paper out of the other boy's hand. "Who asked you anyway, schyt brains."

The glow of the light globe began to fade, but neither boy seemed to notice. The room grew darker and darker until Elodie shivered and had no sense of direction. She fell deeper and deeper into the darkness, walls closing in. Large white birds flapped around her, their black-tipped wings slapping her face. She lifted her arms to shield herself, only to find her wrists were chained above her head.

No. Not again.

She pulled and pulled against the chains, wrists throbbing, until the chains snapped. Her stomach floated as she fell, tumbling through the darkness into a deep hole. There was an old man in the hole, and he cried out in pain. A door lay behind him, and Elodie pushed past into another corridor lined with yellow banners that flapped in a breeze she couldn't feel. She ran past the banners only for more to appear down the never-ending corridor, overwhelming and oppressive. Her view zoomed out and she was standing in the middle of a labyrinth that consumed the entire world.

Her heart pounded in her chest, and hopelessness crashed into her.

The labyrinth began to fade as she thrashed in her blankets and her near waking mind reached for peace. The dream shifted to a memory, and she found herself back in Aluna between one breath and the next. The trip had started badly, and gotten worse, but this time she didn't dream about that dark cave or the blank dead eyes of the man staring up at her. This time Elodie dreamed of the very end of the trip and the weeks she'd spent in the city of Tate. Gedas had suggested she sharpen her bow skills as they were nearly nonexistent, and he asked Silas of Tate to do the job as teacher.

When Elodie had first met him, he'd been several years younger than her, just a little boy of eight who followed the princess and the wizard as they toured his father's estates. But he'd grown up before her eyes, always a few years older each time she saw him. On her last trip, Silas, a few years older than Elodie, was a squire, well on his way to knighthood, and the best swordsmen in his class. In her dream she remembered the scent of leather, soap, and pine needles that crept into her nose as he leaned in with his muscular arms to adjust her grip and help her aim.

She'd hit the target that time.

She felt safe with Silas. He'd seen her in the cave and the mess she made later when the stress made her sick, and he hadn't shamed her for her weakness. Instead, he helped bring her to safety and stood guard so she could sleep soundly.

In the dream, Elodie fired the last of her arrows, then she and Silas wandered out into the practice field to retrieve them. She was bent at the base of a tree picking up arrows, and when she stood, Silas was there, too close for her to move. He reached out and tucked her hair behind her ear, then threaded a brilliantly orange blanketflower into her hair. He smiled down at her and opened his mouth to say something, but a woman's voice came out instead, the memory twisting into the chaos of a dream.

"The mountains are older than those who walk above them, and those who live beneath. They were here before us, and they will be here long after we are gone."

Silas's green eyes flared yellow and Elodie stumbled back.

Her alarm clock blared, and Elodie jumped, heart racing. She groaned and buried her face in her pillow, but the noise didn't stop. With a sigh, she slapped off the alarm.

She wished the dream could have lasted just a little longer. The part at the end had been weird, but she wanted to be back in that meadow. It almost made her want to take up archery lessons and rebuild her strength. Her mom would hate it, thinking it too odd given Elodie's usual tendencies.

When she'd returned from the Twoshy after that trip, all the upper body strength she'd spent months building was gone. Once again chubby and weak, she felt no desire or need to continue working out to build her strength back up. Holding a resolution to work out was hard when it was made in another world.

Elodie got ready for school, letting the water of the shower wash over her and rinse away the dreams until all that was left was a fuzzy memory. She let the solidity of this world close in on her.

The fresh tarragon hanging behind her headboard still hadn't worked. She needed to find a better solution for blocking out her dreams. Gedas liked to tell her she was prone to prophetic dreams and would do well to listen and remember them, but at the moment, Elodie prized peaceful sleep and not screaming her parents awake more than she cared about her future.

The thought of prophecies made her heart race as the warm water ran down her face. She turned the tap cold.

There was a prophecy about her being the catalyst to break the spell she was trapped in. She wasn't alone in the spell. There were others she'd never met, trapped here in the illusion with her, other Misplaced Children. None of them would ever be free to live their lives until Elodie somehow broke the spell.

It wasn't just freedom from the spell she sought. She was heir to the throne of Aluna.

Without her, Aluna had no queen, and the government was slowly deteriorating under the limited power of its steward and council. While she sat comfortable in the spell, people like Silas worried over her kingdom.

She choked down her guilt and finished getting ready. She didn't need to dwell on Aluna and how much her kingdom needed her. The day would be much harder if she started it with that mindset.

She swapped out a cute tank top for something that covered her collarbone a little more. Yesterday she'd worn a top to show her birthmark as a tie-in for her family presentation, but today the desire to be seen for who she really was had left. Once her shoes were on, Elodie made her way downstairs to endure her mother asking her to change into something a little more presentable than jeans and a nerdy T-shirt.

"You have to dress for the job you want after all," Cynthia sang in a much too peppy voice for seven in the morning.

Elodie muttered something under her breath about not being allowed to bring a sword to school. She grabbed her toast from the counter and ran out the door as her mother realized what she'd said and followed her.

"Now, none of that, Elodie," Cynthia called after her in a voice so sugary it sounded brittle. "Remember, think normal, be normal!"

Elodie turned back, halfway down the drive. "Relax, Mom. It was just a joke." She smiled and shrugged before turning back to walk the short block to school.

She passed a trio of paper birch trees just past her driveway. Elodie reached up and pulled a few fruiting catkins off a branch. Crumbling the seed pod in her fingers, she sprinkled the scales of the pod while she walked.

Birch could be used as an antiseptic and diuretic. In the Twoshy, the main power of the birch came from its protective and catalytic properties. Rich families wallpapered their homes during construction with the thin bark, while the wood was used for protection charms and spells.

Ruakh didn't flow through this world like the Twoshy, and Elodie knew the small seeds wouldn't have the same power but crumbling the catkin kept her hands busy while she wrestled with her thoughts.

It was mean for Elodie to tease her mom, knowing she would spend the next several hours thinking her daughter was slipping back into a dark place of mental illness. Elodie hoped she wouldn't worry enough to call her old therapist. It had been a few years since Elodie had to sit in that stuffy office and lie through her teeth to Dr. Abernathy. She didn't want to relive the experience.

She needed to stop goading her parents. She needed to stop thinking and dwelling on the Twoshy and actually take her mother's advice.

Think normal, be normal.

She'd mocked those words for so many years, but for once Elodie wanted to just enjoy the here and now. Normal, being a relative term, could be a hard thing to grasp.

Elodie stopped off at her locker to put her extra books away before class. Matthew Moreno stood in the corner of the hallway leading to Elodie's first class, right in view of her locker. He looked up when her locker banged shut, and Elodie's cheeks burned.

Elodie, math books in arm, walked down the hall toward her class. When she was just about to pass him, Matt straightened and slid his phone in his pocket. He was just a few feet away from her now, looking straight at her. Everything seemed like slow motion as he raised his hand slowly, as if he would reach out and stop her.

And then, just like that, Kelsey Winters was in front of him, blocking Elodie's view.

"Hey Matt, how's it going? Are you ready for the pep rally after lunch today?" she asked as she twirled her long, freshly curled hair.

The butterflies, who a moment ago had been fluttering around so warmly in Elodie's stomach, now felt as though they'd burst into flames and were smoldering her insides to ash. They were remarkably similar to a breed of butterflies believed to be at fault for the burning of a small village outside of Tross in the Twoshy.

Elodie made it the last dozen steps to her math class and darted inside. She sunk into her seat and pulled out her homework, double-checking the problems for something to do. The class began filling with students. Kelsey and her giggling friend made it through the door just before the second bell rang. They sat in their usual seats just behind Elodie and promptly began whispering about what had just happened in the hall.

Much to Elodie's delight, the teacher called the class to order and began going over the homework. It wasn't until the class was set to work on the new assignment that Elodie groaned internally and wished she'd packed her earbuds.

She tried her hardest to ignore Kelsey's whispered conversation behind her as she focused on the quadratic equation on the paper in front of her. "He's gonna ask me out sometime this week. I can feel it."

Elodie didn't honestly care how Kelsey felt. But the thought of Matt asking the other girl out gave her a deep sinking feeling of disappointment. Then another sensation took hold; it was deep inside of her, holding tight to her bones. No, that wasn't her feelings for Matt, it was a different yet familiar feeling. It was the feeling of ruakh, the magical force that filled her home world, bleeding through to this one. The trace she now felt was very faint and soft. She knew that grip well. She felt it every time she traveled to the Twoshy.

She looked to her side and could barely make out a weak shimmer floating near the top of Rachel's head. This happened to her sometimes when the ruakh was close, yet not strong enough to pull her through.

She'd asked Gedas how she could sometimes feel the magic of the Twoshy when she was in the illusion. Gedas explained it to her on a cool night spent under the stars on one of their many trips. She'd been staring at him, but the wizard's eyes gazed into the campfire, as it popped and crackled along the damp wood they'd collected, small mouse-like cindix burrowing through the embers in search of an ash dinner.

"The world you have grown up in most of your life is, of course, an incredibly complex illusion created long, long ago. Someday the spell holding you in this illusion will unravel and you and the other Misplaced Children will be free. Your travels are a symptom of that inevitable break, like hiccups in the fabric of your reality. When you see the ruakh bleeding through to you, that is just another thinning of the fabric of the spell, not quite strong enough to allow you to travel, but allowing the ruakh in to greet you like an old friend."

Elodie had laughed then thinking it was funny. Back then ruakh had felt like a friend, accompanying her on adventures and letting her make potions or perform small spells. It wasn't sentient, but sometimes it felt like it. As she'd grown up, straddling the great chasm between two vastly different worlds, she realized magic didn't always have her best interests at heart. If it had, it would have been easier to hide her double life from those who would use it against her. It wasn't a tool to be used, instead she was the one being used by it.

Sitting in her math class staring at the shimmer in the air over her classmate's head, she wondered if she reached out into the faint sparkle of light would it grab hold of her and pull her into itself.

Did she want to go back to the Twoshy now? How could she long for both normalcy and the fantastic at the same time?

"Elodie, did you have a question?"

Elodie blinked. She looked up at her teacher. Half the class was staring at her. She put her hand down on her desk. "Sorry, no." Her cheeks burned and a few kids around her snorted or whispered.

Stupid. Stop getting carried away and act normal for once.

She gritted her teeth and focused on her paper. Magic hadn't wanted her for the last four years, it wouldn't want her now.

Elodie made it from class to class trying to ignore the sense in the back of her mind that the ruakh was there waiting for her. She'd spent years wishing and hoping for the force to appear and pull her through to her home, but it had been so long now. It was too much work constantly worrying about school life and keeping her parents happy while also fretting over another land's social and economic health and how she would ever break a magical spell while trapped inside. It was all so much easier if she just let the Twoshy sink to the back of her mind.

She didn't need the ruakh acting as a reminder of the world she was trying so hard to ignore.

In English class, the day continued to progress down its shoddy path. Mr. Baker walked around the room, passing out the graded copies of yesterday's oral reports. He slapped the paper down onto Elodie's desk a little harder than necessary.

"Please get this signed by your parents and turn it back in on Monday, Ms. Harper," he said before moving on to the next student. Elodie looked down to see a big D- scrawled across the top of her paper in red ink.

"Schyt!" she said under her breath.

Jackson turned in his seat and howled with laughter when he caught sight of the grade. "Damn Harpy, there goes your four point oh."

It was her own fault. Here she was thinking about how much she just wanted to forget the Twoshy and live a normal life, but she'd still gone ahead and read her story knowing it was a bad idea.

She needed to decide once and for all which world to commit herself to.

The bell finally rang an hour later, and the students cleared out for lunch in under a minute. Elodie stayed in her seat as Mr. Baker made his way back to his desk and began rifling through the papers in his hand. He paused, then gave a small wave indicating Elodie should approach the desk.

"Ms. Harper, what can I do for you?" he asked as though he had no clue.

"Sir, I wanted to ask you about my grade," she said hesitantly, then scolded herself and straightened her posture.

"How about instead, you explain to me how you believe your report fits the assignment I gave you?"

He sat there with his legs crossed, looking back up at Elodie. He had a paper in his hand full of notes with her name at the top and a big red D-. She hesitated.

A small smirk crossed Mr. Baker's face, and he took the opportunity to continue. "To be frank, Elodie, you have been in this school district your entire life. I am very aware of your history. Losing property or disappearing for a few weeks and then telling your stories to get out of trouble. To be honest, I thought your parents had sought the help you needed to get rid of this, as you so accurately termed it, attention-seeking behavior. I really thought this presentation would be a great opportunity for you to be open about your experience."

Elodie took a deep breath and swallowed the words that would get her a detention. He expected her to be rude and disrespectful. She needed to be diplomatic and keep her cool, and maybe, lie a little.

"Mr. Baker, you said it yourself. This is a small town. Everyone knows my past. It's not something I can get free of. When I was young, I had an incredibly active imagination. When I was a child, these characters, this world was real to me. Sometimes more real than my friends and family. The report was to"—Elodie flipped open her folder to find the spot she had marked—"present a personal history. Address your family's story, and how you fit as a part of it."

She looked the teacher in the eyes. He was still smirking, but she kept her voice even and her expression neutral. She set her paper down on his desk. "You said you kept the requirements loose because you wanted us to get creative. I didn't read off a list of facts like a textbook about the adoption process, or my adopted family's history, or how therapy taught me to repress my real feelings so I could fit into society better. That's not what I want to stand in front of a high school class and say. My childhood was a mixture of disappointment and escaping into a dream world to avoid it, and that is exactly what I presented, in the style of my childhood just as I experienced it. I thought my presentation was well written, clever, and creative, but if you didn't like it because I didn't confess to whatever you wanted to hear, then fail me."

Elodie turned on her heel, shouldered her backpack, and left the classroom with her report still sitting on Mr. Baker's desk. It was a power move that could land her in detention or could make the teacher think. She let out a nervous laugh when she was safe in the hallway. The best part of her plan, leaving the paper behind, meant she couldn't get her parents to sign it.

Chapter Five

"WHAT HAPPENED?" Vanessa asked, leaning against Elodie's locker in a pair of brightly colored leggings with cuffed shorts over the top.

Elodie blinked. Now that she was away from her teacher, in the coolness of the hall she could feel her cheeks burning. She wondered how red they'd been during her speech.

"Was it about the report? Did that asshat give you a bad grade?"

"I gave the paper back to him and told him why I deserved a better grade," Elodie said with a small wobbly smile.

Vanessa gasped. "Oh, girl! I'm so proud of you." She hugged Elodie. "It's not like your paper was that far out there, anyway. I presented a painting as my report, and I got a B."

"And you deserved an A."

"But my point is, he can't fail you for being outside the parameters of the report when he didn't really set any."

Elodie shook her head. "He wants me to get the paper signed by my parents by Monday."

Vanessa winced. She knew Elodie's mom and her love for normal very well. "Are you gonna forge it?"

"I left the report on his desk."

They laughed together for a minute, and then Elodie put in her locker combination and started changing out her books.

"Well, I have a story that will make you feel better. Ms. Hensley's second period all got detention after orchestrating a book drop every three minutes. Poor woman. Can you imagine? Every three minutes while you're giving a lecture on quadratic equations your entire class just slams their books down on their desks. After about an hour of it, she grabbed the book off Jackson's desk, you know he sits in front now so she can monitor him, not that it helps though, obviously, and then she just started ripping his book apart! Can you imagine? Pages streaming through the air as she savagely ripped them out! I heard they called in a sub for the rest of the day."

"Are you serious?" Elodie was laughing so hard by the end, it was hard to get the question out. Thank the gods she had math first period. "Well, I wouldn't put it past Jackson to pull that. Ms. Hensley was always a bit of a loose cannon anyway. I thought she was gonna quit after the last time her entire class asked to go to the bathroom one by one and never came back."

The girls made their way to the back hall and pushed open the door to the stairs leading down to the quad. Matt was waiting for them at the top of the staircase as if he could predict Elodie's every move.

"Hey, Elodie," Matt said casually with his hands in his pockets as he moved, blocking her path to the quad. Vanessa waved goodbye with a big wink at Elodie and snuck off down the stairs.

"Hey, Matt," Elodie said back lamely as the butterflies returned in full force, set on destroying her insides.

"So did you hear about Ms. Hensley's second period?" Matt asked, shaking his head. "I always knew she would lose it one day. Those jerks just wanted to see it happen and kept pushing her over the edge."

"Yeah, Jackson has always been the one to start that stuff, it's annoying that since she ripped up his book, he'll get tons of attention for it and probably a formal apology from the school or something."

"I don't think so," he said knowingly. "I work in the office second period and from what I overheard MacAvoy say, he knows it was mostly Jackson and his cronies who started it. Anyway, enough about him." Matt leaned back against the railing in a way that made his T-shirt pull tight against his chest. "I was wondering if you were free tomorrow night, maybe wanted to catch a movie with me or something?"

Her heart pounded out a loud rhythm, and the butterflies in her stomach danced joyously to the beat. Her cheeks were on fire.

"Yeah, that would be fun," Elodie responded in a casual way, feeling everything but casual in that moment. How did girls twirl their hair in that "I like you" way again? She didn't think she would be very convincing with her hair already back in a ponytail and decided not to risk it.

"Great." He smiled. It was a brilliant smile that lit up his warm brown eyes and made a dimple in his cheek stand out. "Um, you know James, right? He's my best friend and also has a date tomorrow he's really nervous about. Would you be open to making it a double date?"

"Oh." Elodie's heart plummeted. James had a date, too? She wanted to go with Matt, but a double date with James and some other girl would be like betraying Vanessa. "I'm not so sure that would be a good idea." Her heart crumbled a little.

"Oh." That perfect smile was gone now, and Matt looked sad, and maybe a little confused. She should take it back and just agree to anything. No. She pushed that thought away. That was never a good idea with boys in high school just because they were cute.

"Really?" Matt asked again. "Vanessa said you would probably say yes."

"Wait, Vanessa said that?"

"Yeah, James asked her out, and she said you would probably be open to a double."

Elodie wasn't sure how long she stood there with her mouth slightly open, trying to connect things in her head. Apparently, all her eloquence had been used up for the day with Mr. Baker.

How had Vanessa not told her about the date? Vanessa had been crazy excited just knowing there was a chance James was open to dating anyone. How did she keep that secret when they had just talked?

Elodie shook her head and smiled at Matt. "Can we start over?"

Matt smiled slightly and nodded. "Elodie, would you like to go on a double date with me and James and Vanessa tomorrow night?"

"Yes, I would love to."

Matt smiled again, and Elodie couldn't help but smile back.

"Great! How about I pick you up at your place around seven? You live in the big house just around the corner from school, right? I think I pass there on my drive home."

"Yep, that's me, big green house on the turn." Elodie didn't know what to do with her hands. What did she usually do with them when she spoke to people? She put them behind her back. It felt wrong but she needed to stop fidgeting.

"Great! I can't wait, see you then, Elodie." He touched her shoulder gently as he walked past, back inside the school. His eyes had seemed to sparkle as they connected with hers and the spot on her arm burned. Elodie gave a small wave and watched him until he disappeared, then she turned tail and half skipped down the stairs, ignoring the few students she passed until she reached Vanessa at their usual lunch spot under the big tree in the center of the quad.

When she reached her friend, Elodie wiped the huge grin off her face and sat calmly as if nothing had happened.

"So? How did it go?" Vanessa asked with an innocent smile.

"Why didn't you tell me James asked you out?"

"Sssssssshhhhhhh! Not so loud."

Elodie laughed. "Vanessa, why don't you want anyone to know? You live for spreading news."

"Exactly," Vanessa giggled. "I wanna see how fast it spreads if I don't tell anyone. It's like a social experiment."

"Ness, I almost said no."

"What? To Matt? Why would you do that?"

"Because he asked if I wanted to go on a double date with James and his date, and I thought it was someone other than you," Elodie drawled.

Vanessa thought about it, then a look of understanding dawned on her face. "You mean you thought James was going out with another girl, and you almost said no like in defense of my honor or something?"

Elodie smiled. "It just wouldn't have been right if it was another girl."

"Aw." Vanessa leaned over until her shoulder rested against Elodie's. "You are literally the best friend a girl could ever hope for. But next time take the date."

Vanessa laughed, and Elodie rolled her eyes at her friend. "Is it weird we're going out on a Thursday?" Elodie asked, smiling. She couldn't seem to stop smiling.

"No, that's my fault. I work Friday and Saturday, and we didn't want to wait until next week."

Vanessa was grinning dreamily now, and Elodie joined her.

There was a small part of Elodie that felt unsure about the date and wondered if Matt had only asked her because of James and Vanessa. She would still go if that were the case, she just wanted to know.

"Do you want to come over after school and we can work on outfits?" Elodie asked.

Vanessa's face lit up and then fell. "No, I can't. I'm working tonight," she said with a big sigh. "But we could do it tomorrow before we go out. I can get my mom to bring me by at like five and we could do hair and makeup."

"Yes, that would be perfect!"

The girls spent the rest of the day talking about shoes and clothes and hair.

Elodie walked the short block home after school. She paused at the corner before turning onto her street. There was a very thick bit of shimmer on the sidewalk in front of her and she sidestepped it quickly. She pushed the feeling of guilt away sharply as she walked past the ruakh bleeding through to this world, trying to call out to her. She readjusted her backpack and walked faster.

She was halfway down the street when Matt drove past in his old vintage red truck and gave her a little wave. Elodie waved back, hoping that wasn't lame.

As she passed the familiar birch trees, someone stepped out from behind a telephone pole and Elodie jumped and let out a little shriek. The smug look on Allen's face made her want to hit him.

"Can I help you?" she asked.

Allen leaned rigidly against the telephone pole with his arms crossed. "So, you're *the* Elodie? Princess of Aluna and Tross. I'm so honored to be in your presence." He gave Elodie a little bow, his blond hair flopping around with his movements. "You've had it quite cushy over the years, haven't you?"

"I—I'm not quite sure I know what you're talking about," Elodie stammered. "I haven't had anything easy."

"Right, so now you're telling me that little speech you gave yesterday was a lie? The legendary Wizard Gediminas, the greatest wizard of our time, hasn't made it his top priority to meet with you and mentor you each time you jump? Do you have any idea what it's been like for me over the years? Each time I jump I end up in, gods know where, without a soul caring to help me."

Elodie's mind was going crazy. Was this kid saying he was one of the Misplaced Children? Could he really be one of the other heirs to the Twoshy who'd spent their life being ripped out of one reality and shoved into another? She couldn't believe it. She'd do anything for a chance to talk with someone else like her, and now here he was, and he was pissed at her.

"Gediminas became my mentor, always taking me on grand adventures," Allen quoted the line from Elodie's story in a high-pitched mocking voice. "My mother was on the council of Pundica when I was misplaced. That means I don't have any inheritance or lands or titles waiting for me back there. There's no kingdom of people who care about me or most of the others when we jump. Tristan, Thomas, Kirk, and Christopher, all of us have had a hell of a time over the years making our own way, and here you are talking about the great Wizard Gediminas guiding you each time you travel back home." Allen turned and started pacing. "I have magic so at least I could head to the Academy when I jump, they have dorms and let me stay and study, even though I'm not technically a student. But Tristan has nothing. He's had to find odd jobs for food or a bed. Sam has a great-nephew who lets her stay with him, but none of us have a welcoming committee or even hope of a life when we return. And here you are, talking of your adventures. And to think you're supposed to be the one the prophecy is about, the one everyone thinks will break this spell."

Allen seemed to have run out of words and just stood there glaring at Elodie with something like disgust.

"So, you're saying you're like me?" Elodie asked, still wanting confirmation.

"Apparently not. Apparently, I'm not as freaking important to the cosmic order of things as you are." Allen threw up his hands and started walking away. Then he stopped and turned back. "Do you have any idea how much I would give just to sit with Wizard Gediminas for an hour and talk about his theories on quantum anomalies? The man is a genius." He looked her up and down. "And you don't seem to have a bit of ruakh on you. I doubt you've even started researching the magic of the spell, I mean look at you. Do you even know how to influence the ruakh when you're in this world?"

Elodie just looked at him. "Of course not, no one can use magic in this world. It's totally separate."

"Right." Allen shook his head. "You are a moron. The others think I'm being too hard on you, Sam is so excited to finally meet you. I'm sure she will be disappointed to find out what a poser you are. You stand up and give a big speech about how you're different, but I've been watching you. You do everything possible to blend in, while saying you're different." Allen looked her in the eyes closely, as though looking for something. Then he sighed and turned away. "Whatever."

He walked up the road without turning back.

Elodie stood on the sidewalk next to the birch trees and the telephone pole. Her whole world felt shaken. She'd never met any of the other Misplaced Children before and never questioned why. Standing in the shadow of the birch, uncertainty surrounded her, closing in. She wavered and let the birch tree catch her. For the first time in Elodie's life, the birch tree didn't feel friendly toward her. It was as if the tree was scolding her for being mean to the boy.

Had Allen used his magic to influence the birches during his speech?

Elodie closed her eyes and put up a wall against the feeling of the trees. She reached instead for her resolution to think normal and to be normal.

Was she a phony trying to be normal?

Elodie shook her head. She couldn't think like that, she just had to try. Once she got her thoughts under control, she made her way up her driveway into her house.

A few years ago, Elodie decided to start lying to her mom and dad and to everyone but Vanessa. For about a year or so, her mom would watch her strangely as if expecting her to break and start telling the world about her magical adventures again, but as more and more time passed with no stories, her mother began to relax and the broken-adopted-kid look in her eyes seemed to fade. Half the time, Elodie still didn't know how to talk to her mom, and the rest of the time, didn't want to talk to her; at this point, that was just another part of their relationship. It was comfortable and expected.

Things with her dad had never really changed. He was a presence at breakfast and dinner and a good companion when she wanted to sit in the same room with someone and read, but he didn't frequently engage other than to suggest a book. It was a straightforward relationship to maintain.

When Elodie entered the kitchen her mom was at the counter talking on the phone with what sounded like a frantic bride. "Yes, Deedra, the flowers will be there fresh. I promise everything will look beautiful." Her mom rubbed her forehead, a look of irritation etched into her face, but her voice never broke character. "No, we won't bring the cake out until after the first dance is done, just like we discussed."

Her mom always seemed so frustrated coordinating weddings. Tensions ran high and there were so many minor details that felt monumental when they didn't work out, but in that world, her mom flourished. The work gave her mom somewhere to be in control of every little facet of a day and situation, and she seemed to love it.

Elodie climbed onto a stool at the kitchen bar and grabbed a piece of fruit, waiting for the phone call to end.

"Yes, I will make sure the DJ knows not to give your mother a microphone after she has had a few. Don't worry, I will make the day perfect for you, Deedra. It's really no problem, call me anytime. All right. Goodbye."

Her mom set down the phone with a deep sigh, then as if reinflating, turned to her daughter and with her usual peppy voice said, "Hi honey, how was your day?"

"Pretty great, actually." Elodie peeled the sticker off her apple as though it was a delicate process. "I was kind of wanting to talk to you about it."

Her mother looked up at her, eyes wide and eyebrows disappearing into her hairline. It wasn't usual that Elodie wanted to share.

"Of course you can talk about it, I would love to hear about your day, sweetie." Her mother's face relaxed, and she leaned against the counter, her total attention on her daughter.

Elodie took a deep breath. She wasn't sure how her mother would respond. They'd never really talked about dating before. They'd never really talked about anything real before.

"Well, I just wanted to let you know that a boy from school asked me out so I have a date tomorrow night," Elodie said, all rather fast, hoping that would make it easier.

Whatever Elodie was expecting from her mother, it wasn't the look of pure, almost manic joy that crossed her face. "You have a date?" she asked, her voice going up several octaves. "Elodie, that is so fantastic. Who is he?"

"Um, his name is Matt, Matthew Moreno. He's a junior and was in my chemistry class last year. He's on the honor roll."

"A smart boy, is he?" Elodie's mother did something weird with her eyebrows as she said this. "Well, what are you two lovebirds going to do?"

Elodie felt a bit embarrassed by the way her mom was reacting. Maybe she should have brought up boys once or twice over the years so her mother could have worked off some of this excitement. "I think we are just gonna go to the movies or something. Vanessa also has a date with Matt's best friend, James, so we are gonna double."

"Oh, that will be so much fun! How are you getting there? Do you need me to drive you?"

"No, Mom, he has a car and a license and everything," Elodie said, mortified at the thought of her mom driving her on a date. "Well, I'm gonna go do my homework."

Elodie jumped down from the stool and ran upstairs as fast as she could before her mother offered to braid her hair or do her makeup.

When her dad got home her mom must have told him about her pending date. After dinner, he ushered Elodie into the living room to show her some basic self-defense.

"Now if he comes at you like this you take your knee and you hit him in the groin as hard as you can, okay? Then, you run. This is very important because when he gets up, he's going to be mad. Run to where you know there are people and call one of us and stay on the phone until we get there."

Her dad was standing off balance. She knew enough self-defense from Silas and a few others over the years to know that much. She could shove her dad to the right with a thrust of her hip and a small push, and he would go down hard.

"Dad, this is stupid. I will be with Vanessa and James all night. I'll be fine."

"And you'll be more fine if you know this. Now, let me show you how to break a wrist hold."

Elodie sighed and let her dad grab her wrist.

This was good. Maybe after her parents saw how normal and well-adjusted her, hopefully, new boyfriend was, they would relax and stop thinking their daughter was a basket case, ready to go off at a moment's notice. Matt was so much easier to explain than some squire living in another world.

Chapter Six

THURSDAY CREPT BY. Elodie spent the day in a constant state of nervousness and excitement. She just had to get through the day, and then she could go out with Matt on her first-ever official date. She alternated between feeling jittery and sick when she imagined their evening.

The only thoughts that could break through her daydreams were about Allen. She was leery of running into him, but still wanted to see if she could get contact information for some of the other Misplaced he'd mentioned. Maybe they would be more friendly, and for once she could talk to someone actually like her, who knew without a shadow of a doubt that she hadn't made up her past. She planned to corner him after English, and she watched the clock, her foot tapping a fast rhythm against the linoleum. Allen was always the first out the door and if she hurries he wouldn't loose her in the crowd.

The bell rang and Elodie jumped from her seat, backpack in hand.

"Elodie, can I have a minute?" Mr. Baker asked.

Elodie stifled a groan and waited for the other students to exit before she approached his desk. He waved her paper in front of her, and she snatched it from the air. The D had been turned into a B. Elodie tried not to grin.

"I expect more out of you next time," he said, before he focused on the papers on his desk, ignoring her.

Elodie turned and rolled her eyes.

When she left the classroom, Allen was nowhere to be seen, so Elodie walked toward her locker to put away her books. Something caught her eye from across the hall. The orange object contrasted with the blue paint on her locker door. Elodie really hoped it wasn't some prank or joke. She didn't have the energy to deal with something new.

As she drew closer, something bubbled up in her chest. The mysterious thing on her locker looked like a flower, but there were too many backpacks and heads in the way. She pushed past some kid a foot taller than her and stepped into the gap in front of her locker.

It was a flower. A single long-stemmed rose someone had stuck upside down into the vent of the door, hanging there for all to see.

There was a note.

Can't wait for tonight.
  —Matt

Elodie giggled. She couldn't help it, the feelings just bubbled up inside of her until they spilled out.

"Oh em gee. Did you just giggle? That is so cute." Vanessa said, screwing up her face in a look that was just on the right side of caring and patronizing. "El, darling, this is like a whole new season of your life, just waiting to burst."

Elodie pulled the rose out of the vent and brought it to her nose. She closed her eyes and took a deep breath. The sweet yet spicy scent floated up around her and filled her with hope and peace and anticipation. "Leave me alone, I have a lot of hormones happening right now and you're not helping."

Vanessa snorted and leaned against the locker next to her. "Should I tell him you don't like roses?"

"Shut up, I do now. It's perfect." Roses stood for many things, love, beauty, the dangers of a pursuit for perfection. They could also be useful, mildly sedative and a great antiseptic. They were also boring and overused in the media. She pushed away the information and facts. This rose was pretty and that was all it needed to be. It was yellow at its base, with each petal darkening to a brilliant red at the edge.

"Don't all the different colors have meanings for roses? Yellow means friendship and red is passion, right? So maybe he's saying he's super passionate to be your friend?"

"Or maybe he just picked it because he liked the smell." Elodie held the bloom out for her friend to inhale. Yellow with red tips stood for falling in love or friendship deepening to more, but Vanessa didn't need to know that.

"Mmm, it is really pretty. He did a good job."

Elodie couldn't help the smile that overtook her face, but she held in the giggle.

People were passing them and watching her. A girl with a rose at school? Yeah, that was big news. Did she get it for herself to make herself look better, or did someone actually give it to her?

Ugh.

Elodie put her books in her locker and tucked the rose inside where it would be safe until after school.

She and Vanessa headed out to the quad and her oak tree for lunch.

Elodie told Vanessa all about her encounter with Allen the day before. The memories took the edge off her excitement.

"He actually said he was one of the Misplaced?" Vanessa asked, her eyes lit with excitement.

"No, he didn't say it like that. It was more like that was already a given, and he was just talking about the Twoshy like he had always been there. Like he said, he's from Pundica. I don't think I've ever mentioned Pundica to anyone. Well, to you, but that's it."

Vanessa thought for a moment. "That's the country where the big magical university is, right? Hogwarts, Twoshy style?"

Elodie laughed. "Yeah, exactly. And he knew the rulers of Pundica are elected so their kids don't inherit a title. No one would know that but one of the Misplaced."

"What are the odds that one of the other Misplaced would turn up here, at our school?" Vanessa asked in awe. She pulled her peanut butter sandwich out of her bag and started eating.

"Statistics have never been my strong point. But I still don't know what I should do about it. He called me a phony. He says I'm not working hard enough at breaking the spell. I mean, what can I even do about it while I'm here?"

Vanessa paused and put down her sandwich. She got a look in her eyes of deep concentration that Elodie only ever saw when Vanessa was saying something she thought truly important.

"El, I get that you have a tremendous amount of responsibility on your shoulders. You live with each foot in a different world, and that kind of existence doesn't allow for you to be all-in in any life. I will be the first to admit I don't want you breaking your spell. I mean, that would cause you to leave me forever, so of course I don't want it. But I do understand what he means. You have such an old soul, and your heart isn't in the whole high school thing. I know you try for my benefit, but you really do suck at being a teen."

Elodie frowned and looked down. A small, perfect acorn sat on the bench next to her. She picked it up and ran her finger over the smooth shell, such a small object to hold so much potential life and magic. "I thought I was doing a good job?"

Vanessa smiled and nudged Elodie in the shoulder. "You were made for greater things than this, but you're still just a kid. It's a sucky place to be." They were silent for a moment as the thought hung between them. "Maybe you should try talking to Allen about what he's learned. Maybe he can help show you how your time in this world doesn't have to be a waste. Just because you'll break the spell doesn't mean you can't have help."

It was a good idea, talking with Allen. If only he didn't hate her so much. She put the small acorn into her pocket.

As she ate the last of her grapes and packed up her trash, she spotted Allen across the quad. He was walking as if on a mission, headed straight for her. It surprised Elodie, she didn't think he would talk to her so openly with Vanessa sitting there. Elodie nudged her best friend and nodded in his direction.

"Look, here he comes."

As they watched the boy cross the quad, Elodie noticed an odd shimmer pop up in front of Allen's path.

"Vanessa! Do you see that? The shimmer?" Elodie pointed, but the girl didn't seem to see it.

"Where is it?" Vanessa asked, peering excitedly in the direction Elodie pointed. "I don't see anything."

Vanessa may not have seen the ruakh hanging in the air, but Allen saw it, if only a few moments too late. He made a movement as if dodging a ball. Then all at once, Elodie saw something she'd only ever felt before. The ruakh seemed to grow dense all around him until he looked up at her, a defeated look in his eyes, and then a moment later he was simply gone. The ruakh dispersing like smoke in the wind.

"What. The. Hell." Vanessa sat perfectly still, staring at the space Allen had been only a moment before.

"I've never seen it from this side before." Elodie looked at Vanessa. "Well, now at least we know he was telling the truth about being a Misplaced Child and not just screwing with me."

A small choking sound came from Vanessa. "That." She took a deep breath. "Was literally the coolest thing I've ever seen." She rubbed a hand over her face and broke out in a huge grin. "Shit, Elodie. He just disappeared like he disapparated or something! Only there wasn't a loud crack. I mean I always believed you and everything, but actually seeing it. I can't even. Does it always happen like that for you? Why didn't I see the shimmer? I was really excited to see that bit. Gosh. This is literally the best day ever."

ALTHOUGH IT ATTEMPTED to move at a snail's pace, eventually her school day ended. Elodie spent the hours her brain should have been thinking about social contracts or negative integers daydreaming about what she would do with Matt. She felt so awkward around him. It felt like her entire past was parading around her head naming her as a freak every time they spoke. But he didn't seem to see any of it, as though he just shrugged off her past as a fun story. They never really talked about it when they were chemistry partners, focusing instead on truly made-up stories in the form of favorite books and movies.

When the last bell of the day rang, Elodie was already standing up and throwing her backpack over her shoulder. Before Elodie retrieved her books and the long stem rose from her locker, she said a quick goodbye to Vanessa, who planned to come over at four with all her makeup.

As she started walking home from school, Elodie went over again what she planned to wear that night. Her mom was forever buying her new clothes, mainly dresses. Although Elodie liked dresses she wasn't the kind of girl who would wear one to school. So, they sat new in her closet.

If Elodie didn't think about her clothing or what was in style or what shoes went with what outfit, she was fine. She was confident enough about how she looked. But as soon as she started thinking about all those details—if she looked good, if something fit right— her insecurities poured in. She needed Vanessa to be the voice of reason. If Vanessa told her she looked good in something, she could believe it and wear it confidently.

There was a particular blue dress she wanted Vanessa's opinion on. She thought it would go great with her eyes, and she knew it would cover her weird birthmark. Everything her mom bought for her covered the mark.

She planned to keep her hair down and maybe curl it a bit. It always made the light tones in her brown hair shine when she curled it.

Elodie imagined standing outside the theater, leaning up against the rough stucco of the building, talking casually to Matt as a lock of her hair fell into her eyes. He would brush it away, maybe make a comment on how beautiful her blue eyes were, then lean down and kiss her. She brought the rose to her nose and inhaled deeply, letting the scent wash over her.

Elodie shook her head as a rough pang of guilt sliced through her stomach. Why should she feel guilt when thinking about Matt? It was honest and innocent. Yes, she might have occasionally thought of another boy who was currently in another realm far outside of her reach, but she'd never sworn herself to him, and other than a few jokes about marriage, she had never said she liked him. Besides, with how time moved between the illusion and the Twoshy, Silas was probably in his sixties and balding. So what did it matter if Matt was just an elaborate part of an illusion. Didn't that make kissing him even more innocent if he wasn't real?

Elodie continued her walk and pushed the confusing thoughts from her mind and instead thought about shoes. She didn't want to wear heels, too showy for a night at the movies. Maybe she would just wear tights under her dress with some simple flats. She kept walking the usual path home, picturing this all in her head, distracting herself from everything else. As she reached the corner turn at the top of her street, the shimmer that had loomed there the day before had grown with force.

She walked into it like a spiderweb in the night, and the ruakh grabbed Elodie with intense strength. But Elodie wouldn't let go this time.

She dropped her backpack and the rose and pulled away as hard as she could.

She wasn't doing this again, letting her life get disrupted just because some unseen force deemed it a good time. She demanded to be in control now, and so she fought hard. The shimmer grabbed tighter and Elodie planted her feet. When the tug came, she was ready for it and braced herself. It held her bones and pulled her so hard to the left that she almost fell to her knees. This took more strength than she expected. She kept resisting, fighting with all she had, but deep down she knew she couldn't break free of this. She gritted her teeth against the magic.

There was another force inside of the shimmer she had not experienced before. It was like a strong and ancient voice she could feel but not hear, it emulated an emotion she didn't understand, and reached her inner self in a powerful, yet gentle, trusting way. She felt vulnerable and naked in its presence, as though she could keep no secrets from it.

The radiating internal light flooded every corner of her soul, and Elodie flinched away from the ancient force. With her flinch Elodie lost her grip on the fight. The ruakh now had her firm in its hands and all Elodie could do was be pulled away.

With a cry of anger and frustration, Elodie surrendered her will and with another pull from the shimmer of a force, she fell to the left.

She fell head over heels for too long: through space and light, thick like water on her skin until she landed hard on her shoulder onto packed eres, dead leaves, and the usual trash that covered a forest floor.

Chapter Seven

ELODIE ROLLED onto her back and groaned. Her shoulder throbbed.

It was stupid to fight so hard against the ruakh. She'd never had any control over her travels before, why on earth or eres did she think she'd be able to fight it this time?

Laying on her back assessing her new bumps and bruises, she tried to reorient herself to her new surroundings. Back home in the illusion it had been warm. Late spring, almost summer. But here it was chillier, maybe early fall. She squinted at the trees, they were wrong for fall. Big purple blossoms filled the branches above, fit for a warming spring day.

Ruakh was heavy in the air, filling her and greeting her like an old friend. She flinched from it.

If Elodie wished it, she could use the ability inside of herself to reach out and bend the ruakh to her will, to create magic and spells. This was the world and the life she was born to. She'd inherited her small gift of magic from her father's line and should have welcomed and embraced the ability. Elodie hated it. She'd learned to live with many facets of this world. She'd even loved using the more practical sides of magic, like herb lore and its medicinal uses for healing, but the flashy sides, like lighting a candle or creating wards of protection, had always seemed too much for her psyche to handle. As if accepting the magic would forever crack the facade of normalcy she tried to sustain in the illusion.

Elodie closed her eyes and took a moment to accept that for a long, undetermined time until the spell decided to pull her back through, she would be here in the magical world of Eres. She wouldn't be going to school or sleeping in her bed. She wouldn't have the luxury of a daily shower or walking into the kitchen to get some ice cream. For however long the fates decided, Elodie would be here at the beck and call of whatever adventure or lesson the old Wizard decided she needed. Elodie took another deep breath and accepted that she wouldn't be going out with Matt tonight.

What a cruel joke.

Hot liquid pooled over her vision and she squeezed her eyes shut tight, letting the tears run down the sides of her face.

She would not cry in front of Gedas.

Her hands clenched into fists at her side, nails biting into her palms. She focused on the sharp pain and breathed through the anger and disappointment.

She let out a shaky breath and wiped her eyes.

The wind blew past her bringing with it the crisp scent of fall. Birds called in the distance and small animals scampered through the leaves. Something was missing.

Where was Gedas?

Whenever Elodie landed in the Twoshy, it would take just a moment for him to pop his pepper and salt beard and gray eyes into her view, but as she looked around from her supine position, she didn't see the old wizard at all.

It didn't matter. She relaxed back on the leaves. The old man would turn up soon. She stared up, examining the purple trees towering over her.

She knew these trees.

The trunks were such a dark purple they looked nearly black, and the big wide leaves spread out above her in every shade of purple imaginable. The large full blossoms filled in the branches with beautiful magenta petals lightening to an almost bright pink center. She'd seen these trees before during one of the trips she'd taken when she was twelve. Unlike most fruit-bearing trees that blossomed in the spring and ripened over the summer months, variant trees didn't follow the seasons. They followed the strength of ruakh flowing through the eres and reached their climax of growth over the winter months.

With the trees above her budding and blossoming, it must be fall.

Elodie pushed herself off the ground and sat up. She rubbed her bare arms and looked around the dim, empty forest. Annoyance crept in. Usually by now Gedas would be leading her to a campsite and a warm fire or would be draping a cloak over her shoulders as they mounted horses and set off toward their destination. He'd never not been there when she'd appeared.

Like echoes from a dream, the smallest bit of worry began to seep into the edges of her mind, and she wrapped her arms around herself.

Gedas studied the ruakh as it shifted through the world, it was how he knew when Elodie would arrive from the illusion. It wasn't something most mages could do. But Gedas wasn't most mages. He was a wizard. The most powerful rank of magic user. Had something prevented him from reaching her? Had their last few arguments been too much for him, and now he'd given up on her, deciding to let her fend for herself for once?

What was she thinking, Gedas would never abandon her. Maybe something had gone wrong with the spell when it dropped her. She'd never fought it so hard before. Maybe her resistance changed her destination somehow, and Gedas hadn't been able to predict it. Either way, it didn't matter. It was cold and Elodie was hungry. She couldn't stay in this forest without supplies. She'd have to fend for herself just like Allen and the other Misplaced did every time they traveled.

The trees around her were old. Their trunks were wide, and their canopy so thick they blocked most of the daylight. If this was the oldest part of the forest, the village of Lottsin would be half a day's ride north of her. Heading for the village would be her best choice.

She could always go south into the Tokke Mountains.

She didn't know where the thought came from, but it was

absurd. The mountains created the south border of Aluna and were the dividing line between the continent of the Twoshy and whatever unknown, uncharted lands lay to the south. There was nothing for her in the south and winter came early in the shadow of the mountains. She would never survive the journey with no supplies. She shook her head. There was no reason to go south. Everyone she knew was north and east of her.

Walking north, even if she were wrong about her exact location, she'd eventually run into a road or village or farm and could orient herself from there.

She took stock of what she was wearing. A light T-shirt and capri jeans had seemed perfect for an end of spring school day, but a bit neglectful for the cool fall day in Aluna. Her look was finished off with her favorite green sneakers. They would start to hurt if she walked too much, and the canvas of her shoes was the opposite of waterproof, but it couldn't be helped. Her biggest worry would be reaching a village before nightfall.

She waited another ten minutes just to see if Gedas would arrive. His absence was so odd that she kept peering through the shadowed trunks around her expecting his figure to appear. Eventually, she set her mind to the long walk and stood. She could just make out the position of the sun through the canopy of leaves above and decided it felt earlier than noon. She started in the direction she hoped was north, winding her way around trees and stepping over brush that reached out and scratched the exposed flesh of her ankles every chance it got.

There was a spell she could use to determine her direction, confirm she was on the right path, but even as her mind thought through the requirements, and her eyes sought the necessary tools around her, she dismissed it. Doing magic would only make it harder to adjust when she returned to the illusion.

She reached the edge of the tree line, cold and a little sweaty, her bare legs covered in scratches. A small road wound around a grove of trees and hills in the distance, and relief rushed through her.

A road meant people and shelter.

A tall wide hill stretched up directly north of her, and the road wound far to the west of the hill. She could follow the winding road, possibly a longer path but the most likely option for finding people and a village, or she could head straight north to the top of the hill where she could see for miles. If there was a village close, it might be quicker than following the winding road.

The soft ground under her sneakers squelched from recent rain. The road would be best if the hills were full of mud. She turned toward the road but hesitated again. A lingering feeling she couldn't yet decipher was bothering her, like cold fingers running down the back of her neck. The road didn't feel like the right choice, and her gut was pointing her to the hills. Decided, she set off straight north toward the hills.

Elodie took one last backward glance to the south, into the thick leaves and blossoms of the variant trees. As she turned back to the open land, she thought she saw something move out of the corner of her eye, high up among the tree blossoms. Spinning back around to get a second look at the reddish-purple blur she'd thought she'd seen, there was nothing. Stories Gedas had once told her of a legendary creature that protected this forest flicked through her mind. She shivered and stepped fully into the sunlight.

When her foot sunk into the first patch of mud, Elodie began to regret her decision to not take the road. Her gut was a moron, and she should stop listening to it. Her socks squished as the water soaked through the canvas of her shoes, and within a few hours of walking, her toes were numb from the cold.

At the top of the hill, Elodie could make out the rough shapes of man-made structures on the horizon. The road would have been a longer distance, but now that she was cold, covered in mud, and being attacked by small hordes of bugs, Elodie didn't think the scenic route had been the wise decision. She hadn't felt the sense of foreboding again after leaving the forest.

The shoulder she'd fallen on bruised and stiffened, the sun was sinking in the sky, and she was hungry. All Elodie wanted in this entire world was to find Gedas and hit him. Her frustration and annoyance were the only things keeping off the chill.

It was fully dark when she reached the edge of the small village of Lottsin. There was more activity than she expected. Men wearing armor rode through the darkness. She saw a three-story building and turned in its direction. With any luck, it would be a tavern with rooms to rent and something hot cooking in the kitchen.

Not wanting the stares that would come from walking through the front door into a full tavern while covered in mud and scratches, Elodie approached the back door of the kitchen in a small alleyway. She gave a hard knock on the door.

"Who be knockin' back here, don't they know we got a house full of hungry payin' customers? Bess, go see who's there."

The door opened and a round-faced woman with brown hair streaked with gray stuck her nose out. Her mouth was rimmed with the blue stains of someone who spent too much of their time self-medicating with cheer sticks. By the look on her face, Elodie thought the woman could use a stick at the moment. She looked startled and maybe afraid to see Elodie standing there in her strange clothes.

Elodie needed to say something before the woman closed the door in her face.

"Hi there, um, I'm Elodie. Uh, Princess Elodie of Aluna, that is. I'm one of the Misplaced Children, and I just got here. Do you have a room I could—"

"No, I'm sorry, I can't help." The woman tried to close the door, looking worried.

"Wait!"

The woman hesitated, fear clouding her face.

"I need help," Elodie said. It should be enough. No one turned down a Misplaced Child in need. There were laws in place to make sure they would always find assistance in their travels.

"Forgive me, Yer Highness, but you need to leave. Now," she whispered and looked over her shoulder. "It isn't safe for you here." She closed the door in Elodie's face.

Elodie was confused. No one had ever met her with fear. She'd always been greeted with joy, wonder, excitement, or at least odd curiosity. She was as close to a celebrity as this world knew. What could possibly make the tavern unsafe? Did the woman just not want to give up a bed for free?

Elodie raised her hand to knock again.

"Psst!"

She turned and saw an older man peeking through an open door. "Over here, quick," he whispered through the night.

Elodie crossed to the man, unsure of his unusual behavior. "What's happening?" she asked. The worry that had been floating through her all day, suppressed by her exhaustion and frustration started to surface in her chest.

Horses clomped down the road near the alley she stood in. They grew closer and the man darted out of his door and grabbed Elodie by the arm startling her. He pulled her inside with more strength than she thought the thin man possessed. She started to protest and he shushed her, closing the door gently behind them. The sounds of horses approached and then faded into the distance. When it was nothing more than background noise in the night, the man let out a small sigh.

Elodie's heart raced and she backed away from the man until she bumped into a workbench covered with leatherworking tools. Was he helping her or was he part of the danger? Should she look for something metal and pokey to defend herself?

The small room was dark except for the glow of a weak fire in the corner. Elodie could just make out the man's face. He was thin and ragged. His hair was gray, or what was left of it; there was none on the top of his head, but the hair at the sides was pulled back into a thin, long braid. His beard was long and intricately braided as was the current style in the Twoshy, even so it was anything but the elegant, elaborate display men usually paraded around the cities, showing off. Everything about this man looked worn and tired, but there was something in his face that felt familiar to Elodie though she was sure she didn't know him.

"It wasn't very wise of ye to come here m' lady."

"Well let me back out that door and I will leave, no problem," Elodie said, fear rising in her chest. All the stranger danger videos her mother had force-fed her as a child were coming back to her in a flood.

"No, ye miss understand me. Gods, but ye don't even know yet do ye? Suspect ye just arrived through that spell did ye?"

Elodie nodded.

"'Swhat I thought. Now ye listen, come with me. Come on now, I won't hurt ye."

He limped across his small one-room home to the side with a bed near the hearth. A small, old cabinet stood in the corner. He opened it to reveal a few belongings and took out an empty and worn pack. He handed it to Elodie.

"I will give ye what I can spare, but ye'll need to leave before sunrise." He pulled out a pile of clothes from the cabinet. "If ye wear normal clothes and try to cover that mark on ye neck, mayhap none of the enemy will spot ye." He pointed to Elodie's collar, barely covering her weird bird-shaped birthmark. The magical sign every member of the royal family wore. It was a mark of honor in most places Elodie traveled in the Twoshy, but apparently not now.

The old man handed Elodie the pile of worn clothes. Thick woolen tights with many darned holes, an old but thick homespun dress, and a threadbare cloak. "These belonged ter me daughter. She left for Tross more'n seven summers back to be a healer in the lower city." His eyes shone with pride, and a spark of remembrance for a girl she'd known flashed through her. She'd had the same dimpled chin and brown eyes as the man.

"Audrey," Elodie said softly, the name coming back to her.

The man's face lit with a wide smile. "She wrote me a letter once about a time the princess came to help at the clinic. No one but the head healer knew until after she was gone. Said she was kind and hardworking."

It had been one of her many trips the year she was twelve. Gedas had left her in the lower city clinic in the hands of a healer while he went on a mysterious trip. It was the only time she didn't spend a trip with him. Audrey had been an apprentice and helped show Elodie the ropes.

That was also the summer she met Callie. The memory of her last visit with Callie filled her heart with sadness and dread.

She pushed away the feelings.

"What are we hiding from?" she asked the old man.

"The soldiers are out looking for ye." He put the clothes in the bag, then added a waterskin.

"Whose soldiers?" Elodie asked, even more confused.

"They're the army. The army of Aluna."

Elodie didn't understand. The man had to be wrong about the danger. The army was *her* army, led by Knight Commander Jesper. Sir Jesper was Silas's knight commander and a friend. If the army was out there looking for her, they would be trying to protect her.

"What makes you think they are a danger to me?"

"Because of the knight who stood in the town square and read a letter on behalf of the steward. Oburleck has named ye a traitor to the crown and says any who help ye will be just as guilty."

Elodie's jaw dropped. She had no words.

"They made their rounds earlier looking for ye, knocking on every door, making sure we all knew not to go letting ye in if ye showed. They might come round again. Ye should hide in the root cellar."

He crossed the small room to a wall filled with kitchen things and leaned over a trap door. He lifted the door to reveal an old ladder leading down into the cool, dark ground. Elodie didn't think the ladder would hold her.

"I can't stay here. If what you say is true and I'm caught, they will execute you," she said flatly.

The old man just shrugged. "I'm not so young as it would make much of a difference. I won't tarnish me soul with the rest of the cowards out there."

He climbed down first and gestured for her to follow. She stepped onto the first rung carefully. The ladder creaked ominously under her but didn't break. She climbed down fast.

It was cooler down here than in the room with the meager fire, but Elodie understood the need to hide and was thankful enough for his help.

The old man looked around at the bare shelves and stroked his beard. He began grabbing the few items he had and put them in the sack. A hunk of hard cheese, some strips of dried meat, and a hard loaf of bread. Elodie tried to stop him, telling the old man she would be fine, but he brushed her off.

"It be me food to do as I wish, and ye will have greater need of it than me." He handed the sack to her and climbed back up, the ladder creaking as he went. He returned with a few thin blankets that Elodie suspected he took off his own bed. "Try to bunker down and get some sleep, I will wake ye round the midhour." He closed the trap door leaving Elodie in darkness.

The floor creaked softly as the man moved above her. The house was silent for a moment before he moved again, and the bed creaked above.

Elodie did her best to change into the spare clothes in the dark. The dress was a style that hung loosely on a smaller person, which was a good thing for Elodie, being that she was a bit on the chubby side. A few weeks of unprocessed food and foraging for everything she ate would put a big dent in her waistline, but for now, the clothes were tight. Folding up her jeans she felt something hard in the pocket and pulled out the acorn she'd found at lunch, a world away. It felt wrong to abandon the small spark of life in this dark cellar, so she transferred it into the pocket of her dress.

The old man hadn't had any shoes to spare so over her stocking-covered feet she put her pink ankle socks and green muddy sneakers back on. Green shoes weren't a great option now that stealth was something she needed, but she would have to worry about that later.

She wrapped herself up in the cloak and thin blankets and laid down on the hard packed dirt. She was way too cold and uncomfortable to sleep. She sighed as the bug bites on her legs, agitated from changing, started to itch.

The last time Elodie had seen Steward Oburleck he was leading a Progress. It was an old tradition for a king or queen to survey the land, connect with the people, and see what needs they could fill. For Oburleck to lead one should have been scandalous, but most of the court had gone along with it. That was how everything ended up with Oburleck. He had a way of twisting things to fit his desires, and you couldn't help but agree. All with the magical help of the dragon's breath, no doubt.

His breath was horrible, worse than any living thing had a right to. Despite this, he was very charismatic and a strong leader. Even those opposed to his politics found themselves agreeing with him, and the country followed where he led. He could control the whole kingdom, get anything he wanted with that magical plant growing outside of his castle.

When she was twelve, the pieces started falling into place, revealing Oburleck's charisma for what it was—a power grab, a magical one. But after her kidnapping, Elodie didn't want to deal with the knowledge or its consequences and left it to other minds to worry over.

Her old friend Callie tried to help her see the truth. Callie was smart and Elodie's guilt over her friend's situation in the bordello still weighed heavy on her. It had taken time, but now Elodie understood Callie's anger. She understood what it felt like to be powerless in a world and feel that no one could break you free of it.

Elodie shivered as the cold of the floor seeped through the blankets into her back.

Over the last few years in the illusion, Elodie had many sleepless nights remembering the kidnapping and Callie's warning. She remembered how she'd gone to Oburleck and asked for his help to free Callie, to stop slavery completely. The man had convinced Elodie it was impossible as long as Aluna had no proper ruler. She had vowed to him she would break the spell that prevented her from taking the throne.

Had that been the threat that broke Oburleck's graceful facade?

Either way it was a bad move. Calling Elodie a traitor broke the Constitution of Sixteen, making Oburleck and Aluna an enemy of every other nation in the Twoshy.

When the Twoshy—the Kingdoms of Sixteen—was founded, the nations' leaders drafted a constitution, binding them together in peace. There were only fourteen nations now, two shy of the magically powerful number sixteen, but still the constitution was upheld. They did not war with each other. They respected the laws of each nation and didn't involve themselves in another nation's business.

Over the centuries as the nations grew, they added new rules to the constitution, such as naming the Great Highway as international property allowing for trade other nations may not consider legal. When the Misplaced Children had first gone missing, her mentor the Wizard Gediminas told the nations' leaders of a prophecy that said their children would one day break the spell, and Elodie would be the catalyst for that end. Believing their children would return to them, the misguided rulers put a new law into the constitution that any Misplaced Child should be helped when encountered, and that their titles and inheritance would be held for their return.

This left many nations like Aluna handicapped without their heir. Aluna's steward could make small changes to laws with the agreement of the council, but he could never make the changes a kingdom needed over decades.

The leaders of the Twoshy hadn't known how long it would take their children to return. Elodie's parents had been dead for decades.

And now, Oburleck who was entrusted to protect Elodie's birthright was calling her a traitor and breaking the constitution. If he did catch her, hurt her in any way, or attempted to name himself king, it was enough reason for any of Aluna's neighbors to go to war. Aluna had always been the largest of the Twoshy, and some of their neighbors would take the opportunity to expand their land if it were presented.

It was hard to say how many hours she'd been walking since landing in the Twoshy, but Elodie figured if she was still in the illusion, she would be home from her date with Matt by now. She wondered how it would have gone. Would they have gone to a movie? Would he have tried to kiss her? Did she even want him to kiss her?

Now that she was in the Twoshy, images of Matt and his brown eyes faded into her memory like a dream, but she didn't want to let it go quietly. She was mad at the spell for interrupting her attempt at a normal life. She didn't want to think about green-eyed squires or the mess her kingdom had become in her absence.

Fear and worry started to overwhelm her. Pressure formed behind her eyes and a sob built in her throat.

Pounding echoed around her.

"Open up," came a muffled shout. Elodie froze in fear.

Chapter Eight

THE BED creaked and the old man shuffled across the floor above her.

"What is this? Ye already searched here hours ago. Hey!"

Torchlight shone through the floorboards as heavy feet pounded above her.

"There's nothing in here," a deep voice said.

"Turn the bed," said a calm female voice.

There was a loud scraping and then a heavy thump.

"Nothin'."

A heavy sigh.

"Let's get to the next one," the woman said.

The footsteps sounded again and then there was the clank of the door.

Silence.

There was a long scuffling mixed with a few grunts and another loud thump as the bed righted. Then a scraping sound. Finally, the old man sighed, and the bed creaked again.

The tears were gone, replaced by a cold, aching fear. Elodie lay curled on the floor in silence for a long time.

AFTER A FEW COLD hours of no sleep, itchy bug bites, bruised shoulders, and troubled thoughts, there was another creak followed by the shuffling footsteps of the old man. At last, the trap door opened letting in the faint glow from the fire.

Elodie stood, put away her old clothes, and folded the blankets nicely, leaving them on one of the empty shelves. The old man wouldn't protest if she took them, but she wasn't about to take the man's only possessions as she ventured out on whatever path was before her. She would be warm enough with the patched cloak.

"Hope ye got a little sleep." The old man handed her a chunk of hard bread when she climbed from the cellar.

She thanked him for his help.

"Make sure ye go out the north side of town," he pointed to his left while he said it. "Keep walking that way straight through the cornfield. Ye will pass through farmland mostly but it'll run into the highway in a day or two, though ye may want to stay away from the road."

"Thank you for everything."

He blushed and squeezed her shoulder one last time. "May Ravid's protection go with ye."

She nodded her thanks and opened the door slipping out into the cool fall night. If she made it through this, she would make sure he was rewarded in some way.

She walked quickly and quietly, making sure to pause at the edges of the old buildings, checking for any sign of life. A few soldiers turned down her path. She hid behind a large barrel with something nasty smelling inside. When they were gone, she left the deserted north side of town and ventured across an empty field. With the road to the south of the town curving far around until it ran north, Elodie could go straight through several miles of farmland, hopefully avoiding the searching soldiers before she connected with the highway. Where Elodie would go from there she wasn't exactly sure. But she had several days' worth of walking to think about it.

Elodie was more appreciative of the moon than she'd ever been before as she set off across the countryside. She sent a quick prayer of thanks up to Ravid, the god who had dominion over travels, wanderers, change, and mischief.

Elodie rarely paid alms or gave attention to the gods. Callie used to stop and pay respects at every shrine she passed, trying to gain the attention of the gods to better her life, but Gedas had always warned Elodie away from their attentions. They usually only made things harder. Looking at Callie's life that certainly was true.

Growing up in a world where technology made nearly anything possible, Elodie had never really felt the need to believe in an all-powerful entity. Her mother, while never denying there was a god, or gods in the world also never drew any attention to them. But here in the Twoshy it was different. Call them what you will, gods, magical creatures, super-powered beings that just liked to meddle in the lives of man, here in the Twoshy they were real, and some said they had power.

Elodie walked through the night on an adrenaline high. Waking up to her alarm clock the previous morning felt like a lifetime ago and she was thankful for the anxiety and fear of discovery that kept her moving long after her stamina normally would have crashed. The night was crisp, the air was still and silent. On and on Elodie walked through wheat field after barley field after cornfield. When Elodie did finally call the end to her march for the night, she collapsed at the base of a wide cedar tree enclosed in privacy by large bushes in between the fields.

Before sleep could come Elodie felt something weird, as though eyes searched for her. A chill ran down her spine that had nothing to do with the cold. She knew what she needed to do, but she'd made the decision years ago not to use magic. At the time it seemed necessary if she wanted to survive in the illusion and going back on that choice now felt like a betrayal.

But still, that tingle on the back of her neck, the small stab of fear in her chest, it frightened her.

Reluctantly she stood, reached up into the branches above her, and broke a few sprigs off the cedar. She found a few rocks and used them to anchor down the small sprigs in a rough circle around her and whispered the words of protection Gedas had once taught her. The sprigs lit up with a tiny spark of sapphire blue fire, drawing on the protection and power in the tree's essence to create a shield around her. The spark of fire dimmed, and a small wave of safety rushed around Elodie. She wrapped her cloak tighter around herself and promptly fell asleep.

ELODIE SAT on a small bench in an enclosed garden reading a book in the sun. The yellow carnations were in bloom, and the fragrant scent filled the air around her. Yellow banners flapped in the breeze, the gray albatross sigil snapping in and out of sight on the fabric. The wind picked up and the flowers shivered on their stems. The pages of Elodie's book kept getting blown, and she had to hold tight to keep her place. With a particularly strong gust of wind, the fabric of the banners snapped and the albatross were launched into the air, set free on the breeze. They glided for a long moment, stretching their wings, and then they dove for Elodie. She screamed and ran.

The birds chased her, swooping whenever they could and slapping her with their heavy wings. She pushed through the bushes at the edge of the garden and fell into a hole. The hole was narrow and deep. When she reached the bottom, it stank of filth and death, not even wide enough for her to lay down properly. Then the world shifted, and the old man was in the hole looking up at her. His gray eyes glowed in the fading light that was his life, and he called out to her.

Elodie rolled over on the cold, dark ground. The dream faded, and she skimmed the surface between sleep and consciousness.

It was a fitful sleep, full of itching bug bites, a throbbing shoulder, and aching feet but not quite deep enough to flood her again with dreams.

Her rest ended with the sun as it rose in the sky and brought workers into the field. Light footsteps crept into the edges of her fitful sleep, followed by a soft rustling, and then something pouring onto the ground in a steady stream.

Elodie jerked awake, and her eyes connected with an old, blond man on the other side of a bush who looked as startled as she did. She screeched and scurried back against the tree while he jumped and fumbled before picking up a large metal scythe and ran from the bushes.

Elodie leaned against the tree breathing heavily. Now that she was awake, she could hear activity all around her like a steady thrumming. She stood slowly and looked out above the bushes to see fields filled with workers. The blond man was slowly jogging back to a place among the wheat, head down and not looking back.

Elodie gave the man a thorough look over as he stopped in the field and continued his work. He was probably the same age as her father, but he looked older. His soft yellow hair didn't seem to have a streak of gray in it, but a lifetime of hard work was etched on his sunbaked skin. His breeches and tunic looked nearly as old and worn as he did. A bright glint of metal at his neck caught Elodie's eye. Her eyes rested on this collar, the thick metal ring that bound him as a slave. Guilt, dread, and anger rose in her stomach at the sight of it.

Elodie took a few deep breaths to calm herself and grabbed her bag out of the dirt.

The small shield of protection around her was weak and faint. It had barely lasted the few hours she'd rested. She kicked one of the rocks and sprigs out of place, ending the spell completely, and walked into the open field. There were workers spread out all around her as far as her eye could see, each one had a glinting ring around their neck, and all of them kept their eyes down as if they didn't notice her.

It was stupid to sleep for so long. This wasn't a vacation.

Elodie pulled the hood of her cloak up over her hair and ducked her head as she wove her way around the lines of wheat and passed the field of slaves watching her.

When she crested the hill on the far side of the wheat field, she could see she had hours of fields and slaves still to walk by. Guilt and regret filled her chest as she dropped her head and continued past the glinting metal collars. She couldn't help but think back to Callie and the summer they spent together.

It was like yesterday, the two of them, young and adventurous, running through the streets of Tross; Callie showing Elodie the hidden side of life in her kingdom. A smile overtook Elodie's lips as she pictured Callie mimicking the noble stepping in a horse pile. She could always make her laugh. But Elodie's heart twisted as she remembered those carefree days before Callie started working in a councilman's household.

Byron was still a bit of a mystery to Elodie. She'd had plenty of opportunities to observe him in social situations over the years, at dinners with Oburleck, in council meetings, or on Progress, and he always kept to himself, spoke little and smiled less. There was something about him that triggered alarm in her instincts. She'd gotten the feeling others had the same sense. Bryon was usually spoken of with respect and maybe a little fear, although there wasn't any clear reason for it.

He was a large strong man who had a fondness for sword work and was rumored to be one of the best fighters in Aluna. He'd never tried to become a knight. Instead, his family had sent him to the magical university in Pundica to train as a mage. According to Gedas, he had very little magical gift and had scraped by with the lowest ranking the university provided. He was rightfully Illusionist Byron, but that title took away more prestige than the low ranking could provide, so nobody used it.

As an influential member of Aluna's council, Byron was seen as good and honorable but Elodie could not agree. She didn't believe for a moment that Callie had attacked him unprovoked while she was in the illusion. There had to be more to the story than Bryon had admitted. Callie was bright and she knew an attack would have meant death. Elodie could never trust someone who made their wealth from slaves. She assumed that Byron only had mercy on Callie because he could make money off her in the long run.

Elodie stuck her hand in her pocket and rubbed her thumb over the bumpy cap of the acorn. Somewhere between waking up in a field full of slaves and walking until her feet wanted to fall off, Elodie decided where she was going. If she kept traveling north, she would meet up with the highway that led straight into Tross. Surely the clinic in the lower city would be the last place Oburleck would think of sending men to look for her. Healer Beathan wouldn't throw Elodie out.

Now that the shock of the morning had worn off, Elodie decided there were a few important tasks she needed to complete before she went any farther. She stopped at the first cluster of bushes she saw with the right shape of leaves. She stripped some of the leaves off the witch hazel bush, and lacking the proper tools for the job, chewed up the bitter leaves until they made a thick paste. She spread the lumpy green mess onto the various bug bites covering her legs, arms, and neck that had been driving her mad all night. Once this was done, she ate a strip of hard, dried meat and broke off a chunk of hard cheese. It was salty and bitter.

Elodie drank down two-thirds of the waterskin, trying to rid her mouth of the foul flavor, before she caught herself and cursed. This was all the water she had at her disposal and to drink it all up now was the biggest mistake she could make. She put her food away and stood, ready to continue her trek. Before she left the cover of the bushes, she collected a few handfuls of witch hazel leaves, folding them into her T-shirt in the pack. They would come in handy when she decided to rest that night and didn't want to scratch off her flesh.

As she walked, Elodie kept an eye out for edible or medicinal herbs and leaves. Her bread and cheese wouldn't last long, and if she was going to be on the road for a while, it would be handy to build up a medical kit. She even picked plants she should use for protection circles and other small spells. It didn't hurt to be prepared.

She walked and walked, stopping only to take the occasional pee break and bite of hard bread or to refill her water at a stream, despite the blisters she felt forming on her poor feet. When night began to fall, she found a secluded tree to shelter under. She removed her shoes and treated her blisters and bug bites with more chewed-up leaves before starting in on the hard cheese. She was so hungry it didn't taste so bitter anymore.

The hair on the back of her neck rose as the sun set, and the fear and dread of her situation crept back in. She was trying hard not to think about what awaited her when she reached Tross. Oburleck couldn't truly convict her of treason. Treason meant death, and she couldn't believe it would ever come to that.

She warded her sleeping area again that night, blocking out the familiar strangeness.

As she lay there, Elodie thought about what she was doing. She needed to get her kingdom out of the corrupt hands of Oburleck so they could heal the damage that had been done since her father had died. But if she did manage to successfully remove Oburleck, what then? She was still trapped in the spell and wouldn't be able to rule. Her kingdom would go back into the hands of another steward. What she really needed was to break this spell. That way she could finally be free to live her life in one reality.

When she was twelve, she'd learned about the prophecy that said she would be responsible for breaking the spell one day. Gedas had been the one to tell the prophecy to her father and the rest of the rulers of the Twoshy, and they had made the decision to put the inheritance, titles, and powers of the Misplaced on hold until their return. But here they were decades later and still trapped. Silas had tried to help her find more information on the spell and help her figure out how to break it, but there were too many people unwilling to help or who just didn't know anything past vague wonderings. The only one who Elodie was sure knew the truth was Gedas, but he had only changed the subject and refused to answer when she'd asked.

SOMETHING SEARCHED for her in the blackness. Something malicious and evil. It had a particular scent to its magic, like rotting flowers and stagnant water. It was a long way off in the darkness, but it *saw* her with its multifaceted eyes. She was petrified in its sight and tried to wake up, but a heavy weight rested at each wrist and each ankle and the chains rattled when she tried to pull free. She closed her eyes tight against the creature, but still, she could feel it looking for her, searching.

The old man was back, calling out to her in the dark. Elodie searched for him, running through halls until she slipped on the smooth surface and slid across the floor, building up speed until she smashed through a stained glass window. The glass burst into birds flapping past her in the air, slicing her skin as they escaped up, and she fell further and further and landed in that deep, dark pit where the light grew dim, seeping away into the night.

Elodie woke up with her back in knots from sleeping on the

hard ground. She rose in a foul temper, drank her water, and ate the last of her food before setting out again, desperate to get to civilization even if it was filled with people looking to find her and imprison her. At least if they caught and executed her, she wouldn't be forced to walk for hours and sleep on the ground anymore. Her mood was morose as she set off north. She was thirsty, itchy, her feet hurt, her shoulder still ached, and now she was beginning to smell. Grumbling for hours as she walked, her determination from the day before gone. She whined to herself, mad at Gedas for not being there to help her, mad at Oburleck for being an ass, mad at whoever trapped her in this stupid spell to begin with, making her used to cars and sitting on her butt all day. She was mad at the ruakh for pulling her into the Twoshy and making her miss her date with Matt. A scream built inside of her, ready to split the silence and loneliness that surrounded her, when fear crept up her spine. That fear of something dark and wrong looking out at her from the shadows. She looked around but saw nothing, no one. She shook away the eerie feeling but only found herself angry again. Angry for not having a better plan, for not being a faster walker, for being so incredibly hungry.

As the day began to turn to evening, the highway was nowhere in sight. Elodie climbed a steep hill and was nearing the top when she turned her ankle on a rock and littered the air with curse words that would have landed her in detention if she was at school. She couldn't take it anymore and yelled into the evening air. With no one around to hear it, she felt free to speak her mind.

"That's it! I'm done. No more." She sat down on the ground and took off her shoe to massage her ankle. "Oburleck! I'm over here! Send your men and take me away. I don't care anymore. One way or another, I'm done walking and dying of hunger. Any takers? Come and get me!"

Elodie felt a bit stupid for yelling and ducked her head looking around cautiously. She really didn't want to get captured. She sighed to herself when she was sure she was alone and carefully began feeling her ankle. It was tender to the touch and already looked a little swollen.

"If you're lookin' to get stolen, I'm up for the job."

Elodie jumped and screeched at the voice. To her right sat a tall lean man laying back on a large rock, propped up on his elbows. His head tilted back, eyes closed as though sunning himself. He had bright platinum blond hair and pale white skin like he wasn't often in the sun. His loose-fitting white shirt was open at the collar and his light tan breeches rolled up to the knees. He would have looked like a beach bum out to soak up some rays, relaxing in the evening sun if he wasn't so pale.

"You know, if you keep making that sound, Oburleck's men will find you." He turned his head and gave her a lazy crooked smile.

"Who the hell are you?" She didn't scream this time, but it was close. There was something odd about this man. He had a strange look about him, as though he wasn't entirely there and if Elodie blinked too fast he might disappear. Yet his rich brown eyes seemed to be the most solid and secure thing in the entire world, and they anchored her in place.

"Now, my love. Don't be like that. I'm only here to help." He leaned back against the rock closing his eyes again and crossed his legs in the air. "You do want help, don't you?"

"Uh, I think, I'm okay actually. I should get going." Elodie wedged her shoe back on her slightly swollen foot, ignoring the aching pain. She stood carefully on her good left foot and then attempted to step onto the right. Immediately regretting the decision, the foot collapsed under her and she fell. The man was now beside her, his strong arms holding her up.

"That wasn't very smart, my love. Come on, sit back down and let me look at your foot."

He moved so fast, and a powerful presence radiated off him. Elodie was at a loss for words as he guided her back to the ground, holding most of her weight and lowering her carefully.

"Now, it's time you and I had a heart to heart. I'm sorry about how things are going right now, but this little story needed to progress so I kinda planted a thought and got things moving in the right direction. It was quite easy. Oburleck is such an impressionable and greedy soul. It only took one little dream to convince him he could take over the throne all on his own."

Elodie's mind was suddenly on overdrive. Something Gedas

had once told her about will and destiny floated into the back of her mind. "Wait a minute. Are you a god?"

The man broke out in a large, crooked grin. "And here I thought you didn't recognize me. Yes, my love, you know me as Ravid, although I've had quite a few names in my life." He lifted her hurt foot and started unlacing her shoe. Pulling it off, he grimaced at the sight of her filthy sock and removed it.

Elodie slowly processed this. "So you're the reason I'm being hunted right now?"

"Technically, Oburleck would have come to the decision to take over eventually. I sped things up a bit to get this whole thing going." The god rested her leg on his lap and gently began to massage her poor aching foot.

She should have been freaking out over a god massaging her stinky foot, but it felt so good, and she was oddly calm about it all. Nothing else was crucial at the moment. She would get back to her trek and her worries in a bit, but right now, she was perfectly content sitting on this rock in the sun and enjoying the foot rub.

"So why should I trust you?"

"Because you need my help." He cracked her ankle sharply. After a sharp pain, her foot no longer ached.

"Wow. That feels amazing." She rotated her foot a few times testing it. Even her blisters were gone. She wondered if it would be wrong to ask the god to massage the other foot too. "I don't understand though. Why are you doing this? Why make Oburleck betray me, then offer to help? What's your endgame in this?"

He started putting her sock and shoe back on, both she noticed with mild shock were now clean. He laced her shoe back up with care and then, to Elodie's glee, unlaced the other dirty shoe.

"Aluna has been in the crapper since your father died. He cared for his people and built the kingdom on principles to last. Since then, Aluna has gone through several stewards, each one more corrupt than the last. I want to help you get things back on track. I want to see this kingdom healthy and vibrant again."

"And what's in it for you?" Now her left foot began to feel that refreshed and blister-free sensation seeping through her skin from the god man's hands. She couldn't help the giddy smile creeping onto her face at the thought of clean feet that weren't covered in bleeding blisters and shoes that no longer smelled like a three-month-old rotting corn beef sandwich.

"Other than the personal satisfaction in a job well done, I was thinking you could make me the national god or something. Aluna thriving and praising me as its benefactor sounds like a great way to spend this next century or so." He smiled at her brightly and put her magically cleaned sock and shoe back on that foot as well. Then he laced the shoe and placed her foot solidly on the ground. In an instant, he was standing in front of her and reached down. She gripped his hands as he pulled her to her feet in one smooth move-ment. "What do you need? Make a request and I will grant it."

Make a bargain with a god? Was that really a good idea? Elodie wasn't sure. Ravid was sometimes known as a trickster as well as the god over travel and change. But his eyes seemed so warm and steady. He was also known for being good to his followers. He usually cared more about the lower classes, rarely helping the nobility.

"I need to find the Great Highway." Elodie thought through her request. She needed more than just the highway. "And I need to find the river. And I want a horse. Oh, and I need a plan to fix things. A good plan!"

Ravid smiled brightly and clapped his hands once. "Excellent. You and I, my love, will make an exceptional team. I see tellers reciting our story time and time again long after your puny mortal life has ended."

With a swirl of his hands that felt all too unnecessary, he turned on the spot and was gone.

"Wait, where's my horse? And my plan?" Suddenly she was feeling stupid. The warm fuzzy peace that had overcrowded the panic was immediately gone. Maybe he'd only been messing with her. Maybe he was just using her.

She heard a soft chuckle right behind her and turned but nothing was there. "Over the hill, love." The disembodied voice was weird, but the humor in it made it feel slightly less creepy. Elodie sighed and resumed her climb, her feet feeling brand new. In five minutes, she made it to the top and groaned at the sight. Only a short way down the other side, lay the Great Highway stretched out far to the east and west. If she followed it west, it would curve around and head straight into Tross. Following it east for a long time, it would eventually curve north out of Aluna into Rohap, one of the neighboring kingdoms. On the other side of the road, Elodie could see the glint of the river poking through the dense foliage of the small forest that stretched to the north. Elodie internally kicked herself. If she'd kept going, she would have run into the highway all on her own.

As she made her way down the hill toward the forest, she muttered her frustration to the god. "There better be a freaking horse and a solid plan waiting in there."

Chapter Nine

PINE, cheer, and maple trees waited for Elodie, but there was no horse. She crouched down to fill her waterskin at the edge of the river when she heard horses approaching from behind. A group of soldiers came into view, and Elodie slipped into a prick bush as they entered the small clearing she'd planned to use as a campsite. She silently thanked the gods, or at least Ravid, that she still had her pack on her shoulder and hadn't begun setting up her camp. She wiggled quietly as she disentangled her flesh from the thick angry thorns and tried to slip off through the trees away from the river. At a safe distance, she peeked through the split trunk of a cheer tree to see who she was hiding from.

There were sixteen men on horseback. They wore the yellow and silver of the Aluna militia with the crest bearing an albatross. Her hand touched her birthmark instinctively. These would be her men if she were in power, they would be fighting for her not against her. But because of the spell they were under the leadership of the steward and were now out hunting for her.

The soldiers were led by a tall knight in leather armor and shining chain mail. He sat atop a handsome gray warhorse with a black mane and legs. The knight scouted the ground as one might before a siege, and his blue roan held his head high just as alert as the knight.

"All right men," the knight said as he removed his helm. "This looks as good a place as any. It will be dark soon, no point continuing the search now. The steward has his mages for that. Set up camp under those trees on the north side, and picket the horses near the stream. Get to work." As the knight turned to dismount, Elodie's stomach lurched so hard she was afraid it would pop out of her throat. She knew that coat of arms, a large tower like a chess rook with two swords crossed under it on the knight's shield, and she knew the green shining eyes looking out from a face a few shades lighter than coal.

He definitely wasn't sixty, and he definitely wasn't balding. The young squire she'd once known was gone and in his place stood this impressive figure.

Sir Silas of Tate.

Elodie ducked down and hid behind the trunk. She could reveal herself to him, seek his help in understanding what was going on. Maybe he knew where Gedas was and could help her get there.

No, if she could describe Silas in one word it would always be honorable. If he gave someone his word or made a vow, he would never in a million years go back on it. He was a knight, sworn to uphold the law and follow the command of its leader. He was out here with these men searching for her, wasn't it proof enough he was under the command of Oburleck? Regardless of any friendship they'd had in the past, Silas would always honor his vows of fidelity.

She let out a heavy breath. It was hard to believe the people she counted on the most had betrayed her. Gedas was nowhere to be seen and now Silas was hunting her.

This was the worst trip yet.

Elodie closed her eyes and put her head against the rough bark of the tree. She knew Silas was only doing his duty and at the end of the day, duty was what he lived by.

Elodie remained crouched behind the trees for a long time. She needed to move while the soldiers were distracted. Once they settled in and someone was set to watch, they would hear any movement she made. Most were near the road on the south side of the camp. She could go deeper into the brush and follow the river, but as soon as night fell, she would have a hard time navigating along the water.

A few feet from her on the other side of the dense bushes came the thump of a saddle being removed and the tinkling of buckles as someone started caring for the horses. If they had sixteen horses to brush and feed, they would be at it for a while, and hopefully the sound would cover her. It was now or never.

Elodie sat up on her knees and slowly got to her feet trying her hardest to place her shoes anywhere but on top of the dry twigs that would give away her position. Despite how careful she was, the leaves at her feet rustled. She held still and listened. The rattling of buckles and the continued shuffling of men told her she was in the clear. She stayed crouched and took a step away from the camp.

She took a few more steps lowering her foot slowly onto another patch of rather crunchy leaves. She cursed silently and held still to listen. She couldn't hear the sound of tack being removed but thought maybe she could hear the strokes of a horse being brushed and chanced another crunchy step.

She froze to listen; she was almost to the rocky part near the river where she could be silent. A horse snorted, another stomped, a few were drinking from the river. Elodie risked another step, and before her foot was down, she was forcefully reminded back to her last trip to the Twoshy when she crashed through the underbrush with the stealth of a warthog. Silas made fun of her inability to walk quietly and then tried to teach her the finer points. He had been able to move so nimbly, he was practically silent. She was reminded of this as the man who'd been tending the horses snuck up on her with the same nimble grace and now stood before her.

He'd removed his helmet and the breastplate of his armor, no doubt to make it easier as he helped his men with the tedious tasks required for setting up a campsite. His forehead was dotted with sweat, shining on his dark skin and his chin was covered with thick black stubble. He looked older. Eighteen? Twenty-something? He was so much more impressive than the fourteen-year-old version of him she remembered. For the first time since landing in the variant forest, Elodie wondered how much time had passed for him since she'd last seen him.

His sword was in his hand, and he seemed completely shocked and yet somehow scared at the sight of her, as though she was the last person he had ever wished to come across helpless in the woods. A second soldier stood just behind him, sword also in hand. This man's russet beard was thick and braided neatly down his chin.

Silas crossed the distance between them in an instant, covering the ground more silently than Elodie ever could have managed. "No, no, no, you cannot be here." He sheathed his sword at his side and held Elodie by her shoulders shaking her slightly in his hysteria.

"Well, it's not like I had much choice in the matter. I picked this campsite first after all," she said sardonically.

Silas shook his head, his face grim and unyielding to the smile she wished to see on the corner of his mouth. "This is no time for jokes." Silas turned to the man behind him. "Rogers, you see nothing. It was a false alarm and there's nothing in the brush but thistle bunnies."

The soldier, Rogers, dropped his guarded stance and sheathed his sword, eyebrows disappearing into his sweaty hairline as he looked pointedly away from Elodie. "Welp, it looks like that was a false alarm," he announced loudly. "I'm gonna go continue tending to the finicky bastards who carried us here while you try and catch that rabbit for dinner, sir." Rogers turned and continued back through the brush to the horses, making a rather lot of noise in the dry leaves.

Silas seemed to deflate a little with relief. "You need to get out of here before anyone else sees you. I trust my men but trusting them and expecting them to commit treason are two different things." He led her closer to the river, shielded by bushes, out of the line of sight of the camp. The horses were just visible through the brush.

"Wait, aren't you going to take me prisoner or something?" Elodie asked, confused.

Silas looked baffled and a little hurt and searched her eyes, his green ones meeting hers with such unveiled conviction. "Do you really think I would do that to you, Elodie?"

Just the way he said her name, so soft and with care to pronounce it just right, flooded her with peace, this was not the cruel, by the book man she feared he would turn into.

She didn't like seeing the hurt in his eyes. "Sir Silas, you are the most honorable man I know, and I can only imagine that has followed you into knighthood." Elodie smiled as she remembered a night that he insisted they couldn't be out after curfew. After he argued that it was improper, Elodie had simply walked off into the evening air, leaving it the duty of the chivalrous squire to catch up and make sure she didn't get lost or trip and break her leg in the dark. "By not turning me in, aren't you breaking your vow to the kingdom?"

His expression had an edge of anger as he turned his face away from her. "I swore my pledge to this kingdom and to its true ruler. Not to the man attempting to take the throne. Oburleck is breaking the laws your father, the last true king, made before he died just by ordering us to bring you in. He is the one committing treason." Silas straightened himself and looked back at her, his face softened. "I am not the only one at court who feels this way. I accepted the assignment to come out here because I had a feeling he was up to worse deeds than throwing you in jail, and I was right. Before I left, Duke Devoss implied that Steward Oburleck would be most pleased if I were to find you, and on the return journey, there was an accident that you did not survive." His face looked bleak. "I am not the only knight that was given those instructions. Dess told me she received the same."

Elodie's stomach dropped and she looked away.

"No, I will not break my higher vows of doing what is right before what is easy on the command of a man who would break any law if it gave him more power or wealth." After giving this speech, Silas seemed to remember himself and where he was. He went back to the line of horses and untied the blue roan warhorse, the largest of the group. He dug through a few saddlebags, heaped in a pile by the river's edge.

Watching the knight sort packs, she was struck again by how much he'd changed and matured. He'd been tall and broad at fourteen, but his build had thickened. His every move was confident and direct, radiating strength and grace. She felt safe with him here, knowing he would help her form a proper plan.

"I'm sorry I missed your knighting," she whispered softly, half hoping he wouldn't hear.

His hands stilled on the packs, his face turned from her. "I left alms at Dima's and Ravid's shrines in the city every day for a week asking for them to make a way for you." He sighed, then turned to face her, a sad look in his eyes. "During the ceremony, I expected you to come shimmering into substance in the middle of the room. An entrance fitting your flair for the dramatic." This time he did give that hidden half smile and her heart filled with warmth.

Elodie grimaced at the thought of the spectacle. "The way you talk, you would think I like the attention much more than I do." She crossed the short distance between them so she could speak in a lower tone. "Still, I wish you didn't have to swear to that smarmy asshat of a steward. Eight years of your life training for your shield and the realm honors you with that mess."

The knight took her hand, a sharp tone to his voice. "I did *not* swear to him. I swore to the realm he stood in place of." To Elodie's horror, he knelt in the dirt before her, head bowed. "I swore to Aluna and her monarch, I swore to you, My Queen, and to no one else."

"Silas, stand up. You're getting your shiny armor all dirty. I'm not your queen, not yet." Elodie hated this show of honor, and it made her feel deeply uncomfortable, she looked away, anywhere but at his eyes. She really wasn't that special, she barely spent five minutes worrying about her country when she was in the illusion. She didn't deserve people like Silas believing in her when she was so near worthless.

"No, Your Majesty, look at me." Elodie had been looking at the trees, safe and dignified, she knew where she stood with trees, unlike passionate young nobles who believed her their sovereign. Elodie looked down into Silas's eyes. The passion and force she found there made her stagger and turn her glance away. He grabbed her wrist and shook it playfully until she looked back. "You, Queen Elodie of Tross, ruler of Aluna, are my future. Do not sell yourself short for you would belittle my life and the lives of everyone in this kingdom. You are why those of us who choose to do so fight."

"But we're friends first, remember?" She thought back to winter nights in a warm library, laughing quietly with Silas and his fellow pages. She valued his honesty and his insight and intelligence, but she also valued his ability to make her smile.

"Yes, always friends first." He gave her wrist one last shake with a small smile and turned back to finish packing a saddlebag, filling it full of supplies. "Give me time. I will rally those who are still loyal to you, and we will win back your rightful standing."

He straightened then, Elodie at a loss for words. So much hung between them. He had so much more faith in her than she had in herself. Even if Oburleck was out of the way, Elodie couldn't rule yet, not as long as the illusion held her in its firm grasp. If Oburleck was dealt with, Elodie would have to place her kingdom into the hands of another and hope that those loyal to her, as Silas was, would keep that balance of power in check in her absence.

"Take Storm, he's a warhorse and will protect you." He patted the neck of the big roan. "Yes boy, you will protect our Elodie, won't you? He will go with you willingly. None of the other horses would trust me giving them away." The big stallion, trained to kill in battle along with his knight, turned into a big puppy at the knight's words and pranced a little with a snort. Silas set the heavy saddlebags on his back and led him and Elodie along the river, away from the camp before securing everything in place. When they stopped, Storm lowered his head to sniff Elodie all over in proper horse greeting, leaving horse love and snot on her clothes. "Where were you planning to go? This isn't a road leading anywhere good for you."

Elodie's head barely came up to the horse's shoulders. A proper horse for a tall knight in full armor but a bit much for a girl her size. "I was thinking of hiding in plain sight and heading to Tross. I have a few friends in the lower city I could hide with and Oburleck would never think to look there."

"You're joking," Silas said as a statement, not letting it even be an option. "That's idiotic," he declared as he adjusted the horse's tact.

Elodie bristled. Where did the respect and adoration that had been in his eyes a moment ago go?

"Silas, where do you expect me to go? I have no idea where Gedas is, and it's not like I can go to my usual suite of rooms at the castle. At least in the lower city, I can be close enough to strike back at Oburleck."

He took Elodie's bag off her shoulder and arranged it with the saddlebags. "No, Elodie, you need to get away from Steward Oburleck. Go out of Aluna and into one of the other kingdoms. No one has heard from Gediminas in months. We had intelligence you would travel near here. In a week when that is believed false, I will return to the castle and find who knew the secret of your traveling. I will try to learn what has happened to Gedas, and then I will gather those loyal to you and leave the kingdom to come find you."

"Silas! You would be a traitor if you leave. You can't do that. This is your future you're throwing away."

"I will not serve a corrupt leader."

Elodie placed her hand on his strong shoulder. He paused in fiddling with her pack. "Silas, please be careful. If anything happens to you . . ." She did not know what she felt exactly, only dread. "I don't know."

The knight stood up straight, towering over Elodie with his height and his strength. "Elodie, you are the most important person in the world to me, and not because of any unavailing prophecy. You are my hope." He took her hand again, his fingers warm and his calluses rough. "If you died without an heir, do you know what state this kingdom would be left in? Nothing can happen to me as long as you are alive and well. Therefore, it is not me you should worry for. Protect yourself, for if you were to perish, I would surely die."

There was a moment, just a moment when Elodie thought he would lean down and kiss her. She could almost feel his soft lips press against hers. Elodie didn't know where the thought came from. Her memories of Matt and high school seemed silly and so long ago now. This was surely the real world and Silas was definitely her future.

But no. Silas would never disrespect a lady with a stolen kiss. To him a kiss was something earned, a treasure to fight for. How could she have ever wanted to give one away to a boy like Matt.

It was Storm who broke the moment, he nudged Silas hard in the shoulder and the spark between them broke in an instant.

"You're right," he said to his horse. "We haven't time for this." He bent down and unhooked a small dagger and sheath from the inside of his boot and handed it over. "Just in case." He made one quick trip back to the other side of the horses by the fallen packs and returned with a bedroll and a bow and quiver, tying them to her pack. "It will get colder as you go. The first of the frosts haven't fallen yet, but they are not far away." Silas looked at the saddle and grimaced. "Rub mud into the saddle and tack as soon as you stop, or anyone who sees it will think it's stolen. Maybe rub it into Storm's coat too. He looks too fine."

He undid his gold purse from his belt and tucked it into an inside pocket of Elodie's cloak when she tried to protest. "You will need more supplies before long. And real footwear," he said as he glanced down at her green sneakers, shaking his head with a small smile. "As soon as you come to a small village with no sign of soldiers, buy some old clothes, hide your hair, and travel as a boy. And Storm"—he turned to his horse—"try your hardest to slouch a little, I know you're more of a noble than I, but try to remember it's to protect our lady. Do your best to look like a mule." The horse let out a disgusted snort and shook his head.

Silas turned back to Elodie ruffling Storm's mane. "Too much pride for one horse, but you are safer traveling if you don't look like yourself. Ward your camp every night. No, don't give me that look, I know you know how, and Oburleck has mages looking for you. Follow this river east, avoid the highway. The river will separate from the road and lead you into Rohap in about a fortnight. Find a tavern by the name the Snarled Cello in Arnav, the capital. Tell the barman you know me. He's a big brute of a man by the name of Graham. He will put you up until I or Dess can meet you there. And for the love of the gods, if you do meet anyone on the road, try to disguise that accent of yours." He chuckled and Elodie smiled. "You will be safe in Rohap, the rest of the Twoshy still holds strong to the laws of Sixteen even if Oburleck, the traitorous swine, thinks he can change things. All right, mount up, you need to get going before my men realize I'm not done with the horses yet."

Elodie looked at the high back of Storm and looked back at Silas. "Yeah, that's a little easier said than done, Sir Silas the wise." The knight laughed and dropped to one knee cupping his hands. Elodie placed one hand on the pommel and one foot in a stirrup. Silas took her other green sneaker-covered foot and launched her onto the horse's back. She groaned as she landed. "Storm, you're as big as a boat."

Sir Silas adjusted her stirrups. "Maybe make sure you only dismount near a pile of big rocks," he said with a smirk. Elodie aimed a kick at his chest now that she was tall enough to hit him, but the nimble knight dodged it easily despite the bits of heavy armor he still wore.

Elodie grew serious again. "You promise to meet me in Rohap?"

Silas stepped closer to the girl and the horse. "I will, or I will send Dess. As soon as I have enough knowledge to be of use in this rebellion against Oburleck," he vowed.

"Rebellion," Elodie mimicked. "Such a strong word for such a noble knight. Are you sure you have it in you?"

"Rebellion against a corrupt system is the truest call of the noble. To sit by and get rich while injustice is being served is wrong. I know I am not the only one who feels this way. Some of the other nobles and myself will make a stand. But it will be much easier to do so knowing you are safely tucked away from the action."

"But the prophecy says I'm—"

"I don't care what the scum-sucking prophecy says. This has nothing to do with breaking the spell. You need to stay safe while I weed the corruption out of your kingdom, Your Highness."

"Please don't call me that." She hated hearing the title come out of Silas's mouth, like a wall between them.

"Then please do not forget it. My pledge of fidelity was to your kingdom, to you. And until you are sitting on that throne, I have no greater calling than keeping that throne, and you, safe." Silas took a deep breath and let it out slowly. "We need to hurry." He placed his hand on Elodie's shoulder, closed his eyes, and prayed. "May the protection of the gods follow you and keep you safe. Ravid, clear her path and give her speed. Dima, protect your daughter with all your love, wisdom, strength, and bitter jealousy."

They opened their eyes and their gaze connected. Silas's green eyes were electric and filled with something Elodie didn't recognize, but before she could puzzle over it, he blinked and turned to the horse. "Storm, protect her with your life, dear friend, just as you protect me." Then he gave the horse a gentle pat on the butt and Storm began carrying Elodie away from the camp and along the river. At the movement of the horse, Elodie nearly lost balance and had to tighten her grip with her knees over the wide back and hang onto the pommel.

By the time she found her balance and turned back to look, Sir Silas of Tate was gone, back to his men, back to his duty, and back to the dangerous game of a spy.

Chapter Ten

AS THEY CLOPPED over the uneven terrain, Elodie thought about little else but keeping her balance. She'd ridden horses constantly while visiting the Twoshy, but with a horse this big and broad, as she traveled over the rough terrain next to the river, it was all she could do not to dig her heels into his sides. Instead, Elodie sat partially hunched over the large warhorse's back, forgetting all her lessons. Her fingers were wrapped simultaneously in Storm's mane and around the pommel while she clung to the wide saddle with her knees. Storm was much more delicate and graceful on the leaf-covered, rocky riverbank than Elodie could ever hope to be. His gate was gentle and smooth for a big horse, but still Elodie clutched with every muscle in her body, trying not to fall. It was late, but she wanted to get a good amount of distance between herself and the soldiers before she stopped for the night.

The sun dipped low in the sky, and the tree line brought a premature gloom to the evening, but Storm didn't seem to mind. He appeared to know exactly where he was going. Elodie was thankful at least one of them did. Slowly, as they ate up the terrain in front of them Elodie began to relax and find her seat.

She loosened the grip of her knees and focused on her balance as her muscle memory took over. After a few hours of clomping along, night had fully set. They'd made so much progress now that she had a horse to speed things up, but they needed to stop for the night. Storm had spent the day carrying around a big knight covered in armor, and even though the big horse was better at seeing in the dark than her, it would be safer to call a halt to their trek. Elodie waited until they came to a place along the river with a large outcropping of rocks surrounded by trees and leaned back in the saddle.

"Woah, boy. Let's stop here for a bit."

Storm let out a breath and stomped his hooves in impatience as he came to a stop.

"Yes, Sir Horse. I'm aware you could keep going all night, but really you should rest after carrying around that heavy load of knight flesh and steel." Elodie carefully dismounted, sliding off the tall horse.

As her feet hit the leaf-strewn ground, her legs buckled and she fell, landing on her butt in the mulch and dirt. Letting the movement carry her the rest of the way, she laid back on the leaves and sticks, resting for a moment. Storm turned his head to look back, his black eye watching her, and gave a snort, clearly unimpressed.

"Just give me a minute, Storm. My legs are tired." She closed her eyes and heard the horse clomp closer to the river to drink. It was stupid of her to ride so tensely. Her knee and thigh muscles felt like jelly after gripping so hard. She needed to get back into shape. She was running for her life and being achy and whiney wasn't going to help. On her last trip to the Twoshy, Elodie had spent weeks practicing her bow work at Silas's instruction. She'd done push-ups and arm strengthening exercises until she was strong enough to shoot one of the heavy longbows. Her competence in archery had grown at the gentle hands of Silas, and her accomplishments made the work enjoyable. Being able to shoot an arrow and actually hit a target had seemed like its own sort of magic. But then the shimmery ruakh had pulled her back into the spell and back into the chubby, out-of-shape body in jeans, and the motivation to work out and get strong again had evaporated at the sight of the couch and TV.

Elodie sighed deeply, preparing herself to stand. Storm stomped over and looked down on her. How could she feel so much reproach from a horse? It took all her willpower to stand and take off his saddle. It was a terribly heavy thing, and she struggled under its weight, nearly dropping it to the ground. Brushing him out was another test of her resolve, and she ran the thick comb over his coat long after her arms wanted to fall off. Eventually, she dropped the brush on the saddlebags and left a grain bag in open view for Storm to chomp. She trusted him not to wander in the night. Horses didn't like being away from their pack, and Storm was better trained than she was.

She detached the bedroll from her pack and stretched it out on a flat spot covered in leaves. Just before crawling in, Elodie thought back to Silas's words about Oburleck sending mages to look for her and she rummaged through her bags looking for the cedar sprigs she'd collected. Once she found them, she crawled around the bed and Storm, making a large lopsided circle as she placed the sprigs. She spoke the words she knew by heart to raise a protection ward and felt a calmness fall over her. Elodie could feel it pulsing below her body as she crawled into the bedroll.

It didn't need to be flashy and obvious to be magic, and it didn't need to be potent and strong to protect her. The land and the things that resided on it could always be used within their natures to do amazing things.

Storm finished his dinner and stomped a few times before he lay at her back. As Elodie snuggled into the blanket that smelled of leather, soap, pine needles, and Silas, she thought over Ravid's words and Silas's plans.

Something dug into her side, and she wiggled until she could reach into her pocket and pull out the acorn. The potential life thrummed against Elodie's fingertips, comforting her. The acorn seemed to like the feel of the ruakh in the Twoshy. The potential life called out to the magic around it.

She wanted to confront Oburleck, to stand before him and denounce him as steward and watch him crumple before her. Then she could appoint a new steward and move on. The calming, comforting presence of Ravid and the bargain he struck with her seemed to only add to the thought that this would be an easy thing. But after Silas's description of the situation, she realized that idea was foolish. Ravid's presence wasn't the sign of a joke he was preparing to play on the corrupt steward. Ravid was here because something big and monumental was beginning to happen. She'd read tales of such shiftings of time and destinies. This was starting to feel like one of those pivotal points in time where choices could make or break a kingdom, and the future was in flux.

Oburleck had control over the army and the kingdom. She feared the only end to this would involve the bloodshed of her people. If this conflict was going to come down to a fight, Elodie was not well prepared. Silas's plan was for her to hide and wait out the conflict, and she would go along with that plan for now, but Elodie had no intention to wait it out when the storm finally hit. When the time came, she didn't want to be the lazy lump she now felt. She needed her endurance back, and if she ever wanted to shoot another arrow, she needed her arm strength back. So, she would stop whining and be the change that she needed in her life. She would start working out and doing exercise.

First thing in the morning she would start. Elodie yawned. Yes, definitely first thing in the morning. With this resolution in her heart, she slept.

"HAVE you ever wondered if ruakh is living?" The two boys were in a library, at a heavy oak table stretched out between the vast shelves of books. The table around them was piled high with heavy tombs and cracking scrolls, and the boy closed the cover on an old book with an iridescent dragon on the cover.

Lan snorted. "You must be joking. Come now, Johna, not even you can be so big a cloud brain as to believe something like that. Even the masters only ever refer to ruakh as a force, a tool for our use and command."

Lan turned back to his book and flipped the page.

"Yes, but we have come to the conclusion before during these little conversations of ours, that sometimes the masters are wrong. That is why we are working so hard to get our wizards accreditation, is it not?"

A girl walked by, she was tall and willowy with bronze skin and thick black hair. "Anna, come join us for a spell, won't you? Johna is so very boring, and I could use some sun in my life."

Anna rolled her eyes and flicked her finger at a heavy book on the top shelf. It flew gracefully into her arms like a pet bird, and she slumped a little when she held its full weight. A strand of straight black hair fell into her eye. She blew at the hair, but it didn't move. "If Beth and I wanted to fail all our exams, we would have joined you earlier." She spun on her heels and glided away, leaving the scent of honeysuckles and vanilla behind.

Both boys sighed as one.

After a long moment staring into nothing, Lan turned back to Johna, the arrogance and elitism gone from his tone and expression. "So tell me more of what you were on about?"

Johna looked out at the dusty books around them, his eyes alight with thought. "Haven't you ever stood silent in the rush of ruakh while you worked your spells and just listened? Felt the rush of power as the ruakh creates and makes? It doesn't always follow the same patterns and formulas. It changes and moves as if on its own. It feels alive."

"Ruakh is just a tool for those of us with a knack to control it, like wood in the hands of a carpenter. It isn't alive, it's only here for us to accomplish our will." Lan smirked. "You only feel as if it has a mind of its own because you do not have as great of control as I do."

Johna rolled his eyes. "Spare me your narcissistic opinions, please. There is no way you truly believe the entire world was created to be used by you or destroyed by your hand. You only say things like that when you are feeling particularly proud of yourself. What are you working on over there?" Johna sat up straighter in his chair to peer over the books between them and grinned.

Lan covered his work with his hand. "Keep your eyes on your own scroll, I will not have you copying. And no, I do not really believe the world is only for me to use or destroy. I also believe the world was created to serve me."

Johna opened his mouth to retort, but instead, an eerie call rang out of his throat. His gray eyes multiplied and turned black and beady as the light globes on the table faded to nothing. And the only light still visible was the glint of the monster's eyes.

Elodie turned and ran from the table through the shelves and stacks of books. The world spun and the shelves started falling in around her. Then her feet hit the ground outside, she was pushing past trees and bushes, warriors in yellow and gray chasing after her.

She clutched the tiara close to her chest. It looked cheap like brittle plastic. If she held it too tightly, it would break apart in her hands. She couldn't let the others smash it, so she fled.

Running through the forest, she stumbled and tripped as logs jumped in front of her and peppermintsteel branches reached out and scratched her flesh trying to trip her. Her green sneakers broke apart like dissolving paper, but her blistered and bloody feet kept moving. A fallen cheer tree lay in her path. Elodie jumped. But the ground on the other side never came. She fell endlessly through the dark.

Cold air swept in at her back and the sudden absence of warmth tore her from her dreams as Storm stood up and clomped his way past the fading wards to the river.

Elodie sighed and ran a hand over her face, but it was no good. She was awake now.

She'd slept badly, tossing and turning among the dreams in her head and the sticks and stones under her bedroll. She'd always had vivid dreams, but this was getting to be too much. She needed to find some tarragon as soon as possible.

Gedas's voice echoed in her head, reminding her of the foolishness in not listening to your own mind's warnings. Worry pounded in her chest. Silas had said he would find out what had happened to Gedas. Did that mean he was unsure of his location, or he didn't know if he was even alive?

She worried for her mentor. He'd always been there for her, and Elodie couldn't imagine life in the Twoshy without his grumpy commentary, his insightful lessons, or his comforting presence after a cold night of camping exactly like this one. Silas's bedroll had been warm, it was the warmest she'd been since arriving in the Twoshy, leaning against Storm's back as she slept, but there had been something else keeping her awake, something searching through the night.

It sapped at her unconscious mind leaving her uneasy. It was more than just the searching spells she'd felt nights past. This had been darker, malicious, and it had sensed her—it was coming for her.

She lay on the cold, hard ground with a rock poking into her shoulder and looked up through the leaves to the sky growing pink with the first hints of sunrise.

Coming down from her dream, she slowed her breathing and focused on the peaceful sounds of the forest around her and the clop of hooves as Storm made his way to the edge of the riverbank and began drinking. Without Storm sleeping at her back, the breeze blowing off the river was cold, such a contrast to the fires of pain that had been covering her body in the dream.

She hurt: her legs, her arms, her stomach. Every muscle in her body cried out, begging her not to move, but she had to. The sun was rising. She had to mount Storm and keep traveling before soldiers found her. Her dreams and the weird presence she'd sensed forced her into motion. She found the acorn lost in her bedding and tucked it back in her pocket.

Moving hurt.

She moved on achy legs to relieve herself in the bushes, then started stretching. First her arms, then her legs. She wanted to stop there, but the bow leaning against the saddle in the middle of the clearing laughed at her. If she ever hoped to draw it, she needed to build up her strength. After three sets of push-ups and sit-ups, she was breathing heavy and her arms were shaking, and she lay flat in the dirt.

She hated this. She wished Gedas were there to help keep her safe so she didn't have to. She wished Oburleck had never tried to move against her. She wished everything were back to normal, and she could relax, ride a normal-sized horse, stop in the next village she came to and sleep in a real bed, take a shower, clean her teeth.

Her waterskin lay just out of reach, her fingertips barely grazing the corner. She gave up and relaxed on the ground, arms spread wide, eyes closed. Something cool and leathery pushed against her hand. Storm had clomped over and nudged her waterskin closer to her. "Ghura, bless you," she croaked as she grabbed the water and drank it down.

When she could feel her arms again and her breathing had calmed, Elodie made herself sit up and stretch again before walking to the muddy bank and drinking as much of the river as she could hold. She filled the waterskin before washing in the chilly fall water. She moved quickly, splashing the frigid water onto her face and the back of her neck. She rummaged through the packs Silas had gifted her and chose a bag of callow nuts for breakfast while Storm munched on some late growing strawberry plants. Once she felt alive again, Elodie packed up the camp and called to Storm who clomped over and let her put on his saddle. She led him to a rocky patch and climbed up to mount. On his back at last, she groaned with the pain of tight muscles, then nudged his side, urging him on through the trees at the edge of the river.

Their progress was more than Elodie could have hoped for when she'd left Lottsin. Their days started early and ended late. Elodie stretched and worked her muscles every time they stopped, and while she didn't feel any stronger, she knew change took time. Each night she warded their camp, but her dreams grew more and more intense, warning her of some danger she felt too ignorant to decipher.

They stole grain, food, and clothes from the occasional lone farm or house they passed, Elodie leaving coins from the purse Silas gave her as payment. Elodie foraged every time they stopped. She found both plants she could eat and use for healing and magic. The only time Elodie was seen was five days into their journey. They came to a small waypoint that marked the turning of the river before it separated from the highway. Just a few small buildings surrounding a roadside tavern and inn.

Elodie eased Storm up near the edge of the tree line. From the outside all appeared quiet, but a large number of horses sporting lively yellow furnishings stood tied to a few stakes outside the building. She was about to turn away and leave when a feed bag, full and forgotten beside the stable, caught her eye. It was a risk, but she didn't want Storm to be on short rations. She ran for it.

Next to a woodpile and an axe, there was a pair of old work gloves, and by the back door sat dirty boots that were a few sizes too big. She stole the boots before running to the clothesline and nabbing a pair of breeches that were too long, but she thought might fit her waist, a length of rope to use as a belt, two white button-up shirts, a gray cap, and a pair of thick socks. She turned with all of this in hand, about to throw the feed bag over her shoulder, and almost screeched at the sight of a boy standing behind her.

"It's you!" the boy said with wide eyes.

Elodie's heart raced. "Please, I just need some clothes." She reached into her inside pocket and pulled out the money pouch Silas had given her. She picked out one of the big gold pieces, more money than this boy was ever likely to see at once, and tossed it to him. He caught it with ease and looked startled when he realized what he held. He looked back up at her, and she made the motion of locking her lips with a key at the boy while holding a pleading look in her eyes. The boy grinned wide and copied the movement of locking his lips with a key before throwing the invisible key behind his back. Then he gave the most noble bow Elodie had ever received from someone not wearing shoes. She gave a formal and stately curtsy in her tattered and grimy clothes making the boy blush.

"May Dima guide you," he said, before turning and heading into a barn. Elodie waited just a moment to see if anyone would come running for her, then picked up the heavy bag, and ran back to Storm and the tree line.

After that, they took large detours around villages or way stations.

The days turned to weeks as they followed the river and it separated from the highway to continue north and east. Elodie didn't hear from Ravid again, and Elodie made sure not to call, pray, or even think of him too hard. She didn't want to risk the god's interference any further, even if she was getting a bit bored without someone who would reply when she talked to them. Storm was great company, but she began to get a bit lonely.

One night a few weeks into their journey, Elodie woke from yet another dream where the multifaceted black-eyed looming presence hunted her. She started to grow worried. Something was off about her dreams, the presence she had felt each night was wrong. It reminded her of something Gedas had told her once, an old legend about a terrifying monster that had been extinct so long as to make it irrational to be afraid. He had called it the bochnid. It was an evil thing, not natural to Eres, something of magic. It hunted by feeding on the psychic energy all people generated and would track its prey until the ends of the eres. There had been an outbreak of them a few decades back on a different continent, and they had been eradicated from the land. Gedas spoke like he had seen them, but he usually did that with everything, so it was hard to tell if it was true. He told her in vivid detail how the bochnid locked onto a target and would stop at nothing until it cracked the skull of its victim with its long powerful jaws and devoured their brain.

Gedas was a good mentor, always telling Elodie stories of terrifying creatures while they sat around a campfire surrounded by the pitch-black of night. He would always end the story by telling you why there was no reason to worry: it was just a legend, the monster didn't exist, or they have never been seen on this continent. But the bochnid had terrified Elodie, and she carried the memory of their tale for most of her childhood.

The bochnid tracked the psychic energy of the unconscious mind, only traveling while their target slept and dreamed. There was no way to hide from it. A person couldn't not sleep.

Gedas had told her they no longer existed, but her faded dreams brought the memories of his story so close to the surface, she couldn't ignore it.

As Elodie was losing count of the days of her journey, it started to rain. They stayed camped under a particularly dense patch of trees for three days, cold and miserable but mostly dry. When the sun finally came out, she mounted up again, and they set out through the mud. The river had risen from the rainstorm, and in patches, the travel was slow and treacherous. They passed a section where the river had risen far over its banks and caused a muddy mess. Storm nearly lost his hoofing and Elodie nudged him further away from the river, into some low-hanging branches. She pushed away the leaves ducking her head, and when they were free, she had a new passenger on her hand, a small fuzzy brown caterpillar.

"Hey little guy," she said, holding it up to eye level. The caterpillar curled up into a pinwheel and rolled down her hand. It fell off and rolled over Storm's back. Elodie tried to catch it, but it bounced off her hand.

Then she noticed a second caterpillar on Storm's flank, and a third on his mane.

A warning echoed in her mind . . . *Caterpillar, caterpillar, brown on red after a flood, you'll be dead or covered in mud.*

Chapter Eleven

SHE HADN'T SEEN the caterpillar's stomach, but if it was red . . . She didn't have time to think.

"Whoa, Storm! I need to check if these are marsh caterpillars."

Elodie slid off the saddle and found a stick to knock off the remaining bugs. They all rolled up and fell off before she could turn them over, but on the last one, she'd seen a hint of red.

She took a deep breath so as not to panic and started quickly removing Storm's saddle. Something itched at the back of her neck, and she swatted, then saw another caterpillar fall to the ground. Panicking she ripped off her cloak and brushed herself off, knocking off another.

She'd ridden right into a nest of marsh caterpillars, all plump from the rain and full of poison. The back of her hand was already covered in a red puffy trail where the caterpillar had rolled, stinging her with its tiny quills. She hadn't even felt the sting.

Her hand shook as she took Storm's reins and pulled him back into the mud. "Come on boy, you aren't going to like this bit." Bending down she scooped up a big glob of mud and rubbed it over her arm, and the back of her neck, tangling the hair falling from her cap. The small stones and twigs in the mud scratched, but she didn't have time to be delicate. She grabbed another handful and picked out the sticks before slathering it on Storm's back where the first caterpillar had rolled. The horse snorted at her, then tried to sidestep away, but she held him firmly. "Come on, you must have encountered marsh caterpillars before, hasn't Sir Studly ever done the same?"

The bug was common enough, fully brown until made plump by feasting on water collected on their plants. The extra water sent their venom production into overdrive. They were dangerous after a heavy rainfall or in dense foliage right along a riverbank. The only reason more people didn't die from them was that the rash they caused was obvious and the antidote was so readily available. Mud left on the sting until it dried pulled the poison from the skin. It took a while for the poison to enter the bloodstream from the skin, but when it did, it took moments for death to occur. There were a few casualties every now and then, a man who'd had one sting him on an open wound or a kid who didn't want to end a game early and tell their mom about a rash.

She'd encountered them before, but it had only been one caterpillar that stung her finger when she tried to hold it, and Gedas had been with her. Not having his calming presence at her side made every danger feel exponential. She rubbed another big handful of mud on Storm's leg. "Come on, be helpful."

Storm snorted and shook his head, then laid down in the mud. Elodie bit back a muttered thanks to whatever god was listening and continued coating the beautiful horse, then gave herself another layer. The leaves had hit her face, and she had no way of knowing if other caterpillars had hit her, so she covered every inch of exposed skin.

While she was coating her ankles, Storm flipped onto his back and rolled around in the mud like a stray dog. Elodie laughed.

"Feel better, my lord?"

Storm rolled around a bit longer, letting out a happy whinny before he stood, shook, and clopped toward the water.

"Oh no you don't. We have to let it dry!" She tried to catch up to the horse, but he dodged at the last moment, and she missed his reins. He trotted along the river snorting as he went, then he flopped down and rolled some more in the mud. "Are we playing now?"

The dignified and regal horse paused and looked up at her.

Elodie laughed. "Your pretty mane is gonna get so tangled doing that, then who do you expect will brush it out?"

Storm whinnied and stood. He clomped back to Elodie, and when he was close enough, lowered his head for a scratch. She reached up as he ducked down and head-butted her in the chest. She went down and landed on her butt in the mud.

"Oh, is that how you're gonna play it?" She grabbed a fist full of mud and threw it at the horse who dodged to the side, whinnied at her, and trotted away.

She gave chase down the river, launching mud and dodging away when he tried to knock her down again. She'd just landed a perfect hit with a mud ball when Storm stopped suddenly and Elodie walked into his side. She staggered for a moment, a hand on his shoulder to hold herself up. Storm stood ridged, his ears cocked to the side, twitching slightly as though listening. She strained her ears but didn't hear anything. Finally, he nipped at her sleeve and clomped to a few large rocks, before he turned back to her and bowed his head.

"Okay, I get it."

She climbed up the rocks and slid onto Storm, almost falling over the other side with nothing but muddy horse to hang onto. He steadied them and started to turn when what had startled him reached Elodie's ears too. Hoofbeats and the jingling of tack. A larger group heading up the road. The foliage was sparse here, trees and leaves overhead, but nothing separating the road from the river as though the small clearing was regularly used as a campsite. Elodie froze as the horse backed up toward the closest trees. If they ran for it, their motion would be noticed.

Her heart pounded. "Ravid, now would be a great moment to do your thing," she muttered under her breath.

Yellow and gray glinted between the trees farther down the road, and in a moment, she could see the albatross crest emblazoned across chests and shields as soldiers headed straight for her. The ground thundered before her as ten horses and riders poured into the clearing. A man startled at the sight of her on Storm's back.

"You, there! Boy! What are you doing?"

"Uh . . . Uh . . ." Elodie tried to make her voice a bit deeper. "Marsh caterpillars. A nest of them."

One of the dismounted soldiers cursed. "Ravid defend. Let's lunch somewhere else, boss."

"Scared of a few worms, Ricktor?"

"More like being smart unless we wanna end up in the same state as that boy," another soldier said as she gestured toward Elodie and Storm. "Druther be under the sun than under trees anyway."

"Fine, let's keep going. 'Tis a pointless search anyhow."

The soldiers remounted and set off along the road in the direction Elodie had come.

"Thanks, Ravid," she murmured.

The yellow and gray disappeared from her view like the flashes in her dreams. Storm decided it was clear long before Elodie's racing heart slowed, and he clomped his way back to his saddle and their bags.

When they got back to their packs, Elodie had a slight dilemma. She couldn't put Storm's saddle back on him while he was muddy. Any little stones or twigs would rub him raw. She could wash off the mud, or at least the mud under his saddle. His fur was thick, and horses were safe from most insect bites and stings, but she didn't want to risk it.

She settled for brushing the mud off his back. It was still wet and would leave a thin layer while removing any small rocks and twigs. They would just ride until it dried, then she could give him a proper brushing, so he didn't get sores. When they set off again along the river, she made sure to keep Storm away from any low-hanging branches. Once the mud dried and they were safe from the caterpillars' stings, Elodie asked Storm to stop so they could clean up. They still had a few hours of light left, but she didn't want Storm to get any sores. She started the meticulous task of removing his saddle, blanket, and every bit of mud from the underside of the leather, then beat out the blanket until it was as clean as she could make it. She was brushing out Storm's coat when the fear of the close encounter with the guards came back to her and her hand stopped its motion as her breathing came in rough breaths. She took a deep breath and tried to calm her mind. The adrenaline had worn into exhaustion while she'd ridden, but this sudden anxiety wouldn't keep her sharp, it would only make her act irrationally.

She took another deep breath and tried to think what was causing the panic. The soldiers hadn't questioned her presence. They believed her a boy because she was so filthy, because Storm looked nothing like a warhorse with mud an inch thick over him. If it hadn't been for the caterpillars, they may have been caught.

Her plan had been to clean Storm, then clean herself before heading back out. Instead, she cleaned Storm's back, all the places his tack would rub, reattached his saddle, and then proceeded to rub mud into all the buckles and fine leatherwork of the saddle. She ground mud into their packs, ripping one a little, making sure the supplies were safe while the equipment looked worthless. The bow was hard to disguise, but she rubbed mud into the limbs and tore strips from one of the old tunics she'd stolen and wrapped it around the grip so the weapon looked old and worn. The string stayed safe in its oiled cloth in the pack. She was still barely strong enough to string the thing anyway. When this was all over and Silas saw what she'd done to his supplies . . . She would pay him back, buy him better equipment, and a fancy new saddle for Storm.

That night she couldn't sleep. The close call with the guards and knowing her dreams waited just on the other side of consciousness was all too much. If Storm wasn't the one who would suffer, she would mount up and ride through the night. She lay awake for a long time thinking of Gedas. She worried about him somewhere in a dark hole, all alone.

Finally, just as the moon was rising, she drifted off to sleep.

SPINDLY LEGS SUNK into wet leaves under the weight of the thing as it moved around a tree trunk. It stank of hunger and malice and rotten things as it navigated the forest. It leaned down, the front half of its brown matted body tipping down, until its long feelers touched the edge of a rock. The long quill-like hairs along its body quivered in anticipation and it sprang to life, launching itself at Elodie.

She jumped awake, breathing heavy and sweating. Storm stirred at her back and flipped his tail. Elodie stood and started packing up their camp. She wasn't sleeping while that thing hunted her.

She'd seen the bochnid, and it was worse than Gedas had ever described. It shouldn't exist, but somehow it did. She paused as she tied the bedroll and counted in her head. It had six or seven legs, so it was still young. Gedas said they grew a new leg every year, growing longer and longer. If cut in half, they could even survive as long as the front half had enough legs to get away and wasn't too badly damaged. Seven legs meant it was young, only three years old. That was good. Young meant it would be slow, likely the only reason she was still alive.

The rock it had inspected looked familiar too, it was one she'd used to mount Storm a few days before. It was closing in fast and Elodie didn't know how to kill it.

First marsh caterpillars and now a mutant spider centipede the size of a dog, with no Gedas to save her and make everything better. This was officially the worst trip she'd ever had, and yes, she was counting the time she'd been kidnapped and chained up in a cave.

She couldn't keep up this pace forever. Storm needed sleep, and if she didn't sleep when they stopped, she would end up sleeping in the saddle. It was close enough to sunrise that they would be fine for now, for a few extra hours on the road. She would make sure to take longer lunches and breaks to give Storm time to rest.

She didn't think they could outrun a bochnid, but she had to try.

Chapter Twelve

SHE WAS by the fire in Gedas's rooms in the castle of Tross, curled up in an overstuffed chair, reading an adventure story about an Aviwoman with green iridescent feathers. The Avi was telling the story of the invasion of the Twoshy, back before Elodie's ancestors had claimed the land as their own and kicked out the Dwarvman and Elvman. The woman spoke of the Tokke Mountains in the south of Aluna as a world unto itself filled with danger and magic. Then the dream shifted in a swirl of yellow.

"Many have found sanctuary and peace in the mountains when the rest of the world has threatened or shunned them," the voice rang out of the mist. Elodie knew that voice and those words, they spoke to her from deep in her memory. When she reached for it, she fell into a pair of gray eyes and sunk into the mist. The mist cleared and she was in a pit as the gray-eyed man's life force slowly bled away into the night.

The bochnid was waiting for her in the dark. She couldn't see it. The hair on the back of her neck rose and she spun around, wanting to face the threat, but it was all around her, growing closer and closer.

She woke herself up, calling out in terror. Storm neighed and nuzzled her shoulder as she tried to slow her breathing.

The bochnid was getting closer. She couldn't outrun it.

She didn't know what to do.

The next few days as the border of Aluna drew nearer, they encountered and hid from three more battalions of soldiers as they passed on the road. It would seem Oburleck knew Elodie had escaped the initial area she was believed to arrive in, and now he was attempting to cut her off before she fled the kingdom.

It wouldn't work. Elodie was determined to beat him. To survive against all odds.

The wings of the albatross flapped in her dreams more and more as they continued their path, and the presence of the creature grew even sharper in the moments just before she awoke.

THEY WERE two days or so from the border when Elodie woke up with a gasp. The bochnid had been inspecting a log, its long coarse hair quivering as it tasted the scents over the bark. Elodie had used that very log as a stepping stool to remount Storm the previous morning. The bochnid was only a day away. When it was close enough, it wouldn't need her sleeping consciousness to follow, it would be able to find her night and day.

It was still early, a few hours before sunrise, but the moon was nearly full. She apologized to Storm and promised him the world when this was all over as she straightened out his blanket and swung the heavy saddle onto his back.

As they headed north fleeing her kingdom with the beast chasing them, reality started to creep into Elodie's mind. The stillness of the early morning would no longer let her avoid the facts.

Her entire kingdom was looking for her, and if they caught her, there was only one punishment for the crime she was accused of. Treason had to be cut off at the head. On the bright side, if the monster found her first, which was likely, she wouldn't have to worry about being executed publicly by her own people. It would do the job privately, maybe without even waking her.

There was no happy ending to this story.

Elodie's only true hope was for the ruakh to come, wrap around her, and take her swiftly back to the illusion where she was safe. It was such a comfortable prison; she'd finally started to prefer it over this dirty, broken world where magic never made anything better.

The river swelled into a lake that they had to circle and the far end was rather marshy. Letting Storm find his own footing, Elodie stared out into the water watching the moon reflect off the placid surface, broken up only by the reeds and brush by the water's edge.

An idea flooded her. It was utterly foolish. The kind of idea that would likely end in her death, but at this point, most of the paths in front of her ended with death.

No, I'm not going to die. Not yet, and not like this.

The prophecy she'd learned about when she was twelve said she would be the one to break the spell that was binding her and the other Misplaced in the illusion. She'd never found the exact translation of the spell, but it didn't matter. Everyone agreed it would be Elodie, heir of Aluna, who would break the spell. That was why Allen had been so disgusted by her. He'd always known about some prophesied princess who would one day set him free, but when face-to-face with Elodie, she wasn't much to work with.

If the prophecy said she would one day break the spell, then the bochnid wouldn't kill her, and Oburleck wouldn't execute her. Either the crazy idea she'd just thought of would work while Silas's plans in the capital paid off, or the ruakh really would come for her and it wouldn't matter.

She took a deep breath and let the resolve sink in before she called Storm to a stop and dismounted, walking toward the water's edge to the plant life sprouting from the marshy ground.

AS THE SUN rose so did their path. They climbed into the hills bordering Aluna. A little after noon, she knew they were very close to Tate, Silas's home. She'd spent a good deal of time there, and his father was a kind lord, who truly cared for his people. She didn't think he would be one to follow Oburleck's orders, but if things ended badly, she didn't want Silas's family to be executed for helping her. If the ruakh was her way out of this mess, Silas would be left to clean up the pieces.

Tate was only a day's ride from Arnav, the capital city in Rohap where Silas had told her to find the Snarled Cello tavern. She was making great time and could keep going until they reached the city, but what then? The border wouldn't stop the bochnid, and she would only be leading it into an unprepared city. More people would die than just her. But if she rode until she and Storm were too exhausted to keep moving, when they finally stopped, she would pass out in a deep sleep. A perfect target for the bochnid.

They stopped that night in the crook of a rocky outcropping, blocked on two sides by stone, a hill rising at her back. The spot, just on the edge of the border, felt safe enough that she started a large fire. The rise of the land around her would block the light, and she prayed the smoke would go unnoticed.

She needed light.

She set out her bedroll and her weapons around her. She didn't know if she should sleep. There was a chance the bochnid was still too far away and wouldn't even reach her that night. But she couldn't keep going. Storm had been tired with their short rest the night before, and their short rests every night since they set out. They had been short on food too. Then they had reached the hills where he had to work twice as hard. She knew he was a strong horse, but she didn't want to ride him into the dirt. He deserved better. He also deserved better than getting killed by a monster.

Storm knew something was happening. He stood unsettled on the edge of the camp as though he were a sentry standing guard. Elodie gave up and lay down fully clothed on top of the bedroll. She covered up with her dirty, disgusting cloak, her boots still firm on her feet, hanging out the bottom. It would be easier than being trapped in the bedroll if she needed to get up quickly.

As she lay there, one hand gripping the long knife Silas had given her, she didn't think she would manage to fall asleep. Before long, something pulled at her mind and consciousness left her like a bird flapping into the night.

SHE WALKED down the hallway of her school. Blue lockers lined the walls, broken up by classroom doors. Each door held a window showing rooms full of students studying. She should be in there with them, but instead she kept walking, dread creeping up her back, her heart pounding. If she was caught, she would get in trouble for being out of class, and getting in trouble felt like the worst possible outcome she could imagine. Fear spiked in her chest.

She couldn't stay here in the school, she needed to leave, but that wasn't allowed. At the sound of a teacher coming, she darted into the bathroom. Heart racing, she leaned against the cold door. Something was wrong, but what?

She shouldn't be here. She needed to leave, to wake up.

She needed to get up. Now.

Sleep wrapped around her like cobwebs pulling tighter as she struggled. She couldn't break free. She reached out into the gauzy muck and tore, trying to free herself. She was suffocating, but it wasn't a physical suffocation, her mind was drowning and had to break the surface. Her shaking hands fought and tore against the cobwebs, pushed and struggled as she had against the ruakh, but this time Storm whinnied loudly and the ground around her head shook as he stomped. She broke free of the dream and lurched awake.

The fire had burned down to low hot flames, still casting light, but not making her small camp as bright as she wished. She rose, knife still in hand, and kicked the logs she'd set out into the fire, stirring up the flames and causing the cindix to stir in the embers.

She looked around the small campsite and saw nothing. Storm too was alert, but not focused on any target. She picked up a small bundle next to her bed and unwrapped the waxed cloth carefully to reveal a brown paste.

Cutting the quills off the marsh caterpillars that afternoon with nothing but rocks, sticks, and a sharp belt knife wasn't the easiest thing she'd ever done, but after grinding up the quills into a thin paste, it was easy enough to coat the knife's blade and the heads of a few arrows. She wouldn't try shooting the arrows, it would be a waste of time—she was barely able to string the damn thing, let alone hold an arrow and aim with her heart racing and her hands shaking. But the arrows were long, and all she had to do was break the bochnid's skin, get the poison into its body.

Storm snorted and Elodie stood, knife in one hand, arrow in the other, and looked at the horse. His head was up, and his ears moved as he listened to the night. She heard it too, a slight scraping of rock. Clicks and scratches reverberated from the rock bringing the image of hard claw-tipped legs on stone. It was coming from above. She looked up at the rocky outcropping above her. Maybe being so near the rocks hadn't been the best plan.

The edge of a long spindled black leg caught the firelight as it moved from behind a boulder ten feet above. As the bochnid stepped into the light, it was worse than her dreams could have warned. The pedipalps around its mouth moved in anticipation as its multifaceted eyes locked on her.

Her mind went blank. There was no way she could survive against this monster. Why had she even tried? If only death would be swift and painless. The weight in her hand started to slip, and she reflexively tightened her grip.

The knife.

She had the knife in one hand, and the arrow in the other, both coated with marsh caterpillar poison. She didn't need to beat the monster with strength, she just had to pierce its flesh. It should be easy. She took a deep breath and let it out in a ragged stream.

She couldn't do this. She pushed the thought away. She *would* do this.

The creature moved to the edge of the ledge, and the front half of its body raised up, front legs in the air. Elodie held her position. The bochnid leapt from the cliff, and she darted to the left.

The bochnid couldn't change its direction in midjump, but instead, it twisted in the air grotesquely. Its long black spindled legs reached for her, and she thrust out the knife and connected. There was a rasping noise as the knife scratched against the hard shell of the spindled leg, and then all she felt was pain as the sharp claw at the end of a leg gouged along her arm.

The knife fell from her hand and she staggered away, backing into a tree. The rough bark supported her and kept her standing. The creature turned toward her, and then Storm was there, blocking its path. The horse kicked at the creature, and the bochnid didn't even seem to identify the being blocking its path, its focus totally fixed on Elodie.

She didn't even scratch the monster. Its chitin armor was too strong, and the blade hadn't done enough damage, it didn't even pierce the shell. Her plan to take the beast down with poison wouldn't work now. She would be killed, and then it would go after Storm.

The bochnid reared up on its back legs, and Storm landed another hard kick on the creature's chest. There was a loud cracking, and a terrible scream came from the beast. It lashed out and attacked Storm with its front clawed legs. Storm screamed and kicked again, but the creature was ready for it and darted under and around the horse, straight for Elodie.

There was no time to think. Her hands clasped the arrow shaft in front of her until she was shaking. The monster launched itself at her. Her hands held firm to the arrow, pointing the poison tip away from her body. There was no time to thrust the arrow out before the weight of the beast pressed her into the tree. She couldn't breathe. Her empty hand came up and met the hard shell of its head. She pushed, her arm shaking, trying to keep it from her.

The bochnid reared its head back before opening its jaw and sinking its teeth into Elodie's shoulder. She screamed. The pain was too much. Her eyes squeezed shut as the monster chewed into her arm. Where was the ruakh, now?

She wouldn't go easily, she wouldn't let this creature eat her. Her eyes flew open.

She released the arrow and raised both arms. Pain seared in her left arm, but she pushed against the monster harder. He would not win. Oburleck would not win.

She could hear the grinding of the monster's teeth as it fought her. It reared back again. Head up, the monster's multifaceted eyes met hers. There was nothing but frantic hunger in its gaze.

The monster fell on its back, its seven legs sticking up in the air, twitching and spasming. Storm screamed and reared up, dropping hard onto the creature's head, cracking it. The legs of the monster shivered and spasmed.

Elodie's eyes stopped on the arrow sticking out of the creature's stomach, wedged perfectly between the cracks in the shell Storm had caused with his first blow. She stood frozen.

The stallion continued to stomp the monster into the dirt, spindled legs twitching with each stomp, dark blood and slime sprayed up to coat the horse. Elodie slowly sank to the ground at the base of the tree. Something tickled her face, and she wiped away tears. Storm had a few nasty cuts on his chest and was getting bug guts into them. She needed to stop him and get him cleaned up. But everything was spinning, and she hurt so much.

Dumb luck. It was only dumb luck she was still alive.

Storm nodded his head up and down at the crushed creature, then kicked dirt on it, and snorted.

She let out a short laugh at Storm's antics, but the laugh turned into a hysterical sob until she covered her mouth with a hand to stop it. Hot tears ran down her face, the fear and shock of her close call escaping with them.

Storm butted his head against her good arm and she lifted it to his mane. Her fingers found bug guts and blood.

"Sir Horse, you are filthy."

Storm neighed, and Elodie rested her head against his for a long moment.

The cold water jolted her and made her wonder if she had led Storm to the river, or if he had led her. They washed off the blood, dirt, and gore. Her right arm had a nasty gash down the forearm and her left shoulder . . . she could barely look at it. When she moved it, pain radiated and her vision wavered black. They climbed out of the river and Elodie collapsed by the saddlebags in the dirt. She sorted through the herbs she'd picked over her weeks of travels and put yarrow into her mouth to chew into a paste. As she chewed, she reached for that small spark of magic within her and fed it into the yarrow to make it stronger.

The first batch of chewed yarrow went into the large gash on Storm's forearm. It wasn't as deep as it looked while covered in blood, but the yarrow would stop the bleeding and encourage healing. The second batch she shoved into the hole in her shoulder. She went on for a time, back and forth treating each of their wounds until each cut was covered in globs of yarrow and blood. She closed her eyes again. She wanted to lie down and sleep. Maybe she would feel better in the morning. Storm nudged her with his nose and she lifted a hand to stroke it. He nudged her again harder then gently bit her good shoulder, and she snapped back to focus. They couldn't stay here. They needed to find a proper healer. She didn't have what she needed to stitch up her shoulder, and she could never manage it on her own.

She gathered every ounce of resolve left in her body and stood, using Storm to steady herself when she swayed. She reached for Storm's saddle, moving her left arm, the pain was so blindingly bad she nearly fell over but for Storm, her tunic in his teeth, helping her to stay on her feet. Her fingers wound through his mane and she leaned against him. She didn't know what to do, she couldn't leave everything behind. She just wanted to curl up in a ball and sleep, and if she didn't wake up in the morning, maybe that would be better too. Storm snorted and nudged her again. She held tighter to him, and he started walking toward a pile of rocks.

Her feet stumbled up the rocks, and she held tightly to the horse, pulling herself up only with her right hand. His back was so wide, and she was so weak that she did not know how she would stay on, but Storm walked slowly, and carefully, and she wound his mane around her hands and held on, slipping in and out of focus as he clomped along under her.

Everything hurt. The pain was all she could think of until her mind stopped feeling even that. Slumped forward, she was vaguely aware when they moved onto a road. The sun had just started to rise, and when people passed, eyes watched her with horror, and when they spoke to her, she only replied with the name of the tavern "Snarled Cello," and the name of the barman "Graham."

She wasn't quite sure how long she rode like that until Storm came to a stop.

"What's your name, boy?"

The voice was rough, and a calloused finger rubbed at the mud still coating her face.

"Graham," Elodie croaked. Her throat was so dry.

"No, Graham is my name, what is yours?" the voice asked again.

"Princess Elodie of Aluna," she muttered. It was hard to think, but she knew her own name.

"I see. Madeline, run and fetch a healer, will you? Tell them we have the princess everyone's looking for down in Aluna, and she's close to death. Hurry up now, girl."

The world seemed to spin a little as she was lifted from Storm's back. She didn't want to let go, but hands had pulled at the mane wrapped around her fingers. Then her shoulder was jostled and she cried out, and everything went black for good.

Chapter Thirteen

THE ROTTEN STAGNANT presence was gone and did not return, but still Elodie sunk into a deep blackness. Under her feet was a grate, and she knew with absolute urgency that something vitally important was down there. She got down on her knees and peered through the grate trying to see past the darkness. Far, far below there was a light in the bottom of the hole. It was so impossibly far below her; she didn't have any hope of reaching it. Slowly the light was fading, waning into the darkness, and Elodie knew when the light faded, she would be all alone.

The fear, the loneliness, and anxiety gripped at her chest. It called to her, whispering in her ear that there was no hope, and hot tears ran down her face.

When Elodie awoke, she was confused. The open wood planks of the ceiling told her she was not at home in her bed in the illusion, and the soft yet scratchy fabric of her bedding told her she wasn't in the castle nor had she been captured. She knew she should be experiencing a little more worry, but as she stretched out on the bed she didn't care. It felt like years since she'd been safe and warm and comfortable. She wanted to roll over and cover her head in a blanket, but a soft noise stopped her. A little girl was peering at her from around the doorframe. Elodie blinked and the girl ran.

She sat up and looked around for a robe or something to pull on over her nightshirt. An older man, hair more on the salt side than pepper, stooped to make it through the doorway. His face, square and long with heavy lines that accentuated his extreme frown, looked down at her.

"Good, you are awake." His voice was deep and strong but not raised. "Madeline, go and fetch some spare clothes from Mrs. Korin. Tell her our guest has awakened at last.," he said to the small mousey girl who'd been hovering near the doorframe.

The girl's light brown face and mess of curls disappeared without hesitation at the man's words.

The man crossed the room with a few strides until he was standing over Elodie, looming down at her with his arms crossed.

"Now, tell me, girl, why were you seeking my establishment in your previous half dead state?"

This must be Graham. Elodie reached her hand tentatively to her shoulder, remembering the gash and torn flesh. The skin felt a little tender but new as if a very good healer had sunk a large amount of magic into her body. It was the sort of treatment usually reserved for the upper class. Healers who tended to regular people focused on using their magic to prompt a person's body into healing itself. It was more economical. A lot of money had to be dropped on a healer for them to heal somebody outright.

"Yes, yes, you're quite fine now. A palace healer was sent if you can imagine it and healed you right up. A good thing too for those scars likely wouldn't have looked very pretty in all your stately ball gowns. Now, Your Highness, if you can tell me why you are here in my humble establishment." He glared at her with expectation, but it was somehow a warm open glare as if his face just always looked hard and stern.

"Silas . . . Sir Silas of Tate told me I should come here. He told me I could trust you."

"Hmph. Someone will have to tell that damn noble I don't like house guests."

"Then why do you run an inn?"

"Let's get you a bath. Where did that girl go?" Graham peered out the door but didn't seem to find what he needed. "Our Meredith is a flighty one. Her previous family taught her that imperfection was rewarded with beatings." He raised one stern eyebrow at Elodie. "I expect you to treat her and the other littles well. It has been my work to teach them not all humanity is worthless and if you are to stay here, I expect your assistance. Though if our knight Silas was the one to send you, I suppose I don't have to worry over much."

Meredith came back and set a small stack of clothing on Elodie's bed before looking out tentatively through her curls.

"Thank you, my dear," Graham said, addressing the girl. "You are a cool autumn breeze in the heat of summer." His words were soft and kind, despite his commanding voice and stern face.

Meredith giggled.

"Now, your arrival to this establishment was not exactly kept quiet, you understand," he said, turning back to Elodie. "One of the Misplaced on the edge of death and requiring a palace healer to survive is not typically the sort of gossip kept quiet, but I don't suppose anyone in your kingdom would dare send someone after you. Crossing the border with the intent of harm, especially to one of the Misplaced would be an extreme breach of the Constitution of Sixteen. And I don't think war is what they want."

Elodie wasn't completely sure if that was accurate, a kingdom could do a lot to ignore an act they didn't want to engage in, but assassins weren't the only worry. She had to tell him that her presence put everyone at the inn at risk.

"They sent a bochnid after me."

"What?" Graham's brow furrowed so far it nearly covered his eyes.

"That's what attacked me. I managed to kill it, but it almost completed the same favor."

"That's not possible. Bochnid haven't been seen on the Twoshy for a hundred years. It's impossible."

"It should still be where I left it, just inside the border of Aluna. On the east side of the road, there's a campsite sheltered in the cliff face. It seemed well used. My packs, my horse's saddle, it should all still be there."

"Indeed."

He didn't look like he believed her, but Elodie would have to go back and fetch her packs soon. There was quite a bit of gold in her saddlebags, and even covered in mud, Storm's saddle was very fine. It would be beneath him to wear anything else.

"Well, child. If you are feeling well, I can have Meredith escort you to the baths, then perhaps some lunch." He gave Meredith a nod and left without another word as though it had not been a suggestion.

Elodie smiled at the little girl. "Lead on."

Being clean was a big improvement for her attitude. The inn had a large bathhouse attached, with exceptional plumbing. After cleaning off several weeks of the road, Elodie looked herself over in a large mirror. The new skin covering her wound was a lighter shade than the rest of her, but all her small scratches and scrapes from traveling had been healed right along with the big ones. It was a waste of magic, but she was so thankful for it.

Once she was dressed, she headed to the stables to check on Storm. She shouldn't have worried. He had been well cared for, the gash on his own leg was healed over with only a slight scar. He whinnied at her indignantly and she leaned against the stall door and stroked his neck.

"We made it, big guy. And it was all you. No way would I have survived that thing if you hadn't cracked its shell." Storm sniffed around her neck, inspecting her for wounds and covering her tunic in horse goop.

"I'm fine, Sir Horse, really." She laughed and gently pushed away his nose.

"Is he yours?"

Elodie turned to see a boy, about twelve or so. He had light skin, his nose covered in freckles, and his hair was light and stuck up in funny directions. He had a jaded look, similar to one she'd seen in the eyes of Meredith and some of the other kids around the inn. But unlike Meredith, he looked well cared for like he got several good meals a day.

"No, he belongs to a friend of mine, but we've been traveling together."

The boy nodded as though he had already known this. "Why did you let him get so muddy?"

"We ran into a swarm of marsh caterpillars," she said a little defensively.

"Oh." The boy's face softened. "He's really beautiful."

Storm, who had been turning his head to the side to let Elodie scratch further under his chin straightened at the compliment. Elodie and the boy laughed. "Yes, and he knows it. Thank you for cleaning him up. You did a wonderful job."

The boy beamed. "I'm junior stableman for the inn, it's my job to make sure our four-legged guests are better cared for than the two leggers."

"And you do a great job." The stables were cleaner than the palace ones in Tross, but there was enough activity around her to show they were well used. "How long have you worked here?"

"About two years. Graham is a good boss. He will give a job to any street kid who doesn't wanna be a street kid anymore, and in a few years, I'll have enough training, I could get a job anywhere."

Meredith slipped in a side entrance and carefully approached. She ducked her head letting her curls fall over her face when Elodie glanced her way. "What's up?" Elodie asked.

"Master Graham says you need to eat lunch before you fall over and someone needs to carry you in." Her voice was soft and mousey, and it was the most Elodie had heard her say so far.

Elodie's stomach growled and Meredith smiled. She turned back to the boy. "What was your name?"

"Ben."

"Ben, this is Storm." She patted the horse on the neck one more time. "Thank you for taking care of him. Storm, be good for Ben." Storm snorted and Ben took her place to pat the horse as Elodie followed Meredith inside.

The kitchens were run by a kind, round-faced woman named Mrs. Korin. She was a little shorter than Elodie and directed the kids who worked in the kitchens with short precise words. The room was full of activity when they entered. There were three older kids, two girls and a boy beating balls of dough, flour billowing around them, two small kids with very sharp knives expertly peeling potatoes by the door, two boys chopping vegetables in a corner, a little girl on a very tall stool stirring a pot that was bigger than her on the wood oven, and a half dozen others doing various tasks around the room.

It was just past lunchtime, and the inn was mostly empty, but based on the amount of food being prepared, an army was expected later. The smells of the kitchen made Elodie's stomach growl louder and the full force of her hunger hit her. Healing took a lot out of a person and it was finally catching up with her.

Mrs. Korin set Elodie down at a corner of the table next to the vegetable choppers and slid a very large sandwich filled with roasted meat and cheese in front of her. Elodie was halfway through the sandwich when a little boy came in with a scowl.

"Mrs. Korin, Meg keeps sneezing over all the tables after I clean 'em!"

Mrs. Korin sighed and set down the cleaver she was using. "Send her in. Girl has the worst hay fever," she muttered to herself. She crossed to the sink and washed her hands as a girl of about fourteen came in. Her eyes and nose were pink and runny. "Grab the bottle for me, Meg."

Meg grabbed an amber bottle out of a cabinet and shook it. "Almost out," she said in a high nasally voice.

"Can I see?" Elodie asked.

Mrs. Korin and Meg turned to look at Elodie as if surprised to see her. Elodie stood up from the table, regrettably leaving her sandwich behind. She opened the bottle and took a sniff. It was old, very old, and probably should have been thrown out, but it wasn't harmful. It was a basic allergy remedy that helped a little with almost anything.

"I can make more if you want. Or I can make something that will help permanently if you can get the ingredients."

"Do you often make such things, Your Highness?" Mrs. Korin asked.

It was the first time she had addressed Elodie formally, and it caught her off guard. Both she and Graham had made a point to address her so casually, and it had made her feel so much more comfortable at the inn.

"Yes, I've apprenticed with a wizard and some other healers for a few years. This is an okay daily remedy, but I know one that, if taken daily for a few weeks will help the body build resistance so the hay fever will go away."

Meg's eyes got big and she looked at Mrs. Korin excitedly. Mrs. Korin sighed. "If you can write down what's needed, I can send someone to fetch it."

Writing tools were received and Elodie turned to Meg. "What are you allergic to?"

Meg rolled her eyes. "What aren't I allergic to?"

Elodie smiled and started writing down supplies.

Elodie finished her sandwich and sat watching the children work and turn ingredients into a meal. Not being alone, her stomach happily and full, it was a welcomed change. When Meg returned with the shopping Elodie was given a corner of the table to work amid the hustle and bustle of the kitchen when an older boy, about Elodie's age, walked up to the open door of the kitchen and rapped his deeply tanned olive hand against the frame. He had a large iron spit in his other hand. His jet black hair was cut into a sleek, high and tight style very foreign to the Twoshy, yet he wore thick breeches, a white tunic, and the heavy apron of a blacksmith and was covered from head to foot in soot.

Mrs. Korin spotted him and rushed over, a big grin on her face. "Oh thank goodness, just enough time for us to put on another roast for dinner." She took the heavy metal from the blacksmith with a grunt and nodded toward Elodie. "Have you met our newest guest?" she asked before carrying the spit to the fire.

Spotting her, he leaned against the doorframe and nodded casually. Elodie's eyes were fixed on his Adidas sneakers sticking out under his breeches.

"Sup?" He gave her a smirk and flexed his arms as he looked her over. The whole look, covered in a thin layer of soot was too much for Elodie and she burst out laughing.

This was obviously not the reaction the boy expected and he straightened and looked around. Mrs. Korin returned, folding a few sweet buns fresh out of the oven into a cloth. The blacksmith leaned close to the cook and whispered. "Is there something wrong with her?"

Mrs. Korin looked Elodie over and handed the blacksmith the buns. "You broke it, you fix it."

The blacksmith stood blankly, at a loss for words.

Elodie reined in her laughter and wiped a tear from her eye. "Does that line usually work on all the maids?"

Graham entered the kitchen and spotted the blacksmith. "Ah Tristan, my good man. Finished already?" He crossed to Tristan and slapped him hard on the back, causing the boy to wince.

"Yep, just finished cooling. I know Korin was itching to get it back, so I brought it right over," Tristan said.

"Spectacular." Graham frowned. "So have you met our resident Misplaced then?"

Triston turned back to her, his eyes wide.

"I'm Elodie," she said, a little nervous. She hoped she hadn't made as bad of an impression as she had on Allen. She probably shouldn't have laughed in this kid's face. "So where are you from?" She knew he couldn't be from Rohap, they didn't have any Misplaced of their own. Tristan must have an interesting story to be working here as a blacksmith.

Tristan's face seemed to harden, and he crossed his arm. "My family was from Pundica, if that's what you mean."

So he definitely knew Allen then. "What are you doing in Rohap? Shouldn't you be off learning the ins and outs of noocratic leadership?"

Tristan's eyes seemed to darken. "The same could be said of you, my lady." His voice held a hint of disgust and Elodie's stomach fell. "Shouldn't you be off learning to embroider and look pretty on a throne? Oh yes, I forgot. Aluna's steward decided robbing the kingdom blind wasn't enough and put a price on your head." He looked down at the herbs she was chopping. "Glad to see you found work to get by."

"Excuse me?"

Tristan bowed. "You're excused." He saluted Graham and turned on his sneaker-covered heels and left out the back door.

Graham sighed and turned to head back into the inn. "Foolish boy left before I could pay him. Now I will have to go traipsing all over town to pay my debt."

"What's his deal?" Elodie asked, choosing to be offended over being hurt by his reaction.

Graham frowned deeply at Elodie, but she saw the softness in his eyes. "That boy has had a hard lot over the years. It is not my place to tell his story, but you would do well to remember how a noocratic nation, such as Pundica, chooses its leaders." Graham gave her a nod and left Elodie with a weight of guilt as she finished chopping her herbs.

Pundica was the hub of all magical activity in the Twoshy. It housed the magic university where any and all with the gift of magic could go to understand and grow their abilities. Their government was made up by sixteen councillors selected by merit, intellect, and wisdom. Elodie personally thought this was a genius idea and a much better plan than Aluna's monarchy. Elodie sure didn't think she should be given full and utter command of thousands of lives just because of her genetic line. That didn't mean she would abdicate her position when it finally came to her, she just thought it was a bad idea.

Because Pundica's leaders were appointed, their positions were not tied up in the amendment of twenty-seven like Elodie's throne was. This meant their country was stable and kept progressing after the loss of the Misplaced. As they had sixteen leaders, it also meant they had a lot more Misplaced than any other country. If Tristan didn't have magic and his family line had ended with him, he might not have anywhere to live in Pundica. It made sense he would travel to Rohap where he could find work.

Elodie didn't always enjoy her time visiting her castle, preferring her time adventuring with Gedas, but at least she always had the castle, her home, to return to when she needed it.

Until now.

She would go and apologize to him in a day or so. She didn't want to lose this opportunity of knowing another Misplaced at last.

Chapter Fourteen

GRAHAM FOUND ELODIE BEFORE DINNER. He'd sent an older boy to the camp where she'd fought the bochnid to retrieve her belongings and wanted her to make sure everything was there. He didn't mention the lumpy form in the small wagon covered in heavy canvas. The smell coming from it was terrible. A tall man in proper mage robes of shiny blue fabric peered under the canvas.

A tall kid, about her age with deep brown skin and pretty brown eyes, showed her the equipment he'd found. His name was Mitchel and when she asked, he said he had been working for Graham since he was eight. He laughed and carried Storm's tack to the stables without another word when Elodie tried to offer him some coins for fetching her things. She was glad she hadn't lost Silas's bow, or his knife, or the few herbs she'd collected along the way.

The mage lowered the canvas, his pale face looking a little green, and crossed to her, giving her a deep bow. "Princess Elodie, I presume?"

Her body tightened. "Uh, yes. That's me."

"It is a pleasure, Your Highness." He bowed again. "I am Sorcerer Johansson of Rohap. Graham tells me you were the one to destroy this beast." His voice went up as he said it, as if not wanting to be rude and imply his clear doubt in her story. Elodie smiled evenly and didn't reply. "How specifically was it killed?"

"Luck, Sorcerer Johansson."

He frowned and bowed his head. "Would you care to elaborate?"

She did not, but that would only lead to more questions. This mage must be ambitious to be a sorcerer at his age, he looked only in his late twenties. "My horse cracked its armor and I was able to stab it with an arrow coated in marsh caterpillar poison."

His eyebrows went up. "I see."

"Luck," she said again.

"How did you know it was coming for you? I've read most victims are usually caught asleep."

Elodie sighed. "Again, it was probably luck, but I dreamed about it. I knew it was chasing me for days."

"Really?" The sorcerer's stoic manner crumbled, and Elodie saw the curiosity and interest that was natural to most mages find its way out. "That's absolutely fascinating. Would you be willing to tell me more of your dreams? Perhaps there's some knowledge to be learned here about the bochnid and how they hunt, especially if they aren't as extinct as previously believed. If the physic feedback of their hunter senses was enough to prompt your dream mind—"

"That's quite enough Han." Graham put a heavy hand on Sorcerer Johansson's shoulder. Johansson seemed to blush a little and dropped his head like a scolded boy, not an established sorcerer. "It's the girl's first day back on her feet, I'm sure she doesn't want to relive the event that nearly killed her so soon."

"Of course." The sorcerer straightened and rearranged his robes, then headed back over to the wagon, taking a deep breath before lifting the canvas again.

"Don't mind him." Graham steered Elodie back into the inn. "He was one of mine until he was old enough to go to the university. Taught him how to read and he spent every spare moment with a book in his hand. The boy likes to learn, but you don't have to give him all your secrets."

"When did you start mentoring street kids?" It was a change of subject, but she wanted to know more about this odd man so full of contradictions. Silas trusted him, and Elodie was beginning to see why.

"Oh, that is a long story, not one to be told through memories. The short version—I found myself as a young man with enough unexpected gold and a desire to start anew. I built an inn. I did everything myself those first few months. For reasons that shall remain untold, I did not want to trust anyone else with my vision. I was not unfamiliar with the streets myself, and when I saw a boy digging through bins, I offered him some work. I realized quickly what I had always known. Those with nothing are very frequently more trustworthy than them with everything, and a little kindness will build a mountain of loyalty in one who has gone without."

They paused in the large open dining room, a boy was picking up chairs and a little girl of maybe five was sweeping under the tables as the boy pointed out spots she missed.

"All the littles need is a safe space to grow up a bit and learn a few skills so they can enter the world and find real work. They offer me more than I can repay in training, coin, food, and shelter."

It made Elodie's heart hurt. If only Callie had found someone she could have trusted, like Graham, instead of someone like the baron.

"Oh, before I forget, now that I have my things, I can pay you properly for my room," Elodie started.

Graham turned from watching the kids work and looked down at her, his eyes stern and imposing. "What do you take me for? The owner of a business trying to earn a livable wage? Your coin is no good here. I know a better way for you to earn your keep." The corner of his mouth turned up just slightly, and the smile alone was the scariest thing she had ever seen. He left her then without another word, and Elodie returned to her room to put away her things, pushing away the looming dread of Graham's smile.

As the evening approached, the tavern filled. Soon the stables were full, every room was booked, and more warm bodies crowded into the dining room than seemed reasonable. When one girl, Kimm, finished making bread for the evening she told Elodie how the Snarled Cello almost always had a teller for the night. Elodie was excited. Tellers traveled gathering stories and reciting them back to any who would listen. The magic of a tale worked to carry images and memories from the teller's mind to the listeners, so everyone who allowed themselves to be pulled into the story saw the tale happening firsthand.

Meredith saved Elodie a seat at a table in the corner of the big room. The table was crammed with travelers from Wedren, who chatted loudly, absorbed in each other's company. As she sat, they didn't ask her who she was or where she was from.

It was wonderful.

Elodie chose the thick, meaty stew for dinner. Potatoes dotted the thick broth in the bowl and the smell of spices and garlic rose with the steam to her nose. It was delicious. When the tavern was full and everyone was eating merrily, Graham stepped up onto the small platform situated against the wall and everyone grew quiet in anticipation of the teller.

"Tonight, for the pleasure of your entertainment"—Graham paused for a dramatic effect that was deeply felt from the absence of his baritone voice—"we have no teller present in the establishment." He said this in a devastatingly final way, and disappointed sighs were born all over the room. Elodie knew the disappointment to be much like a night spent without Wi-Fi. She took a big bite of bread and looked around at the downturned faces.

"But!" Graham's deep voice seemed to shoot itself through the room and embed itself into the attention of every person present. "If we give proper encouragement, I believe we might be able to coerce a tale of her land out of the beautiful and majestic Misplaced Child, Her Royal Highness, Elodie, Princess of Aluna." Graham finished his eloquent pronunciation of her title with a deep bow in her direction and her mouthful of bread seemed to double in size. Elodie's stomach dropped, she wanted to sink into the floor. She chewed as fast as she could as every man and woman in the building clapped their hands in sync to the rhythmic beat associated with an encore. Willing the bread down her throat, she took a large gulp of water before standing to cheers.

She was tired and would prefer a quiet evening listening to someone else tell a tale, then slink off to bed as soon as it was finished, but her telling would be a suitable payment for Graham's kindness and hospitality if not the potential risk in danger he was taking on by housing her. News she was here would travel faster now that she stood before a room of onlookers.

Elodie took a deep breath and pushed down her anxiety and her fear. This wasn't like an oral report at school where everybody was waiting for her to slip up. It was a room full of people eager for a new story, one they'd never heard before and could escape into for the evening. Tales were the entertainment of the Twoshy and if she was less than eloquent, no one would care.

So she called on the small part of her that knew how to stand before a crowd and knew the proper rituals needed for telling a tale and walked to the small stage with at least a semblance of confidence. The room clapped and cheered her progress until she lifted her hands, and the crowd fell silent.

"Thank you, Graham, for the introduction. I'm happy to give you a tale from the illusion. Please, tell me what kind of tale you would like to hear tonight?"

Voices rang out from around the room.

"Tell of a battle."

"Tell an adventure."

"Tell a tragedy."

"One with a lesson."

"How about a comedy?"

But one request seemed to be picked up by a few patrons and carried the mood of the room with it as the words reached her from the waiting watchers. "Tell of a love, a romance."

"All right, a romance it is." Elodie mulled the idea over. She wanted a story she knew well, one she could easily retell. If she told a story from a book she read, she would be sharing the images from her mind, created when she read it. That took a lot more focus and concentration because the images were her subconscious's own creation. She was too tired for that. Instead, she settled on an old story she'd heard a hundred different ways, with images and pictures easily provided by movies.

Elodie closed her eyes and started with the magic words.

"Gather in close while I tell you their tale."

The magic rose around her and flew through the room wrapping around each person who listened eagerly, binding them all together in a wave of magic and memory, thoughts and feelings.

"A man came to the small chattery town filled with lovely chattery young women. The man was arrogant, prideful, and very wealthy. Fiercely loyal and utterly shy, this man's name was Darcy." Elodie continued describing the characters and their achievements and follies. She pictured each scene and moment, the feelings and passion they invoked, and sent it out through the magic to those who listened. Some laughed, some cheered, and some swore to avenge the crushed love of the characters as Elodie wove the plot. At the end, there was a pleased and content silence as all present dwelled on the story and locked the memory of it away in their hearts.

As the magic of the moment dissipated, Elodie bowed and excused herself from the room, leaving the patrons to chat, finish their meals, or make their way to their own rooms and beds. She was exhausted. The magic and focus required for telling the story had left her feeling empty, and she was ready for sleep. Reaching in her pocket her hand found the sprig she'd snuck from the kitchen. She held it close as she prodded it with her magic, encouraging it to full strength to protect her as its nature allowed, before she hung it over her bed. Now the prospect of a dreamless night was too much to resist.

Unfortunately, the tarragon didn't work.

Chapter Fifteen

THE CROWN on her head was heavy, and she had to keep reminding herself to tip up her chin, straighten her posture. Her dress, a sophisticated cut and most elegant, was stitched to fit her with perfection yet made of harsh burlap that scratched at her skin.

She stood tall and proud before the onlookers, men and women of Aluna wearing their finest clothes. They had flower wreaths on their heads and held yellow or gray flags in their hands, everyone prepared to celebrate the day. As she stood before them, not a single person raised a flag, cheered, or waved. Down to the youngest child they stood before her and found her wanting. She took a step toward the crowd, along the path of leaves and flowers scattered just for her. As her first foot landed on the foliage, her dress began to break apart and dissolve, the burlap coming to pieces around her. With each step another piece of coarse brown fiber fell from her shoulders, from around her waist, and from the hem of the skirt.

She did not stop. When she was nearing the middle of the path, her clothes were in tatters, barely enough scratchy material remained to be decent, yet still she walked. The ground covering grew denser, a small patch of woven branches with forget-me-nots strewn about. When she stepped onto the first branch, the trap collapsed under her and she fell into the darkness. Black-tipped white wings flashed around her and far, far below that light grew ever dimmer.

In one final blinding wave of yellow fire, the sky lit up around her scaring away the birds. A voice echoed out of the fire. "The derelict have flocked to the mountains to live out a separate life from their fears, their enemies, and even their own fate."

ELODIE SPENT the next few weeks in Rohap enjoying the city and its people. Each morning she woke sweating and shaking, then took a long bath and let the water wash away each dream and memory so she wouldn't go mad. She did her exercises and when the kitchen was less chaotic, she would spend a little time restocking the inn's medicines. It was something she enjoyed and forced her to pull techniques, recipes, and processes out of her memory from trips long past. She spent afternoons wandering the markets or helping Graham's littles with shopping or other tasks. Occasionally she borrowed a book from Mrs. Korin and found a sunny spot to read.

Her time in Rohap felt weird, like summer vacation only she had an important task she kept forgetting, and if it were put off too long, she would be in trouble. Rohap made her feel safe and protected. She didn't want to think about everything that waited for her across the border.

But each night as sleep took her, the dreams would remind her of the terrifying truth of the situation. Silas told her to wait. He told her to wait in Rohap for him or Dess. She knew he would work diligently to find out who was still loyal or to find Gedas. She just needed to wait, but the anxiety and fear in her heart and her dreams screamed of urgency.

In the evenings, the patrons of the inn asked Elodie for a tale, and she told her stolen and sometimes copyrighted stories. Every night the number of attendees grew and grew as everyone in Rohap wanted to hear the tales of a Misplaced Princess. Some nights a teller would come to the inn to share their stories and hear hers. Sharing stories was nearly as sacred as telling them in the Twoshy.

One night after the tales were over and the patrons were leaving the inn or heading to their rented room, a visiting teller asked Elodie to clarify some of the more detailed points of her story so he could tell the tale again when he traveled. Elodie answered his questions as best she could while trying to recall the old blockbuster movie.

"No, he's the only one worthy enough to pick up his hammer. No one else can lift it," Elodie explained, and then she had to break down the finer points of an alien race's magical technology. She grew fuzzy on a few details, but she was good at improvising.

When he was done asking his questions, he bowed and offered his thanks, but she stopped him before he turned to leave. "Teller Bron, before you go, can I ask you a question?"

"Of course, my lady. How may I serve?" The short man bowed to her again, taking off his cap to show a bald spot on the top of his head.

He'd told a story about an Avi warrior, and it reminded Elodie of the time, when she was twelve, she'd met an Avi chieftain. The Aviman were one of the four races of people who lived on Eres along with the Elvman, Dwarvman, and the Human, like Elodie. The Avi lived in the Tokke Mountains along the southern border of the Twoshy and mostly kept to themselves after the Hu invaded. When she'd met the Avi chieftain and her companion, they joined them for an evening campfire and told them a tale.

Elodie ran her fingers over the acorn in her pocket as she thought over the best way to word her question. "Do you know if it's possible for a teller to show a different story to specific listeners?"

"I'm not quite sure I understand what you mean," Teller Bron said with a kind smile.

The dining room was emptying of its guests and Tristan appeared in the thinning crowd. He approached and leaned against a table nearby. Elodie hadn't seen him since he'd stormed out of the kitchen weeks before. She'd meant to track him down and apologize, but she'd chickened out. She hoped he wasn't here to yell at her more.

She refocused on the teller. "I heard a tale once where it seemed like the teller was sending specific images directly to me. I was in a group of people and the tale started out normally, but then something happened. It was like I was alone in the memories with the teller. I was wondering if that's a common thing, or if maybe I imagined it."

"Hmmm." Teller Bron scratched his chin through his beard. "I've never heard of something like this, but it would be an interesting phenomenon to study. I don't suppose the teller was a mage, were they?" Tristan tilted his head to the side listening, and Elodie ignored him.

Elodie had to think about this. When the Aviwoman's tale changed, yellow fire came with the vision. Human magic was blue, but Avi magic was yellow. "I think they were."

This made the teller frown. "That would likely explain it then. Very few professional tellers have the gift of magic. There's so little money in telling and so much money in magic. I suppose a spell could be devised to do anything, even warp a tale if needed."

The man shrugged as if that was all the answer needed. Elodie thanked him again, and he bowed before leaving for his room for the night.

It was common for nonmagical people to think magic had no limits, but that wasn't true. Ruakh followed clear predictable paths in how it influenced the world. It could be shaped to a specific will by the right combination of thought, words, or objects, but finding out the proper formula to complete your task could be the lifelong pursuit of a single mage. If the average teller didn't know of the ability to focus a telling's message on one mind, maybe it was a gift known specifically to the Avi.

"The mountains are sacred for their ability to isolate and protect," the Aviwoman's words echoed in Elodie's mind.

Tristan left his perch on the table and approached her. She tried to brush off the memories of the Aviwoman's tale and prepared herself for any verbal sparring.

"So do you even understand the concept of copyrights and plagiarism?"

His question confused her for a moment until she realized he was referring to her tale of the night.

"I would love to see the network lawyers serve me here."

He chuckled, then his face dropped. "I wanted to apologize for how I acted the other day." He looked at his feet. "My home life has always been a bit of a touchy subject for me."

"I'm sorry. I wasn't thinking when I brought it up."

He nodded his acceptance, and they stood in silence.

"So anyway, you need to tell me everything about you because I've never had a real chance to talk to another Misplaced before, and I've never met someone on this side of the spell. How often do you travel? And do you know Allen?" Elodie stopped herself before she threw every question she had at him. He looked at her blankly. "I mean you totally don't have to tell me anything if you don't want to. I respect your privacy."

His face cracked into a grin. "No, it's cool. But you've really never met anyone else before?"

Elodie shook her head. "I met Allen a few days before I traveled here, he was a new student at my school, but other than him, no. It's always been just me."

"Yeah, Allen sent a message to our group chat and said he met you. Sam told him to give you the details to join, but I didn't see any messages from you before you left."

"Um, he did mention others, but he walked right into a wall of shimmer before he got back to me about it."

Tristan snorted. "He likely ran for the rift. That dude loves traveling more than anyone I know. I did hear he was back a few weeks ago T-time. I think Sam and a few others are also here. I sent a messenger bird to them a few nights ago after I cooled down from being mad. Again, sorry about that. Most of the Pundica Misplaced hang out there, so if anyone is home, they will get the message."

"You guys have a group chat? How many of us do you know?"

Tristan sighed. "This is gonna take a lot of catch-up. Do you think Graham has any of that stew left?"

He did, and he handed over a large bowl to Tristan with a pleasant scowl. As he ate, Tristan told Elodie a little more about the others. He stayed pretty far away from any of his personal details, but he slowly told her their story in between bites.

"You see, it all started with Diego, a guy from Oskela. Diego was always getting in trouble for running away and making up ridiculous stories for where he'd been." Tristan paused here and gave Elodie a knowing look. Elodie smiled. She understood completely.

"So Diego wises up and stops telling his parents about his magic world, and starts getting into bigger trouble, running with the wrong kids, small crime, things like that. His adoptive parents are rich, so they cover everything up and get him into therapy. One of those really open-minded types. Diego didn't open up to the therapist, because what teen boy wants to tell a concerned adult he's acting out because his life is ruled by a magical spell and that he's constantly questioning his own sanity and just wants some semblance of control in his life?"

Tristan paused again to eat, and Elodie wondered if he too had been in therapy. He definitely knew the language.

"Diego is super into computers, so his therapist tells him to write a blog. Say whatever he wants to say and throw it out into the world. Then Thomas comes along, I think he's the oldest of us, just young enough for the spell to still latch onto him, but he doesn't travel quite as often as the rest of us. He's from Pundica, so he's known most of the other Pundica Misplaced for years. The way he tells it, he was procrastinating while working on a history report and just messing around on Google when he searched 'Twoshy'. He wasn't really looking for anything, but he found Diego's blog. 'Traveling the Twoshy'. He reads a few entries and quickly realized it's another Misplaced he doesn't know and sends a message to the blog owner. Diego didn't believe him at first."

Elodie smiled at the thought. There were times in her life she had deeply questioned her belief in the Twoshy. It would have meant so much for her to have met some of the others in her moments of doubt.

"That's when everything changed. Thomas eventually convinced him he was real, sent a few emails in the common language, or as close as he could come using the regular alphabet. It changed things for Diego. He realized he wasn't alone." Tristan let the moment hang while he ate. He didn't have to tell Elodie how important that moment would have been to Diego.

"When Thomas realized what Diego had been through, he decided to make that his thing. Finding the Misplaced in the other kingdoms and making sure they can find us in the illusion. We all have our things, right? Allen's thing is to figure out how to break the spell, regardless of that whole prophecy saying you'll be the one to crack it. My thing is to learn a trade, so I can make a living when I'm stuck here forever."

Elodie frowned. Making a living in the Twoshy wasn't something she'd ever worried about before.

He brought his bowl to his mouth and drank the last of his stew, then set the bowl down with a thump. "And on that note, I should go to bed. The forge is lit early and waits for no man."

He stood, and Elodie stood with him. He looked tired, and she felt that pang of guilt again. She'd really had things easy over the years, and this trip with no Gedas waiting for her with clean clothes and a warm fire was what the other Misplaced experienced every time they traveled. When he talked about the other Misplaced finding each other, Thomas searching for them, jealousy had started to creep into her. Why hadn't Thomas looked for her in Aluna? But she stamped down on those feelings. Other Misplaced had needed him more. "Thank you for telling me."

Tristan nodded and gave her a crooked smile that felt forced. He wished Graham a good night and left.

Chapter Sixteen

SHE WAS in the hole again. The space was barely wide enough for her to sit, and her legs had been folded under her for so long they ached. She couldn't stretch her arms out to either side. Every limb had to stay folded, curled in on itself. Her muscles cramped and spasmed in the dark hole, and at times, the limitations became so agonizing that she couldn't help but call out, release the tension and pain with her voice. But the sound only reverberated back from the small narrow hole and made her ears throb after so long in the silence. Heat burned behind her eyes, and hot tears fell down her face into her lap.

It was gone, all her hope. Never again would she see the stars or the moon, never again would she feel the light of the sun or brush her fingers against the petal of a flower. Never again would she feel the touch of another human or hear a beautiful song. She'd never know love or feel the rush of heat as someone brushed their lips against hers. Her life would end in this hole, and never again would she know joy.

When Elodie awoke at last, sweaty and twisted in her blankets, she felt trapped as if she was still in that dark hole. She needed to get out. It was still early, the sun not yet beginning to rise. The inn would still be asleep. She dressed quietly in a tunic and breeches and let herself outside through the kitchen door.

Storm stomped his pleasure at the sight of her. Ben dropped

from the loft when she lifted Storm's heavy saddle from its stand. She waved him back to bed and did up Storm's tack herself. If the boy didn't have chores yet, there was no reason he shouldn't get more sleep. She was out of the city just as the sun crested the hills. Her heart was calling her south into Aluna, but it would be suicide. And it would mean breaking a promise she did not want to break. Instead she rode east, along a small road she'd traveled a few times with Storm on mornings like this, when all she needed was air and the smell of growing things to clear her head.

As the cool, crisp morning clashed with the sweat and heat of her body, her muscles relaxed and the grip of the dream loosened. And when the road stretched out empty before her, she let Storm gallop to his heart's content. Then they turned back toward Arnav and the Snarled Cello.

She let Ben feed Storm while she gave him a good brushing. The rhythmic strokes of the brush did just as much for clearing her mind as the ride. When Storm was fed and clean, Elodie left the stables, intent on getting fed and clean herself.

Just before she stepped out of the stables, a shadow fell past her from the sky. She glimpsed a flash of black-tipped white wings and flinched as her dreams rushed back, threatening to overwhelm her. But this wasn't a dream, this was a message. She stepped out from under the awning of the stable and the large gull swooped down and landed on the railing. It was a beautiful bird, a proper seagull with gray and black wings and a light speckling of spots on its neck. There was no reason to fear the bird. She'd been around them all her life. In Aluna, those with money used them as messengers, and those without used them as dinner.

She reached over and untied the roll of paper from the bird's leg and stepped back as it spread its wings and took off into the air.

She held the scroll to her chest, watching the black-tipped white wings as they faded into the distance. When she could no longer see the glint of feathers, she looked closer at the scroll. It had a white wax seal with a symbol Elodie recognized as one used for binding. She placed her thumb on the seal and the charms in the wax snapped in recognition. She unrolled the paper and read the uneven and bumpy handwriting.

E,

I am writing from the saddle, so please forgive the informal tone and quickness of this note. I have been working to root out those among the upper class who are still loyal to the crown, and although public opinion cannot be anything other than the voice of O without serious consequence, there are many who whisper this is treason and work to oppose the rule. There are still many true supporters to the crown who will rise to help fight when the time comes, although most are afraid to move until G has returned to our side. Through whispers and shadows, we have discovered where G has been kept and as I write this we ride for O's home in the west.

As soon as we have found and rescued G, we will head to you at the SC and plan the next leg of this conflict. As we now ride for C, there will be no returning to the guise of a loyal knight under O's rule. Stay safe and I will see you in a few weeks.

Yours always,

S

She read it over three times, panic rising in her chest at each read. Gedas was in Comak, Oburleck's holdings, and Silas was about to openly commit treason. She didn't know how this could possibly end without Silas's head on an executioner's block. Sure, Elodie could disappear back to the illusion at any moment, but Silas had no escape.

And, Silas was going to rescue Gedas *without* her.

Panic, anger, fear, frustration. Emotions cycled through her before she could focus on any one. She closed her eyes and shook her head.

Think. Don't get left behind.

After a bath and food, she got directions from Graham and headed to the forge where Tristan worked.

"I need to work, I can't talk," he said when he saw her.

"Well, can I help? And would you be up for listening while I help?"

Tristan sighed and tossed her the billows. She'd seen them used before, but Tristan had to show her where and when to blow more air into the fire. She was sweating again in minutes but wasted no time in telling him about Gedas and Silas's letter.

"I can't believe Gedas has been in Comak this whole time, that's like, less than a three-day ride from here. I can't just stay safe while Silas fights my battles."

"Well, that's his job, right?" Tristan said in a dry voice as he hit a long strip of metal with a hammer. Elodie rolled her eyes. Something told her Tristan really didn't care about her worries, but she had to talk to someone.

It was hard to tell over the fire and the billows and the pounding of the hammer, but the clamor of many horses came from outside the forge. Elodie turned toward the open door but couldn't see the riders.

"Yo Triskit! Where you at?" a voice called from outside.

Tristan let out a pained sigh but didn't pause in his rhythmic hammering. "Here," he called.

In a moment a crowd of dirty travelers, all in their late teens poked their heads into the small forge and let out a number of greetings. Elodie was immediately overwhelmed. Tristan pretended to ignore them as he worked, but they didn't seem to care. A pretty, tall girl whipped off her hood and shook out her hair in a cascade of glossy black hair as she approached Elodie. Her hair framed her golden-brown face and accentuated her tilted black eyes. She smiled brilliantly at Elodie. "Hi! You must be Elodie! Tristan and Allen mentioned you. I'm *so* glad we have another girl to talk to. Me and Kat were just talking about it."

The tall girl gestured behind her and Elodie saw a shorter girl with rows of pretty braids, soft black skin, and big brown eyes trying to peer into the forge around the other mess of bodies all clamoring for Tristan's attention. She spotted Elodie and gave a small wave.

"I'm Sam," the tall girl said, and gave Elodie a crushing hug. "Oh my gosh, I'm so sorry to hear about your kingdom. That steward must be a total dick. Kirk, he's one of the identical twins over there, not the cute one. Tristan sent him a letter about meeting you, so they left Pundica and picked me up in Leronia on their way."

Elodie laughed, a little nervous. "This is so cool finally meeting all of you, I'm so glad you came."

The twin in a green tunic—Elodie wasn't sure which one he was supposed to be—crossed the small space to Elodie as if to greet her, but Tristan interrupted them. "Guys, I have to finish these rods before the iron cools, why don't you all go play introductions and wait for me in my room?"

"We would never all fit in that hole. We can just wait here," said a boy with an English accent. He had dark brown skin, and straight black hair. His eyes twinkled with laughter.

"Na man, I'm starving, let's go find food," the green-shirted twin said.

"We can head over to the Snarled Cello and eat. That's where I've been staying," Elodie suggested. Tristan agreed to meet up with them when he was done with his work. When they exited the forge, Elodie noticed Allen standing by the horses. She gave a little wave and he pointedly ignored her. They headed to the inn, stabling their horses on the way. Once her horse was in the capable hands of Ben, Sam hooked her arm through Elodie's and they walked together toward the inn.

The green-shirted twin caught up with them and skipped in front of Elodie and Sam, walking backward while he talked. "Hey! So I'm Kirk by the way, and that dude over there who looks exactly like me is Christopher, and the guy in brown is Rick." Rick, the kid with the accent, gave Elodie a little wave, but Christopher only nodded slightly. The twins were identical in every way that she could see, with the same black hair, light brown skin, and copper eyes, but they held themselves differently. Elodie didn't think she would have a problem telling them apart. Christopher was tall and serious, while Kirk slouched a little and was constantly in motion. "We're the resident badasses of this bunch, just in case you were wondering." He smirked, and Elodie could feel Sam rolling her eyes.

"Can you walk literally anywhere else, please?" Sam asked.

"But why would I want to do that? Then I couldn't see your lovely face."

"Exactly."

"Ugh!" Kirk made a fist with both hands as if he held a blade and thrust it into his own chest. "You wound me, Samantha, my moon." He stopped walking so Elodie and Sam almost collided with him. Sam shoved him out of the way with considerable force and he stumbled dramatically making pained sounds. The other girl, Kat, laughed behind them as they entered the inn.

The dining room was empty after the lunch rush. Benches and stools were scattered about in an uneven mess as a kid swept the floors. The afternoon sun shone through the low windows on the west side of the room casting light on the clean tables. Graham and a few of his littles were working at a table cleaning cups with rags. A little girl was showing him her cup and he examined it with the seriousness of a surgeon before nodding in approval. The little girl giggled and grabbed another cup, but Graham spotted Elodie and her companions.

"What in the name of Cooric do you lot think you are doing invading a fine dining establishment like this? Go back to the illusion, the lot of you." Graham called out in his stern voice.

Sam dropped Elodie's arm and pulled the old man into a hug. "Master Graham, it's so great to see you again."

Graham removed himself from Sam's arms and glared down at her. "I do not remember granting you permission to hug me, young lady."

"Missed you too."

"Well, now that we have covered that, what do you want?"

"We were hoping for lunch, but we can put in the labor to pay for it first," Kirk said, picking up a cup and a rag.

"Bah, I'm almost done anyway. Marc!" A small boy came running out of some invisible cranny. "Yes, there you are, my boy. Run and ask Mrs. Korin if we have any scraps, we can feed these disarranged youths, if you please?" The boy scampered off and Graham turned back to them, looking over each of Elodie's companions. "So, I suppose you will also be wanting somewhere to sleep as well," he said in an incredibly offended voice. The others just looked at him expectantly. "Meredith," he barked.

Meredith came in from the kitchens and curtsied before Graham, just as Elodie had taught her, except she kept her head bowed so her curls covered her face. Graham bowed to her in return, formal and stiff, and the little girl's shoulders shook with giggles.

"My dear, will you please help stack these mugs back behind the bar?" Meredith curtsied deeper and picked up an armful of mugs. Graham shook his head after the girl and turned back to the teens with a scowl. "Make yourselves at home. I will go and make arrangements for the night, but I expect a few of you to tell stories this evening." They all thanked him at once, but he waved them away as if annoyed and stormed off.

Marc came back out of the kitchen with a large tray loaded with sandwiches. Rick helped him carry them to the table, and Sam pulled Elodie into a seat next to her while she dug in.

As they ate, Kirk decided to give Elodie his life story. It was a good thing too because Allen made a big show of sitting as far from Elodie as he could, and it had made things a little awkward.

"So I grew up in a group home, right? All of us are adopted and foster kids, so it's not a rare story. Anyway, I was six the first time the ruakh grabbed me up. I was on a swing set at school, and it snatched me right out of the air. So I go spinning through the vortex of doom, you know what I mean, and land on the hard cobbled streets of the city center in Pundica. I'm disoriented and confused and look around and what's the first thing I see? Myself! Or at least I think it's myself, you know a mirror or something, but then the mirror moves, and I totally freak out."

"You just love hearing yourself talk, don't you?" Sam asked and threw a small piece of bread at Kirk. He caught it and ate it.

"Would you like me any other way, babe?"

"Yes, yes I would."

"So anyway, once Christopher and I calm down a little we realize pretty quickly we must be twins. Or at least I realized it, I didn't know what he thought because he was speaking Italian, and I was speaking Spanish."

Elodie chuckled.

"See! She thinks I'm funny," Kirk told Sam.

"It's just because she hasn't known you long enough," Rick said.

They laughed, but Kirk turned to Elodie with a relaxed expression. "Their hate can't touch me."

Elodie snorted.

"So anyway," Kirk said loudly, trying to continue his story. "There we were, two identical boys who didn't speak the same language as anyone around us, including each other, but then we realized we both knew a little English, so we managed until we started to pick up common."

Elodie pushed down a pang of guilt and played with the acorn in her pocket. On her first travel to the Twoshy, Gedas had given her father a translation spell, so she'd never had to learn the common language. She'd also had someone there to tell her exactly what was happening and take care of her. She really did have it made.

"So that's how it was for us every time. We always travel at the same time, so until we were older and found ways to get in contact overseas, we only ever saw each other when we traveled together."

"You always travel at the same time?" Elodie asked.

"Yep, pretty cool right?"

Elodie had to admit, it was cool.

"So when we got older we started emailing and came up with a plan for telling his parents how he met some foster kid who looked just like him. It took some convincing, but eventually they came to visit." He paused and looked over at his brother who was smiling softly. "Now we are working on getting into the same college. So that's me." There was a long pause while Kirk looked around at the others as if expecting someone to jump in and start talking.

No one did. Everyone just looked into their sandwiches or cups.

Kirk turned to Elodie and smiled. "So how about you?"

Elodie took a deep breath. She didn't know where to start.

"Well, my story is a bit different, I guess, because I've always had Gedas with me when I travel."

"That's the wizard, right? Totally wicked," Rick said.

"Yeah. Except he wasn't there this time." She explained about Oburleck accusing her of treason, her soldiers out looking for her, and of Silas's plans to rescue Gedas. "So everything's kind of falling apart in Aluna right now."

"Forget your kingdom, that's not what's really important here," Allen said with a sneer as he leaned forward in his chair. It was the first thing he'd said, and it was about as aggressive as she expected. "Wizard Gediminas is in danger, that's clear. And if this knight of yours is right, he's in Comak." Allen looked around the table to the others seated there. "Guys, Wizard Gediminas is the greatest magical mind of this age. If we have any hope of breaking the spell and ending this torturous jumping back and forth between worlds, we need Gediminas."

"Chill dude. Risking our necks for some wizard isn't gonna break the spell faster. Elodie's supposed to be the one who does it anyway," Kirk said.

"Yeah, everyone talks about this stupid prophecy and how Elodie here is somehow gonna break the spell," Allen rolled his eyes. "But let's be real, she's clearly not gonna do that on her own, if at all, and Gediminas is the only wizard on the continent who may have a shot at helping."

"What makes you think that?" Elodie asked. His words stung, but she was trying not to think about it. There were a few wizards in the Twoshy, maybe three or four. If Allen thought Gedas would be the one to break it, maybe he knew something she didn't.

Allen rolled his eyes. "Because he's the only one I haven't talked to about the spell."

"Because he won't return your letters," Kat cut in. Kirk laughed and Allen looked murderous.

"Laugh all you want, it doesn't make it any less important."

They started arguing on whether they should travel into Aluna or not. The argument degraded fast as arguments do with too many strong personalities who knew each other's weak spots.

"I think we should ride for Comak," Tristan announced. He walked into the room, cleaning his hands on a soot-covered rag. "We need to take real action for once. We know something needs to be done here, and I think rescuing Gediminas is important both for righting the wrong done in Aluna and for eventually breaking the spell. Both of these are important, even if it only involves Elodie's kingdom, we are all a family here and we should help."

They looked at each other, and then one by one seemed to nod in agreement. Warmth flooded Elodie's chest. She'd nearly decided to saddle Storm and ride into Comak on her own, but if she had friends her chance of succeeding rose exponentially.

Rick stood from the table and raised a fist in the air. "Excellent! We will leave at dawn to rescue the wizard," he said passionately.

"Hey, watch it there, Rick," Kirk started to say, but too late. Elodie saw it right as Rick did. The glittering shimmer of the ruakh rose quickly around Rick, and with a gasp, he was gone.

Kirk chuckled. "That kid has the worst timing."

They all laughed, then fell into silence again.

"Comak is only a few days south of here. If we leave in the morning, we will probably get there before Silas." Elodie looked at the others. "I have a friend in the city who we may be able to stay with."

"Are you sure they won't sell us out?" Tristan asked.

"I'm sure. She's in a bound bordello, and she has no love for Oburleck."

"Ew, I forgot Aluna still had slaves and things," Sam said.

Elodie sighed. "It's not something I can do anything about until the spell is broken."

"Well, let's plan then," Tristan said, and he started giving orders. They had enough horses, he could use Rick's, but they needed more supplies, and clothes to blend in. This meant a shopping trip was due.

Sam, Elodie, and Kirk were put in charge of getting clothes for their party. Graham recommended a few second hand stalls he frequented to keep the littles clothed, and they left with Silas's gold in hand, while the others went to find various supplies.

When they were out from under the inn's roof Elodie breathed deeply in the afternoon air. She hadn't known Kirk and Sam long, but she felt like she could trust them. "So be real with me. Is Allen always like that, or does he just really hate me?"

Sam let out a snort and Kirk screwed up his face as if thinking hard. "I don't think he hates you exactly, he just has a lack of care for you as a person," Kirk explained.

Sam tried to ebb her laughter as a few people they passed in the market stared. "Really, Elodie, it's not you. Allen is just a bit stuck up and doesn't really like anyone. Don't take it personally. He's just been jealous ever since he found out that Wizard Gediminas has been a mentor to you. We weren't joking before, I'm sure you could line a room with all the unanswered mail he's sent."

"That doesn't surprise me," Elodie said. "Gedas is prickly and really doesn't like teaching people who ask too many questions. I don't even know why he bothers with me. I'm not strong in magic, but Gedas said he made a promise to my father to look out for me."

"Oh, come on, El, you know you're like the Misplaced golden girl of the prophecy," Sam said. They reached the merchant Graham had recommended, and Sam started digging through the bins. "All of us Misplaced have been hearing about the prophecy all our travels. Apparently, you're the only way we're gonna get free of this divided life. You have to get how important that is. For Allen, meeting you as he did, I think he was just a little disillusioned. When he told us about meeting you, he said he'd always expected you must be incredibly powerful magically, or why else would you be the one and not him."

"We did mention he was stuck up, right?" Kirk cut in. He found a pair of boots in a big bin and set them aside. "I think he was a little surprised to learn you weren't as powerful as he thought and were just as lost in the spell as the rest of us. I mean, I get it, you're just one of us, nothing more nothing less. You may be the one to break the spell, but that doesn't mean you will do it on your own. But for Allen, that's not good enough. He wants to be the one to save the day."

"That makes sense," Elodie said. "But I feel guilty like I haven't been working as hard as I should."

Sam shrugged and picked up a tunic, holding it up for size. "It's never too late to start, and this time you have us." She held the tunic out to Kirk. "Here, this is for Christopher. The blue will really bring out the copper in his eyes."

"Girl, you do realize we're identical, right?"

Sam patted Kirk on the shoulder. "Keep telling yourself that."

"Does Christopher usually do the strong silent thing, or does he not like me either?" Elodie asked.

"Na, he thinks you're pretty cool, and he's excited to see some action on our trip."

Elodie set down the pair of breeches she was looking over and looked at Kirk confused. "When did he say all that?"

"He didn't have to. It's a twin thing." Kirk tapped his forehead and Sam rolled her eyes.

"Kirk got all the talking genes, but Christopher is deadly with knives. They couldn't be more different. Christopher is all suave and so very Italian." Sam got this dreamy look in her eyes, that Elodie was somewhat sure was a joke. Then the look evaporated and she looked at Kirk. "Then there's you."

Elodie laughed as Kirk grew a few inches puffing out his chest. "Hey baby, you don't have to lie, I know you're just intimidated by all this. I'm the older twin, remember? That means I will inherit."

Sam just flipped her hair until it was a shield between her and Kirk and compared a few cloaks.

Kirk deflated and shrugged at Elodie, but she wasn't completely convinced. She had seen Sam's blush as she turned away. She may be two inches taller than the boy, but she clearly felt more for him than she let on.

Vanessa would love these two, watching them dance around each other, displaying their secrets for anyone but themselves to see. The thought made Elodie's heart hurt. Vanessa would love everything about the Twoshy if she could ever travel with Elodie.

Kirk tried to draw Sam into the conversation while he sorted socks. "Sam just thinks she's too good for anyone since she's the best swords person in Leronia. Last time we were in the Twoshy together we were in this tavern in Pundica and this knight from Duum started going on about how women who wore breeches were lower than bordello cleaners. You know how people from Duum think women should behave. Anyway, Sam took him into the alley and let her sword defend her honor."

"The lump was half drunk, it really wasn't a fair fight," Sam clarified.

"Love, it wouldn't have been a fair fight if there had been three of them against you," Kirk said. Sam blushed brighter and dug deeper into a clothes bin. Kirk turned to Elodie. "Her nephew is the current king of Leronia, her older brother was too old for the spell to take him, so the royal line wasn't affected. Now when Sam is home, she helps train his royal guard. He's promised her a position as captain of the guard when the spell breaks. *That* is how good she is."

"If the spell even breaks in his lifetime. There's no telling how long it will take." Sam glanced at Elodie. "Sorry, that wasn't meant to sound like a criticism."

"No, it's okay. I get it."

When they found enough clothes to help them all get by incognito, Kirk did the bargaining. He was pretty impressive to watch. They only paid a fourth of what Elodie would have ended up paying.

Kat, Tristan, and Christopher beat them back to the inn after collecting food and the other supplies. Allen returned later than all of them after getting what he described as "needed supplies."

At dinner, Kirk took to the stage to tell a few tales. They were mostly blockbuster movies from the illusion, but Kirk was gifted with telling. He clearly had a lot of experience with channeling thought and memory, he could paint a picture with words alone. The tales were clear and vivid, and more exciting than the original movies.

That evening Elodie shared a room with Sam and Kat, to save room in the crowded inn. Tristan stayed in his room at the forge, while Allen, Christopher, and Kirk shared another room. They stayed up late talking about life and school and just getting to know each other. It was wonderful. For the first time, Elodie actually felt like maybe she did have somewhere she belonged.

Chapter Seventeen

DARKNESS SURROUNDED her as she knelt again over the dark hole. The light was dimming and when it went out, all hope would be lost. The albatross came for her, carrying yellow banners in their claws that turned into yellow mist, and the voice spoke through the nothingness as if it were in the same room.

"In much the way of my own people, the derelict have flocked to the mountains to live out a separate life from their fears, their enemies, and even their own fate."

The voice faded and Elodie was surrounded again by white wings tipped with black. The small arrows of the men riding the birds pierced her skin until her arms and hands were covered in yellow fletching. The albatross began to swarm as she ran and dived into a cave where the birds couldn't reach her. She crawled on her hands and knees, tiny arrows breaking off in her skin as she dragged herself to the back of the cold, damp cave. She wrapped her arms around herself shivering in the cold, waiting for an attack.

There was another person in the dark, far away from her. He was in pain, but he had known pain before. He'd been foolishly naive and they had trapped him, so he felt in a way that he deserved it. And so, he sat in the dank, cold stone room trying to think through the haze, trying to remember himself long enough to try anything. He had to help and couldn't remain in this cold hard place. Things were in motion too soon, and he had to help. He tried calling out but couldn't remember the words he needed to say. Suddenly he moved just so the light hit his old, weathered face and he opened his eyes wide and stared straight into Elodie's heart, connecting with her for just a moment while the anguish and fear played out in his eyes.

Elodie woke up with a sharp intake of breath.

"What's happening?" A voice asked in the dark.

Elodie gasped before she remembered she was sharing a room with Kat and Sam. She tapped the light globe next to her bed and light burst into the room. Sam was on her feet, sword in hand, steel glinting in the sudden light. Kat sat up blinking on the other side of the room.

"Sorry." Elodie sighed. "It was just a dream."

Kat groaned and stuck her head under her pillow. Sam let out a breath and seemed to deflate. Her shoulders relaxed and her posture drooped. The fierce expression on her face was replaced with one of understanding, and she set her sword back in its place next to her bed. Elodie had thought it funny when Sam had unsheathed the sword and propped it against the bed before they'd gone to sleep, but now Elodie wondered what had caused the girl to adopt the habit and the ability to awaken so suddenly.

Sam crawled back under the blankets. "What was it about? Sometimes it helps to talk about those things."

Elodie let out a deep sigh and pressed her arm over her eyes. "It was mostly a jumble, a bunch of birds attacking me and a whole lot of darkness. I think I dreamed of Gedas."

"Do you dream a lot?" Sam asked, the sound of sleep just audible in her voice.

Elodie chuckled. She uncovered her eyes, then regretted it. The light globe was still unrelentingly bright. She tapped it a few times until it dimmed to a soft glow. "I've had them for years. Gedas thinks they are prophetic, but I don't know if that's true. I've been able to ward them off in the illusion using herbs, but nothing seems to work now."

"Well, if they're prophetic isn't blocking them a bad idea?"

"Probably, but waking up my parents because I'm yelling in my sleep is worse. They'll just stick me back in therapy." She regretted saying it as soon as it was out of her mouth. Sam seemed so perfect: strong, fierce, beautiful, so *together*. Elodie was none of those things and admitting to the complicated parts of her past—therapy, medication, all the labels people put on her back in the illusion—she didn't want Sam and her other new friends looking down on her.

A small smile flashed on Sam's face and she rolled onto her back, running her hand through her thick black hair. "I can understand that. It took me years to get out of the therapy loop. I"—she glanced at Elodie—"I had a hard time when I was younger, dealing with having my life ripped in two every few months, and I expressed it in bad ways. I took it out on my family, my own body. Anyway, on one of my trips back home my great-nephew Rovin, he's the king of Leronia, put a sword in my hand and started teaching me to duel. He was so young then and thought all the world's problems could be solved with a sword. And he was right, of course." As she talked, Sam stretched a hand over her head and stroked the leather on the pommel of her sword. "Rovin told me if I got good enough, he would give me a position leading his soldiers, so I had all the motivation I needed not to give up."

"How did a sword help?" Elodie asked.

A glint of ivory in the dark, Sam was smiling wide as she continued. "It's hard to explain. Something just clicked in my head. I was terrible when I first started, but I felt so powerful, and as I worked with my body, I felt in control for the first time in my life. It also taught me to respect blades."

"So you picked up a sword, and that solved all your problems? I don't know if my mom would go for that, but maybe it's worth a try."

"No, it wasn't quite that easy." Sam trailed off and was silent for a long moment. Elodie thought she had drifted off to sleep when she spoke again.

"When I traveled back to the illusion, I lost all of the progress with my training. It was a big blow, and I didn't have that outlet anymore. I had a big relapse." Sam sighed. "After a few months in a private hospital, I met this girl, she was a few years older than me but was always in and out of those places. She said the trick was to figure out something normal to use as an outlet. Channel yourself into it so the doctors thought you were trying. I was too young to realize if she was right, this girl shouldn't still be there, but I still tried. I picked lacrosse. It was a good cover to rebuild my strength so when I traveled back home, I wasn't totally back at square one with sword training."

Sam kept referring to the Twoshy as "home" when she talked. It was a subtle shift in Elodie's way of thinking and somehow made her heart feel hopeful. "Maybe I just need to find a thing then."

"Do you want to work out with me and Kat in the morning before we leave?" The sudden silence was answer enough, and Sam laughed. "You don't have to. And working out doesn't have to be your thing either. It doesn't work that way for everyone. I just got lucky. But I do like to work out in the mornings and Kat grudgingly agrees to keep me company. Come on, it will be fun."

"Okay, I'll try it. I've been trying to get stronger over the last few weeks anyway, I just got strong enough to draw the bow Silas gave me with any kind of steady hand."

"This Silas, the way you say his name, all soft and breathy like it's some sacred word. You like him, right?"

"What? No!" Elodie said it a little too quickly. Her stomach twisted and did a little somersault.

"Hmm, maybe try thinking on this Silas of yours tonight, see if that helps you get any better dreams."

Elodie wasn't so sure about that. Dreaming of Silas would be nice in the moment, but eventually, she would wake up and reality would slam back into her, washing away all the hope and beauty of the dream. Unless she broke the spell, and soon, Silas would grow old and pass on long before she ever reached marrying age. Then Elodie remembered marrying age in the Twoshy could be as young as sixteen.

She smiled and tapped off the light globe at the head of her bed.

ELODIE AWOKE the next morning to an earthquake. "Waa, what happened?" Elodie asked blinking up into Sam's round face.

Sam stopped shaking her and stepped back. "Time for practice."

She threw Elodie's breeches at her head. "Come on, Kat, no falling back asleep."

"Uuuuuuug. People shouldn't be awake this early, Sam. It's not natural. The sun isn't even awake yet." Kat's voice was muffled through the pillow she held firmly over her head.

"Both of you get up now or I'm getting the water pitcher."

Elodie and Kat both groaned in unison. Elodie sat up and slowly pulled on her breeches while Kat did the same. "You didn't mention your friendly morning workouts were a dictatorship," Elodie growled.

"Why do you think her nephew wants her to run his armies," Kat said before rolling her eyes and pulling on a stocking.

Down in the courtyard, the two girls stood yawning as Sam started leading them through stretches. She ran with them around the stables a few times to warm up before working through a patterned combat dance that was a style similar to martial arts. Kat had apparently been doing this with Sam for the last few days, but a few days didn't make much difference, and she was just as clumsy as Elodie.

"If I can teach you all the steps before you travel back, then you can do it at home by yourself," Sam said brightly. "Either way we should try to get together this summer and hang out. I bet I could have you both fighting by the end of the summer if we worked hard."

Kat let out a shaky breath as she changed positions. "Yeah Sam, that totally sounds like how I want to spend my summer."

Sam looked over her shoulder ignoring Kat's sarcasm. "Tighten your abs through the move, Kat." She showed them the next position to hold. "We are going into a hostile situation where the wrong move could mean life or death. Don't you want to be able to handle yourself?"

"Yeah, but we won't be warrior princesses in three days," Elodie said.

"No, but it's a start."

They kept working until the sun was just beginning to crest the skyline, then Sam called a halt, and Elodie and Kat fell dramatically to the ground and didn't move.

"Whatever," Sam said, stepping over Elodie's legs. "I'm going to take a bath." Elodie and Kat gave each other a side look, then forced themselves to stand up and follow Sam.

The baths were wonderful after the sweaty, dusty workout. Elodie didn't even care about modesty as she slipped into the large bathing pool next to Kat. She soaked in the warmth, trying to will her tight muscles to dissolve into the water like marshmallows in hot cocoa. Sam was the first to climb out of the water and dry off with the strips of linen stocked on the neat shelves along the wall of the bathing room.

"Come on, ladies, it's almost sunrise," Sam announced as she toweled off her long black hair. Across from her, Kat was feigning sleep with her head tipped back hanging her hair out of the bath. Elodie slipped farther into the water until her nose was just above the surface. Sam wrapped her hair in a cloth, tucking another around her securely, then picked up a large pitcher of water and started crossing toward them. Elodie rose quickly out of the pool and the movement cued Kat to the danger. Kat's eyes popped open, and she darted to the side just in time to save herself from the cool sheet of water Sam launched at her.

"Gods, Sam! Not cool! I wasn't getting my hair wet."

Elodie climbed out of the pool and grabbed a drying cloth as Sam snickered and walked back to her stack of clothes. Up close Elodie noticed the thin long scars crossing Sam's thighs. They were old, but there were so many, Elodie couldn't think what would cause it.

Sam blushed and pulled on her underclothes. "No use trying to hide the past. We can only move forward, right?"

"Right." Elodie thought back over her nighttime conversation with Sam, and her respect for the girl and her strength grew.

They made their way into the inn for breakfast. The eating room was surprisingly lively as travelers rose early to set out on the road. Elodie didn't spot any of the boys while they ate, but Mrs. Korin gave them an extra bundle of fresh food to add to their supplies. She thanked the older woman, who waved away the thanks with a flour-covered hand. "Nonsense. You've been a big enough help restocking our medicines the last few weeks. Now go and may Ravid bless you on your journey."

Elodie thanked the woman again and tried not to wince. She hoped Ravid stayed far away from their journey.

The stables were a little hectic as Ben and the other stable boys readied the mounts of guests on their way out of town. Elodie wished Storm a good morning as she grabbed his saddle. She saw Christopher and Allen readying their own horses. Allen was so sleepy eyed that he didn't even scowl at Elodie as he had the night before.

When their horses were saddled, Sam led the way out of the stables. She cleared the entrance and mounted in one smooth motion, her sword on her hip, and her long, glossy black hair swinging in the air around her. She immediately bundled her hair up into a high bun on top of her head.

Elodie led Storm out of the barn behind her but Kirk was blocking her way, arms loaded with packs as he stared dumbstruck up at Sam.

"Did I ever mention I had a huge crush on Mulan as a kid?" Kirk asked, deadpan.

"One more word and I will cut you," Sam said.

"Ooh say it again, baby," Kirk urged.

Sam groaned in disgust and nudged her horse forward.

Elodie led Storm alongside Kirk, grinning. "Mulan? Really?"

Kirk looked at her, his eyes glowing in admiration. "Can you blame me?"

Elodie shrugged and led Storm to the inn's hitching post, Kat rolling her eyes beside her.

Graham waited for them by the hitching post when they returned and helped them adjust their saddlebags. Tristan joined them and loaded his bags on the horse Rick had ridden to Arnav. Once everything was secure, Elodie turned to Graham. He was leaning against the side of the inn examining her with a rather menacing stare.

"Now don't even think of returning here at the end of this little excursion of yours. You have been quite a nuisance and I am very happy to be done with you," he said in his stern voice.

Elodie crossed to him, a smile on her face. "Thank you, Master Graham, for everything." She gave the innkeeper a quick hug and his frown softened just the slightest bit. Elodie would miss the old man. She found a nearby mounting block and climbed onto Storm's back.

"All right, are we ready to set off?" Sam asked, looking over their party and the sleepy faces.

"Off to see the wizard!" Kirk called.

"The wonderful Wizard of Oz!" Kat and Kirk finished together. Elodie snickered while Sam rolled her eyes and mounted up.

Graham walked away shaking his head and muttering something about strange youths.

They set off on the road west of Arnav, singing happy show tunes and laughing together.

Their journey would take a little longer than necessary as they had to give Tate a wide berth. Before they'd gone to bed, Sam spent an hour or so pouring over maps of Aluna and decided their course. As Elodie's presence in Rohap had not been much of a secret, the main highway from Arnav to Tross would likely be watched. Instead, they took smaller roads to the east and tried to blend in with local traffic.

When they crossed the border into Aluna, a heavy weight settled over Elodie. The cheery journey with her new friends seemed to evaporate, and she could no longer hide from the dread and fear and worry. The others seemed to feel it too, for the songs about worlds beyond rainbows started to fade, and they traveled the rest of the day in relative silence. Kirk was the only one who occasionally filled the silence with a joke or a funny story. Elodie was thankful for it as it served as a reminder that hope wasn't gone, and they weren't riding to their doom.

They made their camp a distance from the road, under the shade of a large grove of oak trees, their branches hanging low and craggily. The uneasy feeling from her journey out of Aluna was back, and as Elodie thumbed the acorn in her pocket, she decided to silently set wards for the night. She collected a few leaves from the surrounding oaks and lined their camp. The others were busy setting out bedrolls, starting the fire, and caring for the horses. They didn't notice her movements. When everything was in place, she called to the magic surrounding her and tied it all together, into the trees of the grove and the land beneath them. She let out a deep breath as the unease left her, replaced by the calm and steady nature of the old trees.

"What are you doing?" The voice was sharp and cutting and Elodie jumped. Allen stood next to the campfire but was glaring at her.

"Just setting some wards."

He scoffed and stomped over. "You should have said something. I was planning on setting my own wards once dinner was ready. Now I have to tear down your rudimentary wards before I can reset them." He kicked at one of her oak leaves and winced. The leaf didn't move but had flashed with a spark of dark blue fire. That was odd. Her wards were usually passive, unless Allen had tried to do something to it with his kick. He glared down at the spare leaf as if it was an enemy he needed to destroy.

"Allen, really. Aren't her wards good enough? They kept her safe on the way into Rohap," Sam reasoned, but Allen ignored her. Kat got up and moved toward them. She reached out a hand as if feeling for something in the air she couldn't see, her face puzzled.

Elodie felt self-conscious. She shouldn't have bothered with the wards, but the back of her neck had been prickling as she groomed Storm, and she didn't think they should linger in one place too long without wards of some kind. Now she had two magic users examining her wards for flaws. Elodie didn't even know how to sense magic like they were now doing.

"This is illusionist level spell work," Kat said. Her eyes were closed and she started moving slowly along the ward's boundary. "The way you bound the essence of the plants to reverberate back on the field it's protecting and shielding the presence inside, it's genius."

"It's not illusionist level, it's at least enchanter level," Allen scoffed. "But an enchanter would use five times as many components and drain more magic into the spell than the princess here even owns. This ward is sleek and elegant, weaving a complex idea into so simple a process even a hedgewitch could do it. No way she invented this, this came from the Wizard Gediminas." He looked at her knowingly as if daring her to contradict him.

Elodie crossed her arms, irritation melding with her stress and anxiety. "Of course, Gedas taught it to me. I've never once claimed to be something I'm not."

"And yet we are supposed to believe you are the *chosen one* who will free us all from this spell that not even the head of the magical university will discuss?"

"I never told you to believe it! I've never even said *I* believe it!" Elodie cried.

"Okay, okay." Sam stood up and handed her wooden spoon to Christopher so their dinner didn't burn. She approached slowly, arms out in a placating gesture. "Allen, the prophecy about Elodie came out while all of us were still babies. It's not Elodie's fault they made it public, and it's not her fault she had a wizard tutor her. So how about instead of fighting, we figure out how to work together?"

Allen let out a growl and stalked out of Elodie's wards, deeper into the forest. "I don't need anyone's help," he said just before moving out of sight.

Kat threw an arm over Elodie's shoulder. "Don't worry about him, you still have us."

Sam laughed and put her arm over Elodie's other shoulder. "And really, could you ask for anything better?"

No, Elodie really couldn't.

Tristan cut in front of them, a dirty trowel in his hand. "Not to break up this love fest or anything, but I dug the latrine behind those bushes." He gestured toward some dogwoods and Kat laughed. Tristan rolled his eyes and left to clean up in the stream.

Chapter Eighteen

ON THE SECOND day of travel to Comak, they encountered a party of soldiers. Sam spotted them first. The soldiers had the low ground, so the teens had enough time to get off the road and hide in a small patch of trees. Allen cast a hasty spell—magic way beyond Elodie's level—that used fancy words and hand movements, and when he was done, he slumped to the ground at the base of a tree, exhausted. "They shouldn't be able to see or sense us. But stay quiet when they pass just in case," Allen said, before closing his eyes and seeming to fall asleep.

Sam looked at him warily and drew her sword. "Just in case," she told Elodie when she looked at her. Elodie nodded and unhooked her bow from her saddle. The others all made small movements to arm themselves, except for Kirk who pulled out a small pack of nuts and began eating them and watching the road with amused interest.

Elodie knew a similar spell she could have performed with plants she'd collected on their journey. It wouldn't have exhausted her like Allen's magic had, but it probably wouldn't have been as effective either. Her spell would only work if no one expected to see them hiding under the trees on the edge of the road. If any of the soldiers were looking for them with enough expectation, the spell would have crumbled. She hoped Allen's spell was a little more durable, especially as he wouldn't be so easy to move on short notice.

As the soldiers neared, Elodie's eyes landed on the leader of their pack, a knight in iron chain mail, his helmet fastened to his saddle. The knight was older, maybe in his forties, he had short black hair and wide-set hooded eyes with ample laugh lines in the corners, but he wasn't laughing now. His jaw was clenched and he looked grim and worried. He hadn't even looked half as somber the day he'd been thrown from his horse during a lightning storm and nearly died. That trip hadn't ended so well, and Elodie hoped it wasn't an omen for their current journey.

"I know him," Elodie whispered.

"Friend or foe?" Sam asked, not taking her eyes from the soldiers.

"I mean, he's a friend, but I don't know if that's changed."

"How skilled is he?"

Elodie tried not to laugh. "We wouldn't stand a chance. Sir Jesper is the knight commander of Aluna's army. He taught Silas everything he knows."

Sam's focus grew more intense. She didn't look worried, just alert and maybe a little excited. As the riders approached, they stopped talking and fell into near silence. Storm seemed to tense with anticipation under her, shifting slightly without making a sound. Her heart pounded and she stroked his neck, more to soothe herself than him. Jesper and his men drew near. They were only feet away from them on the road, moving slower than Elodie would have liked. She stared at Sir Jesper trying to read from his face which side he was on. Not knowing if each person she once trusted had now turned against her felt too much like the halls of her high school on some days. Her hands trembled around the bow; she did not want to be responsible for what would happen to the other Misplaced if they were found with her.

Sir Jesper's horse picked up to a gallop with the soldiers in tow and passed without hesitation.

Elodie let out a breath and relaxed her grip on her bow.

"Your army is kind of terrible," Sam said, still keeping her voice low as the riders gained some distance. "I think only two of them even glanced our way, your knight commander didn't look at all."

That didn't seem right. The Jesper that Elodie knew was always observing his surroundings and evaluating them for any movement or danger. Silas did the same thing when he was Jesper's squire, and Elodie remembered thinking it was impressive how he always seemed so aware of everything yet stayed completely engaged in a conversation.

"I believe the knight and his men were trying not to seek as they rode," came a smooth voice from behind Elodie. She looked back a little surprised to see Christopher standing guard in front of Allen's sleeping form. She hadn't even heard him dismount.

He sheathed his daggers and bent down to gently shake Allen. She'd never actually heard Christopher speak before. His Italian accent lent a beautiful lilt to the common language. She glanced at Sam to see a wistful expression on the girl's face. Elodie cleared her throat and Sam jumped.

"Right. Yeah, you're probably right, Christopher." She looked at Elodie. "Should we take lunch here and give Allen time to sleep off his magic coma before we set off again?"

It sounded like a good plan to Elodie. Christopher hadn't had much luck in waking Allen as it was.

COMAK WAS JUST as Elodie remembered it when they arrived a few days later. Unbelievably clean and shiny, the streets glistened with not a speck of muck or horse droppings on the road. The people radiated respectability with no beggars or street kids to ruin the view, but Elodie wasn't fooled. Their lord was a corrupt, power-hungry monster with bad breath, and the streets were not nearly as safe as they looked. She'd been kidnapped from this very market once.

There was a small open-air cafe a short distance from the bordello where Elodie had last visited Callie. Elodie stayed back at the cafe with the others while Tristan and Kat went into the bordello to ask after Calendula, as Callie was known. Elodie sat on the edge of her chair, her hood pulled down low, casting her face in shadows while Kirk ordered food. She was so close to Gedas, it was hard for her to sit still. She understood why Sam thought it a bad idea for Elodie to be the one wandering around the city looking for a known friend of hers, but still, the inactivity was driving Elodie mad.

Kirk's food arrived as Tristan and Kat returned from their scouting mission at the bordello. Callie had indeed moved houses, but she was still in Comak. This time Tristan wanted to stay back and steal bites of Kirk's roasted chicken, and Elodie convinced Sam to let her go. Sam reluctantly agreed and asked Allen to come with them, just in case they needed to hide in a hurry. Elodie tried not to look annoyed as Allen rolled his eyes and begrudgingly agreed.

Callie's new bordello house was on the wealthier side of the city, closer to the castle than any of them would have liked. It was an older wooden building, four stories with fresh paint, and gleaming windows in an overall cute neighborhood. It was disturbing to know the terrible things that could be hidden behind fresh paint.

The main room of the house had thick curtains, eliminating all light except for the muted glow of light globes placed to enhance the mood. In a way, the lower light was to their advantage, as no one would recognize Elodie, especially with her hood up.

On the far end of the room was a small stage with a woman standing amid light globes of every color. She sang a soft melody, and those seated nearby stared transfixed as she danced with a slow, smooth rhythm, her silks and shawls floating around her in a beautiful display.

A man in gold silk and a silver ring around his neck greeted them, asking if they needed a table.

"Actually, we are looking for Calendula if she is available," Sam asked.

"Ah," the man looked down on them with a sympathetic smile. "I'm afraid Calendula only sees our more esteemed patrons, but Hailey will be available after her set if you would like to sit and listen for a time." He gestured to the woman on stage, moving like a butterfly celebrating the morning light.

"Would you please ask her anyway? You can tell her Ellie is

asking after her," Elodie said. The man paid her a little more attention than he had previously, and Elodie drew her cloak further down over her face.

"I'm sure she would appreciate the message," Sam said and held out her hand in a casual gesture. The man moved to take her hand, and Elodie saw a flash of coin.

"I will pass on your message." The man bowed gracefully and excused himself up an ornate staircase.

When he was gone Sam made a disgusted noise in the back of her throat. "Why are we doing this again?" Sam asked.

"To save the Wizard Gediminas and convince him to help free us from the spell," Allen said in a dry voice.

"Right."

Elodie tried not to puke as her stomach twisted and turned. She hadn't told the others that the last time Callie had seen her she told Elodie to go away and forget about her. If Callie rejected them again, where would they go from here? Worse, if she did the lawful thing and told the authorities she'd seen Elodie . . . But that wasn't Callie, and Elodie refused to ever believe her friend could change that much.

Movement from the stairs caught her eye, and Elodie saw a woman descend the steps in a fine blue silk gown. Her hair was brilliantly red, and her face glowed with regal elegance. From her poise alone, the woman could have been from any of the noble families in Aluna. She spotted Elodie and her face lit in a soft smile as she crossed the room.

Elodie's face was still shadowed by her hood, but Callie didn't pause in her approach. "My dearest companion," Callie began. She bowed more gracefully than Elodie had ever managed in her life. When she straightened, she took Elodie's hand. "How good of you to come see me again. Please, will you and your guests join me upstairs?"

Elodie didn't have words, so she nodded instead. Callie did understand her message, didn't she? Callie had known her as Ellie when they were girls running the streets of the lower city in Tross, but the way Callie addressed her now, it was as if she believed Elodie was a regular patron of hers.

Callie smiled brilliantly and tucked Elodie's hand in the crook of her arm and guided her out of the room. They took the steps at a slow, steady pace as if they were two ladies headed to a ball. Allen and Sam followed behind silently. When they reached the top of the stairs, Callie pulled Elodie sharply into a small alcove on the side of the landing.

"What in Cooric's name are you doing here, Ellie?" Callie whispered ferociously at her. Sam moved fast but didn't pull her sword completely out of its sheath before she understood Elodie was in no danger. Callie glanced at the sword, then at Sam and held her gaze for a moment before turning back to Elodie. "I'm glad to know your being at least a little sensible about your safety."

"Callie, I need your help." Elodie pulled down her hood, and Callie's eyes scanned Elodie's face.

"You're still so young." Callie slumped against the wall, all trace of the regal lady gone. "You don't understand the danger you're in, I tried to warn you all those years ago, but it wasn't enough. Ellie, they will execute you if you're caught."

"That's why I need your help, so I don't get caught."

Callie looked her over for a long moment, and her eyes held the full weight of understanding for what Elodie was asking. If it was ever known Callie helped her, she would be killed without question. The life of a slave meant next to nothing. Likely everyone in her bordello would be killed. Elodie's stomach roiled knowing the risk she was putting Callie in, but she didn't know where else to turn.

"What do you need?" Callie asked, letting out a deep breath.

Elodie couldn't help it, she hugged Callie. Callie, who'd come from nothing yet dug around in an artisan's trash heap to find beads to make Elodie a bracelet for luck. Callie, who had so many reasons to give up on the world for being a miserable worthless place but instead had always gone out of her way to tell jokes or do impressions and make others in the lower city smile. Callie, whose greatest sin was trusting those who were charged to protect her.

Callie wrapped her arms around Elodie and returned the hug with fierce strength.

"Could we maybe get on with it already? I'm not standing here for my health," Allen droned.

They broke apart and Elodie rolled her eyes. "He's right. We need a place to hide while we are in the city. We can pay. I have a little gold, but I can get more later."

Callie looked over Sam and Allen again. "Room for the three of you?"

"Actually there are seven of us, the others are waiting a few blocks away."

Callie nodded once and straightened. As she did so she pulled on an air of command and hospitality, a little less regal from the one she'd worn earlier. "We have a set of rooms on the fourth floor usually reserved for parties I can book for you." She led them to another staircase and they ascended.

"Are they clean?" Allen asked with a look of horror and disgust.

Callie stopped their progress on the next landing and turned to Allen. She was so graceful and poised in her silk gown that she seemed to loom over Allen in both stature and worth. "Do you see the gold around my neck, boy?"

The ring was hard to ignore. It was gold all right and encrusted with jewels. A large red ruby sat center stage with smaller yellow and orange stones surrounding it in a sophisticated pattern that surprisingly complimented her hair. She turned in such a way that the stones caught the light from the closest light globe and set off a dazzling display of color.

It was a pretty cage, but still charmed to kill her if she wandered too far just as any slave ring would.

Allen crossed his arms and glared at her. He was maybe an inch taller than her, but the force of her presence dwarfed him. When it was clear she wouldn't move, Allen nodded.

"This is the most elite house in Comak, more reputable than any bordello in Tross. You can bet our floors will be cleaner than your baby-soft mage hands."

"Can you not insult our host, please?" Sam asked, glaring at Allen.

Allen gave a long sigh as if the world were too much for him, but he took a step back. Sam gave Callie an appreciative look. "How did you know he's a mage?" Sam asked.

Callie smirked and started up the next staircase. "You have more in your party, yet only the three of you came. You're obviously the muscle, and Elodie is the diplomat." She looked back at Allen. "He's obviously not here for his winning personality, and he carries no visible weapons, so that leaves mage."

Elodie snorted and Sam nodded appreciatively at Callie. Callie had always been good at observing people, it was why she was so good at impressions.

She took them to the top floor and opened an ornate wooden door with a twist of a key. She bowed them in, holding the door wide.

It was beautiful, not at all what Elodie imagined. The ceilings were high and vaulted with exposed wood beams, and large windows covered the far wall, hung with gauzy curtains that let in the afternoon light. The furniture was tasteful and the carpet looked expensive. The room was open and airy and had a subtle smell of sandalwood and jasmine.

"There are two rooms on the left and a larger one to the right. You have a private bathroom through here"—she gestured to a panel door on the left—"and powder rooms in each bedroom. We can talk price later. We will need a deposit upfront, but I can tell them the customers are nobility and would like to keep their privacy. They will trust my judgment."

"Thank you, Callie," Elodie started. "This is more than I was hoping for, truly, thank you."

"I will need to stay up here as well." As she said it, she seemed to slump a little as if ashamed of the implications.

Sam smiled and poked her head into the first room. "That's perfect. We can have a proper girl's night. You'll like Kat too." She smiled warmly at Callie and ducked into the bathroom. Allen wandered into the larger bedroom.

Callie's mask slipped for just a moment, and she looked surprised. She glanced at Elodie. "They're Misplaced, like you."

Elodie smiled. "Yeah, they are good people, well except Allen."

Callie shook her head. "He's good too, you can see it in his eyes.

There's just a lot of hurt there that stops him from being good sometimes. It's a common condition."

"How did you know they were Misplaced?"

"The accent of course. Although hers is a little different from yours."

Elodie laughed. Callie was way too observant for her own good. Sam was Canadian, so a few of her words sounded different than Elodie's. Callie grew serious for a moment. "Do I want to know what business you have in the city? The steward isn't in residence, you know."

Elodie breathed a sigh of relief. "That's good actually. We need to poke around a little, and if he's not here, maybe that means security will be lower."

Callie eyed Elodie suspiciously. "They have a prisoner up at the castle. No one knows who it is, but there are rumors they are important. I worried it was you until the searches for you didn't stop. That's who you're here for, isn't it?"

Sam stepped out of the bathroom. "Do you know where they are being kept?"

"No. There are jails used to hold criminals and those used to hold fresh slaves, but it's the castle that's being guarded, not the jails."

Elodie thought back to her dreams, and the dark, bleak hole. "Is there a dungeon in the castle? Or caves under Comak, like in Tross?"

Callie shrugged. "I don't know. There are sewers, but not any that people use for travel. In Comak, the criminals walk boldly through the streets, blending in with everyone else, and most of them do their business in public under the guise of more civil trade."

"Charming city," Allen remarked.

Callie glanced at him for a moment, then back at Elodie. "Ellie, the baron has been in residence at the castle for the last few months. If I'm right in believing he is here to guard the prisoner, you shouldn't risk it." Callie brought a hand to her neck and fingered the ruby in her gold ring. "He's more dangerous than you can imagine. There's a reason people fear him, even when they have no reason."

Elodie didn't have to ask which baron Callie meant. Chills ran down her spine.

"Is his threat political, magical, or physical?" Sam asked.

Callie winced. "All three. He's not strong magically, but he's very cruel to those under his power. And he's deadly with a sword."

Silence hung for a moment, and Elodie pushed away guilt for believing Callie was safer with Baron Byron than she had been on the streets. "Callie, you need to make a decision on how invested you want to be in our plans. I don't want to put you in any more danger than you already are."

Callie shrugged. "Treason is treason. If you fail in your plans, I'm dead either way. I may as well help you succeed to the best of my abilities."

Chapter Nineteen

ALLEN WENT to retrieve their friends from the cafe while Elodie, Sam, and Callie talked. Callie knew the taverns and bordellos the baron's people frequented and volunteered to talk with a few friends to see if they could wheedle any information about where the prisoner was kept.

"Be careful though, I don't want anything blowing back on you or them if anyone gets suspicious."

"Don't worry," Callie said. "My friends are very familiar with the behaviors and suspicions of dangerous men."

It didn't reassure Elodie.

That night Callie had dinner delivered to their rooms, it was a grand meal with roasted pheasant and seasoned buttery vegetables. They made plans for the next day while they ate. The twins and Kat would ask Callie's friends for information while Elodie, Sam, and Tristan scouted the castle. Everyone protested when Elodie said she was going, but she absolutely refused to be left behind. "Besides, I'm the only one who's ever been inside the castle. I can offer strategic information."

Sam couldn't argue, and eventually they relented.

The girls took the larger room while the boys divided between the two smaller ones. The house had plenty of extra cots and beds, so everyone slept in comfort. Elodie was tired but had a hard time falling asleep. Her mind wouldn't turn off and let her sink into whatever dream was waiting for her. On their journey to Comak, she'd woken everyone up almost every night until Allen suggested drawing a silencing circle around her bedroll. It was as if Gedas was calling out to her through her dreams. She didn't think it was possible, but what other explanation was there for her seeing him every night?

Elodie rolled over on her bed and saw two blue eyes gazing at her from the bed a few feet away.

"Can't sleep?" Callie asked in a soft voice as to not wake Kat and Sam.

Elodie grimaced. "No, but that's normal at this point. I haven't slept well in weeks."

"Come, let's get tea." Callie rose from her bed and wrapped a light blue shawl over her shoulders. She led Elodie to the sitting room, then told her to wait as she stepped out into the hall. She returned only a few moments later with a tray.

"That was fast."

Callie grinned and set the tray on the table. "They have stations on each floor this time of night." She poured Elodie a cup and handed it over. "There are no stimulants in it, so it won't keep you up."

Elodie brought the cup to her nose and took a deep breath. Lemon, lavender, and chamomile. "It's perfect."

Callie chuckled and folded herself into a corner of the couch, blowing softly on her own cup of tea. "I forgot you could do that, divine out the brew of a tea merchant's secret blend with one sniff."

Elodie smiled, thinking back to her and Callie's days running the streets of the lower city. There was one particularly snooty tea seller in the Odure district who Callie bet an ounce of tea if they could tell her exactly what was in any blend in her shop. Callie traded the tea for three days' worth of dinner after Elodie had won it.

"That merchant was so mad. Didn't she threaten to dump boiling water on you if she ever saw you again after that?"

"Yeah, and she tried too. I saw her a few weeks later, but I was too fast for her and her arthritis."

They laughed for a few moments, then grew silent again. Elodie took a sip of tea. It was warm and soothing. She wished she could bathe in it so that more than just her stomach was soothed.

"Callie, I want to apologize for not doing better by you back then."

"Ellie, stop. What could you have done? Truly. Let the past lie and let's try to make the future better. That isn't what's keeping you up, is it?"

Elodie sighed. "No, it's everything. I'm worried about Gedas, I'm afraid of what the future holds if he's not in it. I'm afraid for all of you, about what happens if Oburleck wins. What if the spell sucks me back in and you and everyone else are left to pick up the pieces? I'm afraid I'm going to succeed in breaking the spell one day, and then I will be queen, and I still won't be able to make Aluna better. I'll just be one more in a long line of royal failures." She pulled the edge of her nightshirt to cover up the cursed birthmark.

"That's a lot of fear to be carrying around."

Elodie sighed and tucked her legs under herself. "But my life is so much better off than most anyone else. Like, there's no excuse for me to whine about life being hard when so many people don't have half of what I do."

"Ellie, just because other people have it worse, doesn't make your feelings less valid. You're allowed to have a bad day. What's important is that afterward you pick yourself back up and figure out how to keep going."

Elodie wanted to cry. Callie's life was far from perfect. She was a slave, a slave in a bordello. As much as Elodie tried not to think about what that meant her life was like, she couldn't deny it. Callie's life was comprised of continual rape, and here she was telling Elodie her fear was valid and encouraging her to keep going.

"I'm also ashamed of myself," Elodie said in a whisper. Callie nodded as if shame was also something she was familiar with. She wanted to confess to Callie, as if saying her worst thoughts, admitting them out loud would make it better. She looked down at her cup, not meeting her friend's eyes. "I've spent the last four years living in the illusion, and a part of me was happy I didn't travel back here, didn't have to worry about all the broken things I can't fix. A part of me just wanted to stay in the illusion forever. To forget this world exists." Her eyes filled with moisture, but she didn't let it fall. "But I do care about Aluna, and I want to make it better. I just feel like any improvement will be an uphill battle."

"That doesn't mean it's not worth the fight."

She was right. That was what leaders did, they found ways to help people. She had to focus on helping people like Callie and others in her kingdom who were suffering. That was where the good resided, within them. She would find a way to help Callie and all the people who'd suffered under men like Byron and Oburleck.

She just hoped the fight wouldn't be futile like the curse of her family demanded it would be. "I just wish there was something I could do now, I don't even know how long it will be until I manage to break the spell. It could be another fifty years for all we know."

They lapsed into silence. Elodie didn't have to tell Callie how time behaved for her. They'd met when they were both twelve, now Elodie was sixteen and Callie was in her early twenties, maybe? She wasn't quite sure, and it felt invasive somehow to ask as if rubbing in the time Elodie had missed of Callie's life. If only someone better had come along back when Callie was a kid, someone better than Baron Byron.

"When I was in Rohap, I stayed at this inn called the Snarled Cello. It's run by this big brash old man named Graham who scowls and acts like everyone on Eres is a bother, but I think he's the most kind and generous man I've ever met in my life."

"How does that work exactly?" Callie asked, a smile on her lips.

Elodie laughed. "I know, it doesn't make any sense. But somehow it works." The inn is run by him and an older woman who oversees the kitchen, and everyone who works for them is an ex-street kid."

Callie's face grew troubled. "Is he good to them?" Her voice was low as if she was afraid of the answer.

"He's the best. He treats the kids with kindness and respect before anything else, and they are fiercely loyal to him. He has a lot of connections in the city, and he helps the kids learn trades so they can get proper jobs. I saw him teaching a little girl how to scrub a table. It was the funniest thing. This giant of a man stooped down explaining about woodgrain in a booming voice. Then he handed her the brush and she made an attempt. He bent down until he was bent in half and his nose was a few inches from the table, and he wiggled his big bushy caterpillar eyebrows as he looked over the work and set the little girl off giggling. And this was the same girl who would flinch whenever I looked at her when I first arrived. None of the kids see him as a threat. It's like they can sense his strength will only ever be used to protect them."

"I like that," Callie said, her gaze directed toward the window overlooking the city, a wistful smile on her face. "Take kids in and teach them a proper trade, keep them off the streets and away from the bound market until they can provide for themselves. We need more people like that in our world. We need a few good people like that in Aluna."

"I agree." But again, it was a dream, a hope that may never be. How did you start something like that without first finding someone with the vision to run it themselves? How could you try to find someone and trust them to do an honorable job, to never use their position in a bad way? And if someone only did a poor job, would that be better than nothing? Even if she did break the spell, how could Elodie ever oversee something like that while also ruling a whole nation? Would it be worth it to even try when her chances of failure were so incredibly high?

Yes, it would always be worth it to try and make the world better.

"Did you ever notice what's missing in Comak?" Callie asked startling Elodie from her thoughts.

"What?"

"The street kids." Her face was angry when she said it, and it surprised Elodie. She had never seen Callie look so angry. "The homeless, the beggars, the poor, the disabled."

Chills ran down Elodie's back. "What does he do with them?"

"He binds them, ships them off to whatever bound service they are best fit for. Not directly of course. The Steward of Aluna would never be involved with such activity. But he owns the binders and the sellers. Then he cuts others like the baron a deal on the merchandise."

"That's disgusting. Oburleck needs to be stopped."

"Think you're up for the challenge?" Callie asked. There was no humor in her voice, and no criticism, simply curiosity, and maybe hope.

"I don't know. Not alone, but maybe with friends by my side." Elodie stretched out her leg on the couch and nudged Callie's knee with her foot.

"I'm yours to command my liege. Direct me." Callie did a little half bow from her seated position. Her expression was so similar to Silas's look of serious devotion she couldn't help but laugh. Callie shushed her with a grin. "Quiet or you will wake up your friends."

She covered her mouth until the giggles subsided. The expression made her wistful to see Silas again. He would arrive in Comak any day. Elodie was worried he would react badly when he saw she'd disobeyed orders. On second thought, he would likely expect it. She'd tried so many times even in this very city to get Silas to do something improper or break the rules.

The thought brought back a memory, and Elodie frowned. "When I was at Comak last, just before I was kidnapped. I asked Oburleck for his help to end slavery."

Callie snorted, it was the same snort and expression Sam often used. "I bet he loved that. Maybe that's why you were kidnapped. Maybe that was the first time he tried to get you out of the way, and when it failed and you didn't return for a few years, he thought up this whole treason plan."

Elodie shook her head. "He's lost his mind. It's the only explanation." She thought of mentioning the god to Callie but decided against it. "If he did actually catch and execute me, he would be in breach of the Constitution of Sixteen, and every other country in the Twoshy would have a fair shot at us. Aluna would be in ruins."

"We have to stop him."

The determination in her eyes gave Elodie hope. Maybe they did have a chance.

Chapter Twenty

THE PROFESSOR RAMBLED on and on, talking about ruakh and its strength at specific times and in specific locations. It was mind-numbing and nothing the listening students hadn't heard before. Lan doodled on the edge of his parchment, drawing spiraling lines and boxes until the black mess started to resemble a maze.

Johna sat to his right in the seat pushed up against the wall, in perfect view of the large windows looking out over the blooming hydrangea garden of the university. Johna was chewing his lip and listening intently as the teacher spoke about the poles of Eres and channels of power flowing under the planet's crust. Finally, Johna had enough. He stuck his hand in the air and waited a long moment. The professor didn't see him at first, and his ink-stained fingers grew self-conscious, curling in on themselves.

Lan saw his hand first and shot a grin at his friend. The kids sitting behind them noticed the distraction next, until eventually, everyone was watching Johna watching the professor.

As if noticing their extreme attention, such an unusual occurrence in his class, the professor turned and called on Johna. "Yes, what is it now, boy?"

"But Professor, what of the gods? You've told us about all the other forms of power known in our world, but what of the gods and how to harness their power?"

On the other side of Lan, Anna's eyebrows went up. She

glanced at a pretty girl next to her with charcoal-black skin and honey-colored hair. They shared a similar disbelieving expression and turned to watch Lan.

"Foolish boy, you do not harness the power of the gods. You are used by the gods for their will and theirs alone. If you are ever in the service of a god, you would do well to remember to be respectful and reverent and do as they say. If you are not in the service of one, you better hope for your own sake that you never are."

"Don't you mean pray that you never are?" Lan drawled, and the rest of the class laughed.

"No, Lanis, that is what I am trying to get through your thick skull. If you are wise, pay your respects and offer your worship, but do not pray, not ever. Not unless you want your life to no longer be your own," the professor warned.

Lan smiled slyly. "I don't know, what do you think, Anna? Beth?"

Anna rolled her eyes, and the pretty girl next to her spoke up. "Don't pull us into this, Lan. You can spend detention on your own."

Lan shook his head. "I think it's worth pursuing. Even if our dear Professor Froggsnar here is too cautious to reach for the more advanced magics, I don't think we should let that hold us back. What about you, Johna?"

Johna grinned at his friend. "Sounds good to me, Lan."

The professor crossed his arms and pursed his lips. "And that would be detention, as Beth has so astutely surmised. Lanis, Johna, you two know the procedure well by now, so if you do not mind, I would like to proceed with the lesson."

The grinning faces of Lan and Johna were the last Elodie saw before she returned to the top of that dark hole. She called into it, looking for any sign of life. Nothing responded. The darkness was overwhelming, radiating hopelessness and death.

EARLY THE NEXT MORNING ELODIE, Sam, and Tristan headed for the castle. After her late-night talk with Callie, she didn't wake up calling out from her dreams. She still had them, and the absence of light in the dark hole left a dread over Elodie's waking mind like a haze clouding her vision, but it was still a relief not to wake everyone else up with the same fear.

The plan for the day was to wander the market close to the castle and get an idea of the area while Kat and the twins talked to some of Callie's contacts to see if they could get a lead on where Gedas was being kept. While they walked, Elodie told them about the layout of the castle, pointing out the kitchens and where the library was in relation to Oburleck's rooms or the great hall.

"The slope of the ground is too steep on this end," Sam observed as she looked at the castle over a rack of printed cloth a bored-looking man was selling. "If they have dungeons, it won't be on this end."

"No, who wants to keep prisoners under the kitchens? It would stink," Tristan said. He was playing his part as the bored friend, not interested at all in the shopping. He did a great job of it.

"Do most of the castles around Aluna have dungeons?" Sam smiled at a merchant selling gloves and asked her for a price before moving on.

Elodie tried to think about it. "Maybe some of the older ones, but not that I've seen. But I've mostly explored libraries when visiting lands around the kingdom."

"Sounds cozy," Tristan said in a falsely positive voice.

"Most of Aluna belonged to the Dwarvman before the founding, didn't it?" Sam asked. "Their castles always had underground sections."

"Not this far east," Tristan cut in. "The Elvman lived along the east."

"How do you even know that?" Elodie asked.

"Because Rohap was once Elv land before us Hu took it. Didn't you see the castle there, all airy and open, like the walls were shaped with living stone? This castle, here, was not Elv made. Probably created after the founding."

"We should make our way to the other side," Sam suggested and started leading the way through the stalls.

A glint of silver in an odd shape caught Elodie's eyes. Peering closer she identified the culprit as a necklace. Just a simple thin chain with a single pendant. So plain compared to the intricate braided gold to its left or the filigree bracelets to its right. The pendant for this necklace was small, no bigger than her thumbnail, and the silver was molded into the shape of a tiny, detailed pinecone.

"Ahh! I see my wares have caught your eye. What do you fancy? The filigree is delicate is it not?" The market vendor picked up the bracelet and waved her over.

"Yes, it's beautiful," Elodie lied. Sam and Tristan had kept walking and Elodie made her excuses and turned to catch up with her friends. She looked for the dark green of Sam's cloak when hands gripped her shoulders and shoved her behind the stalls through the waving shawls and scarves. She tried to elbow her attacker and break free, but iron hands gripped her arms, weary of such tricks, and shoved her past billowing fabrics of every color into a small, dark alley that felt shockingly devoid of life.

Her breath caught in her chest and she was too scared to scream, flashing back to the last time she'd been caught in this very market. Before she could call for help, her back slammed into the wooden wall of the alley. She stilled as she looked into the angry green eyes of her attacker.

"You're dead." He shook her once to illustrate the point.

She was numb as her fear washed over her in a cold wave.

"Are you listening? I have five blades on me, and I could use any one of them to slice open your stomach. I could do anything I want to you right now, and no one in this gods-forsaken city would even look to see who screamed," he whispered, leaning in close to her neck. There was a sharp prick at her side, and she looked down to see a blade pressed against her tunic.

Cold fire washed over her as her heart raced. She'd been caught. Again.

"Do you understand me? Dead. A few ounces of pressure and this blade slices open your liver." His eyes were like green fire and steel.

She'd never seen him this pissed off before, and that was

considering all the time she'd spent intentionally trying to make him lose his temper.

"Silas, you scared me."

"Yes, fear. A little fear and all your thoughts leave your head. What do you do? Do you keep struggling like an idiot?" He shook her again making her back slam into the wall a second time. "Do you step on my foot and hope I magically fall down dead? I'm a trained killer with a blade at your side, and you're completely alone and have clearly forgotten any defensive skills anyone has ever taught you. What do you do, Princess?"

He was right of course, separated in a crowd because she got distracted by something shiny, then she didn't even try any of the hold-breaking moves he'd taught her. How long had he even been in town?

With Elodie's luck, Silas had just entered the city and found her in his first twenty minutes, proving how incapable of stealth she was.

The rage was dimming in Silas's eyes, but he didn't loosen his grip. Clearly, he wouldn't be passing up this teaching moment.

What could she do to get out of his hold?

His feet were in the proper place, so stepping on one like he'd suggested would never work, and he was too close for the one arm move she could remember. She really should have practiced more.

Elodie was about to give up when a crazy idea leapt to the front of her mind. She blamed Sam's influence for the insanity.

Without thinking she lunged forward up onto her tippy toes toward Silas and the blade, leaving her totally off balance. The knife was gone in an instant as Silas moved to protect her and keep her from falling. Her lips collided with his for a moment, just one quick, soft moment where she felt his surprise and then surprise of her own when he didn't pull away. She bit back the immediate regret as she kneed him in the groin and shoved him to the side before running with all her might back into the chaos of the market.

Darting between stalls as fast as she could, she caught a glimpse of the green cloak. She collided with Sam. "Run!"

"Elodie, what happened? Where did you go?" Sam asked as she flagged down Tristan.

"No time," she gasped as Tristan approached, "have to hide."

"Fine." He looked at her oddly and Elodie tried to wipe the smile off her face. "You two head back to the house and I will finish scouting."

With a nod, Sam and Elodie took off in a direction nowhere near the bordello. Elodie knew right away that if she had been on her own, Silas would have found her in minutes. Maybe he would tackle her to the ground in rage, pinning her with the edges of his body so that she couldn't move an inch.

She shook her head to clear those unhelpful thoughts and focused on following Sam's cues for sudden turns.

Lucky for Elodie, Sam knew how to lose a tail. They paused behind a smoking meat cart long enough to catch their breath and see if they were being followed.

"Who are we running from, one of Oburleck's men?" Sam asked, eyes somehow roaming in all directions at once.

Elodie shook her head while trying to pretend she was as aware of their surroundings as Sam. "No. One of mine."

Sam's attention snapped to Elodie. "What?"

"Silas," Elodie sighed. "If he catches me, he will send me back to Graham and the Snarled Cello."

"He found you, already? He wasn't supposed to be in the city for a few more days." Sam was back to watching their surroundings.

"Maybe the bird took longer than he thought, or he sent it from further along on his journey. Or maybe he's just that good."

Sam elbowed Elodie in the side. "Focus, girl. Is it really such a big deal that we lose him? I mean, maybe he knows something we don't."

Elodie shook her head. "I won't let him send me away. I need to be here. I feel it."

"Fine. How motivated will he be to find you?"

"Well . . . I kind of just kneed him in the nuts before I took off."

Sam burst out laughing and quickly covered her mouth to stifle the sound. "We need to move. If he can walk yet, I'm sure he's looking for you, but unfortunately for him, we won't give you up easily."

Half an hour later and after a very convoluted journey, Elodie and Sam returned to the bordello. Elodie was a bit tired from the twisting path they took through the market, but Sam was confident they had not been followed. Inside the darkly lit downstairs room of the bordello, Callie was to the left of the stage speaking to a few guests. She saw Elodie and winked. They climbed the stairs to the fourth floor and Sam pushed the door open.

"How long until the others return do you suppose?" Elodie asked as she pushed past Sam who'd stopped just inside the room.

Elodie's eyes fell on the man sitting on the chair by the large window where Callie had sat the night before. Silas was leaning back on the couch, a book in one hand, and a cup of tea in the other. His feet were propped up on the low table and he looked completely at ease.

Elodie said a bad word.

"Ooh, he is cute," Sam announced. Silas casually set down his drink and tucked a small scrap of paper into the book's pages before closing it with a thump. He rose from the chair.

Sam dropped her voice for Elodie's ears only as the knight crossed the room. "If that bit of man was after me, I wouldn't have run quite so fast."

Now that she wasn't pinned to a wall, Elodie got a better look at him. Her eyes grazed quickly over all the bits she shouldn't be looking at and she felt the phantom scratch of his beard against her face from that brief, impossible moment. Before she knew it, he was standing in front of her, tall and broad. She would have to look up to find his eyes, but she didn't dare.

"Your technique was cute but with no real-world application. All in all, I would say your defensive display was a fail," he said in a short assessment.

Elodie looked up to glare at him and caught his eyes. They were still a mess of green fire and held so much emotion she couldn't read.

She shouldn't have looked up.

"The way I heard it, she managed to get away just fine," Sam said, coming to her defense.

Silas blinked and the fire dimmed for a moment. He glanced at Sam, then back at her. "We need to talk."

Warning bells started to go off in Elodie's mind, but she couldn't remember what to do about it. Instead, she just stood there, staring into his eyes.

"Yeah, I'm definitely not leaving you alone with this one," Sam announced. She crossed the room to the low table and poured herself a cup of tea, then sat in the larger armchair as if ready for a show. Silas took a step back from Elodie, and suddenly she could breathe again. He turned and crossed to the table and fiddled with the tea tray.

Elodie took a tentative step forward. It worked, so she took another step. Sam was grinning over her teacup at her. Elodie glared at Sam, but the girl only grinned wider.

When she reached the couch, Silas turned and bowed, holding out a cup of tea. "My lady."

"Oh, you call her 'my lady'? That's so cute."

He stayed bowed until Elodie took the cup. When he straightened, he was grinning just a little. Elodie sat on the edge of the couch, and as if on cue, Silas sat on the other end. He was way too close.

She brought the tea to her nose and took a long deep breath, letting the mint wash over her and willing the herbs invasive nature to lend her strength and confidence. She took a sip. Silas had added a lot of honey, just like Elodie preferred. When she looked up from her cup, both Silas and Sam were staring at her.

"What?"

Sam turned to Silas. "So what's the plan for rescuing the wizard?"

"The plan is for you lot to stay hidden while I work on the rescuing."

Elodie lowered her cup. "Yeah, that's not gonna work for me."

"My lady, I'm just trying to keep you safe."

"Sir Silas, I don't need you to keep me safe, I need you to help me. I'm not staying safe while Gedas is trapped in some deep, dark hole, his life slowly draining away day by day."

He looked at her closely. "What have you heard?"

"Only what I've seen in dreams. Almost every night. Gedas in a deep, dark hole like an oubliette." Elodie shivered at the thought. "And every night the light of his soul gets dimmer and dimmer as he moves closer to death."

Silas frowned. "My intel says he's being kept in one of the towers, not in an oubliette. I didn't think Comak had an oubliette."

"And prophetic dreams can have multiple meanings," Sam said. She set down her cup with a sigh. "The best plan of action would be to account for both possibilities. One team goes down, one goes up. We can come up with a signal when we find the target." Silas glanced at Sam thoughtfully and her eyebrows went up. "Do you disagree?"

Silas leaned back on the couch. "Who makes up your team?"

"There are seven of us. Two highly skilled in hand-to-hand, two unqualified but very eager mages, one strategist, one loudmouth who can talk the ears off any enemy, and one healer." Silas shot Elodie a small smile, but Sam wasn't finished. "What about you? What do you bring to the operation?"

Silas crossed his arms and tilted his head. "By sundown I will have two knights, a *qualified* mage, and a highly trained squire."

Sam reached out to Silas. He took her hand, and she shook it. "Sir knight, I think we can make this arrangement work."

Silas grinned. "I don't think we have yet been properly introduced."

Elodie rolled her eyes and flapped her hand gesturing between them. "Sir Silas of Tate, may I introduce Princess Samantha of Leronia, future captain of the Leronian Guard, and current Misplaced Child. And Sam, you know the rest."

Silas stood and gave Sam a proper bow. "My lady, it's a pleasure to make your acquaintance."

"Oh yes, please keep doing that around the other boys until they pick it up," Sam said with a grin.

"Especially the loud-mouthed one who talks too much," Elodie added with a smirk. Sam threw her teaspoon at Elodie's head. She missed, which meant she wasn't really trying to hit her.

"Is anyone coming that I know?" Elodie asked once Silas had sat back down.

"Dess will be here at sundown with her brother."

Elodie squealed. "Sam, you're gonna love Dess. She was a few years ahead of Silas in page training. And her brother, he's the mage, right? Jim something?"

"Jinis, yes. He's an enchanter."

"And the squire?"

"Rogers, he's mine. You met him by the river. He should still be tailing your other friends."

Elodie sighed. "Right. And how long were you in the city before you spotted us?"

Silas grinned. "We'd just arrived actually."

Of course, he did.

"And how did you trace us back here?" Sam asked.

"Where else would Elodie go?" Silas asked. "I've kept up with Callie as much as I could over the years. After you . . . distracted me in the market, I came here to see if she'd heard from you. She let me in the room."

Elodie blushed.

"Do you think anyone else will look for her here?"

Silas shrugged. "This is about as safe as anywhere in Comak is likely to be, which is to say, not very. Baron Byron is in the city, and he has sharp senses. He will not hesitate to take care of Oburleck's schemes." Silas got an odd look on his face and reached inside of his cloak. "Excuse me." He pulled out a round glass ball that was emitting a soft glow and a minor humming. Silas squeezed the glass once, and the light stopped, instead there seemed to be something moving in the center of the ball.

"Is that an orb?" Sam asked leaning forward.

"Tim, I'm among allies," Silas said to the ball. Elodie leaned forward and could just make out a face, sandy-brown hair, and a big nose, skewed in the orb to look monstrous.

The man squinted out from within the orb. "Is Dess there already?" The voice from the orb was clear but a little distorted.

"What is that?" Elodie asked.

"No, Tim, I'm here with Elodie and a friend."

"Oh!" The face in the glass straightened his glasses. "Uh, Your

Highness." He disappeared for a moment as if bowing out of the frame. "I'm glad to see you're safe."

The awkward manner stuck a note in Elodie's memory. "Wait, it's Timothee, right? Of Gliedal. How are you doing this? I don't remember you being a mage."

"Uh no, Your Highness, it's a multiway communication matrix bound within the sphere."

"It's like magical FaceTime," Sam said. "Allen was complaining all the way to Rohap because another student was going to teach him the spell before they left to come meet you."

"Tim," Silas cut in. "What have you to report?"

"Right. Um, well, I was going to say there are rumors our princess is no longer in Rohap, but I suppose now the report is that the steward is aware our princess has likely left Rohap."

"Thanks, Tim, keep us updated."

"Will do." A hand filled the view of the orb, then the light dimmed.

"Tim was Lord Riyan's squire, wasn't he?"

"Still is."

"What? Riyan is still alive?"

Silas grinned. "He is. Rumors are starting to go around he has Elv blood or something."

"Do you think it's true?" Elodie asked.

"No." Silas laughed. "I just think the old man is too stubborn to die."

The door burst open, and Silas sprung to his feet, his blade drawn.

Chapter Twenty-One

KIRK STROLLED into the sitting room, followed by Kat, Allen, the twins, and Tristan. "Told you they'd be back," he called over his shoulder. He stopped a few feet into the room. "Woah, who's this?"

Elodie glanced at Silas who was still holding his sword. At her look, he put the blade away but didn't sit. He wouldn't sit until Kat was seated, Elodie guessed. Elodie sighed and made the introductions.

"What did you learn?" Sam asked once they were all seated.

"Not much," Kirk said, pouring himself a cup of tea. "We met this dude who works at a bordello on the other side of town. He says all the guards frequent the establishments on the west side of the castle. It's not much to go on."

"It makes sense," Tristan said. "The east end isn't structured to have any sort of underground holding cells, so the west would work."

"Silas had intel they were keeping him in the tower, which is also on the west side."

"Tower or cellar," Tristan said. He looked at Sam. "You're thinking divide and conquer?"

Sam nodded.

There was a soft knock on the door. Kirk got up to answer it, hopeful for lunch. "What do you want?" Kirk asked the man standing in the doorway.

Silas stood. "He's mine. Rogers, welcome."

Rogers nodded to Silas. "I've moved the horses to the house stable, sir. Storm was quite pleased to see me I think." He winked at Elodie.

"Good, I will have to go down and visit him." Silas made the introductions. "Would you mind if we stay here tonight? We will have two more before long."

Elodie smiled up at him. "Well, I am paying for the rooms with the gold you gave me."

Callie arrived a short time later and gave Silas an elegant curtsy.

"I can't believe you let him into our secret base," Elodie told Callie with a smirk.

Callie only shrugged. "If he already knew you were here, was it really so secret?" She rang for lunch and enough food to feed twice their party was delivered. While they ate, a few maids with iron rings around their necks brought in more beds for the night.

While the others were distracted by the good food and stories of their day, Elodie turned to Silas. "I saw Sir Jesper on the road here."

"Did you talk to him?" Silas asked.

"No, we were magically shielded and he didn't spot us."

"That's probably for the best. He's still pretending to be loyal to Oburleck so we can get more information out of him. If he had spotted you, it might have blown his cover with his men."

"Would some of them rat on him if they knew he helped me?"

Silas looked thoughtful for a moment. "It's hard to say. They are all good people, men and women I would trust with my life, but whether that means they would follow Oburleck's orders and the law or follow Jesper into treason, putting their lives and their family's lives on the line . . . It's hard to tell what one would truly do in that situation."

Silas was doing it. He was sacrificing his whole world for her. If things panned out in her favor, Silas wouldn't be punished, but if things went the other way, he would be killed.

It was common practice to reward treason by executing entire families. Silas didn't have a wife or children, but he was heir to his family's titles. It would depend how spiteful Oburleck was being if he decided to execute Silas's parents, younger siblings, cousins, and the like. Elodie knew Silas's father. He was a good man, and even if he wasn't openly opposing Oburleck, she had no doubt enough investigation would land him with just as many charges of treason as Silas.

She didn't want this brave and amazing man to die on her behalf. Aluna needed more people like him, not less. On her last trip to the Twoshy, Silas had grown from the light-hearted, confident page she'd known into a rigid squire who wouldn't meet her eye. It had hurt. He'd been trying to protect her, and she just saw it as smothering and boring, so she went out of her way to dodge him whenever possible. It wasn't until she was kidnapped and rescued that she realized the danger she was in had been real, and Silas wasn't distancing himself because he found her immature or beneath him. It had been his way to cope with the danger and the duty he was learning to live with.

She'd worried he would grow stiffer with age until his duty consumed him, but that wasn't the case at all, and Elodie couldn't be more relieved. Silas was still capable and smart, kind and noble, but he was also quick to smile. He was perfect, and if anything happened to him, she would never recover from the guilt and heartache.

Dess sent Silas a message on his magic orb and said they'd reached the city a little early. He directed them to the bordello, and they made it in time to eat. Dess was just as Elodie remembered her, if not a bit taller. Her hair was still a golden-blond, sweaty and tied back from their journey, her brown eyes were sharp and held a wicked gleam that showed she liked a challenge. Her brother, Jinis, was also blond, but his face was covered in dark freckles, and his fingers were coated in ink stains.

Allen cornered Jinis before he'd filled his plate with food and asked him about his magical ranking and final exams. Jinis was good-natured about it, and the two seemed to hit it off.

Once the food was mostly gone and everyone was full and happy, Sam called them back to business. "Silas, now that we're all here, is there anything specific we need to factor into our plan?"

"First and foremost, Baron Byron. He is deadly with a sword, and if encountered, it would be best to take him out long range.

Don't engage him in a duel," Silas began. Callie shivered just slightly in her chair by the window, but when Elodie caught her eye, the moment was gone; Callie smiled confidently at her and gave her a reassuring nod.

"So you're saying we should shoot him in the back if given the chance?" Kirk asked, a skeptical look on his face. "That's not very sportsmanlike."

"The baron is one of the key conspirators in this coup," Dess cut in. "He gave me orders directly on where to hunt for the princess and said, were I to find her, there might be a dukedom in my future if she were to not make it to the castle."

"Meaning they would pin the regicide on you so Oburleck would be blameless in his rise to power?" Tristan asked.

"Exactly," Dess agreed. "His death would be a great advantage to our cause. If you knew me at all, you would know I'm the last one to run from a fight, especially if it's the wise move." She grinned at Silas who chuckled and nodded his head in agreement. "But Byron is not a challenge, he is a death sentence."

"What makes him so good?" Sam asked, a sharp look in her eye. Elodie hoped she wasn't thinking of taking on the impossible challenge.

Dess just shrugged. "No one knows."

"What do you mean?"

"Byron makes it a habit to conduct his duels in private. They are not publicly discussed, but one can trace their pathways through the political court of Aluna," Silas explained. "These are deadly, gruesome deaths of strong, skilled swordsmen and women. I've only seen the aftermath of one. The lady was a seasoned and skilled fighter who opposed a business deal that favored Byron. There was talk of her challenging him, but no one saw it happen. Her body was found a few days later, cut to ribbons as if she'd been bled out slowly, and they were all defensive wounds. The healer I spoke with believed they happened before death while the lady was alert and in motion as if he sliced her while they fought."

"Did he have any wounds afterward? Any proof he fought her?"

"No." Silas frowned. "I've only ever known of one person who's left a mark on the baron."

Elodie glanced again at Callie who had gone pale. She still looked regal, holding a teacup with a steady hand. She glanced from Silas and back to Elodie and cleared her throat. "And there is nothing from that encounter I wish to add to this discussion. I have no tactical advice to add, only more rumors I picked up while living in his house." Some glanced at Callie with new eyes. Sam looked at her with grim approval. "I have heard suggestions his magic is what makes him so deadly, but if that is true, I have no evidence."

"Gedas says Byron is a dud. He only got his illusionist ranking as more of a courtesy from the university," Elodie said.

Jinis nodded. "I've heard the same."

The room fell into silence.

"You should also know Oburleck uses a magical method to make himself more persuasive," Silas continued. "Gedas and my old knight master were curious about him for years, but it wasn't until a little discovery of Elodie's that we realized his powers of persuasion were indeed magical. We don't know if he's kept his secrets to himself or if he shared them with others, so you need to be aware of what to look out for just in case. The magic makes him more charismatic until he becomes incredibly persuasive. You'll be speaking to him with your own thoughts, feelings, and opinions, but by the end his way of thinking is the most logical and sound argument, and you aren't sure why you ever thought differently."

"Hey, I like the sound of that. Where did you say he got this magic from?" Kirk asked.

"No." Sam stuck her finger out at him like he was a bad puppy.

Silas smiled. "I very intentionally did not say."

"Hey, but that's serious though, I played a character once with maxed-out charisma. You could do anything and get away with it."

Elodie and a few others from the illusion chuckled.

"That is exactly why we need to be wary. The only protection from his speaking we have discovered is absolute confidence in your convictions and ideas."

"Can you *tell* us what it feels like?" Sam asked.

"Yes, that's a good idea." Silas shuffled in his seat and cleared his throat. "Gather in close and I'll tell you the gods-forsaken tale."

Kirk snickered but Sam elbowed him.

"The council called us in for a special meeting. I was in Tross on other business but was asked to attend," Silas began. With his words, the magic of the tale rose around them and bound them all together. Silas's memories floated through the air to Elodie and everyone else present, she let them take over and fill her mind.

Instead of a tale told from a third-person perspective, she was seeing the world from Silas's eyes, experiencing it just as he had, and his words faded to the background as she lived the moment.

She was walking through the halls of the castle, passing familiar portraits and tapestries of the royal family and their deeds. This royal line was what she had sworn to protect when she took her vow of knighthood.

Unease filled her chest. This request to appear before the council was unusual, and a sense of foreboding slowly crept over her, threatening to overwhelm. She'd heard rumors messengers had been sent out to knights on duty around the kingdom pulling them in or redirecting them to other tasks. Something was happening. And for these orders to come from the council and not Sir Jesper, the captain of the guard, was not a good sign.

She reached the cracking wood door of the council room and pushed it open, taking in the situation in an instant. The full council sat around the large table in the middle of the room, Oburleck sitting in the highest chair reading over a few documents with an even expression. Knights, her colleagues, men and women she trusted were already sitting in the chairs lining the wall. There was a heavy tension in the room, some on the council looked pleased while others, those she trusted the most, had veiled looks of concern.

She caught Lord Riyan's eye and the old man shook his head just slightly. Dess sat in a chair to her left, but Elodie felt showing her allegiances just now would be a mistake. She crossed the room and sat in a corner seat where she could clearly see the door. A few more knights trickled in, Dalene and Albern and Caesper. Then Sir Jesper arrived. His expression was a neutral mask, but Elodie had spent years under him as a squire and knew his temperament well. She could see tension and worry in his eyes. He met Elodie's gaze briefly and sat in one of the few empty seats remaining.

As if on cue, Oburleck looked up and around the room.

"Ah, it looks as though we are all here. Shall we get started?"

"Sounds good to me Oburleck," Devoss called from his seat on the right. "Don't want this meeting running over lunch if you can help it, am I right?" He chuckled and looked at Byron sitting next to him, who looked bored and did not acknowledge him. Devoss took a sip from a flask and tucked it back into his coat pocket.

"Indeed," Oburleck continued as if the interruption hadn't happened. "Welcome all of you, we appreciate that you could make it to this meeting on such short notice. I know our knights have such busy schedules."

He stood from his chair and made a show of walking around the room, greeting all the knights lining the walls. When he reached Elodie, she was prepared for it. She took a slow deep breath so her shoulders wouldn't show the action and held it as the steward approached. He paused before her and reached out to shake Elodie's hand.

"Sir Silas, so great to see you in Tross again." She stood as was proper and took the steward's hand, she was taller than the steward who had to look up to keep eye contact.

"Thank you, my lord," Elodie said in a deep masculine voice. She had to inhale then but did so carefully. The smell was still overwhelming. Oburleck's breath was unnaturally bad and it hit Elodie like a physical force, nearly taking her off her feet. The stench was unbearable, but she felt a little bad for him being afflicted with such a constitution. He was a good man and was just doing his best by the kingdom.

The thoughts were like a cloud enveloping her mind. She expected them and so when she saw them, she knew how to fan them away, to blow them out of her consciousness. Oburleck moved on to the next knight and Elodie sat again. After a moment, she was able to push out the last trace of the foreign thought and could again think clearly.

This wasn't good.

Oburleck's persuasion hadn't hit her this hard in a while. He must have worked to make his stench more potent for the meeting.

When he'd finished moving around the room Elodie saw most of the knights wore pleasant agreeable expressions, while only a few, like Jesper and Dess, still had any sharpness to their eyes.

"Now, I'm sure you are all wondering why we have called you." Oburleck stayed standing and kept moving around the room as he spoke.

Occasionally Elodie would get a wave of nauseous breath and would have to recenter herself. "I'm afraid we have a very troubling development that will lead to some unsettling orders. It has recently come to light that our beloved Elodie, the Misplaced Princess, has committed treason of the highest order."

Cold fire washed over her. Not her princess. No, her future queen would never do something like this. Oburleck must have gotten bad information, or there must be some other explanation, but if it were true . . .

Elodie pushed away the cloud of poison, and rage filled her chest in its place.

How dare Oburleck accuse Elodie of treason. He had no right.

Someone new was talking, and Elodie realized she'd lost the thread of conversation. She focused on Jesper, standing on the other side of the room. "—evidence of such actions?"

"The evidence has been examined most thoroughly by this council and has been found to be satisfactory."

A few heads around the table were nodding as if in agreement.

"We feel it would be best to not make known the specifics of her crimes as we do not want this to be a smear campaign against one who has been so beloved for so many years," Oburleck reasoned.

When they came again—the thoughts about how reasonable and charitable Oburleck was—the rage inside of Elodie burned the thoughts to ash before they could take hold. She would never believe such lies.

"Now as we speak, messengers are heading out to key locations to spread word of this so that none may be taken in by the princess's lies and deceit. We have reason to believe she will again be traveling to the Twoshy in a short time, and we will need each of you to lead scouting missions to trap and catch the princess."

Elodie thought this over. The only one who would know if the princess was arriving would be Gedas. And Gedas had disappeared a month ago with no word as to his location. Usually when he went off on his journeys, his path could at least be traced, but Jesper had heard nothing of the old wizard. Worry found its way into Elodie's mind. Gedas could be prickly, but he was their strongest ally.

The knights around the room had no such worries. They were nodding, their faces troubled yet serious about the development. They had no doubt that the steward's words were truth, and his orders were wise. Every muscle in Elodie tensed. She would stand and call Oburleck out for his lies and manipulation.

A slight movement caught her eye and she saw Jesper on the other side of the room staring at her sternly. He shook his head once. Elodie took a deep breath and forced down her rage. The rage was a tool to burn off Oburleck's magic. She would not let it control her. When her emotion was back in her steel grip, she knew her old knight master was correct. She needed to be wise and strategic. She could play the good knight a while longer, until the moment was right.

The memory started to fade and the magic dissolved around Elodie. She blinked, and a moment later was back in the sitting room squished between Kat and Dess on the couch.

Elodie frowned. From Silas's perspective Oburleck's power seemed obvious, yet she'd never noticed what he was doing in the moment. How many times had she left conversations agreeing with him against her better judgment, and not even being aware of that poisonous cloud he'd overwhelmed her with? She'd needed clues and warning before she'd known what he was capable of.

The room was silent as they all digested what they'd seen.

"Is his breath really that bad?" Kirk asked, still looking a little green.

"Yes," Elodie and Silas said as one.

"Okay got it. Smell something bad, ignore everything anyone says. I can do that." Kirk picked up another pastry and started to inhale it.

"So when is this happening? Have we set a time yet?" Kat asked.

"Midnight," Kirk jumped in. "Isn't that the traditional time for being up to no good?"

"Four in the morning," Silas said, ignoring Kirk. Some of Callie's friends had told them the shift change schedule, and Silas was confident those on watch would be good and exhausted, perfect for their operation.

They unanimously decided to call it an early night.

Chapter Twenty-Two

THE NIGHT AIR was cold and crisp. Winter was approaching and it was coming in strong. Elodie hadn't slept. As soon as she'd closed her eyes she was back in that deep, dark hole and Gedas was there gasping, taking his last few breaths as his light faded to nothing. Yellow lilies rained down from the sky until she was drowning in their overwhelming fragrance. After that, she'd laid awake for the rest of the night until she heard the others start to stir and rose and readied herself for the morning. She made herself a strong cup of tea and channeled her magic into the drink, boosting the caffeine to be as strong as she could make it.

She still had Silas's dagger and the bow he'd lent her, but somehow, she didn't think those would be very effective weapons in her hands. She already had Silas and Christopher at her side looking fierce with their bladed weapons, Allen muttering combat spells to himself, and Kirk, bright, chipper, and ready for anything.

Most of them didn't have proper armor with the exceptions of Silas's party, Sam, and Christopher. Sam's armor was finished off with a pair of pink armguards. When she saw Elodie looking, Sam rolled her eyes. Don't look at me, this was Kat's doing.

"You mean my genius and brilliant sense of style?" Kat asked, coming over to them.

Elodie leaned in for a closer look at the armguards. They were thin fabric secured with basic wooden buttons where the rest of Sam's armor was leather and metal.

"What are they for exactly?" Elodie asked. "Is it to make your hand signals easier to see or something?"

Sam snorted but Kat rolled her eyes, hands on hips.

"It's something I've been working on at the university," Kat said. "They should be as strong as chain mail, but oh so much more comfortable. I've been working on the technique for a few years, whenever I'm here."

A warm presence pressed in on Elodie's left and she looked up into Silas's shining face. He gave her a smile then turned to Sam.

"May I?" he asked. Sam nodded and held her arm out for Silas's inspection. He ran the edge of the material through his fingers. "I've seen similar products. They work well until they don't. Once the magic on the cloth runs out it stops deflecting blows."

"This is different," Kat said, a slight edge of offense lining her voice. "This isn't a spell applied to the cloth. I developed a process to make each fiber of the thread stronger." She glanced at Elodie. "Like magical Kevlar."

At Silas's questioning look, Elodie explained. "It's a fabric from the illusion, they make a sort of armor out of. It can stop projectile weapons stronger than arrows."

Silas's eyebrows rose with appreciation. "Is the color necessary? It leaves something of stealth to be desired."

Kat harrumphed and Sam covered a laugh. "It was a stylistic choice. I suck at sewing so I only made armguards."

"Well, should you make more of the fabric, I would be happy to put it through the paces of testing for you," Silas offered.

Kat smiled dreamily. "Maybe a nice forest-green tunic to match your eyes," she said, before rummaging through her pack for her notebook.

The rest of their party scrounged around until they came up with a semblance of protective gear. Rogers went out the evening before and returned with a mismatched lot of chain mail and boiled leather. Elodie was wearing a chain mail vest Silas wouldn't budge on. It was a bit long and added twenty pounds to her shoulders. She would take a neon pink tunic over the mail any day. On her head, he made her wear a steel helmet that smelled like feet and fit badly until Sam showed her a trick for doing her hair to cushion it.

Kirk wore a thick leather breastplate that was about twenty years old, the leather cracking.

"What kind of protection is this going to offer him?" Silas said, running his finger over an arrow hole in the leather just above Kirk's belly button.

"We're not going into battle, just a stealth rescue mission," Elodie reminded him.

"The armor is there on the off chance it is needed, my lady. It doesn't make it less important."

Elodie rolled her eyes at Silas as she adjusted her helmet.

The other team, headed by Dess, would go through a different entrance leading to the servant workrooms. Rogers was the only one not on a team. When listing their tasks, Silas said only that he would make a diversion and the squire had grinned and nodded.

They snuck through a servant's entrance and moved through the laundry looking for stairs leading down, while Dess's team headed for the tower. Jinis had provided them with charms that would cause others to look away and not notice them, assuming they didn't do anything too alarming, like stab someone. There were workers in the laundry washing clothes even at this late hour, and Elodie couldn't help the pang of guilt and rage as she saw the iron chains around their necks.

They passed silently through servant workrooms, storerooms, baths, and even an armory but found nothing.

"This is getting us nowhere," Allen hissed. "Either he's somewhere other than a dungeon or he's cloaked."

"If he's cloaked, couldn't you detect it, mage boy?" Kirk asked.

"If a cloaking was weak enough that any mage could detect it, it would be pointless."

"Any word from Dess yet?" Elodie asked, trying to stop the arguing before they were caught.

Silas pulled his mage orb from his belt pouch, it was still dim. He shook his head. When either party found evidence of Gedas, they would tell the other so they knew where to go.

"I might have an idea." Elodie looked up at the ceiling above her as if she could see through the floors. "It's kind of crazy, and it might get us all killed."

"Oh, by all means then, let's do it," Allen scoffed.

Silas held up a finger to silence them before someone retorted. "Where's the idea coming from? Your head or your gut?" he asked.

Elodie looked at him and his green eyes reassured her. "My gut, my head's definitely not a part of this one."

Silas nodded. "That works for me. What's your plan?"

Elodie smiled.

She found the servant's staircase and followed it up toward the floors that she had wandered years before.

She was a little shocked at how quickly she found the rooms as if something were guiding her. Unlike her previous visit, no one was guarding the door. The castle was dark, they'd used light globes to light their path so far, but the light coming from under the door was bright. Elodie took a step toward the door, and Silas moved to enter first. Elodie shook her head and waved him off. This was something she needed to do.

She opened the door and light flooded out into the hallway. It took a long moment of blinking for her eyes to adjust. When they did, it was like she'd stepped back in time. The room sported dark-walnut furnishings up against a silver-blue wallpaper with an ornate design, and a woman, tall and elegant, carrying a white vase with yellow and orange mums. That was a little different. The last time she had been carrying yellow lilies.

The woman's hair was pinned up but with locks escaping their pins as if no one had been there to help her undress for the night and she'd slept on it. Instead of a fine gown, she wore a cotton sheath in periwinkle and a fine silk robe tied around her waist. On her feet were ballroom slippers embroidered with beads in the patterns of blooming flowers. She turned from side to side as if confused why the door was open, then seemed to dismiss it, and set the vase on a small table. She looked it over on every side for a long moment. Then picked a book at random from the shelf and sat on the edge of a chair next to the flowers. She opened the book, peering closely at the pages.

Elodie stepped further into the room, Silas behind her, and the others filling in slowly. Elodie slipped off the charm keeping her unseen and approached Lady Madelina, Oburleck's wife. When she was close enough, Elodie noticed the book was upside down, but Lady Madelina didn't seem to care as she chewed a blue leaf and smiled serenely.

Elodie cleared her throat. Lady Madelina looked up as if just noticing her. She smiled brilliantly, showing off her lips and teeth stained blue from the stimulant she chewed. "Oh hello, won't you join me by the fire?"

Lady Madelina gestured to another chair opposite her. The fire was stone cold, not even a cindix rooting in the ashes.

"Thank you, my lady. You are too kind."

Elodie sat in the chair indicated, and Lady Madelina smiled and turned back to her book. Silas crossed the room to the other doors and looked inside before closing and locking each in turn. It was a risk, a more observant person might have noticed him through the charm in such a bright room, but Silas looked calmer when he was done, and Lady Madelina was too far gone from her blue cheer leaves.

"Lady Madelina, do you remember me? We met a few years ago. My name is Elodie."

Madelina looked up suddenly, but not at Elodie, she stared directly across the room to where Silas was standing, but she didn't seem to notice him, her expression joyful and excited. "Oh yes, little Elodie, the princess. I remember her. Poor child, she was lost long ago, but we find her from time to time." She returned to scanning the upside-down book.

"Wow, I've never seen a cheer user so gone before," Kirk said. Allen shushed him.

This was pointless. Elodie turned to Silas, but he nodded. "Keep going," he mouthed.

Elodie sighed. "Lady Madelina, you were just telling me about the dungeons, do go on. That's so fascinating that the castle has an oubliette. Where is it located again?"

Madelina shivered and pulled the shawl from the back of her chair around her shoulders. "No, we would never have a place of forgetting in this castle. Oh no, it would be too gruesome."

"Yes, a place of forgetting, it's a deep hole where a prisoner is left to die. Are you sure there's nothing like that here?"

Madelina shook her head emphatically with big slow movements. "No, would never allow prisoners here, no, definitely not. All filth is kept outside of the castle, out in the pens before they are collared and sold."

All Elodie's sympathy for the woman vanished. Madelina must have faced a lot in her life to try and hide from it so completely with her addiction, but on some level, she'd chosen to hide instead of facing the horror. That would never excuse her thinking it was okay to sell people who were beneath her.

Elodie took a deep breath and tried one last time. "Where would they keep a special guest? One they didn't want to leave?"

Madelina stopped shaking her head and smiled brightly. "In the guest wing. Always in the guest wing, we keep the guests." She picked the book back up and flipped through the pages singing rhythmically. "Guest wing, guest wing, guests go in the west wing, except for the special guests we put in the tower."

Elodie froze. She turned to see Silas just as he reached into his pocket and pulled out his orb, but it was already glowing softly. He squeezed it and Dess's face appeared. "Definitely the tower guys, they have reinforcements here."

There was a scuffling sound from the orb and a loud clanging, and the image went blank.

"We need to get over there," Elodie said.

A door closed with a bang, causing Elodie to jump.

"And who is 'we' precisely?"

Elodie turned cold, colder than Madelina's fireplace. Kirk, Christopher, and Allen parted ways, moving to the edges of the room and out of Baron Byron's path as he stepped slowly into the room.

The lady stood with a jolt, clutching her book tight to her chest. "No, no, no. No, you are not allowed in these rooms, no, you are not." She picked up her vase and flowers and held it tightly in her other arm. "Out, I say!" She stomped once, her whole body trembling, and fled into an inner room, locking the door behind her.

The baron ignored her entirely and pulled his sword from its sheath, his eyes scanning the room with sharp focus. "Your High-ness, please ask your companions to uncloak before I am forced to do something drastic."

Silas moved so fast she didn't see him until he was across the room. His sword came up in a flash, aimed perfectly for the baron's neck, but somehow Byron must have known for his sword moved to match the knight's and their blades connected. Byron could see Silas now, his eyes drilled into the knight and he smirked.

"Ah, Lord Silas. While I am most delighted to see you commit-ting such a clear and deliberate act of treason, I am surprised to see you would allow the princess out into the line of danger."

"I don't allow her anything," Silas snarled. He shoved the baron off his sword with a massive force of strength and took a deep breath. When the air came out, he was calm and steady. They began to move, their swords clashing around each other in a wave of noise and fury.

They were well matched. Silas had height and strength that he wielded with nimble grace, but the baron was good. He moved in step with Silas as if knowing where the knight would move before he did.

"And therein lies the problem, boy. A man of your line and intelligence could have been an asset in the new kingdom, if only you had learned to direct those under your power."

"I believe in power through service," Silas said, his voice deadly calm. His sword came around in a tight arc for an opening in the baron's defense even Elodie saw but something odd happened. Silas's arm jerked to the side and his blade flew wide, just as Byron flicked his wrist and cut the leather strap holding Silas's armor at the shoulder.

"Did you see that?" Allen hissed.

Silas's eyes narrowed and he took three quick steps back, blocking a blow as he moved. He ripped the remainder of the shoulder guard off, the edge of his studded breastplate no longer snug against his chest.

"This is the secret then," Silas said. "You weren't a dud after all I suppose." Blood dotted his light blue tunic along the line where his armor had been cut. It didn't look deep, but Elodie's stomach seized as she thought back to Silas's words the evening before. The baron was going to cut Silas out of his armor, then filet him alive while they fought.

"Can't you do something?" she whispered to Allen.

Allen looked scared. No longer all-knowing, cocky, and brave, but like the sixteen-year-old kid he really was. "Anything I try will likely hit both of them, and I don't know what magic the baron has."

Elodie didn't blame him. She had a bow, but she didn't trust her aim enough to draw it.

They continued their dance. Silas was graceful and smooth with his motions, impressive for someone as tall and muscular as he was, but the baron was like a hawk. He moved economically, picking each strike and blow until he had an opening. Then Silas's sword would go wide, and the baron would be there with a careful slice, cutting laces and leather. When a chunk of armor was so loose as to be a distraction, Silas would remove it, leaving him more open. He already had a number of cuts covering his shirt: one on each shoulder, three across his chest at different angles, and a bad one on his right forearm where Byron had sliced off an armguard. Silas switched sword hands after that to prevent his blood from ruining his grip.

She wanted to move forward, distract the baron in some way, or give Silas an opening, but her lesson in the market had proven Silas's fatal flaw. He would always move to protect her. If she did anything, chances were he would react badly.

Kirk crossed to stand next to his brother, who had drifted slowly around the room and away from Allen and Elodie. Kirk pulled off his charm and dropped his head as if trying to get a better look at a new cut on Silas's thigh.

"Seriously dude. How are you doing that?"

Byron spun around quickly so his back was to Elodie and he faced Kirk, Christopher still hidden at his brother's side. Silas took the opening, and his blade flew right on target to slice off the baron's arm. The baron deflected his blade again with the unseen magic, and Silas only nicked his arm. The baron winced. That made Elodie smile. Silas hadn't winced at any of his cuts.

"Yeah! Just like that!" Kirk called. "How are you doin' it, man? It's like you're Magneto or something, manipulating the metal maybe?"

The side of Byron's lip curled as if in a mock example of a smile. And he attacked Silas again with force, keeping Kirk in his sight. Christopher palmed a dagger in his hand, and worry surged in Elodie's chest.

"Yo! Silas, man, if you beat this dude, I'll totally get your face on a T-shirt or something."

Byron swung wide, and Silas went for the opening. He came in low, and when his sword flew to the side, he let go of it and let the sword fly into the wall, carried by Byron's magical force as Silas dived. A glint of steel flew from Christopher and the dagger plunged into Byron's eye. The baron screamed. Silas rolled and sprung to his feet, a dagger from his boot in hand. He smashed the hilt into the baron's hand, and he dropped the sword. Silas caught the falling weapon and in one smooth, powerful move, spun it around, and sliced off the baron's head.

The head flew and rolled into the empty fireplace as blood splattered the elegant wallpaper. Everything was still for a moment as gravity acted and the baron's headless body crumpled to the ground. Silas pulled the glowing orb from his pocket and tossed it to Kirk who caught it smoothly.

"Yo, where you guys at?" Kirk asked the orb. He looked a little green.

Retching sounded from the corner Allen had been standing in.

"Where are *we* at?" Kat asked, fear heavy in her voice. "We have the wizard and are heading back to the base. Rogers set fire to the stables, and they are still in flames so you have cover to get out."

Elodie barely listened. Her heart was racing and she was out of breath, even though she hadn't been the one fighting. It had been so quick, so sudden. One powerful movement of strength and momentum and . . . She was frozen in place, afraid to move as she watched Silas cross the room and pick up his sword. He wiped the blade clean in a meticulous and routine way and sheathed it along with his dagger. He crossed to Elodie, stepping over the baron's legs and the growing pool of blood, limping slightly. He knelt in front of her, forcing her to look down to meet his eyes.

"My lady," he said. His voice was tight, the only sign of his pain.

That snapped her out of it.

"Silas, get up," she said, trying to grab his arm in a place that wasn't bloody.

"Are you all right?" he asked.

Was he crazy?

"Silas, I'm not the one bleeding all over the rug."

She moved to the table where Lady Madelina had set her flower vase and pulled off the tablecloth, ripping it into long strips.

Silas stood with only the slightest of wobbles as she made it back to him. "That can wait. We need to leave," he ordered.

"The one on your arm cannot wait," she said, holding up her arm to show the bloody handprint he'd left.

Silas gave her a nod of consent and turned to Kirk. "What's the plan?"

Elodie wrapped the fabric around his arm a few times in a passable bandage. She would have to take a closer look back in their rooms.

"Sam said they drew most of the action to the west, so we would be best off going out the kitchens and into the woods before tracking back to the house."

Silas nodded. "Thank you, both." He nodded to Kirk and Christopher.

Christopher nodded back, then he and his brother shared a smile.

"That's how we work best. I distract and he destroys." Kirk said it with a smile, but he still looked a little green. Christopher's expression was as peaceful as ever as he cleaned the blood off his dagger.

"Are we ready?" Silas asked, looking at Elodie.

She rolled her eyes and handed him another folded section of cloth. "Hold this against that gash in your side, Sir Knight, so you don't bleed out while we escape, please."

Silas smiled down at her. It was a silly smile as if blood loss had already addled his brain. "As you command, my lady."

She ignored the warmth flooding through her chest and rolled her eyes.

Elodie led. She knew the path through the kitchens well, as she had taken it a few times before when sneaking out. Allen followed second, a little woozy from getting sick back in Oburleck's rooms. Next was Silas, steady on his feet, almost too steady, holding his bandage to his side while Kirk followed closely, just in case the invulnerable knight passed out. Christopher brought up their rear keeping an eye out.

They all breathed heavily as they went through the back entrance of the bordello so as not to track blood into the house. Silas climbed the stairs in his own power, but when he dropped into a chair in the main room, their allies crowding around to find out what happened, Elodie knew he was in more pain than he let on.

She scanned the faces around the room. There were a few missing, on guard duty, but those she saw looked whole and uninjured aside from minor scrapes and cuts. Silas was without a doubt the worst off.

Dess came out of one of the smaller rooms and closed the door behind her. "What the holy flying razor blades happened to you?" she asked.

"He killed that Byron dude," Kirk said.

Dess looked at him startled, and Kirk made a motion like swinging a baseball bat . . . or maybe a sword if one was uncoordinated.

Dess scowled down at Silas. "What happened to long-range attacks?"

Silas just grinned stupidly.

"Can Jinis heal? If not, he needs stitches," Elodie said, moving toward Silas.

Dess pressed her lips. "He's examining Gediminas, but our host gathered healing supplies."

Gedas. Elodie had forgotten in her anxiety of the moment who they'd gone to rescue.

Silas waved her off. "Go. Check on him."

Chapter Twenty-Three

ELODIE DIDN'T HAVE to ask which room Gedas was being kept in. She could feel the anxiety and tension radiating from it as everyone in the main room seemed to orbit around it. No matter where they looked, their eyes would flicker back to that closed door. Her hand shook a little as she turned the handle and entered. Allen followed her silently. The room was bright, the light globes turned up as high as they could go. It gave the space a slightly sterile feel, but the bedroom was far from being an adequate medical room.

On the far bed, Jinis stooped over a pile of rags while Callie rang out a cloth in a bowl of water. She saw Elodie and smiled sadly.

Elodie stood just inside the room, frozen for the second time that night, too filled with terror to move. Allen huffed and pushed around her.

"He's unconscious," Callie said gently and held a hand out to her. Elodie obeyed and crossed to her friend. The smell was bad, but Elodie had helped in enough clinics that she knew how to push such things away. What hurt was seeing a man she loved so thin it was as if he was just skin draped over bones with nothing remaining inside. His rich black hair, previously swiped through with gray, was now far past salt and pepper, and his olive skin was now pale and green. And his age? Gedas had appeared somewhere in his forties for as long as Elodie had known him. Now his face was wrinkled and withered long past an age where any Hu should still be alive. Callie took the wet cloth and ran it over his sunken cheek, moving down his neck, removing sweat and grime.

"Did they starve him?" Allen asked. His face was grim and Elodie hoped he didn't throw up again.

"They didn't have to. From what I can tell he's been in a magical coma for months," Jinis said. He kept one hand pressed gently against Gedas's forehead, his eyes closed tight in concentration.

"How is that possible?" Elodie asked. "I saw him, he was awake, crying out."

"Scrying or psychic vision?"

"I dreamed it."

Jinis nodded slowly. "Dreams show an interpretation of reality. You also saw him chained in a hole, didn't you?"

"Yes." Elodie ground her teeth. She didn't like being so wrong.

Jinis sighed and removed his hand. He looked at Elodie. "I think what you perceived as a physical cage was, in fact, a magical one. Something's affecting him, some magic keeping him in this state. He wasn't chained, the door wasn't even locked." He glanced at the old wizard again, sadness filling his eyes. "If he had any less magic, he would have been long dead after this much time."

"What can we do?"

Jinis shook his head. "I'm not an expert healer. I've never seen anything like this before."

Her mind raced, her heart pounded so fast she thought it would burst from her chest. "Is it a spell? A poison?"

Jinis kept shaking his head.

She was sinking. The room continued to get bigger and bigger around her as she sunk into the floor and her mind flew in circles.

They could send for healer Beathan, but the healer was too far away. She would never make it in time.

They could look for another healer, one in the city. But would any they found help traitors? They could force one. Suddenly her mind pinged back to reality.

"Lilies," she said.

"What?"

"I need a lily." She turned to Callie. "It's fall, they are out of season. I can't remember what would act as a substitute."

Callie set down the rag. "There's one flower merchant in the city with a hothouse. I can have someone check."

"I only need one," she called as Callie left. "Jinis, do you have willow bark?"

She started rooting around the room collecting things. A glass goblet from one of the bedside tables. An expensive candle, pointless with the light globes, but intended for setting an ambiance. She moved into the sitting room and barely noticed the voices grow quiet at her appearance. There was a healer's kit next to Dess, who paused in cutting Silas's breeches off around the cut in his leg.

Elodie glanced at Silas, assessing he was in good hands and not in immediate danger. She dug around in the kit until she found willow bark. On her way back into Gedas's room she snatched a decorative crystal tray off a table.

Holding the willow bark over the candle until it caught fire, she pulled the bark away and watched it burn. When the tip was black and cracked, she rubbed it against the rough side of the crystal until the ash was ground thin and repeated the process.

"What exactly do you expect to accomplish with flowers and twigs?" Allen sneered.

"Help or leave," she retorted.

He pulled his shoulders back and cleared his throat. "How can I help?"

"You can't," she bit out, hoping he took the hint.

Allen crossed his arms, but he didn't leave.

Callie returned with a single yellow lily in record time.

"Where did you find it?" Jinis asked, watching Elodie's movements with fascination.

"One of my friends is favored by the flower merchant. Her rooms are always full of blossoms."

Elodie filled the goblet three-fourths full of water and scooped the ash into her palm. She closed her eyes and reached for the small spark of magic inside of her, the magic that liked growing things. She grasped the small bit of magic and pushed it into the ash until it felt as though it shimmered. Opening her eyes, she let out a breath and sprinkled the ash into the water until the goblet was dark and murky.

"Thank you," she said to Callie, taking the flower from her hand. She stripped off the leaves and pinched off all but a few inches of the stem, then bent over Gedas. She opened his mouth a crack and pressed the flower gently to his lips.

"This is hedgewitch business, not real magic," Allen scoffed.

Gedas was breathing through his nose. That wouldn't do. She pinched his nostrils, and after a long, heart-stopping moment, his next faint shallow breath came out of his lips and caused the petals of the flower to stir. The faint scent of blueberries rose and wrapped around her. That was odd and seemed to scratch at the back of her memory. She shook away the thought and counted.

One.

Two.

Three.

Four ragged breaths. That would be enough.

Moving back to the goblet, Elodie tipped the flower toward the glass. She felt the others crowding around her, but she ignored it. She lowered the flower until the petals just barely touched the surface of the water. The effect was instantaneous. The ash in the water fled from the petals. She lowered the flower further, and shook it around, stirring the water. When she pulled out the flower the water was clear and pure again, all ash having coated the inside of the glass trying to get as far away from the flower as possible.

"Poison." She spun around and her eyes connected with Silas. "It's poison."

Silas smiled softly. He didn't look any better, but he was standing, or leaning against the doorframe. Elodie frowned at him. She wished he'd sit.

"Are you sure? Could you tell the difference between poison and venom? For example?" Jinis asked.

Elodie stuck her finger into the jar and swiped the ash with her finger. She pulled it out and rubbed it between two fingers. She shook her head. "It's poison. It feels plant-based."

"What if it's a spell that works like poison?" Allen asked.

Elodie shook her head. "It acts differently."

"How differently?" Allen challenged.

Elodie threw up her hands. "I once saw the water burst into flames when a man was cursed. Trust me, Allen, it's poison."

Jinis was shaking his head. "That doesn't help us unless we know the specific kind of poison. Antidotes are very specific."

Elodie frowned. "I think I know one that will work, but I need more supplies." She started looking around. She found paper, but no pencil or even chalk.

"Here." Jinis handed her an oil pencil.

She started scribbling down what she needed but then forcefully slowed herself. The list needed to be legible. "Allen, can you help me shop to speed things up?"

A hand closed over the pencil. "No, he will get all of it, while you stay here."

She looked up at Silas. His eyes, soft and sad, filled her with anger. She yanked her hand away.

"It will be quicker if I help." She kept writing.

"And if you're caught and killed, what are Gedas's chances then?"

A hollowness opened inside her chest, and the anger emptied away. She kept writing the ingredients she needed. When she'd listed them all, she read it three times trying to dig through her memory. It looked correct. She added a list of tools she needed, then handed the paper to Allen.

"High-quality ingredients only."

"I'm not an amateur," he scoffed and stalked out of the room.

"I'll help," Jinis said and followed.

Elodie sat on the empty bed and let out a shaky breath. Being powerless made her feel sick. Silas eased himself down onto the bed next to her with slow controlled movements that reeked of pain. She glanced down at his leg.

"What is that?"

"That's a bandage," he said evenly.

"Why is it bloody?"

"Because bandages cover wounds, and wounds are these things that sometimes bleed."

She turned and took his arm, lifting it to see the bottom. That bandage also had red blots seeping through the cloth. "What did you do to tear the stitches already?"

"We didn't stitch it, just wrapped it tightly. It will be fine until I get to a healer."

"Silas, think. You're wanted for treason. What healer would treat you?" Silas frowned as if the thought hadn't occurred to him. "Did Callie's kit not include the proper tools?" she asked patiently, giving Callie a weak smile.

"Have you seen Dess's mending? Her sewing is always crooked," Silas grumbled.

Elodie sighed. "Did you at least take a blood rejuvenation potion? So many women in this house, they must have one."

"He only sipped it," Callie tattled. She stood and left for the sitting room.

"They taste terrible," Silas whined, but he stopped when Elodie gave him a look.

"So facing down insane magical barons is doable, but taking your medicine is too much to ask?"

Silas shrugged. "Maybe if more healers carried swords it would make things a little more interesting."

"I carry a bow sometimes."

Silas's eyes connected with hers and the corner of his mouth lifted. "I know."

His voice was thick and threatened to distract her from the moment at hand. That would not do.

Elodie scanned her eyes over his body. Silas had changed tunics after Dess patched him up. This one was a darker color, so it was hard to tell if any of his other wounds had opened and bled onto the shirt.

Elodie turned away and took a deep breath. "Take off your tunic please." She rolled up her sleeves and busied herself with getting a clean bowl of water from the powder room. When she returned to Silas, she used all of her will to look at his bandages, and only his bandages. She was already surrounded by distractions and she could not let herself succumb to another, no matter how much she wished to curl up in his strength and forget about everything else like it was a bad dream. So much was riding on her keeping it together. Silas needed patching up and Gedas needed a cure. She could do this if she stayed focused.

She moved his arm closer and unwrapped the bandage so she could get a good look at the cut. The simple motion was enough to break the wound back open.

Callie came back in and handed Silas a bottle. "Drink up, Sir Knight," she said, grinning wickedly.

Silas uncorked the bottle, winced, and downed it in one go. His face screwed up in disgust. He closed his eyes and shuddered.

Elodie took the healer's kit from Callie and started going through it. "Really, it's not that bad. It's like eighty percent dandelion juice anyway."

"You say that like it makes it better."

"Callie, I'm not seeing anything to numb in here. Do you have clove oil or any other anesthetic?"

Callie shook her head. "It's a pretty basic kit."

"I'll be fine," Silas reassured her. "I've had field dressings before."

"Si, you just winced because the dandelion was too much for you." Elodie smiled. Callie cackled and returned to Gedas's side.

"I'll be fine," he repeated. Elodie sighed and examined his arm closer. Dess had done a good job cleaning it, and the ointment she'd applied was expensive and powerful. Definitely not something from Callie's healing bag. It would heal his wounds in record time, as long as they didn't keep ripping open and he got enough rest to let his body heal. She readied her needle and stitcher's string and began. Silas didn't wince as she worked, but his jaw was sharp as he gritted his teeth.

When she was done stitching, she asked Dess for the ointment she'd used and gave Silas's wounds one last coat before wrapping them up again. Jinis and Allen returned as she finished the bandaging. They'd found everything she needed and in large quantities, "In case you mess up and have to start over," Allen explained. Elodie rolled her eyes but thanked them.

When Silas was all patched and covered, she excused herself to wash up in the bathroom. She could hear Silas and Jinis talk over a report Tim had orbed in to tell them that morning. Sir Jesper was returning to Tross on some silent and suspicious orders. Silas suspected it was a plan to quietly get rid of Jesper, who had always opposed Oburleck's politics. Silas told him he had a few messages he wanted to send before he would go out on another errand into the city.

Elodie grit her teeth and dug through the healer's kit again until she found a few ingredients she needed and added them to a fresh goblet of water. She stirred and the potion turned a murky brown color, like weak tea.

"Here, drink this, my lord."

Silas took the glass, smelled it, and drank it in two big gulps. "What is it?" he asked.

"Sleeping draft."

Silas's shoulders sunk and he tilted his head, looking at her with a defeated expression. "That's not very nice."

Jinis snorted. "Come on, my lord. Let's get you to bed before you pass out and no one on eres can move you." Jinis stuck his shoulder under the larger man's armpit and helped guide the knight out.

Elodie turned to the new supplies and started arranging things in the order she would need them for her potion.

She got to work.

Allen watched for a bit, then shuffled off to take a nap. Jinis stayed with her, serving as an assistant. A grand gesture for someone recently certified as an enchanter, but he was the first to admit his specialty had not been healing, and she was their best bet in helping Gedas.

But she was so tired.

Callie brought her tea, and Elodie again fed more of her magic into the leaves to boost their caffeine. When she was done, she looked up to see Jinis examining her closely. She only smiled and sipped her tea. She stopped to eat but spent the rest of the time focusing, making sure she didn't miss a step in the process she'd learned years before. This was a detoxifying potion Gedas taught her when she was twelve. She'd taken some medication back in the illusion that didn't sit well in her body when she returned to the Twoshy and the ruakh reentered her body. When she'd grown sick,

Gedas had brewed the detoxifying potion to help cleanse her body of any foreign substance. It wouldn't have worked on every poison, but she prayed to every god she thought to bother for it to work this time.

She started getting a headache behind her left eye, but some willow bark tea helped it fade into the background where she kept all the other noise, stress, and anxiety that was trying to creep in on her attention.

The last step of the potion involved adding chia seeds and stirring for a very long time. Jinis excused himself after a while, and still Elodie stirred.

Stirring, so very much stirring.

Her mind wandered as she completed the menial task. There was something that kept coming back to her about blueberries, and she couldn't remember what. It gnawed at her over and over.

She felt a light touch on her arm and turned to see Sam. Her friend looked tired and a little pissy, but she tried to cover it with a sympathetic smile. "Are you okay, love?"

"Yeah, I'm fine. Why do you look so miffed?" Elodie asked.

Sam let out a deep breath. "Oh, it's nothing. I'm just annoyed."

"At?"

"Tristan. He didn't check in at the end of our lookout schedule like he was supposed to, so I had to track him down. I should have been back an hour ago and should be sleeping by now. So I kinda yelled at him, and now he's pouting in the other room." She grimaced. "I should apologize, but I'm not ready yet."

"You should go get some rest."

"You should do the same."

"I'm almost done," Elodie said.

"Then you promise to go to sleep after?"

Elodie winced, she didn't want to lie to her friend.

"Elodie, you need sleep. What's wrong?" Sam asked, genuine concern showing through the exhaustion.

She wanted to deny it and say everything was fine, but it was just too much. Heat pounded behind her eyes and she closed them tight.

"I'm afraid of what I will see when I close my eyes."

"But you've been dreaming of Gediminas for weeks. Now that he's here things should ease, right?"

"Or what if instead he dies while I'm asleep and I'm unable to help. What if instead I just have to watch while that light—" She covered her eyes and dropped her head so that Sam wouldn't see the tears fall. But she didn't stop stirring, always stirring.

Sam put her arm on Elodie's shoulder and leaned in, not quite a hug, but a show of comfort and understanding. "All you can do is what you are able, beyond that is in the gods' hands. You've done everything you can, and now you need to sleep and let what comes come."

Elodie nodded. That made sense. She could only do what she was able. She couldn't be expected to do more than she was physically, emotionally, and magically capable of.

Chapter Twenty-Four

WHEN THE POTION WAS FINISHED, Elodie poured it into a few amber glass bottles and corked them. She'd spent all day at her task, making several batches with what she had. Gedas had been ill for so long, his body would need all the help it could get to purge the toxin. She wrote the instructions on the bottles and set them in the bottom drawer of the bedside table. She gave Gedas a quick look over and moved into the sitting room where Jinis and Kat were talking. They looked up when she entered.

"It's finished. It needs to sit for a few hours, four at the minimum, then you can give him as much as he will take. Then keep giving it to him every few hours as you can."

Jinis nodded. "Are you going to bed?"

"Not yet. I just wanted someone else to know—"

The door to the second smallest room burst open.

Elodie jumped spinning to face her attacker, but it wasn't an attacker. It was just a grumpy-looking knight who believed himself invulnerable. His face had wrinkles on it from his pillow, and his hair was flat on one side of his head. His eyes locked on her and he stormed across the room until he towered over her in all his adorable fury.

"My lady, will you please never drug me again?" he asked politely, his teeth gritted.

"Will you please never again get yourself nearly killed and then refuse to give your body the time it needs to heal?"

Silas narrowed his eyes at her, and she glared right back.

"I see we are at an impasse," he said. The corner of his mouth started to lift.

Jinis eased slowly away from Elodie and Silas, but he only caught Silas's attention.

"Jinis, I have a task for you and Rogers, if he isn't sleeping."

"I believe he is still playing lookout, but I can retrieve him," Jinis said.

"I can replace him," Kat volunteered. "I just woke up."

"Excellent. How is Gedas?" Silas asked Elodie.

Elodie sighed. "No change, but I should check on him again."

She returned to Gedas's room and sat by his bed. After a moment, Silas followed silently and knelt by her side.

"I need to be doing something," she said. Being useless made her feel sick and angry. This time when it came, she was too tired to force down the fear and anxiety.

Silas set down a teacup on the bedside table and pulled out a handkerchief. He gently wiped at the tears on Elodie's cheek. Embarrassed, she took the cloth and ducked her head until her hair fell like a shield between them.

"You've already done so much, my lady." He tucked her hair behind her ear. "Until then, we can only pray for Dima to help."

"Please stop calling me 'my lady,'" she said weakly.

"Never," he told her.

She made a noise; she wasn't sure if it should be called a chuckle or a sob.

Elodie looked up at the ceiling and prayed silently in her head. *Ravid, if Gedas dies because of the mess you started, I will never forgive you. Deal or no deal.*

She couldn't imagine the world without Gedas. He was so much more to her than just a great wizard. He was the closest thing to family she'd ever had in the Twoshy. He was her home, her safe place. She couldn't imagine life in the illusion without knowing he was in the Twoshy waiting for her to return. Waiting to take her on one more adventure.

She pulled the acorn from her pocket and turned it over and over between her fingers. The potential life inside was a comfort to her.

"If he was awake now, he would say I was being foolish, crying over an old, useless man like him, then he would come up with some ridiculous number and say eight hundred and thirty-seven was a long enough life for any Hu."

"You don't think he's really that old do you?" Silas asked, a small smile in his voice. Elodie smiled at the thought. He was always dodgy about his age. With enough magic a Hu could live longer than average, and Gedas did have enough magic but only he would know the truth of it. Magical Hu still didn't have the long life of an Elv.

They looked at the old man on the bed and sobered. This Gedas did look ancient, as if his ordeal had sapped decades or even a century from his lifetime.

"What did you need Jinis and Rogers for?" Elodie asked. "And stop kneeling, you will pull your stitches. She pulled on his arm until he relented and sat next to her."

"I have some unfinished business I need to attend to." Silas plucked the acorn out of her fingers and looked it over before handing it back with a small smile.

Elodie rolled her eyes. "I will drug you again if you plan on starting any more duels. Dess and Jinis sent all the messages you needed. You can share the burden of responsibility you know." She leaned until she shoved him with her shoulder, and he smiled. She didn't straighten completely, keeping her shoulder pressed against his. He didn't move, except to accept her weight, a warm strong presence at her side.

"I will work on delegating. I promise. Now, will you be all right while I'm gone?" he asked, his voice a soft rumble.

Elodie knew what he was really asking. *Will you stay safe while I'm gone?* She smiled and nodded. "I'll stay with Gedas."

"Thank you."

Jinis returned and Silas left with him and Rogers, and their rooms once more sunk into silence. A thought kept thumping around in her head and Elodie flopped back on the empty bed to think. Maybe her brain would offer up the idea in the stillness, or maybe she would finally drift off to sleep.

Blueberries.

She jerked awake. She didn't think she'd actually slept. More likely her mind had only just begun to drift that direction before it was startled awake.

She'd smelled blueberries on his breath, and it reminded her of something she'd read long ago. She closed her eyes to think. It was an old story about a poison. She'd read it in a book. It was a small, old book with new but plain binding.

Digging through her memory of past travels was like fishing for pages of a book in a murky lake. Each time she grasped for one, the paper dissolved through her fingers.

The plain binding was important because all the surrounding books in the memory were not plain.

It came back to her in a flash. She'd read it in a book in Oburleck's library, here in this very city. His library was filled with gilded books that made her eyes hurt from the glare, but on the edge of a shelf, she found an old book in plain binding that had beautiful pictures of rare magical plants from across the sea. That was the book where she'd learned about the dragon's breath. But there was another passage in the book that spoke about a poison that left the breath smelling of blueberries. It was odd and stuck in her memory, but try as she might, she couldn't knock any more of the information loose.

Traveling between worlds tended to make the finer details of life and memory iffy at best. Maybe if she found the book and reread the passage, it would hold some clue as to a cure for Gedas.

The sitting room was empty, Silas having left with his team and everyone else either sleeping or on lookout duty. No one had asked her to take a lookout shift. She didn't like being treated differently, given special favors. Sure she made a potion, but she could help more. When she got back, she would tell Silas to put her on the rotation. He would be furious when she returned, if she returned after him. For some reason, the thought made her smile.

"Where do you think you're going?"

She jumped a little. Tristan was sitting on a chair in the corner, tucked into the shadows. He looked annoyed.

"I just have something I have to do real fast."

"You're going out? You're really that stupid?"

She rolled her eyes. Tristan had always been a little distant with her, but he usually wasn't condescending. That was Allen's job. "Just don't tell anyone, okay?"

"Not making any promises there," he said. But he didn't look interested in moving. He pulled his book back up and kept reading, ignoring her. She rolled her eyes and left.

Stepping outside, the cool evening chill rushed over her. The sun had just set and yet it was already colder than it had been the night before. The cold was nice. It helped wake her up. She felt stupid tired, too many nights without sleep.

It was a bad idea to leave so late while enemies were looking for her, when she'd been kidnapped before in this very city. But those memories felt very far away right now, and she had Jinis's charm.

There was a part of her, a very real part that had some childhood belief that bad things didn't really happen. It might have just been her privilege growing up in a safe area so far removed from danger that allowed her to think so, but she pushed away any bits of fear or knowledge that told her otherwise. She owed it to Gedas after everything he'd done for her, her entire life. She owed him this sacrifice if in any way it would help him get better.

Besides, as Sam had said, she was only responsible for what she was capable of, everything else was in the gods' hands. And as the last few months had shown her, risking her neck by sneaking back into the castle was just the sort of thing Ravid would want from her. Who else would have pushed the memories of the blueberries so hard in her mind?

It wasn't hard to avoid her friends' lookout posts. She knew where they were all located, and Kirk was asleep standing up, his head leaning against the stables.

Just seeing him made her feel more tired. She took a deep breath and inhaled the cool air, laced with the scent of fall.

Something sharp and forceful smashed against her head, and after several days of sleepless nights, Elodie finally slept.

Chapter Twenty-Five

SHE OPENED her eyes but was greeted with the same darkness. It surrounded her.

Her whole world shook and jumped, jostling her in every direction. Light filtered through small cracks, casting a dazed light, but still, she couldn't fully see.

Her arm scraped against something rough and hard and she flinched away only to bump into something else. Her heart raced, threatening to jump out of her chest. She felt around, looking for an opening, but she was surrounded by rough pine wood on all sides.

Her heart beat faster.

Her legs were cramped, scrunched up underneath her. She tried to stretch out, but the bottom of the box was just as hard and solid.

She was trapped.

Panic overwhelmed her. She couldn't be trapped again. This had to be a dream. It was just a dream. She breathed deep but before she could exhale the rumbling stopped.

"Do you hear that?"

Elodie froze so she could listen, but her heart was beating so loudly she had to strain to hear over it.

"She's awake. Told you we shoulda got a better mage," a rough male voice said.

It wasn't a dream. Her hands trembled on her legs.

"It'll be fine. Let me fetch him," a second voice said.

Her head spun. And she hoped they were getting Gedas. But no, that was wrong. Gedas was hurt. He was still in a coma. She needed to check on him, see if her potion worked. Her head pounded something fierce. Perhaps from all the caffeine, or the lack of sleep. She didn't understand where she was, or why she couldn't get out.

"Help me," she called. "Please."

The rough voice laughed cruelly. "Yeah, we'll help all right."

Her head ached. She reached up, wedging her arm past the wood, and felt the top of her head. She winced. It was tender and had a large knot. Then she remembered leaving the bordello, set on heading to the castle, and the sharp crack on her head. Cold fire raced down her spine.

She couldn't be in danger. Ravid was supposed to be helping her. This couldn't really be happening.

More voices spoke, low and soft. She couldn't make it out. There was a click like a lock opening, then light flooded in, blinding her. She shielded her eyes and saw the outline of a head. A man leaned in toward her, something in his hand. He looked familiar. Blond curls, blue eyes. He looked like one of the mage apprentices she'd seen around Tross when she was younger.

"Help me, please."

The man grimaced and pressed something cool against her forehead, and again she sank into sleep.

"THIS IS GOING WELL," a voice said out of the gloom.

Elodie sat up. She was sitting on a wooden bench, a large oak tree at her back. The quad of her high school stretched out before her. The space looked odd and foreign with no students milling about on their way to class or eating lunch. The sun was low in the sky, casting a warm glow on her face.

"Don't you agree?"

Elodie turned to her side, and instead of Vanessa on the bench next to her, eating her lunch, there was Ravid sunning himself, stretched out on the narrow bench. He looked carefree and at peace in the sun, leaning back with his legs crossed in a pair of faded jeans, one bare foot dancing in the air to a beat Elodie couldn't hear.

"What are we doing here?"

"Well, we aren't 'here' exactly," Ravid said, looking around them. "Nasty place, this illusion. No ruakh in the air making it livable."

"Why are we here, Ravid?"

"Well if you're just gonna be rude, I'll leave."

"Yes, great. That would be preferable."

"Well fine, I know when I'm not wanted." He stood up and stretched like a cat. "I was going to give you information, relieve your worried mind, all that, but if you don't want to know, I will just see myself out of your mind."

"Wait, where am I actually?" Elodie asked.

Ravid grinned. "See? You do care. You're somewhere between Comak and Tross. The details aren't that important."

"They're kind of important to me."

He sighed exaggeratedly. "You are in a little tiny box on your way to Oburleck, so we could properly spice things up. You and your knight were too good at avoiding him, so I had to make a few adjustments. That Tristan kid really is a good tool, I might need to use him again one day."

"Wait, what?"

"Tristan. He sold you out. Really, can't you follow a basic plot? It didn't take much either, just had him run into a few of the late Lord Byron's men. Nice kill from your knight there, by the way. I was on the edge of my seat watching. It really could have gone either way. But the effortless way he just cut off his head. Beautiful."

Elodie felt sick. She wanted the conversation to end already. She wished she had never agreed to anything with this god. He was only causing chaos.

"Okay great, so thankful for the chat. Is there anything else I should know?"

"Na, just have fun and try to live a little. It's not every day you get to live through attempted regicide, especially when you're the regent. Now get some sleep, cupcake."

With a rush, curtains closed in her mind and she fell back into darkness.

Chapter Twenty-Six

SHE WAS COLD. Her side ached from laying on the hard surface. She rolled over and the clanking of chains brought her fully awake. It was dark, except for one lone point of steady blue light just out of view. Her heart was racing, but she pushed down the panic and stilled herself. She was in control here. She couldn't force herself calm in a dream, but she had power over her waking mind. She was not going to cower.

As she tried to sit up, the rasping sound of chains dragging against stone startled her, she froze. The chains were attached to her, to her ankle. Her body trembled as panic took over, but this time she couldn't push it down. She'd been chained before in a dark hole, and she'd been just as helpless then as she was now. She'd only escaped because Gedas and Silas and Jesper were there to rescue her. But Ravid had said she was somewhere between Comak and Tross. No one would know where to look this time. Gedas didn't have his magic, if he was even still alive.

The thought sobered her and she took a deep breath.

She could do it this time. She could save herself. Her magic failed at breaking chains once before, but she'd spent so many nights back in the illusion after waking from nightmares, reliving that day. She'd thought through how to do things differently, and now she just had to act and not let her panic get the best of her.

She sat up and leaned against a wall and looked over her surroundings. It was hard to tell in the dim light, but the floor was flat, with a thin layer of dirt and the walls looked carved out of stone. It looked oddly familiar.

There was a bucket in the corner with a horrible smell coming from it, and in front of her, there seemed to be an archway or exit where the light was trickling in. She was about to check how long her chain was so she could look further when footsteps echoed in the distance. Elodie cowered as far against the wall as she could.

As the feet grew near, so did the light until a short, round man appeared in the entrance of her alcove. He looked unwell. Sweat beaded on his red face. He held up a light stone in his hand, shining it through the entrance of the alcove, and looked in on her.

"Oh gods, she's awake." He turned away and staggered a little. Propping himself up on the wall, he unscrewed a flask and took a long drink. "Why they had to bring her here, I don't understand," he muttered to himself.

"Duke Devoss? Is that you?" Devoss was one of the councilmen. He supported Oburleck, but she'd never gotten the impression he was particularly dangerous.

"Ah, well, yes, Your Highness. Don't worry, you shouldn't be in there much longer, only a matter of time now until we deal with the matter at hand."

"Can you let me out? Do you have keys?"

"Let you out?" Devoss laughed. It was not a kind laugh. "Dear girl, are you a moron? No, you must be killed before you disappear back into that illusion of yours or Oburleck will have my neck. But don't fret. We will make it quick."

"You, you can't kill me."

"Well, me? No, definitely not." He turned toward her but didn't come any closer. "Byron was supposed to do it of course, but he had to go and get himself killed. I don't like getting my hands dirty. Byron didn't mind. He enjoyed the mess. The messier the better, really," Devoss chuckled like he'd made a great joke.

"Why are you doing this?"

"Well, you have to understand, I didn't exactly start by wanting things to end like this. I just wanted to get richer, but these sorts of things do tend to spiral." He took another deep drink from his flask. "Oh well. There's nothing for it now. I will have to get one of Byron's men to do it. Why they didn't just kill you back in Comak, I will never know, but it's so hard to find good help that can think for themselves. Don't fret Princess, we won't drag out the affair."

Devoss stepped back, and the light receded as he retreated down the hall.

She would not panic.

Her hands shook. Sweat dripped down her face. She took a deep breath. She could panic later, when this was all over. Right now, she needed to think.

The last time she'd been kidnapped she'd tried to use a strawberry seed, blown into the cave on the wind or left behind by an animal. She'd grown the plant using her magic alone and threaded it through the lock trying to break it.

It hadn't worked.

At the time, she'd spent weeks trying to avoid magic. It had been a really hard time in her life with her family, and she thought embracing magic in the Twoshy would make it harder for her to play at being normal when back in the illusion. She wasn't sure if it had helped her in the illusion, but abandoning her magic had made life in the Twoshy harder.

But now Elodie had spent weeks accessing her magic over her journey. Never doing big or grand things but setting wards each night made the path to her magic familiar and easy to travel.

She crossed her legs with one slightly in front of the other and pulled her acorn out of her pocket. She held the acorn in her hand and set her hand on the ground next to the leg irons. Closing her eyes, she took a deep breath and reached down into her magic where the small blue fire lay. She poked at it gently and pulled a long root of it back with her as she returned to her mind and found the small spark of familiar, potential life inside of the acorn. With her spark of blue fire, Elodie asked the ruakh all around her to wake up the acorn and start it on its path of germination.

She closed her eyes tightly and tried to sink into the magic, letting it work around her, shaping and directing it as it went.

It hadn't worked with the strawberry. Strawberries were some-what invasive, but they snuck and crept. They didn't break and destroy.

"I can help with that," a voice seemed to speak into the back of her mind.

Elodie gritted her teeth. "I'm fine, thanks," she said out loud. Ravid didn't speak again, and Elodie returned to her magic.

Oak trees were strong and peaceful, but they could break and destroy over time. The cement in her school quad cracked and buckled where the oak at its center had pushed up roots, the same oak that had dropped this acorn.

As the seedling grew, Elodie felt restricted and pinched. She channeled her will into the tree, making its bark strong. She willed all the strength and power of the future oak tree into that small stretch of bark where wood met the iron of the lock and asked it to grow within, not around.

She didn't know how long she sat there, pushing away thoughts of her body's discomforts, sitting on the cold stone, unmoving and tense. The process was so slow, the tree growing and the metal of the lock expanding. After a long moment, there was a sharp snap and her eyes fluttered open. The room swam before her and she leaned her head back against the hard stone wall. She was exhausted. More than she had been before being kidnapped, after several sleepless nights.

She reached for the lock on her ankle but couldn't move her hand. Something thick and friendly gripped her fingers. It took a few moments of blinking in the near darkness and feeling around to understand what happened. The roots of the oak had grown down and wrapped around her hand, growing between her fingers in the absence of soil.

Gently, she pried her hand out of the webbing, careful not to damage the roots as she let it rest fully on the ground. The tree radi-ated pride and peace, and the simple emotions wanted Elodie to join them and spend the next season in slumber.

It took all her remaining will to stay awake and not drift off. She felt around for the metal of the lock. The tree had grown partly around the metal, but she could just grasp the clasp of the lock and pry it loose. The iron clanked as it fell against the wood of the tree, and Elodie straightened out her leg. Her muscles rebelled as she moved, and she bit back a cry of pain.

She looked down on the black outline of the misshapen oak tree and patted one of its bare thin branches.

"I'll come back for you. Plant you somewhere sunny and warm," she told the tree.

She'd been in one position so long her limbs felt as though they had turned to wood when offering the tree her strength in the fight against the lock. When her feet were under her, it was a struggle to stand. Her legs were cramped and not used to the weight or motion. She braced against the wall of her alcove and breathed. She needed a weapon.

Her first step was a little shaky, but she didn't fall.

Eventually her muscles loosened and she got into a rhythm of walking. Just outside of her alcove, she could finally see the light. It was a small light rock perched on a small stone shelf. She took the rock and shined it down both ends of the small hall her alcove was in the middle of. There were similar alcoves up and down the hall, but they all looked to be empty. Elodie shivered. She didn't know what this place was, but it didn't feel right.

She picked a direction at random and started walking. The floor was mostly smooth, with dirt and grit and the occasional sharp rock making her wince as they stabbed her bare feet.

The hall ended with another intersection, and she wasn't sure where to go. She balled the light rock up in her shirt until its light was extinguished and waited for her eyes to adjust to the gloom, a trick Callie had taught her when teaching her to navigate similar tunnels under Tross. There was a faint light coming from the left, so she removed the stone from her shirt and headed in that direction.

Elodie suspected she was in those very same tunnels Callie had shown her, but if she was right or wrong wouldn't make much difference at the moment. When she reached the end of the next path, an odd smell hit her. It felt familiar somehow and sent chills down her spine. There was a strong glow coming from further down the next turn, with a few light stones perched along the walls. Below the nearest light stone sat a man slumped in a chair before a similar alcove Elodie had been chained in, only this one had an iron grate blocking the entrance.

There was a mop sitting in a bucket leaning against the wall next to her, and Elodie snatched it up, slipping the light stone in her pocket. As she drew closer, she knew her guess was correct. The slumped figure was Devoss, a half-empty bottle of amber liquid in his hand.

She stepped on a sharp rock and winced, the rock scattering on the floor.

Devoss sat up at the sound, blinking in the light. His eyes connected with Elodie and she raised the mop in defense.

"Oh gods." He rubbed a hand down his face and took a long drink from the bottle in his hand. "How did you get free? I could have sworn we locked the cuff properly. Listen, this is really too much, my girl. I've had a terrible day. Can't you just go back into the alcove and wait for someone to come for you?"

This close she could see his eyes were dim and glassy, and he didn't seem able to hold himself up quite straight.

Elodie gripped the mop harder. He didn't have a weapon, so attacking such a miserable mess of a man felt wrong, but she didn't trust him. "Now you're the one who's dim. Why should I let you kill me and take over my kingdom?" Elodie asked sarcastically, but Devoss didn't see the joke.

"Because then we could get rich and put this whole messy regicide plot behind us. Really, Oburleck has talked of little else for the last two years. Always asking for so many favors. It's been quite exhausting if you must know the truth."

"Yeah, that's not gonna work for me." She raised the mop higher but paused before bringing it down.

Something moved in the darkness behind Devoss. It sent a chill down her spine, and she took a step back. Her eyes focused on those metal bars and her heart raced. It took her a moment to realize Devoss had stood.

"Now then, let's just be reasonable and go back to your cell, all right?" Devoss made a shooing motion with his arms, the liquid in the bottle making a sloshing noise. He took a staggering step forward, and Elodie spun the mop. It connected with his chest and she pushed him back. He staggered and tripped over his chair, then fell back against the grate. There was a loud thump and Devoss jostled as if something pushed up against his back. Then a long black chiton-covered arm snaked out of the bars and slashed down at his shoulder and into his skin. Devoss looked down at himself and the blood forming as if confused.

Beady, black eyes and sharp jaws surrounded by pedipalps looked out of the grate at her. There were two, maybe three bochnid locked up in that cell. Elodie took a shaky step back as more spindly claw-tipped legs came out and pinned the duke to the bars.

Elodie turned and fled toward the bright light at the end of the hall as Duke Devoss's screams echoed.

The light grew brighter and brighter until she came to the edge of a ledge. Looking up, she could see the soft glow of a morning or evening sky. It was a sinkhole. Tross was littered with them as the city collapsed in inconvenient places. This one was vast and had wooden scaffolding over it in places.

She was in Tross.

She looked around the walls lining the hole and sure enough came upon a spot where the stone was worn and easy footholds existed. It took her a few tries of gripping the stone before she could lift herself off the ground. Her arms shook with the effort and the rock cut into her bare feet. She climbed ten, then fifteen feet, still far from the light above. She wouldn't make it all the way out, not in one go, but another ledge and tunnel branched off parallel to the surface. It took the last of her strength to reach the new tunnel, and she sat on the edge, breathing heavy.

The tunnel was dark, but when she'd regained her footing, she pulled her light rock from her pocket and walked into the gloom. The path was long, and rose in a steady incline. Her feet left bloody tracks, a clear trail for anyone to follow, but there wasn't anything she could do to prevent it. Eventually she came to a few steps cut into the side of the tunnel ending in a wood panel painted the same dark gray as the stone. Pushing against it, the wood swung to the side, and Elodie shimmied through the opening into a small, dark room that smelled of cleaning herbs and moisture.

She cast her light rock around the closet. There was a door on the other side with light glowing out from the crack at the bottom. She closed the wooden flap behind her and twisted the handle on the door. The light was bright, and it took her eyes a second to adjust. Her nose needed no such time, and the smell of lavender, jasmine, and other perfumes reached her. She took a step into the hall. To her left was the unmistakable sight of the castle bathrooms.

She was in Tross. Her castle. The relief was overwhelming.

Elodie turned and found a mop bucket and puked into it. The stress of it all and the horrible death of Devoss followed by the sharp relief of being somewhere familiar that she associated with safety was too much. It had to come out one way or another. When she was done, she cleaned her face with shaky hands and turned into the larger of the two bathrooms. It was empty. No ladies soaked in the water, and no servants wandered about offering drying cloths or soaps. It was eerie to be there alone. Even in the early hours of the morning, this place always had a few visitors.

Elodie hobbled over to a cabinet that held a small kit of healer's supplies. The rocks were so sharp the cuts barely stung and her feet were cut up more than she'd realized. She cleaned her feet quickly with a strong soap that stung but helped to keep her mind sharp. When she was done, she rubbed a little ointment from one of the jars onto the thin, deep cuts. It was old and wouldn't be very effective, but it should help to keep out infection. She wrapped her feet in strips of drying cloths, making a semblance of slippers, and set off out of the baths before someone discovered her.

She wasn't sure where she was going. The castle was run by Oburleck, and it would be no safer than the tunnels. But the light, the familiar sounds and smells, and the extreme lack of bochnid made it the better choice. The halls were as empty as the baths.

She heard a noise and ducked into one of the laundry rooms. A handful of servants huddled in a corner behind one of the larger wash bins. They watched Elodie with wide eyes as she hobbled in.

"Where is the fighting happening?"

Most of them ducked, but one brave-looking girl with pretty

brown eyes pointed up. Elodie nodded and left. She found a servant's staircase and headed to the next floor. The kitchens were on this end, and that seemed like a fine place to get more directions from any hiding cooks. She turned down a corner and came face to helmet with a knight, sword drawn high over their head.

Chapter Twenty-Seven

ELODIE FLINCHED and lifted the mop, but no strike came.

The knight lifted the visor of their helmet, and Dess's worried blue eyes peered out at her. Relief washed over Elodie, and she sagged.

"Oh my gods, Elodie. What happened to you?"

Elodie looked down. Her tunic was torn and dirty, and her breeches had a big rip in one leg where she'd had to pry it out from within the new oak tree. Her feet looked brutal, all wrapped up in torn cloth.

"I'm fine, where is everyone else?"

"Silas is looking for you still. The others . . . Let's get to Tim."

As Dess led Elodie down the hall, her sword stayed out and she insisted on clearing a corner before Elodie could follow. She explained they'd been in Tross since early that morning tracking her through the city. Silas had been going crazy getting close but not being able to find her. That afternoon, those who Silas had rallied over the last few months started a revolt. Anyone who stood down was not killed, but the key players who'd supported Oburleck without hesitation were being removed permanently.

Oburleck had escaped when Dess's old knight master had cornered him. He convinced those around him he was on their side and barricaded himself in his rooms with a large number of his own personal guard.

Dess and a few others were trying to clear the castle of anyone still under Oburleck's influence. "This whole thing is a mess," she told Elodie. "I don't relish the job the new council will have trying to clean it up."

"How's Gedas?"

"Better. They fed him that potion you made, and he woke up the next morning. Silas was going mad looking for you, and Gedas made him a charm to track you down. We left him in Comak with Allen, Kat, and Tristan."

Elodie grimaced. Tristan had been the one to rat her out. He told her he wasn't making promises about not telling anyone she left, but instead of telling Silas and the others, he'd told Byron's men. Ravid had used him, just like he'd used her. She didn't know where that put him for how she should trust him in the future. She would have to talk to someone about it. Silas, or maybe Sam.

They took a servant's staircase up a few flights to the residential floors where many lords and ladies had rooms in the castle. Elodie had to pause on the top landing, her muscles aching and her breaths coming in ragged gasps. After weeks of travel and exercise, she'd gained good endurance but growing the oak had taken most of her strength.

Moving down a silent corridor, they encountered a guard standing at the top of a hall. Dess nodded to him and he stepped out of the way, his eyes on Elodie as he bowed.

"Guards don't bow," Dess drawled as she passed. The man straightened and blushed.

They moved halfway down the hall, and Dess knocked on a door in a pattern of three knocks followed by two more.

Someone opened the door and Dess moved out of the way and gestured for Elodie to enter first. It was Lord Riyan. His face was cracked with thick wrinkles, but his brown eyes were sharp.

"Your Highness." He bent in a half bow, which looked like quite the feat. Elodie rushed to help him straighten, but he waved her off and grabbed the door for support. "Well don't just stand there gaping. Come in before someone sees you, my lady."

Elodie moved into the room. Bookshelves lined the walls, neat and organized, with wooden chairs and tables set about in convenient locations. On the far end of the room was a desk covered in papers, books, and maps. A familiar-looking man bent over the papers making notes and scribbling fiercely.

"Tim, come greet our newest arrival," the old man called as he walked slowly to a high-backed, wooden chair by the fire.

Tim looked up at them and dropped his quill. "Uh—" He stood up and bowed formally. "Your High—Highness," he stammered.

"Relax Tim, she doesn't like overly formal greetings, remember?" Dess said.

The man looked pained as if unsure of what he should do.

"Where are the others?" Dess asked, and his face relaxed.

He looked down at his notes. "Um, Rogers and Christopher have Baron Gregor tied up on the fifth floor, his men are disarmed and locked in a dressing room. Sam and Kirk are on the third floor heading toward the steward's rooms, and Finley and Jace neutralized two mages by the library but are having trouble with a few soldiers. They need backup."

Dess grimaced. "I will head there now. Message Silas and tell him to get back to us."

Tim nodded. Dess left without another word and Elodie moved closer to the desk as Tim picked up an orb. He gripped it in his hands and closed his eyes tight. The orb lit and he spoke into it. "Silas, are you there?"

Elodie hurried her pace so she could see the knight. "Tim, what do you have to—" The voice cut off sharply and Elodie could see movement in the orb before a sudden bright flash, and the orb went out.

"What does that mean?" Elodie asked, her heart racing.

Tim snorted. "He dropped it, the klutz. It flashes like that when it smashes." Tim realized who he was talking to and his eyes went wide and he ducked his head.

Elodie decided to ignore his awkwardness. "Do you know where he was headed?"

"Um, he was following your trail and ended up on the other end of the practice fields. He thought maybe you were underground and mentioned you told him there were tunnels, so he was looking for a sinkhole," Tim said, shrugging like he thought it was a bad idea.

"Our knight is a smart one. I was in the tunnels. Devoss had me chained up."

"What? We've been looking for him. Is he still down there?"

Elodie shivered. "I don't think we have to worry about him anymore."

The orb on the desk lit up and Elodie crowded in hoping to see Silas as Tim picked it up and squeezed. Instead, she saw Kirk's grinning face.

"Hey man, we're just outside Mister Stink Breath's rooms. A bunch of men just came out, and my fair lady subdued them."

"Kirk!" Sam sighed in the background.

"Anyway, we're gonna head in and see if we can tie up this dude or something."

"No, stand down. Don't engage Oburleck without backup," Tim said.

"Come on man, can't you send some backup or something? Let's just end this already."

"Hold position and stay ready for new orders."

"Will do," Sam said leaning in close to the orb, edging out Kirk's face.

"Come on, woman, you have no sense of adventure," Kirk's voice said faintly before a hand filled the view and the orb went out.

Tim sighed and looked over his notes. Elodie glanced around the tidy sitting room. She needed something to protect herself. She wandered into Lord Riyan's inner rooms and found a cupboard in his dressing room with his armor and weapons. She strapped a belt to her waist and grabbed a dagger, then found a bow and strapped a quiver over her shoulder.

His boots were too big for her, but she stripped off her tied cloth and pulled on a pair of thick socks that had soft grippy strips along the bottom, like the magical version of rubber. It would keep her from slipping on the smooth floors, and as long as she didn't go outside, she would be fine. Entering his bedroom she dug around in a drawer by his bed until she found a small vial of silver powder. Silverstone, it would be perfect.

When she reentered the sitting room, Riyan's eyes followed her.

"Going somewhere, my lady?"

"Sorry for the impertinence, my lord." She blushed as Riyan glanced at the bright yellow socks on her feet. "May I have some of your hot water?"

As she reached for the tea kettle hanging by the fire, his sharp eyes missed nothing. "That is dangerous stuff in the wrong hands."

Elodie picked a fresh teacup and poured an inch of water into the bottom. "Lucky for me, I've had Gedas guiding my hands for most of my life." She took the cork out of the small vial and carefully tapped a finger against the side until a small mist of powder fell into the cup. She tapped it again.

"That's too much," the lord said, reaching for her hand.

"It will be fine. I'm young and my heart is strong." She recorked the vial and handed it back to the lord who tucked it into his breast pocket.

"Your life is not your own, Your Highness. You owe your life to all who fight to stop Oburleck and all those who would suffer if you were to die without an heir."

Elodie swirled the water in the cup until it was murky and gray. She gave it a few blows to cool it. "You're right, my lord. But I don't plan to be the kind of ruler who sits by while others risk their lives for her when she's perfectly able to help."

She put the cup to her lips and tipped it back, drinking it in one go.

"I see," Lord Riyan said.

Elodie turned to the squire. "Tim, tell Sam and Kirk I'm backup and I'm coming."

The squire turned pale. "I don't think that's such a good idea," he began.

"Don't worry. I got this," she said and stepped out the door into the hall. Kirk wouldn't wait to move on Oburleck, he was too impulsive and too sure of his ability to outtalk anyone. Sam would follow orders, unless Kirk talked her out of it and encouraged her that she could do it, that they could do it together. She had to help them.

She turned toward the closest staircase, but the stimulant she'd taken hit her all at once. Cold fire raced up her bones radiating out until her muscles twitched and her skin tingled. It was sensory overload, it was strength, it was power. Silverstone powder was used for the elderly in very careful and very small doses, to help them manage the fading of their life. It would give someone frail and old the strength to do everyday tasks like open a door to friends like Riyan had.

Elodie had taken too much, but she was positive it wouldn't stop her heart.

The fire danced up and down her spine, then into her neck and her skull, then back down to her toes.

She was mostly sure it wouldn't stop her heart.

It was all she could do to hang on as the stimulus worked its way through her system. Eventually, the cold fire fled from her body and she was left shaking on the ground, her knees curled to her chest. She didn't remember falling. It was another minute before she could move, and another still before she could sit up without her head spinning. She used the wall to help herself stand, but when her legs were finally under her, they felt strong. Her mind was alert and sharp, and her body felt wonderful.

The crash would be intense when the stimulant wore off, but until then she would use this to help her friends. She strung her bow with ease and grabbed an arrow to be ready. She walked down the corridor with a renewed bounce in her step. The guard looked at her with open shock as she moved past him and smiled, but he didn't try to stop her. Oburleck's rooms were two floors up and a good bit to the east, closer to Elodie's own rooms.

As she went, she came across men and women lying dead in the halls. It made her stomach turn, but she gritted her teeth and stepped past. The fallen mostly wore the purple and gold of Oburleck's colors, but a few clad in the yellow and gray of Aluna were also down.

It made her sick thinking of men and women dead, all because Oburleck had manipulated his way into a rebellion, and they had followed orders. The arrow in her hand felt heavy and not because her strength was failing.

She made it to Oburleck's floor and was a few corridors away before she encountered anyone living. The soldier wore purple and gold and was about Elodie's age. His armor was a little too small, and something about his posture made him seem younger.

"Stop! I have orders to keep anyone from passing!" His spear shook in his grip.

Elodie notched her arrow and brought the bow up in proper form. She drew back and leveled the arrow at the boy. "I don't want to hurt you," she called.

"S—stop!" he called again and lowered his spear to point at her.

If she engaged, she had to shoot to kill. She wasn't sure she had it in her to kill someone following bad orders, but if she missed, he would kill her. She took a step forward.

"I said stop!" The boy shouted and moved toward her. When Elodie didn't stop moving, he yelled a war cry, running right for her.

Elodie took a deep breath and sighted. She wasn't a great shot, but this was a close distance. Her heart raced but her hands were steady. She released, and the arrow sprouted from the boy's shoulder. He cried out and fell. Elodie rushed to his side and kicked his spear out of the way before kneeling. The wound was in the fleshy part of his shoulder. It wouldn't kill him if he had help soon. She exhaled relief.

"Don't worry," she said to the boy. "This isn't a bad wound. Stay down, don't cause any more trouble, and when this is over someone will be by to bring you to a healer. Okay?"

The boy gritted his teeth, and nodded, his eyes clouded with fear and pain.

"Don't worry." She patted the boy's leg and stood again. She drew another arrow and moved further down the hall. Turning a corner two more soldiers in purple and gold jogged down the hall toward her, alerted by the boy's yelling.

When they saw her, they accelerated. The woman on the left pulled out a sword, and the man held a spear. They weren't young inexperienced fighters. Elodie notched the arrow, not sure who to aim at first.

She decided on the spear. It was longer so it might reach her first. She drew back, took a deep breath, and sighted.

Something large and quick brushed past her jostling the bow, and Elodie stepped aside quickly as a large knight in chain mail and leather dove past her and engaged with the soldiers. He cut the head off the spear and kicked the swordswoman in the stomach in one move, then bashed the spearless man on the head with the butt of his sword causing him to crumble. The woman regained her balance and came for him. The two fighters spun in a cascade of clashes and shining metal. The woman met him blow for blow until Silas got his blade under her guard and the soldier's sword went flying.

Silas caught her in an arm hold and spun the soldier around until his arm was around her neck and he squeezed. After a long moment, the woman grew limp and Silas lowered her to the ground gently.

Silas turned and their eyes connected. His face was furious. "You just had to go wandering off through the market by yourself!" he growled and took a few long strides toward her. He was an intimidating figure wrapped in leather and iron. Elodie's heart raced.

"You say that like I get kidnapped all the time."

"Twice! That's twice, in the same market even!" There was a small vein on his forehead that was pulsing a little, and his eyes glowed green.

Oh, he was so cute when he was mad.

Gods, what was wrong with her?

Another man came running down the hall toward them and Silas disarmed him in three moves, then hit him on the head knocking him out.

"This is going to be a mess to clean up," Silas sighed.

"You'll help me though, right?"

He leaned down until his face was inches from hers. "As long as you have need of me, I will be there," he said, but the fire and anger still lingered.

Another man came around the corner, ruining the moment. "Speaking of which," Elodie drawled. Two more soldiers appeared behind the first.

"Stop!" Silas called, and they hesitated. "The council has spoken. Oburleck's position as steward has been revoked and his honor is no more. Oburleck is accused of attempted regicide. Choose which side you will die on." Silas raised his sword ready for combat.

"The whole council's really on our side?" Elodie whispered.

Silas shrugged. "We killed the ones who disagree, so yes," he said, low enough so only she could hear.

The soldiers glanced at each other, then at their unconscious comrades on the floor. The brown-haired woman was the first to lower her sword. She sighed. "You speak the truth, yes? We don't have to fight anymore?"

"On my honor," Silas said boldly.

"Mine too," Elodie added. "I can promise I've never committed treason. Oburleck just wanted to kill me because he wanted more gold and power."

The woman looked at the redhead beside her, and he shrugged. "Thank the gods," she announced.

Silas nodded. "Tell your comrades to stand down. Any who leave now will not be harmed."

The soldiers sheathed their swords and turned back down the corridor they came from. "Will do!" the redhead called back.

"Thanks for sparing us, Sir Knight!" said the woman.

Elodie glanced at Silas who smirked. "Like I said, the people were never really behind Oburleck to begin with. Once they are out of his reach, it doesn't take much to convince them."

"Maybe not for you," Elodie remarked. "I don't think it would take much convincing for anyone to follow you."

He turned and looked at her, his green eyes now calm and curious. "What is that supposed to mean?"

Elodie grinned. "I don't think we have the time for me to explain."

"Right." Silas got back to business. "Where are you heading? You weren't planning on taking out Oburleck on your own, were you?" He was grinning a little. Elodie would have hit him if his armor wouldn't have hurt her hand.

"Sam and Kirk were outside of Oburleck's rooms waiting for backup, but I didn't think they would wait long enough for real backup."

Silas looked down at Elodie's yellow socks. "And you thought you would help?"

Elodie shrugged. "It was between Riyan and me, who would you have sent?"

Silas grew thoughtful. "Hmm, I might have to think on that one."

Elodie did hit him then, and it did hurt her hand, but she hid the wince. When she met Silas's eyes again, he was watching her as if looking her over for wounds. "Shall we go rescue your friends?"

"You mean you aren't going to lock me in some safe room while you go do the things?"

Silas shrugged and straightened an armor strap on his arm. "Then I would waste time trying to find someone big enough and courageous enough to keep you from escaping while I rescued your friends, and I don't think there's anyone on eres capable of that."

"Fair enough. Shall I lead?"

Silas nodded, and Elodie started down the hall.

Chapter Twenty-Eight

SHE TRIED to clear the corners like a properly-trained person, but she was sure Silas was grinning behind her. With a bow, it made sense for her to go in front, so she didn't accidentally shoot Silas, but he was the one with experience.

More bodies lined the halls the closer they came. Some were breathing shallowly, just unconscious, but others were bloody and still. The hall outside of Oburleck's rooms was clear. Elodie and Silas exchanged glances. Sam and Kirk must have gone inside. Either they were under Oburleck's power, or they had captured him.

"Remember," Silas said to her. "You know what's true. Remember that and his breath won't work on you."

Elodie nodded once and notched the arrow on her bow. She drew it back to a firing position, and Silas kicked in the door with one powerful blow. The door blew open, and a wave of rancid breath rushed over Elodie.

"Stop," a voice called to her.

Elodie stopped. She lowered the bow, not wanting to hurt anyone.

"Ah, Princess, so wonderful to see you. And you brought your favorite knight. How charming. Won't you come in?"

Elodie nodded to Oburleck and stepped into the room, Silas at her back. She stopped. She needed to be on guard, but it was a little hard to remember why. Oburleck was so gracious, he was just being nice, even if his breath did stink.

Silas shook his head oddly, then bumped into her harshly. The action jolted her for a moment, and she remembered. Oburleck was the enemy. He wasn't friendly, and he couldn't be trusted.

His persuasion had never been so strong before. Oburleck used reason and arguments just as much as magic to win people to his side, but this was a different level than he'd reached even in Silas's shared memories.

Elodie raised her bow again and glanced around. Kirk sat tied to a chair, a gag in his mouth and his eyes frantic. Sam stood by, smiling softly at Elodie.

"Ah, none of that, please," Oburleck said, and a rush of stench rushed over her again. "Your Highness, would you mind giving your bow over to your lovely friend?"

Sam walked to Elodie and held out her hand. It was so nice of Sam to take it for her. She wanted to keep it, but if Oburleck wanted Sam to have it, that was probably best. He was just helping. She handed the bow over.

"Elodie, don't," Silas ground out. But Sam already had the bow in her hand and took it back over to the other side of the room.

"Ah, Sir Silas. You want to do what you can to protect this kingdom, right?" Oburleck asked. Silas frowned but nodded. Oburleck took a step closer to them and another wave of stench washed over them. His blue tunic was torn at the collar. Elodie hoped he was okay. Oburleck was a good man. "Protecting this kingdom, keeping it safe, it's one of the most important things in the world to you, isn't it?"

Another step, and another wave of stench. Elodie rocked back slightly on her heels trying to avoid it. Her eyes watered.

"Yes," Silas ground out.

Another step. "Good, very good. That is after all, what we all want here. To protect the Kingdom of Aluna, to make it better." Another step. "All I want is for this kingdom to prosper, for Aluna to prosper and blossom into the best empire it can be. That doesn't sound so terrible. Does it, Sir Silas?" Another step.

The smell was starting to lessen, or at least Elodie was beginning to get used to it. Oburleck was making a lot of sense, but Silas stood quiet at her side, his sword in hand, but in a resting position. He was being a bit rude not responding to Oburleck.

Muffled cries drew Elodie's eyes back to the other end of the room where Kirk sat thrashing against his binds, his eyes wide. Sam stood nearby looking down at him, concerned. Elodie rolled her eyes. Kirk was always saying stupid things. Maybe Sam had tied him up to be funny. She hoped he hadn't offended Oburleck.

"Sir Silas, you are by far one of the most courageous and intelligent knights in Aluna's arsenal. You know the state of the kingdom better than many others. While our heir is tied up in magic and spells the kingdom suffers. We must rectify this."

Elodie's heart deflated. He was right. Her kingdom suffered because she couldn't be there for it. She sometimes didn't even want to be there for it. Even if they did break the spell, Aluna would be so much better off without her.

"Don't you agree, my lord," Oburleck asked.

"Yes," Silas agreed with a surety that made Elodie's heart fall.

"Good, very good," Oburleck took the last few steps to them. He reached out and put his hand under Elodie's chin until she looked at him. "You do understand the kingdom would be better off without you, don't you?"

Something hot and warm rolled down her cheek. His words were so gentle, so right. She nodded.

"Good. See, Sir Silas? Even she agrees it is in Aluna's best interest if you remove her from the equation."

Elodie frowned. She looked up at Silas. The sword was still in his hand, and he was looking at her with intense concentration; his green eyes were a little glassy, but fixed so completely on her.

"Sir Silas, help us make Aluna a better place. Do what's right by your kingdom," Oburleck ordered. "Princess, tell him to do it."

Elodie shook her head slightly. Silas wouldn't. He could never hurt her, even if it was better for everyone else. But the knight lifted his sword. His focus on her it made her heart race. She trusted him completely.

"Tell him," Oburleck commanded, the words wrapping around her like a physical force.

Tears fell down her face. She had to obey, she had to do what was best for Aluna. "Silas, save Aluna," she said.

Silas lifted his sword and moved in one powerful moment. The sword glinted through the air as it flew and sliced into its target with a solid finality. Hot wet liquid sprayed Elodie, as Oburleck's head thudded on the ground. Elodie let out a shaky breath and Silas dropped his sword. He reached out and pulled her into an embrace. She wrapped her arms around him, not even minding being smashed against the metal of his armor. His hand stroked the back of her head gently as her mind cleared of the fog, and her body shook from the adrenaline.

"What," a weak voice sounded behind them. Muffled yelling filled the air, suddenly louder as if someone had turned off a noise machine.

Elodie took a step back and Silas released her but didn't move away. Sam stood next to Kirk, a confused expression on her face.

"Sam, are you back with us?"

"I—" Sam looked at Kirk tied to the chair and then down at Oburleck's body and the growing red stain. "I can't believe I—" She put a hand over her mouth, her face contorting in pain.

Kirk made a noise that sounded an awful lot like "Helloooo?"

Sam blinked and started untying the knots.

Elodie looked down as the warm puddle spread. "Ew, I think I ruined Riyan's socks."

Silas took her hand and helped her step around the puddle. "I don't think he will mind. Sam, do you have an orb still?"

"Uh, it's in Kirk's front pocket, I think."

Silas reached into his pocket to remove the orb while Kirk kept talking nonsense through the gag.

"Shouldn't we remove that first?" Elodie asked, pointing at the gag.

"No, I think that's best where it is," Sam said. She untied another knot and one of the ropes went loose.

Kirk managed to pull out an arm and removed the gag. "Seriously guys? I'm the only one who keeps my head, yet you think censoring me is the right choice?"

"I think Oburleck's the only one who really lost their head," Silas added.

It was too much, Elodie started laughing and stripped off her bloody socks.

Silas grinned at her then turned and started communicating through the globe to Tim.

"So what happened exactly?" Elodie untied one of Kirk's legs. She looked at Sam who only shook her head, frowning.

"Well, we decided to come put a stop to Mister Stink over there, but my girl here started losing her head when he told her he was a friend and on our side. Apparently, his magic didn't work on me so well, you know, since I'm so charismatic myself. Anyway. He tells Sam to tie me up, and I don't wanna fight her, so I let her do it."

Elodie glanced at Sam, who was frowning. Sam shook her head. "I don't know. It was a bit of a blur. But I do remember being a little more forceful than strictly necessary with getting him in the chair."

Kirk rubbed his head. "Hey, no hard feelings. You're still my number one."

Sam rolled her eyes while she fought off a grin.

CLEANUP WOULD TAKE A LONG TIME, Elodie knew. They took care of the wounded first, Elodie helping with healing and stitching as needed. When she patched the shoulder of the boy she'd shot, he was terrified to learn who she was. She didn't try to talk to him, to help ease the awkwardness.

After the wounded were found, the dead were retrieved. Too many men and women had died because of Oburleck's plans, and they wouldn't be the last.

Silas and Jesper led the cleanup. Tim had organized the operation not only in Tross but also in a few key cities around Aluna, while Silas and Jesper relied on men and women they trusted to carry out the acts. Captives, those who supported or actively assisted Oburleck were being brought into Tross. There would be trials for some and executions for many. Elodie would watch as was her duty, even if it would only create a few more years' worth of nightmares and horrors for her to get over.

Elodie kept working for another twelve hours, tending to soldiers who'd fought for her and others who hadn't. She didn't care which end the injured were on, men and women following orders or brainwashed by magic shouldn't be held accountable for the actions of those giving the orders. She was cleaning a wound on the arm of a kitchen maid who'd tried to stop one of Oburleck's men from hurting a boy when the silverstone in Elodie's system finally wore off, and she passed out.

Chapter Twenty-Nine

WHEN SHE AWOKE, she felt safe. She didn't know anything at first, except for the familiar sound of pages turning and slow, even breathing. It was almost enough to send her back into a peaceful snooze, until she realized why the breathing brought her peace. She turned over and wedged open her eyes to see Gedas sitting in the big chair by her bed reading. It was such a familiar scene her eyes watered with relief. She buried her head in her blankets until she had more control, then surfaced again. He still looked old and frail, like Riyan, but seeing him alive and awake was such a comfort.

She peeled back the blankets and climbed from the high padded bed. Her legs were a little unsteady, but she lowered herself to the floor next to Gedas's feet and took his hand.

"There now, my Gull," he said. Hearing the endearment again, when she feared for so long that she wouldn't see him again made her eyes sting, and she buried her face in the blanket covering his knees. They sat like that for a long moment while he stroked her back gently.

She was home at last, in a safe and warm place. The relief was overwhelming.

There was a soft knock and Elodie wiped her face quickly on her nightshirt as the door opened and Mistress Piera, Elodie's old maid, entered carrying a tea tray. When she spotted Elodie, she curtseyed.

"Your Highness, I'm glad to see you awake at last." She set the tray on a small table.

"It's good to see you too," Elodie said with a smile. "How long have I been out?"

"You mean after draining yourself magically and then taking several doses of silverstone until you dropped?" Gedas said, a little steel back in his voice.

"Three days, Your Highness." Mistress Piera bowed again, with a dry expression. "I will leave you to it."

Elodie winced.

Gedas sighed. "Will you make the tea?"

Elodie rose and crossed to the tea tray. She felt great for being out for three days. A nice long bath and she would be as good as new. After handing Gedas a cup of tea, she settled on her bed, cross-legged with her own cup. She covered her legs with a blanket to ward off the chill.

"So, tell me what I missed. What happened to you?"

Gedas closed his eyes and took a long sip of tea. He held the silence for a long time, but Elodie didn't interrupt. If she did, he probably wouldn't tell her anything. She brought her own tea to her nose and inhaled deeply. Peppermint rose around her and she let its peace seep into her.

"As you can likely guess, I was a fool and suffered for it by getting myself poisoned."

"Valo's peace," Elodie said. "I remembered, much later, reading about it in the same book that talked about the dragon's breath. It created a death-like paralysis and makes the breath smell like blueberries."

Gedas's eyebrows went up. "Well, that is one mystery solved then. Your potion was enough to help wake my body, and as my magic replenishes itself, I will only become stronger."

Elodie's eyes ran over his face again. He looked so frail that a strong breeze would blow him away. "You should have stayed in Comak until you're stronger."

"And miss seeing you, and what a beautiful young woman you are growing into? Never."

Elodie offered a weak smile.

"Don't worry about me, my Gull. I am stronger than I look." Elodie met his eyes, and he smiled sadly. "I stayed a few days longer in Comak than your knight did. I had your friend Kat to keep me company, and that unfortunate boy Allen to talk my ear off and keep my mind sharp."

"What about Tristan?"

Gedas's left eyebrow went up. "Ah, that one. He confessed he may have had a role to play in your disappearance, and Kat, fierce little thing that she is, threatened to curse him if he didn't leave."

Elodie sighed. "I feel bad. It was one of the gods. He's had this whole thing planned out and said he used Tristan to get me back to Tross."

Gedas stilled as alarm and something else crossed his face. On any other person she would have thought it was fear, but Gedas wasn't afraid of anything. "My Gull, you must be very careful when dealing with the gods. They will go to great lengths to get what they want from us."

"Yeah, I noticed that when the last one told me he prodded my steward into regicide just to shake things up a little."

Gedas closed his eyes for a long moment. When he opened them again, he looked sad. She didn't like him looking sad.

"So Allen got on your nerves then? You're like his biggest hero, if you didn't notice."

Gedas grimaced. "I thought he was just a score scavenger before I realized he does have a genuine thirst for knowledge and understanding. Not that it will do him much good. That boy is so busy convincing himself he's right, he doesn't have any time to learn anything from me or anyone else."

"That sounds about right. He hates me because of the prophecy. He doesn't see how someone as unskilled as I am in magic could ever break the spell." She didn't want to push the topic of the prophecy, she had in years past and Gedas always dismissed her questions. She didn't want to fight with him now. Not when he looked so ill and so old.

His face darkened.

"I have something I must tell you, my Gull. And I fear you may hate me for it."

"Gedas, I could never hate you."

"Don't make absolute statements before you know all the facts, my Gull."

Elodie smiled. It was such a Gedas thing to say, it made her hopeful her old mentor was still in there somewhere, under the gray and the wrinkles.

Gedas set down his tea and fiddled with his book, as if it was hard to get started. "I was a young man when the spell that took you entered the world, and when I spoke of the prophecy to your father, it was my interpretation I shared, not a true prophecy. This is why I wished you not to dwell on it. In so doing, I was afraid you would be locked on a course for your life, that mixed with your family curse would only ever cause you to fail disastrously."

A cold fear started to prick at the back of Elodie's mind and she itched at the birthmark on her collar. This birthmark, this family curse. Elodie had dismissed it when it came to breaking the spell, because she believed so completely that the prophecy said she would be the one to break it; she would not fail.

"What did the original prophecy say, Gedas? Who gave it?"

He still didn't meet her eyes. "The prophecy I referenced was never about the spell that traps you. It was about the man who cast it. The prophecy spoke of his ambition and his eventual downfall. The prophecy only stated that after a wrongdoing by the seabird king, the daughter of Aluna would be his undoing. At the time I believed the wrongdoing to be an act of your father's. I believed you would be the one to bring his undoing. But I was wrong."

"Who is he?"

"He is someone I knew a long time ago."

"But if my father wronged him, can't that mean I'm still the one from the prophecy?"

Gedas shook his head slowly. "I believe not. I don't believe your father ever really wronged the mage. Your father's actions were just and wise with hindsight."

"What were my father's actions?"

Gedas took another long sip of tea. This was the most information she'd gotten from him about her family and the spell, maybe ever. She hoped he didn't clam up again and go back to his usual methods of avoidance.

"The mage was looking for a position in Aluna, and your father turned him down. When the mage went to the next kingdom, your father sent a message warning them the mage may not be entirely safe. Given that the mage eventually cast a spell, trapping you and the other Misplaced in the illusion, I believe your father's actions were in the right. He sensed something in the mage's personality that had not yet made itself fully known."

"But he still could have done something, something small that was wrong and got the mage hurt. I could still be the one."

Gedas let out a breath slowly and then looked Elodie in the eyes for the first time. "My Gull, do you not see? The prophecy never spoke of the illusion or you breaking the spell. Only that the mage would have his downfall met by one of your line. Even if it is you, it does not mean you will ever break the spell."

The full weight of his words began to sink in. Allen would be so smug to know he was right.

"Fine," she said a little harshly, then softened her voice. "Fine. There is nothing saying I will break the spell. Maybe it will be one of the others, and I just help." It didn't matter if she wasn't destined to free them all. She could still try. "Gedas, can't you tell me what you know of the spell? Please?"

A tear fell out of Gedas's clear gray eye and rolled down his cheek. "My Gull," his voice cracked and Elodie's heart began to break. He cleared his throat. "I fear the spell cannot be broken. I have spent decades trying to unravel it. It has become my life's work, of which I am a failure. The spell cannot be broken. The cost is too high."

Elodie let his words soak in. Gedas was a wizard. One of the most powerful and knowledgeable Hu in the world. If he'd spent decades, how long would it take her and Allen? Hopelessness fell over her, but Elodie wouldn't accept it. She would be in control of her own destiny. That was all Gedas had told her. There was no prophecy guiding her steps. She would make it all on her own.

She got off the bed and wrapped a dressing gown around her shoulders before opening the door to her sitting room. As she suspected, a guard stood outside. Silas was sure to be a bit overprotective for a time. The man saw her and looked startled, then bowed.

"Would you ask Sir Silas to gather the remaining council for a meeting tomorrow at noon, and ask him to come as well?"

"Yes, Your Highness."

"Thank you." She closed the door and moved back to her bed. "Gedas, I know you will never take the post, but are there any mages in Aluna you trust for the council position?"

"I may have a few suggestions," he said, eyeing her wearily.

"I would appreciate them." She sighed. "I don't hold anything against you, Gedas. I don't begin to understand everything you know or why you haven't shared it sooner, but I trust you. And I'm not going to stop trusting you until you give me a reason to."

"That is very generous of you, my Gull." His voice sounded guarded, and he watched her closely as though unsure if she would attack. She didn't like feeling authority over him.

Elodie snorted. "I don't know if it's generous. Gedas, you're my oldest friend. The closest thing to family I have." His expression softened. "I would appreciate it if you agreed to correspond with Allen, tell him what you know of the spell, but I won't demand it." She sighed again. "We have a lot of work to do."

"Well one thing to cross off the list is killing the bochnid in the tunnels under the castle," Gedas said, changing the subject quite efficiently.

Elodie glanced up suddenly. She'd forgotten about the bochnid, and really didn't want to think about them again. "What happened?" she asked.

"Sir Silas took soldiers into the tunnels yesterday. They killed the bochnid and cleaned up some pincer fodder." Elodie blanched, but Gedas didn't pause to lament over the death of Devoss. "They happened across an oddly shaped oak tree with a pair of shackles half embedded in the bark."

Elodie grinned. "I promised the tree I would plant it somewhere sunny."

Gedas nodded. "It will be done then. A fitting reward if I do say so."

"I need a bath, but after, do you want to join me for lunch?" she asked.

"I think I might be better off taking an afternoon nap if you don't mind." Gedas braced himself on the arms of the chair and rose shakily. She'd seen him do it a hundred times, but the shaking had always looked like an act to play down his strength and rank. It wasn't an act this time.

"Sleep well, Gedas."

He put an old, wrinkled hand on her shoulder and then left.

Elodie took a long bath in the rooms at the base of the castle. When she was sparkling clean and smelling of lavender, she had a long lunch with her old friend, the head seamstress of Aluna, Charmaine. After lunch Charmaine asked if she wished to be naked for the rest of her stay, or if she wanted to shine. Elodie gave in and let her friend fit her for a few gowns and more practical dresses and clothes. Elodie griped over the fitting but was thankful. She always felt more confident in Charmaine's clothes.

She hadn't brought any assistants, instead she set Elodie's pins herself and talked to her about nonsense. It felt insanely normal and made Elodie want to cry. Before she left, Charmaine gripped Elodie in a tight hug and didn't let go. Elodie relaxed into the embrace and breathed in the rose scent from Charmaine's bright red hair. Elodie did cry then, and Charmaine wiped the tears away with the sleeve of her beautiful gown before kissing Elodie on the forehead.

Elodie invited the remaining Misplaced to dinner, and everyone except Allen came. Apparently, he had a dinner invitation from Gedas. Elodie hoped her old mentor would come through and tell Allen something that would help them break the spell.

Kat told them about Tristan's betrayal. None of them could quite muster the ability to be truly pissed at him. They were mad. Kirk called him a few bad names, but in the end none of them really blamed him for making a deal that Elodie survived from. They had all done things, either in the illusion or in the Twoshy, that they were less than proud of to survive.

Elodie didn't tell them the truth of the prophecy. It was still too new and tender to think about, and she didn't want to ruin the dinner. Instead, they made plans to get together back in the illusion. Elodie promised to visit Sam over the summer in Canada. She wasn't really sure she could convince her parents, but she would try.

Elodie didn't know what the future held with no prophecy to guide her now, but she relaxed in her friend's company, feeling a little less alone.

Chapter Thirty

JOHNA STORMED into his room and threw a book against the wall.

Lan strolled in behind him, a small smirk on his face. "Oh come on, you're not still pouting, are you?"

"If you're going to be an ass, just leave."

"Now, now, don't take your anger on me just because you're mad at the teachers." Lan waved a hand and the book flew into it. He fingered the bent cover. "I don't understand why you get so worked up by them to begin with. The teachers mean nothing to us. They're just a means to the end."

"Now that doesn't sound narcissistic at all."

"It's not narcissistic if it's true. We're more powerful than them."

Johna rolled his eyes. "Please, they know so much more than us."

"Of course they know more, they're older, they've had years to learn and we're just getting started. But I'll tell you, we're catching up fast. I'm not talking about knowledge, I'm talking about power. Don't roll your eyes at me Jo, you see the way they look at us when we do remedial spells. You, me, Beth, Anna, we're not just more powerful than everyone in our class, we're more powerful than everybody in this university."

"You're mad," Johna said but something glimmered in his eyes.

"I'm not mad, watch the next time you're assessed. There's fear in their eyes. That's why they're so hard on us. That's why Professor Froggsnar keeps trying to tear us down. He wants us to think we are weak, that we know nothing so they can control us."

"Now you're just being paranoid."

"Am I? Truly, if we're so powerful why should we listen to them?"

"They are teaching us how to become mages. We need them, Lan."

"How to grow up and be docile, kept mages? Sorcerers and enchanters who can sit in some stuffy castle and make some noble's life safer and more enjoyable? It's absolute nonsense. We can do so much better. We should be the ones leading not some king or elected official who's been spending their life learning about politics but has never known true power a day in their life."

"Right, Lan, tell me how you really feel."

"How I really feel is that we could change this world for the better."

"Oh yeah, what did you have in mind? Being some traveling sorcerer granting good deeds to any who passes on the road?"

"Oh, I don't plan to stop at sorcerer."

"Careful there, Master Lanis, that sounds a lot like pride," Johna said in a perfect imitation of Professor Froggsnar. "There's been what? One wizard accredited in the last century on the continent?"

Lan shrugged. "And when we graduate there'll be four more."

"Four? You really think the four of us have what it takes to be wizards?"

"Yes."

Such a simple short statement. Johna froze, his mouth open and ready to argue. It closed with a snap and he got a faraway look on his face. "Making the world a better place, it's not really possible as long as people have free will and are able to make choices that hurt themselves and others."

"Ahh, now who's a narcissist? Think you know what's best for everyone else?"

The door opened and two beautiful girls walked in without knocking. Both boys straightened and came to attention.

"Beth had a lovely idea for how we should spend the upcoming summer. What do you boys think about going on an adventure together?" Anna asked, a small smile gracing her pink lips.

"What did you have in mind?" Lan asked.

Johna dropped his eyes and sat on the bed to sulk.

"Well, we're all of age, we could get away and tell our families we're going somewhere safe and culturally enriching, while actually going somewhere that would make our teachers' heads spin."

"I'm in," Lan said without thought.

"Sounds boring," Johna said in a dry voice.

"Come on, Johna, do you really want to spend another summer stuck in university pouring over dusty books?" Lan asked.

"Beth and I are scholarships, we can't afford to go off for the summer. I've already signed up for three tutor positions just so I can have pocket money next year." His cheeks went red.

"And I have enough family wealth to support the four of us," Anna said. She crossed the room and put a hand on Johna's shoulder. "Come on and accept a little charity for once in your life. We are in this together, wasn't that our pact? If you meant it then, you should also mean it now and let me pay for an adventure."

"There will still be illusionists failing their classes and in need of tutoring next year, Jo." Beth grinned, her eyes shimmering with mischief. "Besides, you haven't even heard where I think we should go yet."

A sound from behind drew Elodie's attention, and she turned from the four mages and moved into the hallway of the university. An Aviwoman stood in the middle of the hallway, her blue feathers reflecting the glow from the light globes with an iridescent sheen.

"While one may hide from their destiny in the mountains, another may find it and break the chains that keep them separate from the world," she said, reaching out to Elodie with her pale hand. Elodie took the offered hand and sunk deeper into sleep, free from the stress and anxiety of nightmares for the first time in months.

THE NEXT MORNING, Elodie woke early and had a long soak in the castle baths. Her body was still a little achy after everything she'd put it through, but she would be fine in no time. She needed rest, and maybe a few dreamless nights. She was tired from dreams she didn't understand and from so many days and nights in a state of fight-or-flight. Maybe in a few weeks when the trials and executions were over, she would head south for the mountains and try to seek out why she was being called there, what her dreams of the four students meant. Maybe Sam and Kat would go with her. She would need an escape after the executions. Silas would understand, maybe.

She wished it was possible to skip the executions. She'd been taught they were a necessary thing. The crown had to appear as the most powerful force, and treason must be seen as the worst act, but Elodie's heart wasn't in it. When had the crown been powerful, made an impact, or given back to its people in Aluna's living memory? Things had to change, and if she couldn't rule now and make the changes necessary, she would find someone who could.

When she returned to her rooms, Mistress Piera insisted on brushing her hair out beside the fire until it was dry and glossy. Piera braided a few sections and pinned it up in an elegant updo that made her face look a little slimmer and a little older.

When she was done, she helped Elodie dress in one of the finer dresses Charmaine had made her. It was yellow silk with silver and gray embroidery. The neckline ran just below Elodie's collarbone, showing off her albatross birthmark. A surer sign of her position as heir than any tiara ever could be.

Sam was reading a book in her sitting room when she entered. Sam catcalled. "Where are you going, hot stuff?"

Elodie smiled. "I have a council meeting. Do I look good?"

"Oh yes. You look powerful and fierce. I don't know what it is exactly. You look in charge and like five years older."

Elodie laughed. "Charmaine is magic with thread and fabric."

"Well, you go tell those councilmen who's boss, girl!"

Elodie let out a sigh, that carried with it her anxiety. "Thanks. Are we still on for dinner tonight?"

"Always," Sam replied before returning to her book.

The council room was small with a few tiny west-facing windows. The walls were lined with maps showing the different regions of Aluna and the surrounding kingdoms of the Twoshy. Elodie sat on the tallest chair in the room, the one usually reserved for Steward Oburleck. Sixteen other chairs sat around her, with even more lining the walls for aids and assistants. The room was blessedly empty, and she wished it would stay that way.

She was clean. Cleaner, it felt, than she had been in months. She'd soaked so long in the baths below the castle, and now she wanted to go back to bed and sleep for a few more days. But she had things to do. Responsibilities. Her kingdom needed her.

Her dress pulled tight along her shoulders and arms. It reminded her to sit up straight. Slouching in such a fine dress ruins the lines, Charmaine had told her.

It didn't feel real, sitting in this beautiful gown, clean and smelling like lavender soap as if everything she'd been through was just her imagination. She would have scars after everything that happened, but they wouldn't show on her skin.

The door opened and Silas entered. He was also clean and wearing a green tunic and brown silk doublet. He looked so good, noble and strong, and when he saw her, he smiled. He crossed the room to kneel at the side of her chair.

"My Queen," he said from the floor.

"Silas, stop it. You know I hate it when you kneel."

He looked up at her and smirked. The small expression filled her chest with light. "Get used to it," he said, cocking an eyebrow.

"Besides, I'm not queen yet." And may never be. She didn't say it, but the words Gedas had said came back to her, and the warmth in her chest vanished.

Concern replaced the smirk, and Silas reached out and took her hand. "What's wrong?"

Before she could answer, the door opened, and Silas stood and greeted the only men left on the council. Baron Reginald, Lord Pauric, Lord Riyan, Sir Jesper, and a few others. Each man bowed to her as they entered and took their seat. She nodded to each in turn, giving Jesper an extra smile.

That was another problem. They were all men and had been for as long as Oburleck had been steward. It hadn't always been that way, and it was one of the things she hoped to change.

The council had all moved to sit on the far end of the table, avoiding the chairs to her sides. Before Silas could move away, she grabbed his sleeve. "Sit beside me," she asked. He obeyed.

Elodie sat straight in her chair. No sighing, no slouching. She was in control and had to make the men before her believe it.

"I know my words hold no power over this council or over this kingdom until we break the spell. But I'm going to make a few requests and I expect you as my council to follow through with them." She looked at each man in turn leaving no room for exceptions. They all met her gaze directly as if sizing up her resolve. "After the executions are complete in a few days, there will be a lot of land, positions, and roles left empty in this kingdom that need to be filled. For the majority of these, I trust you to make wise and charitable decisions, but I have a few requests. Squire Timothee and Squire Rogers will be knighted and given a barony each. I believe between the lands of Baron Byron and Duke Devoss, we can make it work."

The men before her shifted uncomfortably. The two squires were not of noble birth. For them, a squiredom was a full-time job, one they would never rise past. But Sam had told her how Tim had really been running the show behind the scenes and how Rogers had saved most of their lives a few times, without them even realizing it. Aluna was short of knights after some recent beheadings, and she hoped these men would be the first in a long line of fresh blood that would help make their kingdom better.

"For Lady Knight Candescence, I request she be given a seat on this council." Dess would hate it, but Elodie knew she would be a powerful force for change. "Lastly, I request you swear in Sir Silas of Tate as Steward of Aluna until he resigns, or the spell is broken." She met each man's eyes again, except for Silas at her side. "See to it this is done." She suspected right now these men would do whatever she asked and wouldn't protest her appointments. That devotion or faith wouldn't last long, but she would do what she could before it faded.

She rose from her chair, and the men around the table rose with different reaction times. She left without another word. Her head high and her posture impeccable. She didn't slump until she reached the stables.

She was not yet happy to be confined within the stone walls of the castle for so long after being trapped under the city. She'd always had an easier time clearing her head when she was in open places.

Storm was happy to see her. He was fed and well-groomed, back in his permanent stall. She looked down at her skirts and shook them out. Charmaine was a skilled seamstress and would never make Elodie anything that wasn't up for a little hard work. The skirts were wide enough she could ride in them. She asked a stable girl to help her saddle the big horse. She didn't want to totally ruin the dress if she could help it. The stable girl tore her eyes off the albatross birthmark showing at her collar and agreed with a bow.

Elodie rode out to the north. The air was a few degrees warmer than it had been, and her dress had long sleeves made of warm silk, but still the cold air bit into her exposed skin, waking her up in the afternoon air. There was a small cliff that overlooked the city a ways into the hills, and it only took an hour or two for her to find the path. She led Storm to the edge of the cliff and dropped the reins so he could munch the grass. She was confident he wouldn't wander off, not after protecting her for so long.

There used to be a log on the edge of the cliff, perfect for sitting, but that had been more than fifty years before, and it was long gone. Elodie sat in the fallen leaves and wrapped her arms around herself, looking out at the view of Tross. From so far away, you could barely tell one side of the castle was made of wood, and that the streets were dirty and half flooded in filth from the water backing up after a recent rain. From the cliff, she could almost imagine Tross was a proper city with a proper castle. One she would actually rule someday, instead of watching it slowly crumble into ruin as the decades passed with her barely aging.

His soft footsteps padding over the leaves pulled her from her thoughts. He must have been trying to alert her of his approach, or she never would have heard him.

A cloak fell over her shoulders, still warm from his body, and she pulled it tight at her neck as Silas dropped to the ground next to her. He folded his legs and looked out over the view.

"How did you find me?" she asked.

Silas held up his wrist and a small silver pinecone hung from a fine chain. "Gedas cast a charm on this to track you."

"Really?" Elodie smiled. Tim had mentioned a charm, but she hadn't expected to see the pinecone again. She reached up and felt the small charm. The edges were smooth and warm from being next to Silas's skin. "What does it use as a focus?"

"Uh, Gedas explained it, but it was complicated." Silas's face grew darker, a soft red tint to his cheeks as he blushed. Elodie didn't press the issue. "I bought it for you, back in the market that first day after you kneed me."

Elodie smiled. She'd been looking at the exact pendant when he'd caught her in the market. "Sorry about that, by the way."

Silas chuckled. "I let you catch me unprepared. I deserved it. Master Driard would be ashamed of me."

An image of Silas's old sword instructor came back to her and Elodie smiled. Silas had been the best, and one of the youngest pages in his class. She couldn't imagine Master Driard being anything other than proud of the man he'd become. Unless Master Driard had been one of Oburleck's supporters. That would be unfortunate.

"You can keep it," she said, letting go of the small charm. Silas dropped his arm. "At least until we break the spell. That way you'll know when I'm back."

"Elodie, about me being steward."

Elodie shook her head. "Don't try to get out of it. It's the easiest decision I've made in a long time."

"I can't get out of it." Silas ran a hand over his head. "They swore me in as soon as you left the room. They were practically eager. Cooric knows none of them wanted the job." He looked bewildered and Elodie laughed.

"Good. You can help rebuild things while I'm gone. I always said you'd make a great king."

Silas grinned, his eyes going to some far-off place. She'd told him once, that he'd make a great king. He'd teased her about being too young to marry, but now here they were, her calling on him to officially look after Aluna in her stead. Not rule exactly, but to care for and protect her people.

The responsibility, the expectations hung between them now.

Would their timing ever be right? Or would Elodie always be playing catch-up as Silas aged in her absence, eventually passing on the role of steward to another? How many generations would pass before she could finally live her life? Oburleck hadn't been Aluna's first steward.

"We will break the spell," Silas said as if reading her thoughts.

Elodie sighed, and she told him about the prophecy and what Gedas had said.

"I'm not destined to break the spell, I'm not destined for anything," she finished.

Silas took her hand and met her eyes, his gaze filled with so many things, sympathy, confidence, passion. "Just because you don't know what the future holds doesn't make the journey any less important."

She smiled and dropped her eyes, looking back over the view. "I'm not giving up. Just because we don't have a prophecy saying we will break it, doesn't mean we won't still pull it off. I think Allen may be our best help."

Silas frowned. "Maybe I can put together a task force for it."

"Just be gentle with Gedas. I think what he told me took a lot for him to admit."

"And if he had told us sooner, we wouldn't have spent so much time spinning our wheels."

Elodie nodded. "I don't disagree, but if anyone comes accusing him, he will clam up. He won't tell us anything."

"And you care about him and don't want to see him hurt worse," Silas added.

Elodie nodded more slowly. "Yes."

"I have something for you." Silas reached behind himself and pulled out a single sprig of fairies' breath. The stem was light green, winding up in a corkscrew pattern with a single soft lavender bloom at the end. The stamen at the center of the flower glowed softly.

Elodie took the flower gently and brought it to her nose. It had a soft and clean scent. "When did you get this?" she asked in awe. Fairies' breath only grew in very specific parts of the Twoshy. It only bloomed at dawn and dusk, but if picked at that moment stayed in bloom.

"I picked it the night you decided to go out and get yourself kidnapped," he said, lacing the words with as much scorn and derision as he could.

Elodie rolled her eyes. "What were you doing out in the woods, Sir Knight?"

"I may have found that tree with the dragon's breath growing over it and chopped it down."

"You what?"

"And then I set fire to it."

Elodie laughed. "So it's gone for good?"

"Yes."

Elodie brought the flower to her nose again and breathed deeply. "So you're saying you woke up after losing too much blood and having half your body stitched up, only to go traipsing into the woods to cut down a big tree?" She would make the potion to knock him out stronger next time. Make him sleep for a week so he could heal properly.

"I had Rogers and Jinis help."

"Rogers deserves his knighting."

Silas smiled. "He does."

"You didn't even know if I was still alive when you went after me, but you still brought a flower across the country?"

"I knew."

Elodie smiled. "There are a few more things I need you to do for me."

He bowed from his sitting position. "I am yours to command, my lady."

There's a girl who works in the lower city clinic, Audrey. Her father lives in Lottsin near the variant forest. I don't know his name."

She could see Silas's mind working, trying to keep up with her words. "Okay," he said.

"He helped me when I first arrived. Hid me from the soldiers sweeping the town when others turned me away."

"Who turned you away?" he asked sharply.

Elodie put a hand on his arm. "Forget about it. That's not important. Just make sure he's taken care of, okay?"

"Of course. What else?"

Elodie sighed. "I need you to make sure some of Byron's businesses are awarded to Callie for her help." Silas looked at her with surprise. "I know she won't thank me for it, she may just see it as me trying to buy her all over again, but I don't care. Tell her that. Tell her I don't care what she thinks about it. She can have all of Byron's bordellos and all his property within them, living and not. She can do whatever she wants with them. I trust her."

Silas grinned and looked out onto the city below them. "That's brilliant."

They sat for a time longer, happy to be in each other's presence with no conflict or battles waiting to be fought. He told her his plans, to get the other council members appointed in the next few days, people he thought would be good additions for their intelligence or reluctance to settle for second best. They wouldn't make any announcements until after the executions were finished. They would mourn for a week, then they would celebrate the new knights and the other promotions and rewards. Elodie would bring up her trip to the mountains later when she wasn't enjoying the peace and presence of her old friend quite so much.

As the sun threatened to set, Silas rose and reached down for her. Elodie put her hands in his, and he pulled her gracefully to her feet. They were inches away for a long moment, as he smiled down at her. He broke the contact and bent down to retrieve her fairies' breath. She took it and thanked him and turned to find where Storm had drifted off to.

A shimmer rose around her like twinkling stars in the evening light. She spun to Silas. He reached for her hand but missed.

The ruakh snatched Elodie up, ripping her from her life, her home, her future, and tossed her through the spinning chaos of nothing with no promise of when it would return her. She was powerless to stop it as the magic pulled her to its whim.

After a long disorienting moment, Elodie landed hard on the cement sidewalk. The sun was bright and jarring, and the sudden absence of a corset made her feel naked in a T-shirt and jeans. She ran a hand over her face, trying to reorient herself. To her right rest two flowers on the cement: a long-stemmed, red-tipped yellow rose and a corkscrew sprig of fairies' breath still glowing gently from the lingering ruakh.

A red vintage truck rumbled down the road toward her and pulled to a stop along the curb next to her. A door slammed shut, and someone came into her line of sight. "Elodie, are you okay? Did you fall?"

Elodie looked up into the boyish face of Matt Moreno and cried.

Acknowledgments

Thank you to everyone who listened to me complain about writing and then nodded encouragingly before walking away swiftly.

In all seriousness, thank you to everyone who read and reviewed book one. Thank you for picking up this book and getting this far.

Thank you to every person who helped in making this book happen. The list is long and in no particular order, but shoutout to the following people:

To Mom, Kody, Karlye, Jesse, Keith, Victor and Eden, Krystal, Julie and Mikey, thank you for your love and support. To Junior, for all the idea bouncing and brilliant improvements. To Michelle, Kristina, Camila, Danielle, Emma, Carl, and Jeremy, for reading this first and helping make it better (Double thanks to Michelle for reading it twice). Thank you Rachel and Michelle, for making Elodie look and sound perfect.

Elodie's story doesn't end here. Keep an eye out for the next book in The Misplaced Children series: A Misplaced Life, coming soon.

About the Author

Heather Michelle is an emerging author of young adult fantasy. She lives in Acworth, GA with her cats; Fitzwilliam, and Mister Bingley, and a slew of unique roommates.

Growing up, Heather Michelle spent more time living in her imagination than outside of it. Small town life sandwiched between the redwood forests and the Pacific ocean provided a rich scope for the imagination. Before the age of twelve, Heather Michelle was not a reader, but a chance encounter with a rented audiobook launched her into the vast world of the printed word, and she never looked back.

For exclusive content, pronunciation guides and a guide to the Twoshy by Kirk, visit our website:

www.authorheathermichelle.com

 instagram.com/heathermichely